The Master & Margarita

MIKHAIL BULGAKOV

The Master
&
Margarita

TRANSLATED BY
Diana Burgin & Katherine Tiernan O'Connor

ANNOTATIONS & AFTERWORD BY
Ellendea Proffer

PICADOR

First published 1995 by Ardis Publishers, Dana Point, California

First published in Great Britain 1997 in paperback
and simultaneously in hardback by Picador

This edition published 2010 by Picador
an imprint of Pan Macmillan, a division of Macmillan Publishers Limited
Pan Macmillan, 20 New Wharf Road, London N1 9RR
Basingstoke and Oxford
Associated companies throughout the world
www.panmacmillan.com

ISBN 978-0-330-54393-4

Translated by Diana Burgin and Katherine Tiernan O'Connor
Copyright © Diana Burgin and Katherine Tiernan O'Connor 1995

Annotations and Afterword by Ellendea Proffer
Copyright © Ellendea Proffer 1995

Originally published in Russian in 1966

5 7 9 8 6 4

A CIP catalogue record for this book is available
from the British Library.

Printed and bound by CPI Group (UK) Ltd, Croydon, CR0 4YY

Visit **www.picador.com** to read more about all our books and to buy
them. You will also find features, author interviews and news of any author
events, and you can sign up for e-newsletters so that you're always first to hear
about our new releases.

CONTENTS

PART II

Translators' Note

All aspects of the work on this translation were done equally by the two of us, and the order of our names is purely alphabetical. We would like to thank Marina Khazanov of Boston University for the assistance she provided as a first speaker of Russian in clarifying certain difficult and obscure words and phrases.

In realizing this translation, we strove, first of all, to produce what has been lacking so far: a translation of the complete text of Bulgakov's masterpiece into contemporary standard American English. At the same time, our translation aims to be as literal a rendering of the original Russian as possible. Challenged by the third of Goethe's well-known ideas on translation (as articulated in his notes to the *West-Ostlicher Divan*), we have "associated ourselves closely with our original." We have made every effort to retain the rhythm, syntactic structure, and verbal texture of Bulgakov's prose. We have often eschewed synonyms in favor of repeating the words that Bulgakov repeats, and we have tried, as far as possible without sacrificing clarity, not to break up Bulgakov's long sentences and to adhere to his word order. In sum, we strove for an accurate, readable American English translation of *The Master and Margarita* that would convey the specifically Bulgakovian flavor of the original Russian text.

Diana Burgin and Katherine O'Connor

...and so, who are
you, after all?

—I am part of the power
which forever wills evil
and forever works good.

Goethe's *Faust*

Part One

I

Never Talk to Strangers

ONE hot spring evening, just as the sun was going down, two men appeared at Patriarch's Ponds. One of them—fortyish, wearing a gray summer suit—was short, dark-haired, bald on top, paunchy, and held his proper fedora in his hand; black horn-rimmed glasses of supernatural proportions adorned his well-shaven face. The other one—a broad-shouldered, reddish-haired, shaggy young man with a checked cap cocked on the back of his head—was wearing a cowboy shirt, crumpled white trousers, and black sneakers.

The first man was none other than Mikhail Alexandrovich Berlioz, editor of a literary magazine and chairman of the board of one of Moscow's largest literary associations, known by its acronym, MASSOLIT, and his young companion was the poet Ivan Nikolayevich Ponyryov, who wrote under the pen name Bezdomny.

After reaching the shade of the newly budding linden trees, the writers made a beeline for the colorfully painted refreshment stand bearing the sign: BEER AND COLD DRINKS.

And here it is worth noting the first strange thing about that terrible May evening. Absolutely no one was to be seen, not only by the refreshment stand, but all along the tree-lined path that ran parallel to Malaya Bronnaya Street. At a time when no one, it seemed, had the strength to breathe, when the sun had left Moscow scorched to a crisp and was collapsing in a dry haze somewhere behind the Sadovoye Ring, no one came out to walk under the lindens, or to sit down on a bench, and the path was deserted.

"Give me some Narzan water," said Berlioz.

"There isn't any," replied the woman at the refreshment stand, taking umbrage for some reason.

"Got any beer?" inquired Bezdomny in a hoarse voice.

"The beer will be delivered later," the woman answered.

"So what have you got?" asked Berlioz.

"Apricot juice, only it's warm," said the woman.

"Well, give us that then!..."

The apricot juice generated an abundance of yellow foam, and the air started smelling like a barbershop. The writers drank it down and immediately began hiccuping, paid their money, and went over and sat down on a bench facing the pond, with their backs to Bronnaya Street.

Here the second strange thing happened, which affected Berlioz alone. He suddenly stopped hiccuping, his heart pounded and stopped beating for a second, then started up again, but with a blunt needle lodged inside it. Besides that, Berlioz was seized with a groundless fear so intense that he wanted to run away from Patriarch's Ponds that very minute without looking back.

Berlioz looked around miserably, not knowing what had frightened him. He turned pale, wiped his forehead with a handkerchief, and thought, "What's wrong with me? This has never happened before... my heart's playing tricks on me... I'm overtired. Maybe it's time to throw everything to the devil and go off to Kislovodsk..."

And then the hot air congealed in front of him, and out of it materialized a transparent man of most bizarre appearance. A small head with a jockey cap, a skimpy little checked jacket that was made out of air... The man was seven feet tall, but very narrow in the shoulders, incredibly thin, and his face, please note, had a jeering look about it.

Berlioz's life was so arranged that he was unaccustomed to unusual happenings. He turned even paler, opened his eyes wide, and in a state of confusion thought, "This can't be!..."

But, alas, it was, and the tall transparent man swayed from left to right in front of him, without touching the ground.

At this point Berlioz was so overcome with terror that he shut his eyes. And when he opened them, he saw that it was all over, the mirage had evaporated, the man in checks had vanished, and the blunt needle had dislodged itself from his heart.

"What the devil!" exclaimed the editor. "You know, Ivan, I think I almost had a sunstroke just then! Maybe even something like a hallucination." He tried to smile, but alarm still flickered in his eyes and his hands were shaking. Gradually, however, he calmed down, fanned himself with his handkerchief, managed a fairly cheerful "Well then...," and resumed the conversation that had been interrupted by the apricot juice.

This conversation, as was learned subsequently, was about Jesus Christ. The fact is that the editor had commissioned the poet to write a long antireligious poem for the next issue of his journal. Ivan Niko-layevich had composed the poem, and in a very short period of time at that, but unfortunately it had not met with the editor's approval. Bezdomny had painted the central character of his poem, that is, Jesus, in very dark colors, and yet, in the editor's opinion, the whole poem had to be rewritten. And so now the editor was giving the poet a kind of lecture on Jesus in order to point out to him his basic error.

It is hard to say what had ultimately led Ivan Nikolayevich astray—the descriptive power of his pen, or his complete ignorance of his subject matter, but the Jesus whom he portrayed emerged as a, well, totally life-like figure, a Jesus who had once existed, although, admittedly, a Jesus provided with all sorts of negative traits.

Thus Berlioz wanted to prove to the poet that the important thing was not what kind of man Jesus was, good or bad, but, rather, that Jesus, as an individual, had never existed on earth at all and that all the stories about him were mere fabrications, myths of the most standard kind.

It should be noted that the editor was a well-read man and in his speech he made very clever allusions to ancient historians such as the famous Philo of Alexandria, and the brilliantly educated Flavius Josephus, neither of whom had said a word about the existence of Jesus. With a display of solid erudition, Mikhail Alexandrovich also informed the poet, in passing, that the passage in Book 15, Chapter 44 of Tacitus's famous *Annals*, where mention is made of Jesus's execution, is nothing but a later, fraudulent interpolation.

The poet, for whom everything the editor said was a novelty, stared at Mikhail Alexandrovich with his sharp green eyes and listened to him attentively, hiccuping only occasionally and cursing the apricot juice under his breath.

"There is not a single Eastern religion," Berlioz was saying, "where an immaculate virgin does not, as a matter of course, bring forth a god into the world. And the Christians, displaying no originality whatsoever, followed the same pattern when they created their Jesus, who, in fact, never existed at all. That's where you have to put your main emphasis..."

Berlioz's high tenor resounded along the deserted path, and as Mikhail Alexandrovich ventured into that maze, which only a highly educated man can explore without risking his neck, the poet learned more and more interesting and useful things about the Egyptian Osiris, the kind god and son of Heaven and Earth, and about the Phoenician god Tammuz, and about Marduk, and even about the lesser known terrible god Uitzilopochtli who had once been venerated by the Aztecs in Mexico.

And just as Mikhail Alexandrovich was telling the poet how the Aztecs had modeled figures of Uitzilopochtli out of dough, the first man appeared on the pathway.

Afterward, when, frankly speaking, it was already too late, various agencies filed reports describing this man. If one compares them, one cannot help but be astonished. For example, one says that he was short, had gold teeth, and was lame in his right foot. Another says that he was hugely tall, had platinum crowns and was lame in his left foot. Yet a third notes laconically that he had no distinguishing characteristics whatsoever.

We should add that all of the reports were worthless.

To begin with, the subject was lame in neither foot, and he was neither short, nor hugely tall, but simply tall. As for his teeth, the left ones had platinum crowns, the right—gold. He was dressed in an expensive gray suit and wore foreign-made shoes of the same color. A gray beret was cocked rakishly over his ear, and under his arm he carried a walking stick with a black knob shaped like a poodle's head. He looked to be a little over forty. Slightly crooked mouth. Smooth-shaven. Dark brown hair. Right eye black, left—for some reason, green. Black eyebrows, but one was higher than the other. In a word—a foreigner.

As he passed the bench where the editor and poet were sitting, the foreigner looked at them out of the corner of his eye, stopped, and suddenly sat down on a neighboring bench two feet away.

"A German," thought Berlioz.

"An Englishman," thought Bezdomny, "I bet he's hot with those gloves on."

The foreigner looked around at the tall buildings that formed a square border around the pond, thus making it obvious that he was seeing the place for the first time and that it interested him.

He rested his gaze on the upper stories of the buildings and on the windowpanes' blinding reflection of the broken sun that was departing from Mikhail Alexandrovich forever. Then he lowered his gaze, to where the windowpanes were turning dark in the dusk, gave a condescending smile, narrowed his eyes, placed his hands on the knob of his walking stick, and rested his chin on his hands.

"Some things, Ivan, you described very well and satirically," Berlioz was saying, "for example, the birth of Jesus, the son of God, but the fact is that a whole host of sons of God were born even before Jesus, like, say, the Phoenician Adonis, the Phrygian Attis, the Persian Mithras. But, in short, none of them, including Jesus, were ever born or existed, and so, instead of describing his birth or, say, the coming of the Magi, you should describe the nonsense that was said about all this. Otherwise your account seems to suggest that he really was born!..."

Bezdomny held his breath in an effort to stop the hiccups that were tormenting him, which only made them louder and more excruciating, at which point Berlioz stopped talking, because the foreigner suddenly got up and came over to them.

They looked up at him in amazement.

"Please, excuse me," he said, speaking correctly, but with a foreign accent, "for presuming to speak to you without an introduction... but the subject of your learned discussion is so interesting that..."

Here he politely removed his beret, and the friends had no choice but to raise themselves slightly and bow in response.

"No, more likely he's French," thought Berlioz.

"A Pole?" thought Bezdomny.

It should be added that the poet found the foreigner loathsome from the moment he opened his mouth, whereas Berlioz rather liked him, or, if not liked him, then... how shall we say it... at least took an interest in him.

"May I join you?" asked the foreigner politely, and the friends moved apart involuntarily; the foreigner deftly seated himself between them and immediately joined their conversation.

"Was I mistaken when I heard you say that Jesus never existed on earth?" asked the foreigner, focusing his left green eye on Berlioz.

"No, you were not mistaken," Berlioz replied courteously. "That's exactly what I said."

"Ah, how interesting!" exclaimed the foreigner.

"What the devil is he after?" thought Bezdomny with a scowl.

"And do you agree with your friend?" queried the stranger, turning to Bezdomny on his right.

"A hundred percent!" confirmed Bezdomny who loved pretentious, figurative expressions.

"Astonishing!" exclaimed the uninvited discussant, and then, looking around furtively for some reason, and muffling his already low voice, he said, "Excuse my persistence, but did I understand you to say that you don't believe in God either?" He made his eyes pop in mock fright and added, "I swear I won't tell anyone."

"That's right, we don't believe in God," answered Berlioz with a faint smile at the tourist's fear, "but we can talk about it freely and openly."

The foreigner leaned back on the bench and practically squealed with curiosity as he asked, "You mean you're atheists?!"

"Yes, we are," answered Berlioz with a smile, while Bezdomny thought in irritation, "He's sticking to us like glue, the foreign pest!"

"Oh, how delightful!" cried the amazed foreigner, turning to look first at one writer and then the other.

"In our country atheism comes as no surprise to anyone," said Berlioz in a polite and diplomatic way. "The majority of our population made a conscious decision long ago not to believe the fairy tales about God."

Here the foreigner made the following move: he got up, pressed the astonished editor's hand, and uttered these words, "Allow me to thank you with all my heart!"

"What are you thanking him for?" queried Bezdomny, blinking.

"For very important information that I, as a traveller, find extraordinarily interesting," explained the eccentric from abroad, raising his finger in a meaningful way.

The important information had apparently made a really strong impression on the traveller, since he anxiously scanned the surrounding buildings, as if in fear of spotting an atheist in every window.

"No, he's not English..." thought Berlioz, while Bezdomny wondered, "Where in hell did he learn to speak Russian like that, that's what I'd like to know!"—and he scowled again.

"But, may I ask," resumed the guest from abroad after a moment's troubled reflection, "what do you make of the proofs of God's existence, of which, as you know, there are five?"

"Alas!" answered Berlioz regretfully, "all of those proofs are worthless, and mankind has long since consigned them to oblivion. Surely you would agree that reason dictates that there can be no proof of God's existence."

"Bravo!" exclaimed the foreigner, "Bravo! You've said just what that restless old sage Immanuel said about this very same subject. But here's the rub: he completely demolished all five proofs, and then, in a seeming display of self-mockery, he constructed a sixth proof all his own!"

"Kant's proof," retorted the educated editor with a faint smile, "is also unconvincing. No wonder Schiller said that only slaves could be satisfied with Kant's arguments on this subject, while Strauss simply laughed at his proof."

As Berlioz was speaking, he thought, "But, who is he anyway? And how come his Russian is so good?"

"This guy Kant ought to get three years in Solovki for proofs like that," blurted out Ivan Nikolayevich, completely unexpectedly.

"Ivan!" whispered Berlioz in consternation.

But the suggestion that Kant be sent to Solovki not only failed to shock the foreigner, it positively delighted him.

"Precisely so, precisely so," he cried, and his green left eye, which was focused on Berlioz, sparkled. "That's the very place for him! As I told him that time at breakfast, 'As you please, professor, but you've contrived something totally absurd! True, it may be clever, but it's totally incomprehensible. People will laugh at you.'"

Berlioz's eyes popped. "At breakfast... with Kant? What kind of nonsense is this?" he thought.

"However," continued the foreigner, unflustered by Berlioz's astonishment and turning to the poet, "he can't be sent to Solovki for the simple reason that for more than a hundred years now he's been somewhere far more remote than Solovki, and there's no way of getting him out of there, I assure you!"

"Too bad!" responded the poet-bully.

"I couldn't agree more!" concurred the stranger, his eye agleam, and he continued, "But this is what disturbs me: if there is no God, then, the question is, who is in control of man's life and the whole order of things on earth?"

"Man himself is in control," was Bezdomny's quick and angry reply to what was, admittedly, a not very clear question.

"I'm sorry," replied the stranger in a soft voice, "but in order to be in control, you have to have a definite plan for at least a reasonable period of time. So how, may I ask, can man be in control if he can't even draw up a plan for a ridiculously short period of time, say, a thousand years, and is, moreover, unable to ensure his own safety for even the next day? And, indeed," here the stranger turned to Berlioz, "suppose you were to start controlling others and yourself, and just as you developed a taste for it, so to speak, you suddenly went and... well... got lung cancer..."—at which point the foreigner chuckled merrily, as if the thought of lung cancer brought him pleasure. "Yes, cancer," he repeated, narrowing his eyes like a cat as he savored the sonorous word, "and there goes your control! No one's fate is of any interest to you except your own. Your relatives start lying to you. You, sensing that something is wrong, run to learned physicians, then to quacks, and maybe even to fortune-tellers in the end. And going to any of them is pointless, as you well know. And it all ends tragically: that same fellow who not so long ago supposed that he was in control of something ends up lying stiff in a wooden box, and those present, realizing that he is no longer good for anything, cremate him in an oven. Why, even worse things can happen: a fellow will have just decided to make a trip to Kislovodsk,"—here the foreigner narrowed his eyes at Berlioz, "a trivial matter, it would seem, but he can't even accomplish that because for some unknown reason he goes and slips and falls under a streetcar! Would you really say that that's an example of his control over himself? Wouldn't it be more correct to say that someone other than himself is in control?"— and at this point the stranger laughed a strange sort of laugh.

Berlioz listened with rapt attention to the unpleasant story about cancer and the streetcar, and uneasy thoughts began to trouble him. "He's no foreigner... he's no foreigner..." he thought, "He's a real oddball... but who exactly is he?"

"You'd like a smoke, wouldn't you?" said the stranger unexpectedly turning to Bezdomny. "Which brand do you prefer?"

"You have assorted brands, is that it?" glumly inquired the poet, who had run out of cigarettes.

"Which do you prefer?" repeated the stranger.

"Well, how about 'Our Brand,'" was Bezdomny's sneering reply.

The stranger immediately pulled a cigarette case out of his pocket and offered it to Bezdomny: "'Our Brand.'"

Both the editor and the poet were astonished not so much by the fact that the case did contain "Our Brand," but, rather, by the cigarette case itself. It was enormous, made of pure gold, and as it was being opened, the blue and white fire of a diamond triangle sparkled on its cover.

The writers had different thoughts at this point. Berlioz thought, "No, he's definitely a foreigner!" and Bezdomny thought, "Oh, to hell with him!"

Both the poet and the owner of the cigarette case lit up, but Berlioz, a non-smoker, declined.

"That's how I'll refute his argument," decided Berlioz, "Yes, of course man is mortal, no one would deny that. But the point is that..."

But before he could utter these words, the foreigner went on to say, "Yes, man is mortal, but that isn't so bad. What's bad is that sometimes he's unexpectedly mortal, that's the rub! And, in general, he can't even say in the morning what he'll be doing that very same night."

"What an absurd way of posing the question..." thought Berlioz and retorted, "Well, that's a bit of an exaggeration. I know more or less precisely what I'll be doing this evening. It goes without saying, of course, that if a brick were to fall on my head on Bronnaya Street..."

"The brick is neither here nor there," interrupted the stranger in an imposing fashion, "it never merely falls on someone's head from out of nowhere. In your case, I can assure you that a brick poses no threat whatsoever. You will die another kind of death."

"And you know just what that will be?" queried Berlioz with perfectly understandable irony, letting himself be drawn into a truly absurd conversation. "And you'll tell me what that is?"

"Gladly," replied the stranger. He took Berlioz's measure as if intending to make him a suit and muttered something through his teeth that sounded like, "One, two... Mercury in the Second House... the moon has set... six—misfortune... evening—seven..." Then he announced loudly and joyously, "Your head will be cut off!"

Bezdomny glared fiercely and malevolently at the impertinent stranger, and Berlioz asked, with a crooked smile on his face, "By whom, namely? Enemies? Interventionists?"

"No," replied his interlocutor, "by a Russian woman, a member of the Komsomol."

"Hmmm..." grunted Berlioz, irritated by the stranger's little joke, "Well, excuse me, but that's highly unlikely."

"No, please excuse me," replied the foreigner, "but that's how it is. By the way, I wanted to ask you, what will you be doing this evening, if it's not a secret?"

"It's not. First I'm going home to my place on Sadovaya and then at ten there's a meeting at MASSOLIT which I'll be chairing."

"No, that can't be," firmly protested the foreigner.

"And why is that?"

"Because," replied the foreigner, narrowing his eyes and looking up at the sky where the blackbirds were circling noiselessly in anticipation of the evening coolness, "Annushka has already bought the sunflower oil and not just bought it, but spilled it as well. So the meeting won't take place."

At this point, as one might expect, silence fell under the lindens.

"Excuse me," resumed Berlioz after a pause, looking at the nonsense-spouting foreigner, "but what's sunflower oil got to do with it... and who is this Annushka?"

"Here's what the sunflower oil has to do with it," interjected Bezdomny suddenly, evidently deciding to declare war on their uninvited interlocutor. "You haven't by any chance spent some time in a mental hospital, have you?"

"Ivan!" softly exclaimed Mikhail Alexandrovich.

But the foreigner was not the least bit insulted and he burst out with a hearty laugh.

"I have indeed, I have indeed, and more than once!" he exclaimed, laughing, his unsmiling eye still focused on the poet. "And where haven't I been! I'm only sorry I never managed to ask the professor what schizophrenia is. So you'll have to ask him yourself, Ivan Nikolayevich!"

"How do you know my name?"

"Goodness, Ivan Nikolayevich, who doesn't know you?" At which point the foreigner pulled the previous day's *Literary Gazette* out of his pocket, and Ivan Nikolayevich saw a picture of himself on the front page and underneath it some of his poems. But the evidence of his fame and popularity which had so delighted the poet the day before now gave him no pleasure whatsoever.

"Excuse me," he said and his face darkened, "but could you wait a minute? I'd like to have a word with my colleague."

"Oh, by all means!" exclaimed the stranger. "It's so pleasant here under the lindens, and besides I'm in no hurry to go anywhere."

"Look here, Misha," whispered the poet after taking Berlioz aside, "he isn't a tourist at all, but a spy. He's a Russian emigré who's managed to get back here. Ask to see his papers or he'll get away."

"You really think so?" whispered Berlioz anxiously, thinking to himself, "He's probably right..."

"Mark my words," hissed the poet in his ear, "he's playing the fool in order to pump us for information. You heard how well he speaks Russian," said the poet, looking at the stranger out of the corner of his eye to make sure he did not run off. "C'mon, let's grab him or he'll get away."

The poet took Berlioz by the arm and led him over to the bench.

The stranger was no longer seated on the bench, but was standing near it, holding a small booklet bound in dark gray, a thick envelope made of good quality paper, and a visiting card.

"Excuse me," he said with importance, looking intently at the two men of letters, "but in the heat of our discussion I neglected to introduce myself. Here is my card, my passport, and my invitation to come to Moscow as a consultant."

They became embarrassed. "Damn, he's heard everything," thought Berlioz, and he made a polite gesture to show that a presentation of papers was not necessary. When the foreigner thrust them at the editor, the poet managed to make out the word "Professor" written on the card in foreign letters and also the first letter of his surname—the double V, a "W."

Meanwhile the editor mumbled an embarrassed "I'm very pleased to meet you," and the foreigner shoved the documents into his pocket.

Thus relations between them were restored, and all three again sat down on the bench.

"So, you've been invited here as a consultant, Professor?" asked Berlioz.

"Yes, that's right."

"Are you a German?" queried Bezdomny.

"Who, me?" replied the professor and suddenly grew pensive. "Yes, I suppose I'm a German," he said.

"Your Russian is first-rate," observed Bezdomny.

"Oh, in general I'm a polyglot and know a great many languages," answered the professor.

"And what is your field?" inquired Berlioz.

"I'm a specialist in black magic."

"Well I'll be..." flashed through Mikhail Alexandrovich's head.

"And... and is it in that capacity that you've been invited here?" stammered Berlioz.

"Yes, it is," affirmed the professor, and he went on to explain, "Some authentic manuscripts of the tenth century master of black magic, Gerbert of Aurillac, have been discovered here in your State Library. And I've been asked to examine them. I'm the only person in the whole world who's qualified to do so."

"Ah! So you're a historian then?" asked Berlioz with great respect and relief.

"Yes, I'm a historian," confirmed the scholar and added, apropos of nothing, "This evening some interesting history will take place at Patriarch's Ponds."

And again both the editor and the poet were completely dumbfounded. The professor motioned to both of them to come closer, and when they had, he whispered, "Keep in mind that Jesus did exist."

"You know, Professor," answered Berlioz with a forced smile, "we respect your great knowledge, but we happen to have a different point of view regarding that issue."

"No points of view are necessary," replied the strange professor. "He simply existed, and that's all there is to it."

"But surely some proof is required" began Berlioz.

"No, no proof is required," answered the professor. He began to speak softly and as he did, his accent somehow disappeared. "It's all very simple: Early in the morning on the fourteenth day of the spring month of Nisan, wearing a white cloak with a blood-red lining, and shuffling with his cavalryman's gait..."

II

Pontius Pilate

E ARLY in the morning on the fourteenth day of the spring month of Nisan, wearing a white cloak with a blood-red lining, and shuffling with his cavalryman's gait into the roofed colonnade that connected the two wings of the palace of Herod the Great, walked the procurator of Judea, Pontius Pilate.

More than anything in the world the procurator loathed the smell of rose oil, and everything now pointed to a bad day, since that smell had been pursuing him since dawn. It seemed to the procurator that the palms and cypresses in the garden were emitting a rose scent and that even the smell of leather gear and sweat coming from the escort contained a hellish trace of roses. From the outbuildings at the rear of the palace, the quarters of the first cohort of the Twelfth Lightning Legion, which had accompanied the procurator to Yershalaim, smoke was drifting across the upper terrace of the garden into the colonnade, and this acrid smoke, which signaled that the centuries' cooks had begun to prepare dinner, contained an admixture of that same oily rose scent.

"O gods, gods, why are you punishing me?... Yes, there's no doubt about it, it's back again, that horrible, relentless affliction... the hemicrania that shoots pain through half my head... there's no remedy for it, no relief... I'll try not to move my head..."

An armchair had been set out for him on the mosaic floor near the fountain, and the procurator sat down in it and without looking at anyone, put his hand out sideways. His secretary respectfully handed him a piece of parchment. Unable to hold back a grimace of pain, the procurator gave a fleeting sidelong glance at what was written on the parchment, handed it back to the secretary, and said with difficulty, "The accused is from Galilee? Was the case sent to the tetrarch?"

"Yes, Procurator," replied the secretary.

"And what did he do?"

"He refused to give a judgment in the case and sent the death sentence pronounced by the Sinedrion to you for confirmation," explained the secretary.

The procurator's cheek twitched, and he said quietly, "Bring in the accused."

Two legionaries immediately left the garden terrace, proceeded through the colonnade and came out onto the balcony, escorting a man of about twenty-seven whom they stood before the procurator's chair. The man was dressed in a light-blue chiton that was old and torn. He had a white bandage on his head that was held in place by a leather thong tied around his forehead, and his hands were tied behind his back. There was a large bruise under the man's left eye, and a cut with dried blood on it in the corner of his mouth. The prisoner looked with anxious curiosity at the procurator.

The procurator was silent for a moment, then he said quietly in Aramaic, "So it was you who incited the people to destroy the temple of Yershalaim?"

The procurator sat stonelike, moving his lips only slightly as he spoke. The procurator was stonelike because he was afraid to move his head, which was seared by hellish pain.

The man whose hands were bound took a few steps forward and began to speak, "My good man! Believe me..."

But the procurator, perfectly still as before and without raising his voice, interrupted him on the spot, "Is it me you are calling a good man? You are mistaken. Word has it in Yershalaim that I am a savage monster, and that is absolutely true." In the same monotone, he added, "Bring centurion Ratkiller to me."

It seemed to everyone that it became dark on the balcony when Mark the centurion, nicknamed Ratkiller, who commanded the first century, came and stood before the procurator. Ratkiller was a head taller than the tallest soldier in the legion and so broad in the shoulders that he blocked out the sun which was still low in the sky.

The procurator addressed the centurion in Latin, "The criminal calls me 'good man.' Take him away for a moment and explain to him how he should address me. But don't maim him."

Everyone except the motionless procurator stared at Mark Ratkiller as he gestured to the prisoner to follow him.

Because of his height, Ratkiller was usually stared at by everyone wherever he went, and those seeing him for the first time also stared because of his disfigured face: his nose had once been smashed by a German club.

Mark's heavy boots stamped on the mosaic, the bound man followed him out noiselessly, complete silence ensued in the colonnade, and one could hear the doves cooing on the garden terrace by the balcony and the water in the fountain singing a pleasant and intricate tune.

The procurator felt the urge to get up, put his temple under the water, and freeze in that position. But he knew that even that would not help him.

After leading the prisoner through the colonnade and out into the garden, Ratkiller took a whip from the hands of a legionary standing at the foot of a bronze statue and struck the prisoner a mild blow across the shoulders. The centurion's stroke was casual and light, but the bound man sank to the ground instantly as if his legs had been knocked out from under him. He gasped for breath, the color left his face, and his eyes glazed over.

With just his left hand Mark lifted the fallen man into the air lightly as if he were an empty sack, stood him on his feet, and began speaking in a nasal voice, mispronouncing the Aramaic words, "Address the Roman procurator as Hegemon. Do not use other words. Stand at attention. Have you understood me or do I have to hit you again?"

The prisoner swayed on his feet but got control of himself. His color returned, he caught his breath and answered hoarsely, "I understand you. Don't beat me."

A minute later he was again standing before the procurator.

A flat, sick-sounding voice was heard, "Name?"

"Mine?" the prisoner responded quickly, demonstrating with all his being his readiness to answer sensibly, and not to provoke more anger.

The procurator said softly, "Mine—I know. Do not pretend to be more stupid than you are. Yours."

"Yeshua," the prisoner replied hurriedly.

"Is there a surname?"

"Ha-Notsri."

"Where are you from?"

"The city of Gamala," answered the prisoner, indicating with a toss of his head that somewhere far away, off to his right, in the north, was the city of Gamala.

"Who are you by birth?"

"I don't know exactly," the prisoner replied readily. "I don't remember my parents. I've been told that my father was a Syrian..."

"Where is your permanent residence?"

"I have none," answered the prisoner shyly. "I travel from town to town."

"That can be expressed more succinctly in one word—vagrant," said the procurator. Then he asked, "Do you have any family?"

"None. I am alone in the world."

"Are you literate?"

"Yes."

"Do you know any language besides Aramaic?"

"Yes. Greek."

One swollen lid was raised, and an eye glazed by suffering stared at the prisoner. The other eye remained closed.

Pilate began speaking in Greek, "So you intended to destroy the temple building and were inciting the people to do this?"

Here the prisoner again became animated, the fear disappeared from his eyes, and he began in Greek, "I, goo—," the prisoner's eyes flashed with horror at having again almost said the wrong thing, "Never in my life, Hegemon, have I intended to destroy the temple nor have I ever tried to instigate such a senseless action."

A look of surprise crossed the face of the secretary, who was bent over a low table, writing down the testimony. He raised his head, but then immediately lowered it to the parchment.

"All kinds of different people flock into the city for the holiday. Among them are magi, astrologers, soothsayers, and murderers," said the procurator in a monotone. "And liars as well. You, for example. It is plainly written: He incited the people to destroy the temple. People have testified to that."

"Those good people," began the prisoner, and after hastily adding, "Hegemon," he continued, "are ignorant and have muddled what I said. In fact, I'm beginning to fear that this confusion will go on for a long time. And all because he writes down what I said incorrectly."

Silence ensued. Now both pained eyes gazed at the prisoner seriously.

"I will tell you again, but for the last time: stop pretending to be crazy, villain," said Pilate in a soft monotone. "Not much has been recorded against you, but it is enough to hang you."

"No, no, Hegemon," said the prisoner, straining every nerve in his desire to be convincing, "There's someone who follows, follows me around everywhere, always writing on a goatskin parchment. And once I happened to see the parchment and was aghast. Absolutely nothing that was written there did I ever say. I begged him, 'For God's sake burn your parchment!' But he snatched it out of my hands and ran away."

"Who is he?" asked Pilate distastefully, touching his hand to his temple.

"Levi Matvei," the prisoner explained willingly. "He was a tax collector, and I first met him on a road in Bethphage at the place where the fig orchard juts out at an angle, and I struck up a conversation with him. At first he treated me with hostility and even insulted me, that is, he thought he was insulting me by calling me a dog,"—here the prisoner laughed. "I personally have no bad feelings about dogs that would cause me to take offense at the name..."

The secretary stopped writing and cast a furtive, surprised glance not at the prisoner but at the procurator.

"...However, after he heard me out, he began to soften," continued Yeshua, "and finally he threw his money down on the road and said that he'd come traveling with me..."

Pilate laughed with one side of his mouth, baring his yellow teeth. Turning his whole body to the secretary, he said, "O, city of Yershalaim!

What tales it can tell! Did you hear that, a tax collector who throws his money on the road!"

Not knowing how to respond to that, the secretary deemed it obligatory to smile as Pilate had.

"But he said that money had become hateful to him," said Yeshua in explanation of Levi Matvei's strange behavior, and then he added, "Since then he has been my traveling companion."

His teeth still bared, the procurator glanced first at the prisoner, and then at the sun, which was rising steadily over the equestrian statues of the hippodrome located far below to the right, and suddenly, as an agonizing wave of nausea swept over him, the procurator realized that the simplest way to get this strange miscreant off his balcony was with two words, "Hang him." Get rid of the escort too, leave the colonnade, go inside the palace, order the room to be darkened, collapse on the bed, ask for some cold water, call piteously for the dog Banga, and complain to him about his hemicrania. Suddenly the thought of poison flashed seductively through the procurator's aching head.

He looked at the prisoner with lusterless eyes and was silent for awhile, trying desperately to recall why this prisoner with a face disfigured by beatings was standing before him in Yershalaim's pitiless morning sun, and what other pointless questions had to be addressed to him.

"Levi Matvei, did you say?" the sick man asked in a hoarse voice and shut his eyes.

"Yes, Levi Matvei," came the high voice that was tormenting him.

"But still, what was it that you said about the temple to the crowd in the marketplace?"

The voice of the man answering seemed to pierce the side of Pilate's forehead. Inexpressibly tormenting, that voice said, "I said, Hegemon, that the temple of the old faith will fall and that a new temple of truth will be created. I said it that way to make it easier to understand."

"Why did you, a vagrant, stir up the crowds in the marketplace by talking about truth, when you have no conception of what it is? What is truth?"

And here the procurator thought, "O my gods! I am questioning about something irrelevant to the case... My brain isn't working anymore..." And again he had a vision of a cup of dark liquid. "Poison, give me poison..."

And again he heard the voice, "The truth is, first of all, that your head aches, so badly, in fact, that you're having fainthearted thoughts about death. Not only are you too weak to talk to me, but you're even having trouble looking at me. That I, at this moment, am your unwilling executioner upsets me. You can't think about anything and the only thing you want is to call your dog, the only creature, it seems, to whom you are attached. But your sufferings will soon end, and your headache will pass."

The secretary looked goggle-eyed at the prisoner and stopped writing in the middle of a word.

Pilate raised his martyred eyes to the prisoner and saw that the sun was already high above the hippodrome, that one ray had penetrated the colonnade and was creeping toward Yeshua's tattered sandals, and that he was trying to step out of the sun.

The procurator then got up from his chair and pressed his head with his hands, a look of horror appearing on his yellowish, clean-shaven face. But he immediately suppressed it with an effort of will and again lowered himself into the chair.

Meanwhile the prisoner went on talking, but the secretary no longer wrote any of it down, he just craned his neck like a goose, not wanting to miss a single word.

"Well, then, it's all over," said the prisoner, looking kindly at Pilate, "and I'm very glad that it is. I would advise you, Hegemon, to leave the palace for a short while and take a stroll somewhere in the vicinity, perhaps in the gardens on Mount Eleon. There will be a thunderstorm..." the prisoner turned and squinted his eyes at the sun, "...later on, towards evening. The walk would do you a lot of good, and I would be happy to accompany you. Some new ideas have occurred to me which may, I think, be of interest to you, and I would be especially happy to share them with you since you strike me as being a very intelligent man."

The secretary turned deathly pale and dropped the scroll on the floor.

"The trouble is," continued the bound man, whom no one was stopping, "that you are too isolated and have lost all faith in people. After all, you will agree, one shouldn't lavish all one's attention on a dog. Your life is impoverished, Hegemon," and here the speaker allowed himself a smile.

The secretary now had only one thought: whether or not to believe his own ears. There was no other choice but to believe. Then he tried to imagine in exactly what fanciful way the procurator would express his anger at the prisoner's unprecedented insolence. But the secretary could not imagine this, even though he knew the procurator very well.

Then the procurator's hoarse and cracked voice was heard, saying in Latin, "Untie his hands."

One of the legionaries in the escort tapped his spear, handed it to someone else, and went over and removed the prisoner's bonds. The secretary picked up the scroll, decided not to write anything down for the time being and not to be surprised at anything.

"Tell the truth," said Pilate softly in Greek, "are you a great physician?"

"No, Procurator, I am not a physician," answered the prisoner, rubbing his mangled, swollen, reddened wrists with pleasure.

Pilate looked probingly at the prisoner from beneath his brows, and his eyes, no longer dull, gave off their familiar sparkle.

"I did not ask you before," said Pilate, "but do you, perhaps, know Latin too?"

"Yes, I do," answered the prisoner.

Pilate's yellowish cheeks filled with color, and he asked in Latin, "How did you know that I wanted to call my dog?"

"That was very simple," replied the prisoner in Latin, "You waved your hand in the air," the prisoner repeated Pilate's gesture—"as if you were petting something, and your lips..."

"Yes," said Pilate.

They were both silent for awhile. Then Pilate asked in Greek, "And so, you are a physician?"

"No, no," was the prisoner's animated reply, "Believe me, I am not a physician."

"Well, all right. If you wish to keep it secret, you may do so. It has no direct bearing on the case. So you maintain that you did not incite them to tear down... or burn, or in any other manner destroy the temple?"

"I repeat, Hegemon, I did not incite them to any such actions. Do I look like an imbecile?"

"Oh, no, you do not look like an imbecile," replied the procurator softly, breaking out in a fearsome smile. "So swear that you did nothing of that kind."

"What would you have me swear by?" asked the unbound prisoner excitedly.

"Well, by your life," answered the procurator. "It is most timely that you swear by your life since it is hanging by a thread, understand that."

"You do not think, do you, Hegemon, that you hung it there?" asked the prisoner. "If you do, you are very much mistaken."

Pilate shuddered and answered through his teeth, "I can cut that thread."

"You are mistaken about that too," retorted the prisoner, smiling brightly and shielding himself from the sun with his hand. "Don't you agree that that thread can only be cut by the one who hung it?"

"Yes, yes," said Pilate, smiling. "Now I have no doubt that the idle gawkers of Yershalaim followed at your heels. I do not know who hung up your tongue, but he did a good job. By the way, tell me: is it true that you entered Yershalaim through the Shushan Gate astride a donkey and accompanied by rabble, who shouted their welcome to you as if you were some kind of prophet?" Here the procurator pointed to the scroll of parchment.

The prisoner looked uncomprehendingly at the procurator.

"I have no donkey, Hegemon," he said. "I did enter Yershalaim through the Shushan Gate, but on foot, and accompanied only by Levi Matvei, and no one shouted to me since no one in Yershalaim knew me then."

"Don't you know these people," continued Pilate, keeping his eyes fixed on the prisoner, "a certain Dismas, Gestas, and Bar-rabban?"

"I do not know those good people," answered the prisoner.

"Is that the truth?"

"Yes, it is."

"And now tell me, why do you keep using the words 'good people?' Do you call everyone that?"

"Yes, everyone," replied the prisoner. "There are no evil people in the world."

"That is the first time I have heard that," said Pilate with a laugh, "but maybe I know little of life! You don't have to write down any more," he said to the secretary, although the latter had not been writing anything down, and then he continued speaking to the prisoner, "Did you read that in some Greek book?"

"No, I came to that conclusion on my own."

"And that is what you preach?"

"Yes."

"But what about the centurion Mark, whom they call Ratkiller, is he—a good man?"

"Yes, he is," answered the prisoner, "but he's an unhappy man. Ever since good people disfigured him, he's been cruel and hard. I'm curious to know, who mutilated him?"

"I'll gladly tell you," retorted Pilate, "because I was a witness. Good people attacked him the way dogs attack bears. The Germans grabbed him by his neck, arms, and legs. An infantry maniple had been ambushed, and if the cavalry turma under my command had not broken through from the flank, then you, philosopher, would not have had to talk with Ratkiller. It happened in the battle of Idistaviso, in the Valley of the Maidens."

"If I could just talk to him," interjected the prisoner wistfully, "I'm sure he would change drastically."

"I imagine," rejoined Pilate, "that the legate of the legion would have little cause to rejoice if you took it into your head to talk to one of his officers or soldiers. Fortunately for all of us, however, that will not happen, and I'm the one who will see that it doesn't."

At that moment a swallow darted into the colonnade, flew in a circle under the gilded ceiling, swooped down, its pointed wing almost grazing the face of one of the bronze statues in the niche, and then took cover behind the capital of the column. Perhaps it had decided to build a nest there.

During the swallow's flight, the following thought was taking shape in the procurator's now bright and clear head: the Hegemon had looked into the case of the vagrant philosopher Yeshua, called Ha-Notsri, and found the criminal charges against him to be unsubstantiated. Specifically, he found no connection whatsoever between Yeshua's actions and the recent disorders in Yershalaim. The vagrant philosopher turned out to be mentally ill. In consequence of which, the procurator does not confirm the death sentence pronounced against Ha-Notsri by the Lesser Sinedrion. However, in view of the fact that Ha-Notsri's insane, utopian speeches might cause unrest in Yershalaim, the procurator is removing Yeshua from Yershalaim and sentencing him to confinement in Strato's Caesarea on the Mediterranean, that is, the site of the procurator's residence.

All he had to do was to dictate it to the secretary.

The swallow's wings whirred above the Hegemon's head, the bird made a dash for the basin of the fountain and flew out into freedom. The procurator looked up at the prisoner and saw a column of dust swirling up next to him.

"Is that all there is against him?" Pilate asked the secretary.

"Unfortunately, no," replied the secretary unexpectedly, and he handed Pilate another piece of parchment.

"What else is there, then?" asked Pilate with a frown.

After he read the parchment, his face changed even more. Either because of the dark blood suffusing his neck and face, or because of something else, his skin lost its yellow cast, turned grayish brown, and his eyes seemed to sink in.

The blood pouring and pounding into his temples was probably also responsible for what had happened to the procurator's vision. He seemed to see the prisoner's head float off somewhere, and another head appear in its place. On top of this bald head was a gold crown with widely-spaced points. On the forehead was a round sore, eating away at the skin and smeared with ointment. The mouth was sunken and toothless, with a capricious and protruding lower lip. Pilate had the feeling that the rose columns on the balcony had disappeared as had the roofs of Yershalaim in the distance below the garden, and that everything around him had drowned in the thick greenery of the Capreaean gardens. And something strange had happened to his hearing too—trumpets seemed to be sounding softly and menacingly in the distance and a nasal voice was clearly heard, haughtily intoning the words, "The law pertaining to insults to the sovereign..."

Brief, strange, disconnected thoughts sped through his brain, "He is lost!"—then, "We are lost!" And included among them was a totally absurd notion about some sort of immortality, and for some reason this immortality evoked a sense of unbearable anguish.

Pilate pulled himself together, drove away the vision, directed his gaze back to the balcony, and the eyes of the prisoner again appeared before him.

"Listen, Ha-Notsri," began the procurator, looking at Yeshua rather strangely: the procurator's face was menacing, but his eyes were anxious. "Did you ever say anything about the great Caesar? Answer! Did you? Or... did you... not?" Pilate drew out the word "not" a bit longer than was appropriate at a trial, and his eyes transmitted a certain thought to Yeshua, which he seemed to want to suggest to the prisoner.

"It is easy and pleasant to tell the truth," observed the prisoner.

"I do not care," retorted Pilate in a choked and angry voice, "whether you find it pleasant or unpleasant to tell the truth. But you will have to tell the truth. And when you speak, weigh every word, unless you want a death that is not only inevitable, but excruciating as well."

No one knows what had come over the procurator of Judea, but he permitted himself to raise his arm, as if shielding himself from the sun, and, using his hand as a shield, to shoot a meaningful glance at the prisoner.

"And so," he said, "answer the question: do you know a certain Judas from Kerioth, and if so, what exactly did you say to him, if you said anything, about Caesar?"

"It happened like this," began the prisoner willingly, "the day before yesterday in the evening, I met a young man near the temple, who called himself Judas, from the town of Kerioth. He invited me to his house in the Lower City and offered me his hospitality..."

"Is he a good man?" asked Pilate, and a diabolical spark flashed in his eyes.

"A very good man and eager for knowledge," assented the prisoner. "He expressed a great deal of interest in my ideas, gave me an enthusiastic welcome..."

"Lit the candles," said Pilate through his teeth, speaking in the same tone of voice as the prisoner, his eyes glittering.

"Yes," continued Yeshua, somewhat surprised by how well-informed the procurator was. "He asked me to express my views on the power of the state. That question was of great interest to him."

"And what did you say?" asked Pilate. "Or will you reply that you forgot what you said?" But hopelessness already sounded in Pilate's voice.

"Among other things," continued the prisoner, "I said that every kind of power is a form of violence against people and that there will come a time when neither the power of the Caesars, nor any other kind of power will exist. Man will enter the kingdom of truth and justice, where no such power will be necessary."

"Go on!"

"There was nothing more," said the prisoner, "because it was then that they rushed in, tied me up, and took me off to prison."

Trying not to miss a word, the secretary quickly scribbled everything down on the parchment.

"There is not, never has been, and never will be any greater and finer power on earth than the power of the Emperor Tiberius!" Pilate's broken and ailing voice swelled forth.

For some reason the procurator looked at the secretary and the escort with hatred.

"And it is not for you, insane criminal, to debate it!" Pilate then began shouting, "Remove the escort from the balcony!" And turning to the secretary, he added, "Leave me alone with the criminal, this is a matter of state."

The escort raised their spears and, clacking their heavily soled caligas in unison, marched off the balcony into the garden. The secretary went out after them.

For a short while the only thing that disturbed the silence on the balcony was the song of the water in the fountain. Pilate saw the plate of water swell up over the small pipe, break off at the edges, and fall down in rivulets.

The prisoner was the first to speak, "I see that a calamity has occurred because I talked to the young man from Kerioth. I have a premonition, Hegemon, that misfortune will befall him, and I feel very sorry for him."

"I think," replied the procurator with a strange laugh, "there is someone else in the world you ought to feel sorrier for than Judas of Kerioth, someone whose fate will be far worse than Judas's! And so, Mark Ratkiller, a cold and confirmed executioner, the people, who as I can see," the procurator pointed to Yeshua's disfigured face, "beat you for your preaching, the outlaws Dismas and Gestas, who, along with their gang, killed four soldiers, the filthy traitor Judas—are they all good people?"

"Yes," answered the prisoner.

"And the kingdom of truth will come?"

"It will, Hegemon," replied Yeshua with conviction.

"It will never come!" Pilate shouted in such a terrible voice that Yeshua recoiled. Many years before, in the Valley of the Maidens Pilate had shouted to his cavalrymen in the same voice, "Cut them down! Cut them down! They've got the giant Ratkiller!" He raised his voice—cracked from giving commands—even higher, shouting out the words so they would be heard in the garden: "Criminal! Criminal! Criminal!"

And then, his voice lowered, he asked, "Yeshua Ha-Notsri, do you believe in any gods?"

"There is one God," replied Yeshua. "I believe in Him."

"Then pray to him! Pray as hard as you can! But," here Pilate's voice dropped, "it won't help. Have you no wife?" asked Pilate, sounding somehow depressed, not comprehending what was happening to him.

"No, I'm alone."

"Hateful city..." Pilate muttered suddenly, his shoulders hunched as if he were chilled, and he wiped his hands as if he were washing them. "You would have been better off, really, if they had cut your throat before you met Judas of Kerioth."

"Couldn't you let me go, Hegemon?" asked the prisoner suddenly, and his voice became anxious. "I can see that they want to kill me."

Pilate's face convulsed in a spasm, he turned the inflamed, bloodshot whites of his eyes toward Yeshua, and said, "Do you suppose, you poor wretch, that the Roman procurator will release a man who said what you said? O gods, gods! Or do you think that I am prepared to take your place? I do not share your ideas! And listen to me: if after this you say even a word, or try and talk to anyone, beware of me! I repeat: beware!"

"Hegemon..."

"Be quiet!" screamed Pilate, his crazed eyes following the swallow that had flown back onto the balcony. "Come here!" he shouted.

When the secretary and the escort returned to their places, Pilate announced that he was confirming the death sentence passed by the Lesser Sinedrion upon the criminal Yeshua Ha-Notsri, and the secretary copied down what Pilate said.

A minute later Mark Ratkiller stood before the procurator. The procurator ordered him to hand the criminal over to the chief of the secret service and in doing so to pass on the procurator's orders that Yeshua Ha-Notsri be separated from the other condemned men, and that, in addition, the secret service command be forbidden, under threat of severe punishment, to converse with Yeshua on any subject or to answer any of his questions.

At a signal from Mark the escort closed ranks around Yeshua and led him off the balcony.

Next to appear before the procurator was a handsome, blond-bearded man with eagle feathers in the crest of his helmet, gold lion heads gleaming on his chest, gold studs on his sword belt, triple-soled sandals laced up to his knees, and a crimson cloak thrown over his left shoulder. He was the legate in command of the legion.

The procurator asked him where the Sebastian cohort was currently stationed. The legate informed him that they were on cordon duty on the square in front of the hippodrome, where the sentences pronounced on the criminals would be announced to the people.

The procurator then directed the legate to detach two centuries from the Roman cohort. One, under the command of Ratkiller, was to escort the criminals to Bald Mountain along with the wagons carrying the executioners and the equipment for the execution. When the escort reached its destination, it was to join the ranks of the upper cordon. The other century was to be sent to Bald Mountain immediately and to commence formation of a cordon without delay. To assist in this task, that is, the securing of the mountain, the procurator asked that the legate send an auxillary cavalry regiment—the Syrian ala.

After the legate left the balcony, the procurator ordered the secretary to invite to the palace the president of the Sinedrion, two of its members, and the head of the temple guard of Yershalaim, but in giving the order, he added his request that he wished to speak to the president in private prior to his meeting with all of them.

The procurator's orders were executed swiftly and precisely, and the sun, which had been scorching Yershalaim with unusual fury in recent days, had still not reached its zenith when, on the upper terrace of the garden, near the two white marble lions guarding the staircase, the procurator met with the president of the Sinedrion and high priest of Judea, Joseph Kaifa.

It was quiet in the garden. But after emerging from the colonnade onto the sun-drenched upper terrace of the garden with its monstrous, elephant-legged palm trees, the terrace that looked out over the whole city of Yershalaim, which he detested, with its hanging bridges, fortresses, and, most important, the utterly indescribable block of marble with golden dragon scales instead of a roof—the temple of Yershalaim,—the procurator's sharp ears picked up a sound coming from below and far away, from the direction of the stone wall that separated the lower terraces of the palace garden from the city square. It was a low rumbling sound, above which would shoot from time to time feeble, thin, half moans, half screams.

The procurator knew that there on the square a countless multitude of Yershalaim's inhabitants had already gathered, stirred up by the recent disorders, that the crowds were impatiently awaiting the pronouncement of the sentences, and that restless water-sellers were circulating and shouting out their wares.

The procurator began by inviting the high priest onto the balcony to escape from the merciless heat, but Kaifa politely declined, explaining that he could not do that on the eve of a holiday. Pilate pulled his hood over his slightly balding head and began the conversation. It was conducted in Greek.

Pilate said that he had reviewed the case of Yeshua Ha-Notsri and had confirmed the death sentence.

Thus, three outlaws, Dismas, Gestas, and Bar-rabban had been condemned to death and were to be executed that day, along with Yeshua Ha-Notsri. The first two, who had conspired to incite the people to rebel against Caesar, had been forcibly detained by Roman authorities and were under the procurator's jurisdiction, and, consequently, no more would be said about them. The last two, Bar-rabban and Ha-Notsri, were apprehended by local authorities and sentenced by the Sinedrion. In accordance with both law and custom, one of these two criminals would have to be released in honor of the great holiday of Passover beginning that day.

And so, the procurator wanted to know which of the two criminals the Sinedrion intended to free: Bar-rabban or Ha-Notsri?

Kaifa inclined his head to signify that he understood the question, and replied, "The Sinedrion asks that Bar-rabban be released."

The procurator knew very well that this would be the high priest's answer, but his task was to appear astonished by such a reply.

Pilate did this with great skill. The eyebrows on his haughty face arched upwards, and the procurator looked at the high priest with amazement.

"I must admit, your reply astonishes me," began the procurator softly. "I fear there may be some misunderstanding here."

Pilate went on to explain. The Roman government did not infringe upon the rights of the local religious authorities, as the high priest well knew, but in this particular instance an obvious mistake seemed to have been made. And, naturally, the Roman government had an interest in correcting that mistake.

In point of fact: the crimes committed by Bar-rabban and by Ha-Notsri were not comparable in terms of seriousness. The latter, clearly a deranged individual, was guilty of making absurd speeches that incited the people of Yershalaim and other locales, but the former bore a far heavier burden of guilt. Not only had he made direct calls to rebellion, he had even killed a guard in the attempt to arrest him. Bar-rabban was incomparably more dangerous than Ha-Notsri.

In view of all the above, the procurator was asking the high priest to review the decision and to release the less dangerous of the two condemned prisoners, which was, without question, Ha-Notsri. And so?...

Kaifa said in a quiet but firm voice that the Sinedrion had reviewed the case very thoroughly and again reiterated its intention to free Barrabban.

"What? Even after my petition? A petition made by a spokesman of the Roman government? Repeat it, High Priest, for the third time."

"I am informing you for the third time that we are freeing Bar-rabban," said Kaifa quietly.

It was all over, and there was nothing more to be said. Ha-Notsri was departing forever, and there would be no one to cure the procurator's horrible, savage headaches. There would be no remedy for them, except death. But it was not this thought that struck Pilate at that moment. That same incomprehensible anguish, which had come over him on the balcony, pierced his entire being once again. He immediately tried to explain this anguish, and the explanation was strange: the procurator had the dim sense that there was something he had not finished saying to the condemned man, or perhaps something he had not finished listening to.

Pilate dismissed that thought, and it flew away as fast as it had flown in. The thought flew away, and the feeling of anguish remained unexplained, for it could not be explained by a second brief thought that flashed like lightning and immediately died out, "Immortality... immortality has come..." Whose immortality has come? The procurator did not understand this, but the thought of that mysterious immortality made him turn cold despite the broiling sun.

"Very well then," said Pilate, "So be it."

Then he looked around, surveyed the world that was visible to him and was amazed at the change that had occurred. The rose bush, laden with flowers, had vanished, as had the cypresses bordering the upper terrace, and the pomegranate tree, and the white statue in the foliage, even the foliage itself. In place of all this floated a crimson sediment in which seaweed began to sway and move somewhere, and Pilate moved along with it. Now he was engulfed by the most terrible rage of all, rage that choked and burned him—the rage of powerlessness.

"I'm suffocating," said Pilate. "Suffocating!"

With a cold, damp hand he tore the clasp off the collar of his cloak, and it fell on the sand.

"It's stifling today, a thunderstorm is brewing," rejoined Kaifa, staring intently at the procurator's reddened face and foreseeing all the torments yet to come. "What a terrible month Nisan has been this year!"

"No," said Pilate, "it's not the sultry weather that's making me suffocate, it's you, Kaifa." And, narrowing his eyes, he smiled and added, "Beware, High Priest."

The high priest's dark eyes flashed, and no less artfully than the procurator had earlier, he put a look of astonishment on his face.

"What am I hearing, Procurator?" replied Kaifa proudly and calmly. "Are you threatening me over a sentence you confirmed yourself? Can that be? We are accustomed to having the Roman procurator choose his words carefully before he speaks. What if someone overheard us, Hegemon?"

Pilate looked at the high priest with dead eyes and bared his teeth in a smile.

"What are you saying, High Priest! Who could possibly overhear us here? Do I look like the young, vagrant holy fool who will be executed today? Am I a boy, Kaifa? I know what I'm saying and where I'm saying it. The garden is cordoned off and the palace is too, so there's not even a crack for a mouse to squeeze through! And not just a mouse, but that, what's-his-name... from Kerioth. By the way, do you know such a person, High Priest? Yes... if someone like that were to get in here, he would regret it bitterly. You don't doubt what I'm saying, do you, High Priest? Know, then, that from now on you shall have no peace, High Priest! Neither you nor your people," said Pilate, pointing far off to the right, where the temple blazed on the heights. "It is I who am telling you this—Pontius Pilate, Knight of the Golden Spear!"

"I know, I know," fearlessly replied the black-bearded Kaifa, and his eyes flashed. He raised his hand up to the sky and went on, "The people of Judea know that you hate them with a fierce hatred and will cause them many torments, but you will never destroy them! God will defend them! He will hear us, the almighty Caesar will hear us, and he will protect us from the scourge of Pilate!"

"Oh, no!" exclaimed Pilate, feeling more and more at ease with every word he spoke: he did not have to pretend anymore, he did not have to choose his words carefully. "You have made too many complaints against me to Caesar, and now my time has come, Kaifa! Now I shall relay word, not to the governor-general in Antioch, not to Rome, but straight to Capreae, to the Emperor himself, word about how you are shielding known rebels from death. And then it will not be water from Solomon's Pool that I shall give Yershalaim to drink, as I had wanted to do for your benefit! No, it will not be water! Remember how, because of you, I had to take the shields with the imperial insignia off the walls, to transfer troops, and remember how I had to come here myself to see what was going on! Remember my words: what you will see here, High Priest, will not be one cohort in Yershalaim, oh, no! The entire Lightning Legion will be at the city walls, so will the Arabian cavalry, and then you will hear bitter weeping and groaning! Then you will remember the Bar-rabban you saved and you will regret that you sent to death the philosopher who preached peace!"

The high priest's face had become covered with blotches, his eyes burned. Like the procurator, he smiled, baring his teeth, and replied, "Procurator, do you yourself believe what you just said? No, you do not! It was not peace that that rabble-rouser brought to Yershalaim, and you, Knight, know that very well. You wanted to release him so that he would stir the people up, do violence to their religion, and subject them to Roman swords! But I, High Priest of Judea, shall not, so long as I live, allow the faith to be profaned, and I shall protect the people! Do you hear, Pilate?" And here Kaifa raised his hand threateningly, "Take heed, Procurator!"

Kaifa fell silent, and again the procurator heard what sounded like the sea rolling up to the walls of the garden of Herod the Great. This noise rose from below up to the procurator's feet and into his face. And behind him, beyond the wings of the palace was heard the anxious blaring of trumpets, the heavy crunch of hundreds of feet, and the clanking of iron. The procurator now realized that the Roman infantry was already moving out, in accordance with his orders, heading toward the pre-execution parade that was so terrifying to outlaws and insurgents.

"Can you hear, Procurator?" quietly repeated the high priest. "Are you really telling me that all this,"—here the high priest raised both his hands, and the dark hood fell from his head—"was caused by that miserable outlaw Bar-rabban?"

The procurator wiped his cold, damp forehead with the back of his wrist and looked down at the ground. Then, squinting up at the sky, he saw that the scorching ball was almost directly overhead, and that Kaifa's shadow by the lion's tail had shrunk away to nothing. He said quietly and indifferently, "It's not long till noon. We got carried away by our conversation, but we must proceed."

After making intricately worded excuses, Pilate asked the high priest to sit down on a bench in the shade of the magnolias and wait while he summoned the others needed for the brief, final meeting and gave one last order regarding the execution.

Kaifa made a polite bow, his hand pressed to his heart, and remained in the garden while Pilate returned to the balcony. There he ordered the waiting secretary to summon to the garden the legate of the legion, the tribune of the cohort, two members of the Sinedrion, and the chief of the temple guard, all of whom were awaiting his summons on the lower terrace in the round gazebo with the fountain. Pilate added that he himself was about to go out to the garden, and then he disappeared inside the palace.

While the secretary gathered people for the meeting, Pilate was in a darkened room, shuttered against the sun, meeting with a man whose face was half-covered by a hood, even though the sun's rays could not possibly have bothered him in that room. This meeting was extremely brief. The procurator said a few quiet words to the man who then left, and Pilate returned to the garden through the colonnade.

There, in the presence of everyone whom he had wished to see, the procurator solemnly and dryly acknowledged his confirmation of Yeshua Ha-Notsri's death sentence, and formally asked the members of the Sinedrion which of the criminals they wished to spare. After receiving the answer that it was Bar-rabban, the procurator said, "Very well," and ordered the secretary to enter it in the official record, squeezed the clasp which the secretary had picked up off the sand, and said solemnly, "It is time!"

All present then started down the wide marble staircase between the walls of roses that exuded an overpowering scent. They descended lower and lower to the palace wall, to the gates that opened out onto a large, smoothly paved square, at the far end of which could be seen the columns and statues of the Yershalaim hippodrome.

As soon as the group emerged from the garden onto the square and mounted the vast stone platform that dominated it, Pilate surveyed the scene through narrowed eyelids and assessed the situation. Although the space he had just traversed, that is, from the palace walls to the platform, was empty, he could no longer see the square directly in front of him because it had been devoured by the crowd. The crowd would have engulfed the platform and the open space as well if it had not been held back by the triple row of Sebastian soldiers on Pilate's left and the soldiers of the Ituraean auxiliary cohort on his right.

And so, Pilate mounted the platform, clutching the superfluous clasp mechanically in his fist and squinting. But the procurator was not squinting because the sun burned his eyes. No! He was squinting because he did not want to see the condemned men who, as he knew very well, were now being led up onto the platform behind him.

As soon as the white cloak with the crimson lining appeared atop the

stone cliff, high above the edge of the human sea, a wave of sound—
"Ah-h-h-h"—assailed the ears of the unseeing Pilate. It began softly, orig-
inating somewhere in the distance near the hippodrome, then attained
a thunderous volume, which lasted for several seconds before beginning to subside. "They've seen me," thought the procurator. Rather
than ebbing completely, the wave unexpectedly began to swell once
again, rising even higher than before, and on top of this second wave,
like seething foam on the crest of a breaker, whistles and women's
screams were heard above the thunder. "They've been led onto the
platform," thought Pilate, "and there are screams because several
women were crushed when the crowd surged forward."

He waited for a few moments, knowing that no force could silence
the crowd until it had released all its pent-up emotions and quieted
down by itself.

And when that moment came, the procurator threw up his right
arm, and the noise of the crowd finally subsided.

Then Pilate took as much of the scorching air into his lungs as he
could and began to shout. His broken voice carried over the thousands
of heads, "In the name of the Emperor Caesar!..."

His ears were immediately assailed by a choppy, metallic din, repeated several times, that came from the soldiers in the cohorts as they
threw their spears and insignia up into the air and shouted out in fearsome tones, "Hail Caesar!"

Pilate craned his neck and looked straight up at the sun. A green
flame flared up under his eyelids, setting his brain on fire, and the
hoarse Aramaic words flew out over the crowd, "Four criminals, arrested in Yershalaim for murder, incitement to rebellion, and abuse of
the laws and the faith, have been sentenced to the shameful death of
hanging on posts! And the execution shall take place shortly on Bald
Mountain! The names of the criminals are Dismas, Gestas, Bar-rabban,
and Ha-Notsri. Here they stand before you!"

Pilate pointed to the right, without seeing the prisoners, but knowing that they were there where they were supposed to be.

The crowd replied with a prolonged roar that seemed to signify either surprise or relief. When it quieted down, Pilate continued, "But
only three of them shall be executed, for, in accordance with law and
custom, in honor of the Passover holiday, one of the condemned, as
chosen by the Lesser Sinedrion and confirmed by the power of Rome,
shall have his contemptible life restored to him by the magnanimous
Emperor Caesar!"

While Pilate was shouting out these words, he was also listening to
the deep silence that followed in the wake of the roar. Now not a sigh or
a rustle reached his ears, and there was even a moment when it seemed
as if everything around him had disappeared completely. The city he
detested had died, and he was standing there alone, being scorched by

the rays that were shooting down on his upturned face. Pilate held onto the silence for awhile and then began to shout out, "The name of the one whose release you are about to witness is..."

Pilate paused again, holding back the name, making sure that he had said everything he was supposed to, because he knew that once he had pronounced the lucky one's name, the dead city would spring to life and nothing he might say subsequently would be audible.

"Is that everything?" Pilate whispered wordlessly to himself. "Yes, everything. The name!"

And, rolling the "r" out over the silent crowd, he cried out, "Bar-rab-ban!"

It then seemed to him that the sun began ringing and burst overhead, engulfing his ears in flame. And raging inside this flame were roaring, shrieks, groans, laughter, and whistling.

Pilate turned and walked back along the platform to the steps, looking at nothing but the multicolored tiles beneath his feet, so as not to stumble. He knew that a hail of bronze coins and dates was raining down on the platform behind him, and that people in the roaring crowd were climbing on each other's shoulders, crushing each other, trying to see the miracle with their own eyes—a man who was already in the hands of death, had been torn from its grip! To see the legionaries remove his bonds, unintentionally causing him searing pain in his arms which had been dislocated during his interrogation; to see him grimacing and groaning as he smiled an insane, senseless smile.

Pilate knew that the escort was now leading the three men with bound hands over to the side stairs in order to bring them out to the road heading west, out of the city, to Bald Mountain. It was only when he was down on the ground, with the platform at his back, that he opened his eyes, knowing that he was safe—the condemned men were out of sight.

Blending with the wail of the crowd, which was beginning to die down, were the piercing cries of the various heralds, repeating—some in Aramaic, others in Greek—what the procurator had just proclaimed from the platform. In addition, he could hear the staccato clatter of horses' hooves approaching, and the short, cheerful blast of a trumpet. Echoing these sounds were the sharp whistles of the boys on the rooftops of the street that led from the marketplace to the hippodrome square, and by shouts of "Watch out!"

A soldier, standing alone in a cleared part of the square with a badge in his hand, waved at them anxiously, and then the procurator, the legate of the legion, the secretary, and the escort came to a halt.

The cavalry ala, picking up speed, galloped out onto the square in order to cut across it diagonally. Bypassing a throng of people, it headed down the lane along the vine-covered stone wall, the shortest route to Bald Mountain.

Flying by at a gallop, the commander of the ala, a Syrian, small as a boy and dark as a mulatto, shouted out something in a thin voice as he passed Pilate and drew his sword from its sheath. His vicious, sweaty, raven-black horse shied and reared up on its hind legs. After sheathing his sword, the commander struck his horse across the neck with a whip, steadied it, and rode off down the lane at a gallop. Behind him in a cloud of dust rode the horsemen, in rows of three, the tips of their light bamboo lances bobbing up and down. The faces that streamed past the procurator with gaily bared, flashing teeth looked especially swarthy beneath the white turbans.

Raising a cloud of dust, the ala tore down the lane; the last one to ride past Pilate was a soldier with a trumpet on his back that glowed in the sun.

Shielding his face from the dust with his hand and frowning with dissatisfaction, Pilate moved on, heading for the gates of the palace garden, and following behind him were the legate of the legion, the secretary, and the escort.

It was about ten o'clock in the morning.

III

The Seventh Proof

"YES, it was about ten in the morning, my esteemed Ivan Nikolayevich," said the professor.

The poet passed his hand over his face like a man who had just revived and discovered that it was evening at Patriarch's Ponds.

The water in the pond had turned black, and a small rowboat was skimming across it; the splash of an oar could be heard from the boat, along with a woman's giggling. There were now people on the benches along the paths, but once again only on the other three sides of the square, not on the side where our friends were having their chat.

The sky over Moscow seemed to have paled, and high overhead, shining clearly and distinctly, was a white, not yet golden, full moon. It had become much easier to breathe, and the voices under the linden trees now sounded softer, as often happens in the evening.

"How come I didn't notice that he managed to spin out a whole tale?" thought Bezdomny in amazement. "Why it's already evening! But maybe he didn't really tell it, maybe I just fell asleep and dreamed it all?"

But he had to believe that the professor had told the story because otherwise it would mean that Berlioz had dreamed the same thing since the latter, looking attentively into the foreigner's face, said, "Your story is extraordinarily interesting, Professor, even if it bears no relation whatsoever to the gospel accounts."

"I beg your pardon," replied the professor, with a condescending smile, "You of all people should know that absolutely nothing written in the gospels ever happened in actual fact, and if we start citing the gospels as an historical source..." He smiled again, and Berlioz stopped short because he had been saying the very same thing to Bezdomny when they were walking down Bronnaya Street on their way to Patriarch's Ponds.

"That's true," Berlioz remarked, "but I'm afraid no one can confirm that what you told us actually took place either."

"Oh, no! There is someone who can confirm it!" retorted the professor in broken Russian with total self-assurance and suddenly, with a mysterious air, he motioned the two friends to come closer.

They both leaned toward him, one on either side, and he said, without any trace of the accent which seemed to fade in and out, the devil knows why, "The fact is..." at this point the professor looked around nervously and began speaking in a whisper, "I myself witnessed the whole thing. I was there on Pontius Pilate's balcony, and in the garden when he was talking with Kaifa, and on the platform too, but I was there in secret, incognito, so to speak, so I beg you—keep it quiet, and don't breathe a word to a soul! Shhh!"

Silence fell, and Berlioz grew pale.

"You... you've been in Moscow how long?" he asked, his voice trembling.

"I just this minute arrived," replied the professor absently, and it was only then that the friends had the sense to look straight into his eyes, whereupon they decided that his left eye, the green one, was completely mad, and the right one was vacant, black and dead.

"Well, that explains everything!" thought Berlioz, in confusion, "He's a crazy German who just arrived, or else he just went off his rocker here at Patriarch's Ponds. That's the story!"

Yes, indeed, that did explain everything: the highly bizarre breakfast with the late philosopher Kant, the idiotic talk about Annushka and the sunflower oil, the predictions about a head being cut off, and all the rest of it—the professor was a madman.

Berlioz knew immediately what had to be done. Leaning back against the bench, he started winking at Bezdomny behind the professor's back, as if to say, "Don't contradict him," but the flustered poet did not understand the signals.

"Yes, yes, yes," said Berlioz excitedly, "but of course, it's all possible! More than possible, the whole thing, Pontius Pilate, the balcony, and all the rest of it... Did you come here alone or with your wife?"

"Alone, alone, I'm always alone," the professor replied bitterly.

"But where are your things, Professor?" Berlioz asked in an insinuating tone. "At the Metropole? Where are you staying?"

"Where am I staying? Nowhere," answered the half-witted German, his green eye wandering sadly and wildly over Patriarch's Ponds.

"What? But... where will you be living?"

"In your apartment," replied the madman with sudden familiarity and he winked.

"I... I would be delighted," stammered Berlioz, "but you would no doubt be uncomfortable at my place... Besides, the rooms at the Metropole are superb, it's a first-class hotel..."

"And the devil doesn't exist either?" the sick man suddenly inquired cheerily of Ivan Nikolayevich.

"And the devil doesn't..."

"Don't contradict him!" mouthed Berlioz in a soundless whisper, as he dove behind the professor's back and made a face.

"There is no devil!" exclaimed Ivan Nikolayevich, blurting out what he shouldn't have because all the nonsense going on had made him flustered. "What a nuisance you are! Stop acting like a loon!"

At this point the madman produced such a laugh that a sparrow darted out of the linden tree overhead.

"Well, now, this is really getting interesting," cried the professor, shaking with laughter. "What is it with you? Whatever comes up you say doesn't exist!" Suddenly he stopped laughing, and, as often happens with the mentally ill, he went from laughter to the other extreme: he became irritated and shouted harshly, "So, then, you're quite sure he doesn't exist?"

"Calm down, calm down, calm down, Professor," muttered Berlioz, afraid of exciting the sick man. "Just sit here for a moment with comrade Bezdomny while I run to the corner and make a call, and then we'll take you wherever you want to go. After all, you don't know the city..."

It has to be said that Berlioz's plan of action was the correct one: to run to the nearest telephone and inform the office in charge of foreigners that a visiting consultant from abroad was sitting at Patriarch's Ponds in an obviously deranged state. And that measures should be taken to prevent any unpleasantness.

"You want to make a call? Fine, go ahead," the sick man said, giving his sad consent and suddenly making an impassioned plea, "But as we part, I implore you, at least believe that the devil exists! I ask no more than that. Keep in mind that for this we have the seventh proof, the most reliable of them all! And you are about to get a demonstration."

"Fine, fine," said Berlioz in an insincerely placating way, and after winking at the dismayed poet, who was by no means enchanted by the idea of guarding the mad German, he made for the exit from Patriarch's Ponds that was located at the corner of Bronnaya Street and Yermolayevsky Lane.

Then suddenly the professor seemed to recover and cheer up.

"Mikhail Alexandrovich!" he shouted after Berlioz.

Berlioz shuddered and turned around, but comforted himself with the thought that the professor had learned his name and patronymic from reading the newspapers. Cupping his hands like a megaphone, the professor shouted, "Wouldn't you like me to have a telegram sent to your uncle in Kiev right away?"

And once again Berlioz was given a jolt. How did the madman know that he had an uncle in Kiev? That certainly hadn't appeared in any newspaper. Perhaps Bezdomny's right after all? And what about those fake documents of his? What an oddball he is! Get to a phone! Get to a phone! Call right away! It won't take them long to figure out who he is!

And without listening to another word, Berlioz ran off.

Just then, at the exit to Bronnaya Street, a man got up from a bench and walked over to the editor. He was none other than the same fellow who earlier, in broad daylight, had materialized out of the dense heat. Only now, he was no longer made of air, but of ordinary flesh and blood, and in the gathering twilight Berlioz could clearly see that his wispy mustache looked like chicken feathers, his beady little eyes looked ironical and half-drunk, and his checked trousers had been yanked up so high you could see his dirty white socks.

Mikhail Alexandrovich drew back with a start, but comforted himself with the thought that it was a meaningless coincidence and that now was not the time to think about it anyway.

"Looking for the turnstile, Mister?" inquired the fellow in the checked trousers in a cracked tenor, "Right this way! Go straight ahead and you'll come out at just the right place. How 'bout a little something for showing you the way... enough for a pint... help a former choirmaster get back on his feet!" Squirming and grimacing, he swept off his jockey cap with a theatrical gesture.

Berlioz did not stop to listen to the begging and simpering choirmaster, but ran instead to the turnstile and grabbed hold of it with his hand. He turned it and was about to step across the tracks when a red and white light splashed in his face—the words in the glass box lit up: "Caution! Streetcar!"

Just then the streetcar started hurtling toward him as it turned onto the newly-laid stretch of track running from Yermolayevsky Lane to Bronnaya Street. After coming out of the turn onto the straightaway, the streetcar lit up inside with electric light, let out a roar, and picked up speed.

Even though the ever-cautious Berlioz was standing in a perfectly safe place, he decided to return behind the barrier, he shifted his hand on the revolving gate, and took a step backward. Just then his hand slipped and lost its grip, his foot slid uncontrollably, as if on ice, over the cobblestones that led down to the track, his other leg shot up in the air, and he was thrown onto the rails.

Trying to grab hold of something, Berlioz fell flat on his back and hit the back of his neck lightly against the cobblestones. He just caught a glimpse of the gilded moon high above, but he could not tell whether it was on his right or his left. He managed to turn on his side, and at the same time to draw his legs frantically up to his stomach. When he turned, he saw the absolutely white, horror-stricken face and the crimson armband of the woman streetcar driver bearing down on him with irresistible force. Berlioz did not scream, but the whole street around him began squealing with women's despairing voices. The driver pulled on the electric emergency brake, the car pitched forward, then jumped instantaneously, and the glass flew out of the windows, crashing and shattering. Then a voice in Berlioz's brain cried out in despair, "Can this be?" Once again, and for the last time, the moon flashed, but it was already breaking into splinters, and then it became dark.

The streetcar covered Berlioz, and a round dark object was propelled under the railing of Patriarch's Ponds path onto the cobbled slope. After rolling down the slope, it began bouncing over the cobblestones of Bronnaya Street.

It was Berlioz's severed head.

IV

The Chase

THE women's hysterical screams died down, the police whistles stopped drilling, and two ambulances drove off, one to the morgue carrying the headless body and severed head, the other—the beautiful streetcar driver who had been injured by the shattered glass. Street cleaners in white aprons cleared away the broken glass and sprinkled sand on the pools of blood, and Ivan Nikolayevich, who had collapsed onto a bench before reaching the turnstile, stayed where he was.

He had tried to get up several times, but his legs would not obey him—Bezdomny seemed to be paralyzed.

As soon as he heard the first scream, the poet had rushed to the turnstile and seen the head bouncing over the pavement. This made him so deranged that he collapsed onto a bench and bit his hand till it bled. He had forgotten all about the mad German, naturally, and was trying to make sense out of just one thing: how could it be that he had just been talking to Berlioz and a minute later—the head...

Distraught people kept running down the path past the poet, shouting various things, but Ivan Nikolayevich could not comprehend what they were saying.

But then, suddenly two women collided with each other right in front of him, and one of them, sharp-nosed and bareheaded, shouted to the other practically in the poet's ear, "Annushka, our Annushka! She was coming from Sadovaya Street! It's her doing! She got some sunflower oil at the store, then went and smashed a liter of it on the turnstile! Made a mess of her skirt... she swore and swore! And he, poor man, must have slipped and fallen on the rails..."

Of all the words the woman had shouted, only one impressed itself on Ivan Nikolayevich's disordered brain, "Annushka..."

"Annushka... Annushka?" the poet mumbled, turning around anxiously, "Excuse me, excuse me..."

Attached to the word "Annushka" was "sunflower oil" and then, for some reason, "Pontius Pilate." The poet rejected Pilate and began forming a chain, beginning with the word "Annushka." The chain was formed very quickly and led straight to the mad professor.

He was to blame! Hadn't he said the meeting wouldn't take place because Annushka had spilled the oil? And now, if you please, it won't take place! And that was the least of it: hadn't he said straight out that Berlioz's head would be cut off by a woman? Yes, yes, yes! And the streetcar driver was a woman! What was all this about? Huh?

There was no longer even a shadow of a doubt that the mysterious consultant had known beforehand, and in exact detail, the entire scenario of Berlioz's horrible death. Two thoughts then penetrated the poet's brain. The first was, "He's certainly no mad man! That's all nonsense!" And the second was, "Could he have engineered the whole thing himself?!"

But how, pray tell, did he do it?!

"Yes, that's what we'll find out!"

Ivan Nikolayevich exerted great effort, got up from the bench and rushed back to where he had been talking with the professor. And, fortunately, it turned out that he was still there.

On Bronnaya Street the streetlights had come on, and a golden moon was shining over Patriarch's Ponds. In the moonlight, which is always deceptive, Ivan Nikolayevich thought he saw the professor standing there, holding a sword, rather than a walking stick under his arm.

The unctuous retired choirmaster was sitting exactly where Ivan Nikolayevich had been sitting not long before. Now the choirmaster had an obviously useless pince-nez perched on his nose. One lens was cracked, and the other was missing. This made the checked fellow look even more repellent than he had when he was showing Berlioz the way to the tracks.

Feeling his heart grow cold, Ivan walked over to the professor and looked him straight in the face. He was convinced that it showed no signs of madness, and never had.

"Confess, who are you?" Ivan asked hollowly.

The foreigner frowned, looked as if he were seeing the poet for the first time, and answered hostilely, "No understand... no speak Russian..."

"The gentleman doesn't understand you," interjected the choirmaster from the bench, although no one had asked him to explain the foreigner's words.

"Don't play games!" said Ivan in a threatening tone and felt a chill in the pit of his stomach. "You were speaking Russian perfectly before. You're not a German and not a professor! You're—a murderer and a spy! Show me your papers!" screamed Ivan in a fury.

The enigmatic professor squeamishly twisted his already twisted mouth and shrugged his shoulders.

"Citizen!" said the loathsome choirmaster, butting in once again, "Why are you disturbing a foreign tourist? You can be severely penalized for that!" And the suspicious professor then put on an arrogant face, turned, and walked away from Ivan.

Ivan felt as if he were losing his mind. Gasping, he turned to the choirmaster, "Hey, citizen, help detain a criminal! It's your duty."

The choirmaster became very animated, leaped off the bench and yelled, "What criminal? Where is he? A foreign criminal?" The choirmaster's beady eyes sparkled mirthfully. "This one here? If he's a criminal, then the first thing to do is shout 'Help!' Or else he'll get away. C'mon, let's do it together! Both at once!" at which point the choirmaster opened his jaws wide.

The flustered Ivan obeyed the buffoonlike choirmaster and shouted "Help!" but the choirmaster fooled him and didn't say a word.

Ivan's hoarse and solitary shout accomplished nothing. Two girls recoiled from him, and he heard the word "drunk."

"Ah, so you're in league with him?" shouted Ivan, becoming enraged, "What are you trying to do, make fun of me? Let me by!"

Ivan went to the right, and the choirmaster followed suit. Ivan went to the left, and the scoundrel did the same.

"Are you purposely trying to trip me up?" screamed Ivan, furious. "I'll turn you over to the police too."

Ivan tried to grab the rascal by the sleeve, but missed and caught hold of nothing. The choirmaster seemed to have vanished into the ground.

Ivan groaned, looked off into the distance and saw the hateful stranger. He was already at the exit to Patriarch's Lane, and he wasn't alone. The more than dubious choirmaster had managed to catch up with him. And that wasn't all: the third member of the company, who had appeared out of nowhere, turned out to be a cat, big as a hog and pitch-black, like a crow, or like soot, and sporting a mustache like a reckless cavalryman's. The threesome set off down Patriarch's Lane, with the cat walking on his hind legs.

Ivan rushed off in pursuit of the villains and soon realized that catching up with them was going to be very difficult.

The threesome tore down the lane in a flash and were on Spiridonovka. No matter how much Ivan quickened his pace, the distance between pursuer and pursued never shortened. Before the poet could realize what was happening, he had left the peaceful Spiridonovka behind, and found himself at Nikitsky Gates where his plight worsened. Here there was a huge crowd, and when Ivan ran into one of the passersby, he was showered with curses. It was here, moreover, that the villainous gang resorted to that favorite outlaw strategy—they split up and went in different directions.

With great agility the choirmaster corkscrewed himself into a moving bus going to Arbat Square, and disappeared. After losing one of the pack, Ivan focused all his attention on the cat. He saw the bizarre feline walk over to the steps of an "A" streetcar that was standing at the stop, rudely push aside a woman who let out a shriek, grab onto the handrail, and even try to thrust a ten-kopeck piece at the conductress through the window, open because of the heat.

The cat's behavior so amazed Ivan that he froze in his tracks next to a grocery store on the corner, only then to become even more amazed by the behavior of the conductress. As soon as she saw the cat climbing onto the streetcar, she began shouting with such fury that she shook all over, "Cats aren't allowed! No passengers with cats! Shoo! Get off, or I'll call the police!"

But neither the conductress nor the passengers were amazed by the most important thing of all, namely, that a cat was not merely getting on a streetcar, which wasn't so bad, but that he intended to pay his fare!

The cat turned out to be not only a fare-paying beast, but a disciplined one as well. At the first yell from the conductress, he stopped in his tracks, got off the streetcar, and sat down at the stop, stroking his whiskers with his ten-kopeck piece. But no sooner did the conductress pull the cord and the streetcar start to move, than the cat did just what anyone who has been kicked off a streetcar and still has somewhere to go would do. He let all three cars go by, then jumped onto the coupler in back of the last one, grabbed on to a piece of tubing that stuck out of the back with his paw and sailed off, saving himself ten kopecks in the bargain.

Preoccupied with the revolting cat, Ivan almost lost track of the most important one of the three, the professor. But, fortunately, he had not managed to slip away. Ivan caught sight of his gray beret in the midst of the crowd swarming into Bolshaya Nikitskaya or Herzen Street. In the flash of an eye Ivan himself was there, but to no avail. Although he quickened his pace and began running at jogging speed, jostling pedestrians in the process, he never managed to get any closer to the professor.

However distraught he was, Ivan Nikolayevich could not help but be struck by the supernatural speed of the chase. Twenty seconds after leaving Nikitsky Gates, he was blinded by the lights on Arbat Square, and a few seconds after that, he was on a dark side street with sloping sidewalks, where he fell with a crash and hit his knee. Again a brightly lit thoroughfare—Kropotkin Street, then a side-street, then Ostozhenka and yet another side street, bleak, nasty, and poorly lit. It was here that Ivan Nikolayevich finally lost the man who was so important to him. The professor had vanished.

Ivan Nikolayevich grew discouraged, but not for long. It suddenly hit him that the professor would definitely turn up in building No. 13, and without fail in apartment 47.

Ivan Nikolayevich tore through the entranceway and flew up the stairs to the second floor. He found the apartment immediately and rang the bell impatiently. He did not have to wait long because a little girl of five or so opened the door for him, and then went off without a word.

The vast and extremely neglected entrance hall was dimly lit by a tiny corner lamp that hung from a ceiling black with dirt. A bicycle without tires hung on the wall, and on the floor there was an enormous iron-studded chest; on the shelf above the coatrack there was a winter hat, with long drooping earflaps. Behind one of the doors a booming masculine voice was angrily declaiming verses on the radio.

Ivan Nikolayevich was not in the least bit flustered by these unfamiliar surroundings and headed straight for the hallway, reasoning thus, "Naturally, he's hidden himself in the bathroom." It was dark in the hallway, and as he bumped against the wall, Ivan saw a faint streak of light coming from under the doorway. He grabbed the doorknob and gave it a slight tug. The latch unfastened, and Ivan found himself precisely in the bathroom, and thought what luck that was.

But it wasn't the right kind of luck! The moist warmth of the bath enveloped Ivan, and in the light of the coals smouldering in the water heater, he could see large basins hanging on the wall and a bathtub, pitted with horrible black spots where the enamel had chipped off. There in the tub stood a naked woman, covered in soap and with a loofah in her hands. She squinted nearsightedly at Ivan's intruding figure, and clearly mistaking him for someone else in the hellish light, said softly and cheerily, "Kiryushka! Quit fooling around! Have you gone out of your mind? Fyodor Ivanovich will be back any minute. Get out of here this instant!"—and she waved her loofah at Ivan.

It was an obvious misunderstanding, and Ivan Nikolayevich was, of course, to blame. But not wanting to admit it, he yelled reproachfully, "Whore!..."—and then somehow ended up in the kitchen. There was no one there. Standing silently on top of the stove in the semidarkness were a number of unlit primus stoves. A single ray of moonlight filtered through the dusty window, which had not been cleaned for years, and feebly illuminated the corner, where amidst the dust and cobwebs hung a forgotten icon, the stubs of two wedding candles still sticking out of its case. Tacked to the wall beneath the large icon was a small paper one.

No one knows what thought possessed Ivan at that moment, only that he grabbed the paper icon and one of the candles before running out the back door. With these objects in hand, he left the strange apartment, mumbling in embarrassment over what had just happened to him in the bathroom, and wondering, despite himself, who the insolent Kiryushka might be and whether the repulsive hat with the earflaps belonged to him.

Ivan looked all around for the fugitive in the dreary, deserted back street, but he was nowhere to be seen. Then Ivan said to himself firmly, "But, of course, he's on the Moscow River! Onward!"

Perhaps Ivan Nikolayevich should have been asked why he thought the professor was on the Moscow River and not somewhere else. But there was, alas, no one to ask him. The foul and odious street was completely deserted.

In no time at all Ivan Nikolayevich could be seen on the granite steps of the amphitheater by the Moscow River.

After taking off his clothes, Ivan entrusted them to a pleasant-looking fellow with a beard who was smoking a hand-rolled cigarette. Next to him was a torn, white Tolstoyan-style shirt and a pair of worn-down, unlaced shoes. Waving his arms in order to cool off, Ivan plunged into the water like a swallow. The water was so cold it took his breath away, and the thought even flashed through his mind that he might not be able to surface. But surface he did, and, puffing and snorting, his eyes bulging with terror, Ivan Nikolayevich began swimming in the black, oil-reeking water between the broken zigzags of light cast by the streetlamps along the bank.

When a wet Ivan came tripping up the steps to the spot where the bearded fellow had been safeguarding his clothes, it soon became clear that not only the latter had been kidnapped, but the former as well, that is, the bearded fellow himself. Where the pile of clothes had been, there was now only a pair of striped long johns, a torn Tolstoyan-style shirt, a candle, a paper icon, and a box of matches. After shaking his fist at someone in the distance in a gesture of feeble outrage, Ivan proceeded to put on what had been left behind.

It was then that two thoughts began to plague him: first, his MASSOLIT ID, which he was never without, was gone, and second, would he be able to walk around Moscow the way he was dressed without being stopped? Long underwear was a bit... True, it was nobody's business, but someone might make a fuss or try to stop him.

Ivan tore the ankle buttons off his long johns, thinking that might make them look more like summer trousers. He then gathered up the icon, candle, and matches and set off, saying to himself, "To Griboyedov! No doubt he's there."

The evening life of the city had already begun. Trucks sped by in clouds of dust, their chains rattling, and on their platforms men lay on sacks, their stomachs sticking up in the air. Everyone's windows were open, and shining in each one was a lamp with an orange shade; from all the windows, doors, gateways, rooftops, attics, cellars, and courtyards came the hoarse strains of the polonaise from the opera *Eugene Onegin.*

Ivan Nikolayevich's fears were completely justified: passersby took one look at him and laughed and turned to stare. As a result he decided to abandon the main thoroughfares and make his way through the side streets and back alleys where people were less nosy, and there was less chance that a barefoot man would be pestered about long johns that stubbornly refused to look like trousers.

So Ivan plunged into the mysterious network of back alleys around the Arbat. He slinked along the walls, casting fearful glances and turning around every minute. From time to time, he hid in entranceways. He avoided intersections lit up by traffic lights, and the plush doorways of embassy residences.

Throughout his difficult journey, he was, for some reason, inexpressibly tormented by the omnipresent orchestra accompanying the deep bass who was singing of his love for Tatyana.

V

The Incident at Griboyedov

O N the ring boulevard there was an old cream-colored two-storey house that stood in the depths of a withered garden which was separated from the sidewalk by a carved wrought-iron fence. The small area in front of the house was paved over with asphalt, and in winter a mound of snow with a shovel on top towered above it; in summer it was shaded by a canvas awning and became the outdoor pavilion of a summer restaurant.

The house was called "Griboyedov House" because it was supposed to have been owned at one time by an aunt of the writer Alexander Sergeyevich Griboyedov. Whether she owned it or not, we don't know for sure. I even seem to recall that Griboyedov did not have an aunt who owned property... However, that was what the house was called. What's more, a certain Moscow prevaricator would relate how the famous writer read excerpts from his *Woe from Wit* to this very same aunt while she reclined on a sofa in the round colonnaded hall on the second floor. And, the devil knows, maybe he did, but that's not the point!

The point is that at the present time the house was owned by that very same MASSOLIT which had been headed by the unfortunate Mikhail Alexandrovich Berlioz before his appearance at Patriarch's Ponds.

Following the example of MASSOLIT's members, no one called the place "Griboyedov House," but simply—"Griboyedov": "Yesterday I hung around Griboyedov for two hours." —"Well, so how did you make out?" —"I managed to get a month in Yalta." — "Good for you!" Or, "Go talk to Berlioz, he's seeing people at Griboyedov today from four to five," and so on.

MASSOLIT's quarters at Griboyedov were the best and most comfortable imaginable. The first thing a visitor saw upon entering Griboyedov were the notices of various sports clubs, and the individual and group photos of MASSOLIT members which hung on the walls of the staircase leading to the second floor.

The first room on the upper floor had a sign on the door in bold letters which said, "Fishing and Dacha Section," accompanied by a picture of a carp jumping into a net.

The sign on Room No. 2 was not entirely clear, "Creative Day-Trips. See M. V. Podlozhnaya."

The next room had a brief but utterly baffling sign, "Perelygino," and the array of signs that adorned the rest of the aunt's walnut doors would make your eyes swim, "Sign up with Polevkina for supplies," "Cashier. Personal Accounts for Theatrical Sketch Writers..."

If one cut through the very long line that began downstairs in the entryhall, one could see the sign, "Housing Concerns," on a door that people were constantly bombarding.

Behind "Housing Concerns" was a lush poster depicting a horseman in a Caucasian cloak riding along the crest of a mountain cliff with a rifle slung over his shoulders. Lower on the poster were palm trees and a balcony, and on the balcony a young man with a cowlick was seated and looking upward into space with incredibly alert eyes while holding a fountain pen in his hand. The caption read, "Creative Package Vacations from two weeks (for a short story or novella) to one year (for a novel or trilogy). Yalta, Suuk-Su, Borovoye, Tsikhidziri, Makhindzhauri, Leningrad (Winter Palace)." This door also had a line, but not a very long one, only about one hundred and fifty people.

Then there followed, conforming to the whimsical curves, rises, and falls of Griboyedov House—"MASSOLIT Administration," "Cashiers: Nos. 2, 3, 4, 5," "Editorial Board," "MASSOLIT President," "Billiard Room," various auxiliary offices, and finally, that same colonnaded room where Griboyedov's aunt had enjoyed listening to her brilliant nephew's comedy.

Any visitor who came to Griboyedov immediately realized, unless, of course, he was a complete ninny, how good life was for the fortunates who were members of MASSOLIT. He would soon become green with envy and curse the heavens for not having blessed him at birth with literary talent, without which, naturally, one could not even dream of possessing the brown, gold-bordered MASSOLIT membership card that smelled of expensive leather, and was known to all of Moscow.

Who will say anything in defense of envy? As a feeling it falls into the category of worthless, but even so, one has to put oneself in the position of our visitor. After all, what he saw on the upper floor was merely the icing on the cake. The entire bottom floor of the aunt's house was occupied by a restaurant, and what a restaurant it was! Griboyedov was considered the best restaurant in Moscow and with good reason. Not only because of its layout in two large rooms with vaulted ceilings that were adorned with lilac-colored, Assyrian-maned horses, or because each table had its own shawl-shaded lamp, or because it was exclusive and closed to the general public, but also because it served better-quality food than any restaurant in Moscow and at reasonable, by no means prohibitive, prices as well.

This explains why the author of these most truthful lines found nothing surprising in the following exchange which he once overheard at Griboyedov's wrought-iron fence:

"Where will you be dining today, Amvrosy?"

"Why, what a question! Here, of course, my dear Foka! Archibald Archibaldovich let me in on a secret: the à la carte special today is perch *au naturel*, a real virtuoso dish!"

"You know how to live, Amvrosy!" sighed Foka, a skinny and unkempt fellow with a carbuncle on his neck, to Amvrosy, a pudgy-cheeked, rosy-lipped, golden-haired giant of a poet.

"I don't have any special talents," retorted Amvrosy, "just an ordinary desire to live like a human being. Now you'll say, Foka, that you can get perch at the Coliseum. But a serving there costs 13 rubles, 15 kopecks, and here it's only 5, 50! Besides, at the Coliseum the perch is three days old, not to mention the fact that at the Coliseum there's no guarantee you won't get smacked in the kisser with a bunch of grapes by the first young scamp who bursts in from Theater Passage. No, Foka, I'm categorically opposed to the Coliseum," boomed the gourmet Amvrosy for the benefit of the whole boulevard. "Don't try to change my mind!"

"I'm not trying to, Amvrosy," squeaked Foka. "One can also dine at home."

"Thank you, no," trumpeted Amvrosy, "I can just imagine your wife, trying to cook perch *au naturel* in the frying pan of your communal kitchen! Ha-ha-ha! *Au revoir*, Foka!" And, humming a tune, Amvrosy headed for the canopied veranda.

Ha-ha-ha... Yes, those were the days! Oldtime residents of Moscow still remember the famous Griboyedov! As for the perch *au naturel*, that was nothing, my dear Amvrosy! What about the sterlet, the sterlet in a silver pan, the sterlet filets layered with crayfish and fresh caviar? And the eggs *en cocotte* with mushroom puree? And didn't you like the filet of thrush? With truffles? The quail *à la genoise*? Ten rubles fifty! And the jazz, and the gracious service! And in July, when the whole family's away at the dacha and pressing literary matters keep you in the city—out on the veranda in the shades of twisting grapevines, a bowl of soup *printanier* sitting in a sunspot on the most immaculate tablecloth imaginable? Do you remember, Amvrosy? Well, why ask! I can see by your lips that you do remember. So much for the whitefish and perch! What about the snipe, great snipe, jacksnipe, woodcock in season, quail, and sandpipers? The Narzan water fizzing in your throat?! But enough, your eyes, dear reader, are becoming glazed! Follow me!

At 10:30 p.m., on the evening when Berlioz was killed at Patriarch's

Ponds, the lights were on in only one of the upper rooms at Gribo-yedov, where the twelve writers who had been summoned to a meeting languished, as they waited for Mikhail Alexandrovich to arrive.

They were sitting on chairs, tables, and even on both windowsills of the MASSOLIT administration room and were suffering intensely from the stifling heat. Not a breath of fresh air came through the open windows. All the heat that had accumulated on Moscow's pavement during the day was being released, and it was clear that the night would bring no relief. The smell of onions wafted up from the basement of the aunt's house, where the restaurant kitchen was, and everyone was thirsty, edgy, and irritable.

The fiction writer Beskudnikov—a quiet, neatly dressed man with keen, yet unfocused eyes—took out his watch. The hour hand was creeping towards eleven. Beskudnikov tapped his finger on the dial, and showed it to his neighbor, the poet Dvubratsky, who was sitting at the table and shuffling his yellow rubber-soled shoes out of boredom.

"Well, really," muttered Dvubratsky.

"The lad must have gotten held up on the Klyazma," said the thick-voiced Nastasya Lukinishna Nepremenova, an orphan from a Moscow merchant family, who had become a writer and turned out naval battle stories under the pen name "Bosun George."

"If I may!" boldly began Zagrivov, an author of popular sketches. "I too would rather be sipping tea on the balcony than stewing around here. Wasn't the meeting called for ten?"

"It's nice on the Klyazma now," said Bosun George, egging everyone on because she knew the writers' colony in Perelygino on the Klyazma was a universal sore spot. "The nightingales are probably singing by now. Somehow I always work better in the country, especially in spring."

"For three years now I've been paying in money, so I can send my wife to that paradise for her Grave's disease, but so far it's no go," said the novelist Hieronymus Poprikhin venomously and bitterly.

"It's just the luck of the draw," rang out the critic Ababkov from the windowsill.

Joy blazed in Bosun George's little eyes, and softening her heavy contralto she said, "No need for envy, comrades. There are twenty-two dachas in all, and only seven more are being built, and there are 3,000 of us in MASSOLIT."

"3,111," interjected someone from the corner.

"Well, there you have it," continued the Bosun, "what's to be done? It's natural that the most talented people got dachas..."

"The generals!" cut in the dramatist Glukharyov, joining the fray.

Beskudnikov gave a theatrical yawn and walked out of the room.

"Five rooms in Perelygino all to himself," said Glukharyov in his wake.

"Lavrovich has six," exclaimed Deniskin, "and an oak-paneled dining room!"

"Right now that's not the issue," rang out Ababkov, "the issue is that it's eleven-thirty."

It got noisy, something like a mutiny was brewing. They put in a call to the hateful Perelygino, got the wrong dacha, namely, Lavrovich's, where they learned that Lavrovich had gone off to the river. That threw them into a complete muddle. For no reason at all they called the Commission for Belles Lettres (extension 930) and naturally found no one there.

"He could at least have called!" shouted Deniskin, Glukharyov, and Kvant.

Alas, they were shouting in vain: Mikhail Alexandrovich could not call anywhere. Far, far from Griboyedov, in a cavernous room illuminated by 1000-watt bulbs, on three zinc tables lay the remains of what once had been Mikhail Alexandrovich.

On the first table lay his naked body, covered in dried blood, with a broken arm and crushed rib cage; on the second lay his head with smashed-in front teeth and glazed, wide-open eyes, undisturbed by the most glaring light; on the third lay a pile of encrusted rags.

Standing near the headless body were a professor of forensic medicine, a pathologist and his dissector, members of the investigating team, and the writer Zheldybin, Mikhail Alexandrovich Berlioz's assistant at MASSOLIT, who had been called away from his wife's sickbed.

A car had gone to get Zheldybin and to take him first (this was around midnight), together with the investigators, to the apartment of the deceased, where the latter's papers were put under seal, and then, to the morgue.

And now they were all standing around the remains of the deceased, discussing how best to proceed: should they sew the severed head back on the neck or lay the body out in Griboyedov's hall with a black cloth drawn tightly up to the chin?

Yes, Mikhail Alexandrovich was unable to make any calls; so Deniskin, Glukharyov, Kvant, and Beskudnikov ranted and raved in vain. At precisely midnight all twelve writers quit the upper floor and went down to the restaurant. Here again they had cause to think unkindly about Mikhail Alexandrovich: naturally, all the tables on the veranda were already taken, and they were forced to have supper in the beautiful but stuffy rooms inside.

At exactly midnight, something in the first room crashed, followed by ringing, shattering, and thumping sounds. And at once a thin male voice began to shout despairingly to the music, "Hallelujah!" These were the sounds of the renowned Griboyedov jazz ensemble. Sweat-covered faces seemed to light up, the horses painted on the ceiling seemed to come to life, the light in the lamps seemed to glow brighter, and suddenly, as if freed from their chains, both rooms started to dance, with the veranda following suit.

Glukharyov began dancing with the poetess Tamara Polumesyats, Kvant began to dance, as did the novelist Zhukopov, with a movie actress in a yellow dress; Dragunsky, Cherdakchi, tiny Deniskin, and gigantic Bosun George all danced, and the architect Semeikina-Gall, a beauty, danced in the tight embrace of an unknown man in white burlap trousers. The regulars danced and so did their guests, Muscovites and out-of-towners too, the writer Ioann from Kronstadt, someone called Vitya Kuftik from Rostov, who was apparently a director and had a purple birthmark covering his entire cheek; representatives of the poetry subsection of MASSOLIT, that is, Pavianov, Bogokhulsky, Sladky, Spichkin, and Adelfina Buzdyak; young men of dubious profession wearing jackets with shoulder pads; and a very elderly man with a piece of green onion stuck in his beard, who danced with an anemic girl in a crumpled orange dress.

Bathed in sweat, the waiters carried foaming mugs of beer above the dancers' heads, yelling hoarsely and venomously, "Sorry, sir!" Somewhere, orders were being shouted through a megaphone, "One shashlyk! Two zubrovkas! Tripe *polonaise!*" The thin voice no longer sang but wailed, "Hallelujah!" The crash of the jazz band's bold cymbals was sometimes muffled by the crash the dishes made as the dishwashers sent them down a slide into the kitchen. In a word, hell.

And at midnight a vision appeared in hell. A handsome, dark-eyed fellow with a dagger-shaped beard stepped out onto the veranda in full dress and cast an imperial glance over his domain. They said, the mystics did, that there was once a time when this handsome fellow wore a broad leather belt with pistols instead of a tailcoat, and tied his raven hair with red silk, and the brig he commanded sailed the Caribbean under a black flag with skull and crossbones.

But no, no! The seductive mystics lie, the Caribbeans of this world are gone—desperate marauders do not sail across them, chased by corvettes, and cannon smoke does not hang low over the waves. There is nothing, and there never was anything! The stunted linden tree over there is all there is, and the iron fence, and the boulevard beyond it... And the ice melting in the little bowl, and someone's bloodshot bulllike eyes at a neighboring table, and it's awful, awful... O gods, my gods, give me poison, poison!

And suddenly the name "Berlioz" fluttered up from a table. The band broke off abruptly and fell silent, as if punched with a fist. "What, what, what, what?"—"Berlioz!!!" And people jumped up and started screaming...

Indeed, a wave of grief surged up in response to the terrible news about Mikhail Alexandrovich. Someone ran around yelling that a collective telegram had to be composed right then and there, before anyone could leave, and sent off right away.

But what kind of a telegram, may we ask, and where should it be sent? And why send it? And indeed, where? And what use is a telegram to a man whose flattened occiput was at that very minute being squeezed by the dissector's rubber gloves and whose neck a professor is probing with curved needles? He is dead and has no need of telegrams. It's all over, so let's not burden the telegraph system.

Yes, he's dead, he's dead... But we are alive!

Yes, a wave of grief did arise and lasted for a time, but then it began to subside and one fellow had already returned to his table and, furtively at first, but then openly downed some vodka and taken a bite to eat. And indeed, why waste *suprème de volaille*? How can we help Mikhail Alexandrovich? By staying hungry? After all, we are alive!

Naturally, the piano was locked shut, the band went home, and several of the journalists went off to their offices to write obituaries. Word spread that Zheldybin had returned from the morgue. He ensconced himself in the upstairs office of the deceased, which started the rumor that he would be Berlioz's replacement. Zheldybin summoned all twelve members of the board from the restaurant, and at the meeting which began immediately in Berlioz's office they moved to discuss a number of urgent matters: decorations for the colonnaded Griboyedov hall, transport of the body from the morgue to the hall, the establishment of visiting hours, and various other things connected with the regrettable occurence.

Meanwhile, the restaurant resumed its usual nighttime routine, which would have gone on until closing time, that is, 4 a.m., if something had not happened that was truly out of the ordinary and made a much bigger impression on the patrons than the news of Berlioz's death.

The first to become agitated were the cabdrivers on call at the entrance to Griboyedov. One of them climbed up on the coach box and was heard to cry, "Wow! Take a look at that!"

It was then that a small light suddenly flashed near the wrought-iron fence and began moving toward the veranda. People who were seated got up to have a look and saw that a white apparition was accompanying the small light as it moved toward the restaurant. When it got as far as the trellis, everyone stiffened in their chairs, bits of sterlet stuck on their forks and their eyes opened wide. The doorman, who at that moment had emerged from the restaurant coatroom in order to go out into the courtyard for a smoke, stamped out his cigarette and was about to move toward the apparition with the intention of barring its entrance to the restaurant. But, instead of doing this, he stopped, for some reason, a foolish smile on his face.

Thus the apparition passed through the opening in the trellis and stepped unimpeded onto the veranda. Then everyone saw that it was no apparition at all, but Ivan Nikolayevich Bezdomny—an extremely well-known poet.

He was barefoot and dressed in white striped long johns and a torn, once-white Tolstoyan peasant blouse which had a paper icon with the faded picture of an unknown saint pinned to its front with a safety pin. He was carrying a lighted wedding candle in one hand. There was a fresh scratch on his right cheek. It would be hard to measure the depth of the silence that reigned on the veranda. Beer could be seen spilling onto the floor from a mug that one of the waiters was holding sideways.

The poet raised his candle over his head and said in a loud voice, "Greetings, friends!" after which he glanced under the nearest table and exclaimed in anguish, "No, he isn't here!"

Two voices were heard. A basso said pitilessly, "A clear-cut case. The DT's."

The second, a frightened woman's voice, said, "How could the police let him out on the street looking like that?"

Ivan Nikolayevich heard that and replied, "They tried to stop me twice, in Skatertny Lane and here, on Bronnaya Street, but I jumped over a fence and, as you see, scraped my cheek!" Here Ivan Nikolayevich raised the candle and cried out, "Brothers in literature!" (His hoarse voice grew strong and impassioned.) "Listen to me everyone! He has appeared! Catch him immediately or else he will do indescribable harm!"

"What? What? What did he say? Who has appeared?" came voices from all sides.

"The consultant!" answered Ivan, "And he's the one who killed Misha Berlioz at Patriarch's Ponds."

At this point people from the inner room began to pour out onto the veranda and a crowd gathered around Ivan's candle.

"Sorry! Give us more details," said a soft and polite voice above Ivan Nikolayevich's ear. "Tell us, how was he killed, and who killed him?"

"A foreign consultant, a professor and a spy!" replied Ivan, looking all around.

"And what's his name?" people whispered in his ear.

"That's the problem!" Ivan cried in anguish, "If only I knew his name! I couldn't make out the name on his visiting card... I only remember it began with 'W'! But what was the name beginning with 'W'?" Ivan asked himself, clutching his forehead. Suddenly he began to mumble, "W, W, W! Wa... Wo... Washner? Wagner? Weiner? Wegner? Winter?" Ripples ran through his hair from the tension he was under.

"Wolf?" a woman cried out sympathetically.

Ivan got angry.

"Fool!" he yelled, trying to locate the woman. "What's Wolf got to do with it? Wolf is beside the point! Wo, Wo... No! I just can't remember! But this is the main thing, citizens: call the police right away and tell them to send five motorcycles armed with machine guns to catch the professor. And don't forget to mention he's got two accomplices: a tall fellow in checks... with a cracked pince-nez... and a fat black cat. Meanwhile I'll go search Griboyedov... I have a feeling he's here!"

Ivan became agitated, pushed aside the crowd of onlookers, began waving his candle around, covering himself with wax, and then peering under the tables. At this point a voice called out, "Get a doctor!" and there appeared in front of Ivan a tender, fleshy, clean-shaven, well-fed face with horn-rimmed glasses.

"Comrade Bezdomny," said the face in a voice suited to anniversary celebrations, "Calm down! You're upset over the death of our beloved Mikhail Alexandrovich... Misha Berlioz, to us. We all understand perfectly. You need rest. Now your comrades are going to take you to bed, and you'll go to sleep."

"You," interrupted Ivan, baring his teeth, "Don't you understand that the professor must be caught? And here you are weaseling up to me with your nonsense! Cretin!"

"Comrade Bezdomny, forgive me," he replied, turning red and edging away, already regretting that he had gotten involved in the affair.

"No, I'll forgive anyone but you," said Ivan Nikolayevich with calm hatred.

A spasm contorted his face, he quickly switched the candle from his right hand to his left, took a broad swing, and punched the sympathetic face on its ear.

At this point they decided to take Ivan by force, and they did. The candle went out, and his glasses fell off and were immediately trampled. Ivan let out a terrible battle cry which was heard to everyone's titillation even on the boulevard. Then Ivan began to defend himself. Dishes clattered to the floor, women began to scream.

While the waiters were tying the poet up with towels, the commander of the brig was conversing with the doorman in the coatroom.

"You saw, didn't you, that he was in his underwear?" asked the pirate coldly.

"But, Archibald Archibaldovich," replied the doorman timidly, "how could I not admit the gentleman if he is a member of MASSOLIT?"

"But you saw he was in his underwear?" the pirate repeated.

"For pity's sake, Archibald Archibaldovich," the doorman said, turning crimson, "What could I do? I know there are ladies on the veranda..."

"The ladies are not the issue, they don't care," replied the pirate, his eyes literally setting the doorman on fire, "but the police do care! A man in his underwear can tramp around Moscow only if he's in police custody, and only if he's going to one place—the police station! And you as a doorman should know that when you see such a man, you should begin blowing your whistle without a moment's delay. Do you hear me? Do you hear what's happening on the veranda?"

Here the half-crazed doorman could hear the oohs and ahs, crashing dishes, and women's shrieks coming from the veranda.

"Well, how should you be punished for what you did?" asked the pirate.

The skin on the doorman's face took on a typhoid tinge and his eyes became dead. The pirate's black hair, now parted down the middle, seemed to be covered with fiery silk. Gone were his dress shirt and dinner jacket, and sticking out of his leather belt was the butt of a pistol. The doorman imagined himself hanging from the foremast. With his own eyes he saw his tongue hanging out and his lifeless head slumped on his shoulder, and he could even hear the waves splashing against the side of the ship. His knees gave way from under him. But just then, the pirate took pity on him and extinguished his piercing gaze.

"Watch out, Nikolai! This is the last time. We don't need that kind of a doorman in this restaurant. Go be a watchman in a church." Having said this, the commander gave quick, precise, clear orders: "Get Pantelei from the pantry. Call a policeman. Write a report. Order a car. Send it to the asylum." And he added, "Blow your whistle!"

A quarter of an hour later a flabbergasted crowd—not only inside the restaurant, but outside on the boulevard and in the windows of the buildings overlooking the restaurant pavilion— watched as Pantelei, the doorman, a policeman, a waiter, and the poet Ryukhin came out of Griboyedov's gates, carrying a young man swaddled like a doll, with tears running down his face, who tried to spit on Ryukhin, and was screaming the length of the boulevard, "Bastard! Bastard!"

The driver of the van had a malicious look on his face as he started the motor. Alongside him a cabdriver urged on his horse, beating her hindquarters with lilac-colored reins, and shouting, "I'll go fast! I've taken guys to the nuthouse before!"

The crowd buzzed as they discussed this unprecedented event. In short, it was a filthy, vile, titillating, beastly scandal which ended only when the van carting off the unfortunate Ivan Nikolayevich, the policeman, Pantelei, and Ryukhin drove away from the gates of Griboyedov.

VI

Schizophrenia, as Predicted

I T was one-thirty in the morning when a man with a small pointed beard and a white coat entered the reception room of the famous psychiatric clinic that had recently been built outside of Moscow on the banks of the river. Three male nurses were keeping a vigilant eye on Ivan Nikolayevich who was sitting on the couch. The distraught poet Ryukhin was also present. The towels which had been used to tie Ivan Nikolayevich up were lying in a heap on the couch. Ivan Nikolayevich's arms and legs were free.

When he saw the man walk in, Ryukhin turned pale, coughed, and said in a timid voice, "Hello, Doctor."

The doctor bowed to Ryukhin but in doing so, looked not at him, but at Ivan Nikolayevich. The latter was sitting completely still, with his eyebrows raised and an angry expression on his face. He did not stir even when the doctor walked in.

"Doctor," began Ryukhin in a kind of conspiratorial whisper, looking timidly over at Ivan Nikolayevich, "this is the prominent poet Ivan Bezdomny... well, as you can see... we're afraid it might be a case of delirium tremens..."

"Has he been drinking heavily?" asked the doctor through his teeth.

"No, he did drink, but not enough to..."

"Has he been trying to catch cockroaches, rats, little devils, or running dogs?"

"No," replied Ryukhin with a shudder. "I saw him yesterday and this morning too. He was completely fine..."

"And why is he in his underwear? Did they get him out of bed?"

"That, doctor, is the way he arrived at the restaurant."

"Aha, aha," said the doctor with great satisfaction. "And why the cuts and bruises? Did he get in a fight with somebody?"

"He fell off a fence, and then he hit someone in the restaurant... and there was someone else too..."

"I see, I see, I see," said the doctor, and turning to Ivan, he added,

"Hello!"

"Hello, you wrecker!" replied Ivan in a loud, angry voice.

Ryukhin felt so embarrassed that he could not even look at the polite doctor. But the latter was not in the least offended. He removed his glasses in a practiced, graceful manner, and after lifting the hem of his smock, he put the glasses in the back pocket of his trousers. He then asked Ivan, "How old are you?"

"All of you can go to the devil!" Ivan bellowed rudely and turned away.

"But why are you angry? Have I said something unpleasant to you?"

"I'm twenty-three," said Ivan excitedly, "and I'm going to file a complaint against all of you. You in particular, scum!" he said, addressing Ryukhin separately.

"And what is it you wish to complain about?"

"That I, a healthy man, was seized and dragged by force to a madhouse!" Ivan replied angrily.

Here Ryukhin took a good look at Ivan and turned cold: there was absolutely no sign of madness in his eyes. They had looked lackluster at Griboyedov, but now their customary clarity had returned.

"My goodness!" thought Ryukhin in fright, "Can it be that he is completely normal? What nonsense this is! Whatever possessed us to drag him here? He's normal, normal, only his mug's been scratched up..."

Sitting down on a gleaming white stool, the doctor began calmly, "You happen to be in a clinic, not an asylum, where no one will keep you if it is unnecessary."

Ivan Nikolayevich looked mistrustfully out of the corner of his eye but nonetheless muttered, "The Lord be praised! Finally there's one normal person among all the idiots, chief of whom is that booby and hack Sashka!"

"Who is this Sashka-hack?" inquired the doctor.

"He's right here," answered Ivan, pointing a dirty finger in Ryukhin's direction.

Ryukhin flared up in indignation.

"That's what I get instead of thanks!" he thought bitterly, "All because I was concerned about him! There's a bastard for you!"

"He has a typical kulak mentality," began Ivan Nikolayevich, who obviously felt an urge to expose Ryukhin, "and even worse, a kulak who tries very hard to masquerade as a proletarian. Look at his glum face and compare it to the sonorous verses he concocted for New Year's! Heh-heh-heh... 'Soar!' and 'Unfurl'... then take a look inside him and see what he's thinking in there... and you'll gasp!" And Ivan Nikolayevich let out a sinister laugh.

Ryukhin was red, breathing heavily, and thinking of only one thing, that he had nursed a viper to his breast and shown kindness to someone who turned out to be a vicious enemy when put to the test. And worst of all, there was nothing he could do—you could hardly exchange insults with a madman, could you?!

"And why were you brought here?" asked the doctor after he had listened attentively to Bezdomny's accusations.

"May they rot in hell, the blockheads! They grabbed me, tied me up in rags, and dragged me off in a truck!"

"May I ask you why you went to the restaurant in your underwear?"

"There's nothing surprising in that," Ivan answered, "I went for a swim in the Moscow River, and someone took my clothes and left me this junk! I couldn't very well walk around Moscow naked! I put on what was available because I was in a hurry to get to the restaurant at Griboyedov."

The doctor gave Ryukhin a quizzical look, and the latter mumbled gloomily, "That's the name of the restaurant."

"I see," said the doctor, "and why were you in such a hurry? Did you have a business meeting?"

"I was trying to catch the consultant," answered Ivan Nikolayevich, looking around anxiously.

"What consultant?"

"Do you know Berlioz?" asked Ivan pointedly.

"You mean the composer?"

Ivan became flustered. "What does the composer have to do with it? Oh, I see. No, not the composer! He has the same name as Misha Berlioz!"

Ryukhin did not want to say anything but was forced to give an explanation. "Berlioz, the secretary of MASSOLIT, was run over by a streetcar this evening at Patriarch's Ponds."

"Don't lie about things you don't know anything about!" said Ivan, angry at Ryukhin, "You weren't there but I was! He deliberately set it up so he'd fall under the streetcar!"

"Did he push him?"

"What does 'pushing' have to do with it," Ivan exclaimed, furious at how dense everyone was. "Someone like that doesn't have to push! He can do things that would make your flesh crawl! He knew in advance that Berlioz would fall under a streetcar!"

"And did anyone besides you see this consultant?"

"That's the trouble, only me and Berlioz."

"I see. And what did you do to catch this murderer?" At this point the doctor turned around and glanced over at the woman in a white coat who was sitting at a table off to the side. She took out a sheet of paper and began filling in the blank spaces in the columns.

"Here's what I did. I took a small candle from the kitchen..."

"This one here?" asked the doctor, pointing to the broken candle that was lying next to the icon on the table in front of the woman.

"Yes, and..."

"Why the icon?"

"Well, the icon..." Ivan turned red, "The icon was what scared them most of all," he poked a finger in Ryukhin's direction again, "but the fact is that he, the consultant, that is, let's speak frankly... he's in league with evil powers... so you won't have an easy time catching him."

For some reason the attendants stood stiffly at attention and did not take their eyes off Ivan.

"Yes," Ivan continued, "he's in league with evil powers! That's an incontrovertible fact. He personally conversed with Pontius Pilate. And there's no reason to look at me like that! It's true, I tell you! He saw it all—the balcony and the palm trees. He was there with Pontius Pilate, you have my word on it."

"I see, go on..."

"So I, well, pinned the icon on my chest and ran after him..."

At this point the clock struck 2 a.m.

"Uh oh!" exclaimed Ivan and got up from the couch, "it's 2 a.m., and here I am wasting time talking with you! Excuse me, where's the phone?"

"Let him use the phone," the doctor ordered the attendants.

Ivan grabbed the receiver while the woman asked Ryukhin in a whisper, "Is he married?"

"No, single," Ryukhin replied, frightened.

"A member of the union?"

"Yes."

"Is this the police?" Ivan screamed into the receiver, "Is this the police? Comrade dispatcher, see to it that five armed motorcycles are sent on the double to catch the foreign consultant. What? Come get me and I'll go with you... This is the poet Bezdomny speaking from the asylum... What's your address?" whispered Bezdomny to the doctor, cupping his hand over the receiver. Then he again screamed into the phone, "Do you hear me? Hello!... What an outrage!" Suddenly, Ivan let out a wail and threw the phone against the wall. Then he turned to the doctor, extended his hand, said a chilly "good-bye" and started to leave.

"Excuse me," said the doctor, looking Ivan in the eye, "where do you wish to go in the middle of the night in your underwear? You're not well, stay here with us!"

"Let me by" said Ivan to the attendants who were blocking the doors. "Are you going to let me by or not?" screamed the poet in an awful voice.

Ryukhin shuddered, and the woman pressed a button on the table, whereupon a small shiny box and a sealed ampule popped out on its glass surface.

"So that's how it is?!" said Ivan looking around wildly, like a hunted animal. "OK then! Good-bye!!" and he dove headlong at the blind covering the window.

A fairly loud crash was heard, but the glass behind the blind didn't even crack, and Ivan was soon thrashing about in the attendants' arms. He became hoarse, tried to bite, and screamed, "So that's the kind of windows you have here! Let me go! Let me go!"

A hypodermic syringe flashed in the doctor's hands, and in a single motion the woman ripped open the bedraggled sleeve of Ivan's Tolstoyan shirt and grabbed his arm with unfeminine strength. There was a smell of ether, Ivan grew weak in the arms of the four attendants, and the agile doctor took advantage of the moment and plunged the needle into Ivan's arm. They held on to Ivan a few seconds longer and then lowered him onto the couch.

"Bandits!" shouted Ivan and jumped up from the couch, but was deposited on it again. As soon as they let go of him, he was about to jump up again, but this time he sat back down himself. He fell silent for a moment, looking around wildly, then yawned suddenly, then grinned maliciously.

"So they've locked me up after all," he said, yawned again, and then suddenly lay down, putting his head on the pillow and his fist under his cheek like a child. In a sleepy voice, free of malice, he mumbled, "Well, and very good too... You'll pay for what you've done. I warned you, so now do as you wish!... Right now what interests me most is Pontius Pilate... Pilate..." and here he closed his eyes.

"A bath, Room 117—private—and post a guard," ordered the doctor while putting on his glasses. At this point Ryukhin shuddered again; the white doors opened noiselessly onto a corridor lit by blue night lights. A rubber-wheeled gurney rolled into the room from the corridor, and the sedated Ivan was transferred to it and wheeled down the corridor, the doors closing behind him.

"Doctor," whispered the shaken Ryukhin, "is he really sick?"

"Oh, yes," replied the doctor.

"But what's the matter with him?" Ryukhin asked timidly.

The weary doctor looked at him and replied listlessly, "Speech and motor excitation... delirious episodes... clearly a complicated case... Schizophrenia, one must assume. And alcoholism too..."

Ryukhin did not understand anything the doctor said except that Ivan Nikolayevich was obviously in a bad way. He sighed and asked, "And what was all that about a consultant?"

"He probably saw someone who excited his disturbed imagination. Or perhaps he was hallucinating..."

A few minutes later the truck was carrying Ryukhin back to Moscow. It was getting light, and the streetlights along the highway cast a glow that was both unnecessary and unpleasant. The driver was angry that the night had been wasted, and he drove the truck so hard that it skidded on the turns.

Then the forest fell away and remained in the background, the river disappeared to the side, and a highly varied panorama came out to meet the truck: fences with sentry boxes, stacks of wood, towering poles and masts threaded with spools, piles of crushed stone, land slashed by canals—in short, one had the feeling that it, Moscow, was lying in wait just around the next bend, and was about to fall on one and engulf one.

Ryukhin was having a bumpy ride, since the stump he was sitting on kept trying to slide out from under him. The towels from the restaurant, which the policeman and Pantelei had tossed into the truck before leaving earlier on the trolleybus, were sliding all over the floor of the truck. Ryukhin had started to try and pick them up, but for some reason he hissed in fury, "The devil with them! Why am I making an ass of myself?"—and he kicked the towels aside and stopped looking at them.

The passenger was in a terrible mood. It was obvious that his visit to the insane asylum had had a most oppressive effect on him. He was trying to understand what was tormenting him. Was it the corridor with the blue lights that had stuck his mind? Was it the thought that there was nothing worse in the world than to lose your mind? Yes, yes, of course, it was that too. But that, after all, was a universal response. There must be something else. But what was it? It was the insult, that was it. Yes, yes, the insulting words that Bezdomny had thrown in his face. And the worst thing was not that they were insulting, but that they were true.

The poet had stopped looking off to the sides, and staring at the dirty, rattling floor of the truck, he began muttering and whining, gnawing away at himself.

Yes, his poetry... He was thirty-two! What did lie ahead? He would go on composing a few poems a year. Until he was old? Yes, until he was old. What would these poems bring him? Fame? "What nonsense! At least don't deceive yourself. Fame never comes to someone who writes bad poetry. But why are my poems bad? It was true what he said, true!"—Ryukhin showed himself no mercy—"I don't believe in anything I've ever written!"

Poisoned by this attack of neurasthenia, the poet gave a lurch as the floor beneath him stopped shaking. Ryukhin raised his head and saw that he had long since arrived in Moscow, and, moreover, that a new day was dawning over the city, that the cloud above was outlined in gold, that his truck was stuck in a column of traffic at the turn onto the boulevard, and that close by there was a metal man on a pedestal, his head slightly bent, looking indifferently at the boulevard.

Strange thoughts poured into the stricken poet's head. "There's an example of real luck..." Here Ryukhin stood up in the truck and raised his fist in an attack against the cast-iron man who wasn't harming anyone. "Whatever step he took in life, whatever happened to him, everything worked to his advantage, everything added to his fame! But what did he do? I don't get it... What's so special about the words: 'Storm with mist the heavens covers...'? I don't understand!... He was lucky, lucky, that's all!" Ryukhin concluded with sudden venom, just as he felt the truck stir beneath him. "He was shot, shot by that white guard, who smashed his hip and guaranteed his immortality..."

The column of traffic began to move. Not more than two minutes later, the poet, utterly ill and visibly older, was stepping onto the veranda of Griboyedov. It had already cleared out. There was a group in the corner, finishing up their drinks, presided over by a master of ceremonies Ryukhin knew who was wearing an embroidered skullcap and holding a glass of Abrau champagne in his hand.

Ryukhin, laden with towels, was met politely by Archibald Archibaldovich and immediately relieved of the accursed rags. Had Ryukhin not had such an agonizing time at the clinic and in the truck, he probably would have enjoyed recounting what had happened at the hospital, embellishing the story with a few details of his own invention. But now he wasn't in the mood for it and however unobservant Ryukhin was, now, after the torture in the truck, he looked sharply into the pirate's face for the first time and realized that despite his inquiries about Bezdomny and even his exclamations of "How awful!" he was at heart completely indifferent to Bezdomny's fate and did not even feel sorry for him. "Good man! That's right!" thought Ryukhin with cynical, self-lacerating malice. Cutting short his story about schizophrenia, he asked, "Archibald Archibaldovich, may I have a little vodka?"

The pirate put on a sympathetic face and whispered, "I understand... right away," and he signalled a waiter.

A quarter of an hour later Ryukhin was sitting all by himself, hunched over a plate of carp, downing glass after glass. He was coming to realize and to acknowledge that he could not rectify anything in his life, he could only forget.

The poet had wasted his night while others were feasting and now he realized it could never be brought back. He had only to raise his head from the table lamp up to the sky to realize that the night was gone forever. The waiters were hurriedly pulling the tablecoths off the tables. The cats nosing about the veranda had a morning look about them. Day was bearing down on the poet with full force.

VII

The Evil Apartment

I F on the following morning anyone had said to Styopa Likhodeyev, "Styopa! You'll be shot if you don't get up this minute!" Styopa would have replied in a numb, faintly audible voice, "Shoot me, do whatever you like to me, but I'm not getting up."

It wasn't just a matter of getting up—he didn't even think he could open his eyes, because if he did, lightning would strike and blast his head to bits. A heavy bell was clanging inside his head, brown spots with fiery-green rims were floating between his eyeballs and his closed lids, and to cap things off, he felt nauseated, and his nausea seemed to be related to the sounds coming from a persistent phonograph.

Styopa was trying to remember something, but the only thing he could remember was that yesterday—he didn't know where—he had been standing, napkin in hand, trying to kiss a lady and promising he would visit her the next day at noon on the dot. The lady had refused him, saying, "Don't, don't, I won't be home!"—but Styopa had been insistent, "I think I'll just come anyway!"

Who this lady was, what time it was now, or what the day or month—Styopa hadn't the slightest idea. Even worse, he couldn't remember where he was. That, at least, he tried to figure out by ungluing the lids of his left eye. In the semidarkness something glowed dimly. Styopa finally recognized the mirror, and realized he was in his own room, lying flat on his back on his own bed, that is, in the bedroom on the bed that used to belong to the jeweller's widow. At this point his head started to pound so badly that he closed his eyes and began groaning.

Let us explain: Styopa Likhodeyev, the director of the Variety Theater, regained consciousness that morning in the apartment that he shared with the late Mikhail Alexandrovich Berlioz in a large six-storey building on Sadovaya Street.

It should be said that the apartment—No. 50—had long had, if not a bad, then at least an odd reputation. Two years before it had belonged to the widow of the jeweller de Fougeret. Anna Frantsevna de Fougeret, a very businesslike and respectable woman of fifty, let out three of her five rooms to lodgers. One of them was apparently named Belomut— the other's name has been lost.

And it was two years ago that inexplicable things began happening in the apartment: people started disappearing without a trace.

Once, on a day off, a policeman appeared, summoned the second lodger (whose name has been lost) into the front hall, and said that he had been asked to come down to the police station for a minute in order to sign something. The lodger told Anfisa, Anna Frantsevna's longtime, devoted housekeeper, to tell anyone who called that he would be back in ten minutes, whereupon he went off with the policeman who was correctly attired in white gloves. Not only did he not return in ten minutes, he never returned at all. And the most astonishing thing was that the policeman evidently disappeared along with him.

The pious and, to be blunt, superstitious Anfisa came right out and told the distressed Anna Frantsevna that it was witchcraft pure and simple, and that she knew exactly who it was that had spirited away both the lodger and the policeman, only she didn't want to say because it was almost nighttime.

Well, as everyone knows, once witchcraft gets started, there's no stopping it. The second lodger disappeared, I recall, on a Monday, and on Wednesday Belomut vanished as if he had fallen through the earth, albeit in different circumstances. In the morning a car came to take him to work as usual, and the car did leave with him, but it did not bring anyone back, and never returned again.

Madame Belomut's grief and horror defied description. But both, alas, were of short duration. On the night when she and Anfisa returned from her dacha, where Anna Frantsevna had hurried off to for some reason, she discovered that Belomut's wife was no longer in the apartment. And what is more, the two rooms occupied by the Belomuts had both been sealed.

Two days passed somehow. On the third, a sleepless Anna Frantsevna again left hurriedly for her dacha... It hardly needs to be said that she did not return either!

Left all alone, Anfisa cried her eyes out and then went to bed after one in the morning. What happened to her after that is a mystery, but the residents of the other apartments said they thought they had heard knocking sounds in No. 50 all night long and they thought the lights were on until daybreak. In the morning it turned out that Anfisa was missing too!

All kinds of tales circulated in the building about the accursed apartment and the people who had disappeared. For example, according to one of them, the dry and pious Anfisa had allegedly worn a chamois pouch on her emaciated breast which contained twenty-five large diamonds that had belonged to Anna Frantsevna. According to another story, the dacha which Anna Frantsevna had hurriedly visited allegedly had a woodshed where priceless valuables were found, including those same diamonds as well as tsarist gold coins... And there were other such stories. But we cannot vouch for what we do not know.

In any event, the apartment stood vacant and under seal for only a week, and then who moved in but the late Berlioz and his wife and the aforementioned Styopa and his wife. Not unexpectedly, as soon as they settled into the accursed apartment, devilish things started happening to them, too. In the space of a month, both wives disappeared. But not without a trace. Berlioz's wife was said to have been seen in Kharkov with a ballet master, and Styopa's wife supposedly turned up on Bozhe-domka Street, where, word had it, the director of the Variety Theater had used his many connections to get her a room, on the condition that she never set foot on Sadovaya Street again...

And so, Styopa groaned. He wanted to call Grunya the maid and ask her for some Pyramidon, but he was sufficiently in touch with reality to realize that was pointless, since she naturally would not have any Pyramidon. He tried calling Berlioz for help, groaning two times, "Misha, Misha," but as you yourself can understand, he got no reply. The most total silence reigned in the apartment.

After wiggling his toes, Styopa could tell that he was still in his socks. He palpated his thigh with a trembling hand to determine if he had his trousers on, but he couldn't be sure. Finally, seeing that he was abandoned and alone and that there was no one to help him, he decided to get up, whatever the superhuman effort it cost.

Styopa unglued his eyelids, looked in the mirror and saw a man with hair sticking up all over his head, with swollen eyelids in a bloated face covered with black stubble; the man was wearing a dirty shirt with a collar and tie, long johns, and socks.

That was how he saw himself in the mirror, and next to the mirror he saw a man he did not know who was dressed in black and wearing a black beret.

Styopa sat down on the bed and tried as hard as he could to focus his bloodshot eyes on the stranger.

It was he who broke the silence, intoning in a low, somber voice with a foreign accent, "Good day, most kind Stepan Bogdanovich!"

There was a pause, after which Styopa made a huge effort and said, "What do you want?" He was shocked not to recognize his own voice. The word "what" came out in a treble, "you" in a bass, and "want" did not come out at all.

The stranger gave a friendly smile, took out a large gold watch with a diamond triangle on the cover, listened to it ring eleven times and then said, "Eleven o'clock! I've been waiting for you to wake up for exactly an hour because you told me to be here at ten. And here I am!"

Styopa felt for his trousers on the chair next to the bed and whispered, "Excuse me...," put on his trousers, and asked hoarsely, "Would you kindly tell me your name?"

It was hard for him to talk. With every word he spoke, someone stuck a needle in his brain, causing him hellish pain.

"What? You've forgotten my name too?" Here the stranger smiled.

"Sorry..." croaked Styopa, sensing that his hangover was blessing him with a new symptom: the floor by the bed seemed to him to have vanished somewhere, and he was just on the verge of flying headfirst down to the devil's mother in the underworld.

"My dear Stepan Bogdanovich," said the visitor with a piercing smile, "pyramidon will not help you. Follow the wise old rule: cure like with like. The only thing that will restore you to life is two shots of vodka with some hot and spicy hors d'oeuvres."

However sick he was, Styopa was shrewd enough to know that once he had been found in such a state, it was better to admit to everything.

"To be honest," he began, barely able to move his tongue, "yesterday I may have had a bit too..."

"Not another word!" the visitor replied, moving his armchair over to the side.

Styopa, his eyes bulging, saw a small table and a tray, covered with sliced white bread, pressed caviar in a glass bowl, white marinated mushrooms on a plate, something in a saucepan and finally, vodka in a mammoth decanter that had belonged to the jeweller's wife. Styopa was particularly struck by the fact that the decanter was sweating with frost, which was understandable since it had been placed in a shallow bowl packed with ice. In a word, the table was set flawlessly, impeccably.

The stranger prevented Styopa's astonishment from assuming morbid proportions by deftly pouring him half a glass of vodka.

"Won't you have some?" squeaked Styopa.

"With pleasure!"

Styopa raised his glass to his lips with a wobbly hand while the stranger downed the contents of his in a single gulp. As he was munching on some caviar, Styopa managed to get out the words, "Wouldn't you like some hors d'oeuvres?"

"Thank you, I never eat hors d'oeuvres," the stranger replied and poured a second round. They uncovered the saucepan and found sausages in tomato sauce.

And soon the accursed greenness which had been floating in front of Styopa's eyes melted away, words started to come out, and most important of all, Styopa began remembering things: namely, that yesterday he had been in Skhodnya at the dacha of the sketch writer Khustov and had been taken there in a taxicab by Khustov himself. He even remembered that they had hired the taxicab at the Metropole and that some actor had been there too, or maybe he wasn't an actor... with a portable phonograph. Yes, yes, yes, it had all happened at the dacha! Then he recalled that the dogs had howled because of the phonograph. Only the lady whom Styopa had wanted to kiss remained a mystery... the devil only knew who she was... maybe she worked in radio, maybe not.

Thus the events of the previous day gradually became clearer, although at the moment the present day interested Styopa more, especially the stranger in his bedroom, with vodka and hors d'oeuvres to boot. It would be a good idea to clear that up!

"Well, I hope you can remember my name now?"

But Styopa merely smiled shamefacedly and shrugged.

"Really! I have the feeling that you drank port after vodka! Forgive me, but how could you do such a thing!"

"May I ask that this go no further?" said Styopa obsequiously.

"Of course, of course! But, naturally, I can't speak for Khustov."

"Do you know Khustov, too?"

"I saw the man briefly in your office yesterday, but one quick look at his face was enough to convince me that he's a bastard, a wrecker, a toady and a yes-man."

"Absolutely true!" thought Styopa, who was struck by the accuracy, precision, and pithiness of this characterization of Khustov.

So, although the previous day was reassembling itself, piece by piece, the director of the Variety still felt anxious. There was still a huge, gaping hole to be accounted for. And there was no way that Styopa could have seen the stranger in the beret in his office yesterday.

"Professor of black magic, Woland," said the visitor weightily, seeing Styopa's consternation, and he gave him a precise account of what had happened.

He had arrived in Moscow from abroad yesterday and had gone to see Styopa immediately to propose a performance at the Variety Theater. Styopa had phoned the Moscow Regional Entertainment Commission to receive approval (Styopa grew pale and blinked his eyes), signed a contract with Professor Woland for seven performances (Styopa's mouth opened) and arranged for Woland to come by this morning at ten o'-clock to iron out the details... And so Woland had come! When he arrived he was met by the maid Grunya, who explained that she came in daily and had only just arrived herself, that Berlioz was not at home, and that if the visitor wished to see Stepan Bogdanovich, then he could go into his bedroom himself. Stepan Bogdanovich was such a sound sleeper that she would not try to wake him up. Seeing the condition Stepan Bogdanovich was in, the artiste sent Grunya to the nearest specialty store for vodka and hors d'oeuvres, to the drugstore for ice and...

"Let me settle up with you," whispered the crushed Styopa as he tried to find his wallet.

"Oh, don't be silly!" exclaimed the guest artiste and would hear nothing more of it.

And so, the vodka and hors d'oeuvres were accounted for, but even so, it was still painful to look at Styopa: he had absolutely no recollection of a contract and could have sworn that he had not seen this Woland fellow yesterday. Yes, Khustov had been there, but Woland had not.

"May I have a look at the contract," asked Styopa softly.

"By all means, by all means..."

Styopa took a look at the paper and froze. Everything was in order. First, there was Styopa's own dashing signature! And then a note written slantwise in the margin in the financial director Rimsky's hand, authorizing an advance payment to Woland of ten thousand rubles from the thirty-five thousand due him for seven appearances. Finally, there was Woland's signature confirming his receipt of the ten thousand ruble advance!

"What is all this?!" thought the miserable Styopa, and his head began to spin. Was he beginning to have ominous memory lapses? But, it goes without saying, after he had been shown the contract, any further expression of surprise would be simply impolite. Styopa asked his guest's permission to step out for a moment and, as he was, in his socks, he ran to the phone in the front hall. On the way he shouted in the direction of the kitchen, "Grunya!"

But nobody answered. Here he glanced at the door to Berlioz's study, which was close to the front hall, and at that point, he was, as they say, struck dumb. There was a huge wax seal hanging on a string attached to the door handle. "Oh, great!" roared a voice in Styopa's head. "That's all I need!" And at this point Styopa's thoughts began racing down two tracks, but as always happens in a catastrophe, they were both going in the same direction, and only the devil knows where they were headed. It is hard even to convey the confusion that reigned in Styopa's head. First there was the devilish character with the black beret, the cold vodka, and the improbable contract, and now, if you please, to top it all off, a seal on the door! If you told anyone that Berlioz had done something bad, no one would believe it, truly, no one would believe it! But a seal is a seal! Yes indeed...

And here some highly unpleasant little thoughts began stirring in Styopa's brain regarding an article which, as luck would have it, he had recently foisted on Mikhail Alexandrovich for publication in his journal. And just between us, it was a stupid article! And pointless too, and it paid a pittance...

The recollection of the article triggered another recollection, of a questionable conversation which had taken place here in the dining room on the evening of April 24th when Styopa was having supper with Mikhail Alexandrovich. That is, of course, one would never call the conversation "questionable" in the full sense of the word (Styopa would never have entered into such a conversation), but it had been a conversation on a needless topic. It would have been just as easy, citizens, for him not to have engaged in it at all. Before the seal appeared, that conversation could doubtlessly have been considered totally inconsequential, but after the seal...

"Oh, Berlioz, Berlioz!" Styopa's brain was seething. "The thought would never have entered my head!"

But this was not the time for prolonged grief, and Styopa dialed the office number of Rimsky, the financial director of the Variety Theater. Styopa was in a delicate situation: first of all, the foreigner might be offended that Styopa was checking up on him after he had shown him the contract, and besides, it was extraordinarily hard for him to broach the subject to the financial director. After all, he could hardly come right out and ask, "Tell me, did I sign a contract yesterday for thirty-five thousand rubles with a professor of black magic?" That would hardly do!

"Yes!" sounded Rimsky's sharp, unpleasant voice in the receiver.

"Hello, Grigory Danilovich," said Styopa softly, "this is Likhodeyev. This is the situation... umm... umm... I have this, uh, artiste Woland here and I, uh... I wanted to ask about this evening?"

"Oh, the fellow who does black magic?" echoed Rimsky's voice in the receiver, "The posters will be ready right away."

"OK," said Styopa in a weak voice, "Well, bye then."

"Will you be in soon?" asked Rimsky.

"In half an hour," Styopa replied and, hanging up the phone, he pressed his hands to his burning head. Oh, what a nasty business it all was! And what, citizens, was happening to his memory? Huh?

However, it was becoming awkward to stay in the hall any longer, and Styopa devised a plan on the spot: do everything necessary to conceal his incredible forgetfulness, and now, first of all, subtly pump the foreigner for information regarding the kind of act he intended to perform that night in Styopa's Variety Theater.

As Styopa turned away from the phone, he looked in the hall mirror, which the lazy Grunya had not cleaned for some time, and distinctly saw a weird-looking fellow—thin as a lath and wearing a pince-nez (oh, if only Ivan Nikolayevich had been there! He would have recognized the fellow right away!). His reflection appeared and disappeared in an instant. Anxious, Styopa peered into the depths of the hallway and reeled a second time, for he saw a hefty black cat pass by in the mirror and also disappear.

Styopa's heart skipped a beat, he lost his balance.

"What's going on?" he thought, "Could I be losing my mind? Where are these reflections coming from?!" He peered into the hall and shouted in fright, "Grunya! What's that cat doing in our house? Where did he come from? And who's the fellow with him?"

"Don't be upset, Stepan Bogdanovich," a voice sounded, not Grunya's, but that of the guest in the bedroom. "That cat belongs to me. Don't be nervous. And Grunya isn't here, I sent her to Voronezh. She was complaining that you hadn't let her go on vacation for a long time."

These words were so unexpected and absurd that Styopa decided he had not heard them correctly. In a state of total confusion, he trotted back to the bedroom and froze in the doorway. His hair stood on end, and fine drops of sweat appeared on his brow.

His guest was no longer alone in the bedroom but had been joined by a retinue. Sitting in the other chair was the same oddball who seemed to have appeared in the hall. Now he was clearly visible: a feathery mustache, one lens of his pince-nez glistening and the other missing entirely. But there were worse things to be seen in the bedroom: sprawled in a relaxed pose on the pouffe that had once belonged to the jeweller's wife was a third creature, namely, a black cat of horrific proportions with a glass of vodka in one paw and in the other a fork on which he had speared a pickled mushroom.

The light, dim as it was in the bedroom, began to fade altogether in Styopa's eyes. "So this is what it's like to go crazy!" he thought and grabbed onto the door frame.

"Do I note a touch of surprise, my dearest Stepan Bogdanovich?" Woland inquired of Styopa whose teeth were chattering, "But there is nothing to be surprised about. This is my retinue."

At this point the cat drank down his vodka, and Styopa's hand began to slip down the door frame.

"And my retinue needs space," Woland continued, "which means that one of us in this apartment is superfluous. And I think that someone is—you!"

"It's them, it's them," crooned the thin checked man in a bleating voice, referring to Styopa in the plural. "In general, they've been acting like swine lately. They get drunk, use their position to have affairs with women, don't do a damn thing, and can't do anything because they don't know the first thing about their jobs. They hoodwink their bosses!"

"And he runs the official car ragged!" tattled the cat while chewing on a mushroom.

And at this point, the fourth, and last, phenomenon occurred in the apartment, just as Styopa, who had already slid down to the floor, was clutching feebly at the door frame.

Right out of the mirror stepped a short, but unusually broad-shouldered man. He was wearing a bowler hat and had a fang sticking out of his mouth, which made his already loathsome face look even uglier. To top it all off, he had fiery-red hair.

"I," the newcomer joined in the conversation, "don't really understand how he ended up a director," the redhead's voice became more and more nasal, "He's as much a director as I'm a bishop!"

"You don't look like a bishop, Azazello," noted the cat as he piled his plate with sausages.

"That's just what I'm saying," said the redhead through his nose, and turning to Woland, he added respectfully, "May I have permission, Messire, to throw him out of Moscow straight to hell?"

"Shoo!!" roared the cat suddenly, his fur standing on end.

And then the bedroom began to spin around Styopa, he hit his head on the door frame, and as he was losing consciousness, he thought, "I'm dying..."

But he did not die. He opened his eyes slightly and saw that he was sitting on something made of stone. A sound could be heard nearby. When he opened his eyes properly, he realized that it was the sound of the sea and that a wave was, in fact, breaking at his very feet, that, to be brief, he was sitting at the end of a jetty, and that a blue sky was sparkling above him, and behind him was a white city nestled in the hills.

Not knowing the proper behavior in such circumstances, Styopa raised himself on his shaky legs and set off down the jetty to the shore.

A man was standing on the jetty, smoking a cigarette and spitting into the sea. He gave Styopa a strange look and stopped spitting.

Then Styopa resorted to the following maneuver: he dropped on his knees in front of the unknown smoker and said, "Please tell me, what city is this?"

"Are you kidding?!" said the heartless smoker.

"I'm not drunk," Styopa replied hoarsely, "Something's happened to me... I'm sick... Where am I? What city is this?"

"Well, Yalta..."

Styopa sighed softly, fell over on his side and struck his head against the warm stone of the jetty. He lost consciousness.

VIII

The Duel between the Professor and the Poet

AT precisely the time when Styopa lost consciousness in Yalta, that is to say, around 11:30 a.m., Ivan Nikolayevich Bezdomny regained it as he awakened from a long, deep sleep. He spent some time trying to figure out how he had ended up in this unfamiliar room with white walls, an amazing night table made out of bright metal, and a white window shade that was keeping out the sun.

Ivan shook his head, realized that it did not ache any more, and remembered that he was in a hospital. This, in turn, brought back the memory of Berlioz's death, but today Ivan was not as strongly affected by it. After a good night's sleep, Ivan Nikolayevich was calmer and had begun to think more clearly. He lay motionless for a while on his immaculate, soft, comfortable spring-cushioned bed, and then noticed the bell button by his side. Due to his habit of touching things on impulse, Ivan pressed it. He expected to hear something ring or to have someone appear after he pressed the button, but something quite different happened.

At the foot of Ivan's bed a frosted-glass cylinder lit up that said, "DRINK." After staying put for a while the cylinder began to turn until the word "NURSE" appeared. It goes without saying that the ingenious cylinder made quite an impression on Ivan. The word "NURSE" was replaced by "CALL THE DOCTOR."

"Hmm..." murmured Ivan, not knowing what else to do with the cylinder. But then he had a stroke of luck: he pressed the button a second time at the word "DOCTOR'S ASSISTANT." The cylinder rang softly in reply, stopped, and then went blank. A stout kind-looking woman in a clean white robe came into the room and said to Ivan, "Good morning!"

Ivan did not answer because he considered the greeting inappropriate under the circumstances. They had, in fact, put a perfectly sane man in the hospital, and yet were still pretending that it was the right thing to do!

Meanwhile, without changing her kindly expression, the woman pressed the button once to raise the shade, and the sun streamed into the room through a light, widely spaced grille that extended down to the very floor. Beyond the grille there was a balcony, and beyond that, the banks of a winding river with a cheery pine forest on its opposite shore.

"Time for your bath," said the woman invitingly, and beneath her hands, the interior wall moved aside, revealing a bath compartment and a splendidly equipped bathroom and lavatory.

Although Ivan had resolved not to talk to the woman, he broke down when he saw the water rushing into the bathtub from the gleaming tap, and said ironically, "My, my! Just like at the Metropole!"

"Oh, no," answered the woman with pride, "much better. Even abroad you can't find equipment like this. Doctors and scientists come here especially to inspect our clinic. We have foreign visitors here every day."

When he heard the words "foreign visitor" Ivan immediately recalled the consultant from the day before. His mood darkened and he scowled and said, "Foreign visitors... How impressed you all are with foreign visitors! But they come in many different varieties. Take the one I met yesterday, for example, he was a real charmer!"

He was on the verge of telling the woman about Pontius Pilate, but he restrained himself when he realized that it wouldn't mean anything to her, and she wouldn't be able to help him anyway.

After his bath, Ivan Nikolayevich was given everything a man needs after a bath: a freshly ironed shirt, long underwear, socks. But that wasn't all: after opening the closet, the woman pointed inside and asked, "What would you like to wear—a bathrobe or pajamas?"

Since he had been attached to his new abode by force, Ivan nearly clasped his hands in dismay at the woman's free-and-easy attitude, and he pointed silently to a pair of red flannel pajamas.

After that Ivan Nikolayevich was led down an empty and soundless corridor into an office of immense proportions. Having made up his mind to respond to everything in this marvelously appointed building with irony, Ivan mentally christened the office the "factory-kitchen."

And with good reason. It had cupboards and glass cabinets with shiny nickel-plated instruments, there were chairs of unusually complex construction, potbellied lamps with gleaming shades, a multitude of vials and gas burners and electric wires and gadgets that would mystify absolutely anyone.

In the office Ivan was attended to by three people—two women and one man, all wearing white. First, Ivan was led over to a small table in the corner with the obvious intent of getting some information out of him.

Ivan began to consider his situation. He had three choices. The first choice was especially tempting: he could lunge at the lamps and the intricate gadgets and smash them all to hell, and thus protest their holding him for no reason. But the Ivan of today was dramatically different from the Ivan of yesterday, and this first choice seemed dubious to him: it might even strengthen their conviction that he was a raving lunatic. And so, Ivan rejected this first choice and considered the second: give an immediate account of the consultant and Pontius Pilate. However, yesterday's experience had shown that people either did not believe this story or they distorted its meaning. And so Ivan decided against the second choice and opted for the third: seek refuge in proud silence.

As it turned out, however, this was not fully possible since, willy-nilly, he ended up answering, albeit curtly and sulkily, a whole series of questions. Ivan was questioned about absolutely everything relating to his past life, including such things as his scarlet fever fifteen years ago. After filling up a whole page on Ivan, they turned it over, and the woman in white proceeded to questions about Ivan's relatives. It was a lengthy business: who died, when and how, did the deceased drink or have venereal diseases, and all that sort of thing. They concluded by asking for an account of what had happened yesterday at Patriarch's Ponds, but they did not badger him, nor did they show any surprise at what he said about Pontius Pilate.

At this point the woman turned Ivan over to the man, and he took Ivan through another kind of exam altogether and asked him no questions at all. He took Ivan's temperature, measured his pulse, and looked into his eyes with some sort of light. Then another woman came to assist the man, and they injected something, painlessly, into Ivan's back, made tracings on his chest with the handle of a small mallet, tapped his knees, so that his legs jerked up, pricked his finger and took some blood, stuck a needle into the crook of his arm, and put rubber bracelets on his arms...

Ivan just smiled bitterly to himself and reflected on the stupidity and grotesqueness of it all. Imagine! He had just wanted to warn everybody about how dangerous the foreign consultant was, and try to catch him, and the only thing he had accomplished was to end up in some mysterious office where he had to tell a lot of rubbish about his Uncle Fyodor, who had been a chronic drunk in Vologda. Intolerable stupidity!

Finally they let Ivan go. He was taken back to his room where he was given a cup of coffee, two soft-boiled eggs, and white bread and butter.

After he had eaten and drunk everything, Ivan decided to wait for one of the top brass of the establishment to show up who would finally listen to him and treat him fairly.

And show up he did, very shortly after Ivan's breakfast. Suddenly the door opened, and in walked a bunch of people in white coats. At the head of them all came a man of forty-five or so, who was as cleanly shaven as an actor and had pleasant but very penetrating eyes and a polite manner. The entire entourage showed him attention and respect, and his entrance was therefore a very solemn affair. "Just like Pontius Pilate!" thought Ivan.

Yes, this was unquestionably the head man. He sat down on a stool, while all the others remained standing. "Doctor Stravinsky," the seated man introduced himself to Ivan and looked amiably at him.

"Here, Alexander Nikolayevich," someone with a neatly trimmed goatee said softly, and handed the head man Ivan's sheet, which was covered with writing on both sides.

"They've put together a whole case!" thought Ivan. The head man cast an experienced eye over the sheet of paper, mumbling "Uh-huh, uh-huh" and exchanging some words in a little-known language with the people around him.

"And he even speaks Latin, just like Pilate..." thought Ivan sadly. Here one word made him shudder, and that was the word "schizophrenia"— which had, alas, been uttered yesterday by the damned foreigner at Patriarch's Ponds and was repeated here today by Professor Stravinsky.

"And he knew that, too!" Ivan thought anxiously.

The head man had obviously made it a policy to agree with and be delighted by everything the people around him said, and to express his delight with the words, "Splendid, splendid..."

"Splendid," said Stravinsky, returning the sheet to someone, and addressing Ivan, "You are a poet?"

"Yes, a poet," replied Ivan gloomily and for the first time he felt a sudden and inexplicable aversion to poetry, and the poems of his which came to mind seemed somehow distasteful.

Wrinkling his face, Ivan responded by asking Stravinsky, "And you are a professor?"

To this Stravinsky gave an obligingly polite nod.

"And are you the person in charge here?" Ivan continued.

Stravinsky nodded again.

"I must speak with you," said Ivan Nikolayevich in a meaningful way.

"That's why I'm here," replied Stravinsky.

"This is the situation," began Ivan, feeling that his hour had come, "They've decided that I'm crazy, and no one wants to listen to me!"

"Oh, no, we'll give you our full attention," said Stravinsky earnestly and soothingly, "and we certainly won't let anyone say you're crazy."

"Then listen: yesterday evening at Patriarch's Ponds I met a mysterious person, perhaps a foreigner, perhaps not, who knew about Berlioz's death before it happened and who knew Pontius Pilate personally."

The entourage listened to the poet in silence, without moving a muscle.

"Pilate? The Pilate who lived in the time of Jesus Christ?" asked Stravinsky, narrowing his eyes at Ivan.

"Yes, the very same."

"I see," said Stravinsky, "and this Berlioz was killed under a streetcar?"

"Yes, he was the man I saw cut in two by a streetcar at Patriarch's Ponds yesterday when this most mysterious fellow..."

"The one who knew Pontius Pilate?" asked Stravinsky, whose powers of comprehension were obviously very high.

"Precisely," confirmed Ivan, studying Stravinsky, "As I was saying, he knew ahead of time that Annushka had spilt the sunflower oil... And it was there on that very spot that he slipped and fell! How do you like that?" Ivan asked meaningfully, hoping that his words would produce a big effect.

But they did no such thing, and Stravinsky simply asked the following question, "And who is this Annushka?"

This question disconcerted Ivan somewhat, and he grimaced.

"Annushka is of no importance in this matter," he said nervously. "The devil knows who she is. Just some foolish woman from Sadovaya Street. Don't you understand, the important thing is that he knew in advance about the sunflower oil! Do you understand me?"

"I understand you perfectly," Stravinsky replied in a serious tone and, touching the poet's knee, he added, "Don't get excited, go on."

"I will," said Ivan, trying to imitate Stravinsky's tone and knowing from bitter experience that staying calm was the only thing that would help him. "So this horrible character, who is lying, by the way, about being a consultant, possesses some kind of extraordinary power... For example, if you chase him, you can't ever catch him. And he's got quite a pair with him who have their own special charm: a tall guy with broken eyeglasses, and a tremendously huge cat who rides streetcars by himself. What's more," Ivan spoke with greater fervor and conviction when no one was interrupting him, "he was on Pontius Pilate's balcony himself, no doubt about it! What do you make of that? Huh? He should be arrested right away or else he'll cause indescribable harm."

"So you are trying to have him arrested? Have I understood you correctly?" asked Stravinsky.

"He's clever," thought Ivan, "You have to admit, there are some smart people even among the intelligentsia. No denying that!" and he replied, "Absolutely correctly! Judge for yourself, what else is there to do! But meanwhile they're holding me here by force, shining lights in my eyes, washing me in tubs, and asking me questions about my Uncle Fyodor! And he's been dead for years! I demand to be released immediately."

"Well, splendid, splendid!" replied Stravinsky, "It's all clear now. And, really, what sense is there in keeping a sane man in the hospital? So, I'll release you immediately if you tell me you're normal. You don't have to prove it, just say it. So, then, are you normal?"

There was complete silence. The fat woman who had taken care of Ivan that morning looked at the professor with pious respect, and again Ivan thought, "Very clever."

The professor's offer was very attractive, but before answering, Ivan thought very hard, wrinkled his brow, and finally said firmly, "Yes, I am normal."

"Well, that's splendid," Stravinsky exclaimed with relief, "and if you are, let's reason this out logically. Take yesterday, for example," at this point he turned and was immediately handed Ivan's sheet, "while trying to find a stranger, who told you he was an acquaintance of Pontius Pilate, you did the following," here Stravinsky began bending his long fingers, looking first at the chart, then at Ivan. "You hung an icon on your chest. Is that right?"

"Yes," Ivan agreed sullenly.

"You fell off a fence and hurt your face. Right? Appeared at a restaurant with a lighted candle in your hand, wearing only underwear, and then hit one of the people in the restaurant. You were tied up and brought here. Once you got here, you called the police and asked them to send machine guns. Then you tried to throw yourself out the window. Is that right? Now I ask you: is it possible to catch anyone or arrest them by acting that way? And if you're a normal person, you can answer that yourself: no it isn't. Do you wish to leave here? Be my guest. But may I ask where you will go?"

"To the police of course," replied Ivan, but not so firmly as before and losing his composure a bit beneath the professor's gaze.

"Straight from here?"

"I guess so."

"And won't you stop off at your apartment?" asked Stravinsky quickly.

"No, there's no time for that! While I'm going to apartments, he'll get away!"

"I see. And what's the first thing you will tell the police?"

"About Pontius Pilate," answered Ivan Nikolayevich, and his eyes clouded over.

"Well, a splendid idea!" exclaimed Stravinsky agreeably, and turning to the fellow with the goatee, he gave the order, "Fyodor Vasilyevich, please issue a release for citizen Bezdomny so that he can return to the city. But leave his room unoccupied and don't change the sheets. Citizen Bezdomny will be back here in two hours. Well," he turned to the poet, "I won't wish you success because I don't for a minute believe you'll have any. See you soon!" And he stood up while his entourage began to stir.

"Why do you think I'll be back?" Ivan asked anxiously.

Stravinsky seemed to be waiting for that question because he resumed his seat and began talking. "Because as soon as you appear at the police station in your long underwear and say that you met a man who was personally acquainted with Pontius Pilate—they'll have you back here in an instant, and you'll find yourself in this very same room."

"What does my underwear have to do with it?" asked Ivan, looking around in distress.

"The main problem is Pontius Pilate. But the underwear doesn't help. We'll have to remove your hospital clothes and give you back your own. And you were brought here in long underwear. And you had no intention of stopping off at your apartment although I hinted that you should do so. Then comes Pilate... and the case is complete!"

At this point something strange happened to Ivan Nikolayevich. His will seemed to give way, and he felt that he was weak, that he needed advice.

"So what should I do?" he asked, but timidly this time.

"Now that's splendid!" Stravinsky replied. "A most reasonable question. Now I shall tell you what really happened to you. Someone gave you a real fright yesterday and upset you with that story about Pontius Pilate and other things. And so you, a morbidly sensitive and nervous individual, went around the city talking about Pilate. It's completely natural that you should be taken for a madman. Only one thing can save you now—and that's complete rest. You definitely need to stay here."

"But he has to be caught!" exclaimed Ivan imploringly.

"Fine, but why do you have to run after him yourself? Write down all your suspicions and accusations against this man on a piece of paper. There's nothing simpler than to send your statement to the proper authorities and if, as you claim, we are dealing with a criminal, that will soon be apparent. But there's one condition: don't overstrain yourself, and try to think less about Pontius Pilate. All sorts of stories can be told! Not all of them have to be believed."

"I understand!" Ivan announced decisively, "Please give me some paper and a pen."

"Give him some paper and a short pencil," was Stravinsky's order to the fat woman, and to Ivan he said this, "I advise you not to write today."

"No, no, it has to be today, absolutely today," Ivan squealed in agitation.

"Well, all right. Only don't overtire your brain. If it doesn't work out today, it will tomorrow."

"He'll escape!"

"Oh no," Stravinsky retorted confidently. "He won't go anywhere, I assure you. And remember that here we shall assist you in every way that we can, and without that nothing you do will work out. Do you hear me?" Stravinsky asked abruptly, lending special significance to his words, and grabbing hold of both Ivan Nikolayevich's hands. As he held them in his own, he stared long and intensely into Ivan's eyes and repeated, "You'll be helped here... do you hear me?... You'll be helped here... you'll get relief. It's quiet here, everything is peaceful... You'll be helped here..."

Ivan Nikolayevich unexpectedly yawned, and his expression softened.

"Yes, yes," he said quietly.

"Now that's splendid!" concluded Stravinsky in his usual fashion and got up. "Good-bye!" He shook Ivan's hand, and as he was walking out of the room, he turned to the man with the goatee and said, "Yes, and try oxygen... and baths."

A few moments later Ivan was alone, without Stravinsky or his entourage. Beyond the window grille the joyous and vernal wood on the opposite bank looked radiant, and nearer by, the river sparkled in the noonday sun.

IX

Korovyov's Tricks

NIKANOR Ivanovich Bosoi, chairman of the house committee of 302B Sadovaya Street in Moscow, the residence of the late Berlioz, found himself inundated with problems, which had started during the night between Wednesday and Thursday.

At midnight, as we already know, Zheldybin arrived as part of a commission which summoned Nikanor Ivanovich, informed him of Berlioz's death, and then went with him to apartment No. 50.

There the papers and belongings of the deceased were put under seal. Neither Grunya, the maid, nor the frivolous Stepan Bogdanovich was in the apartment at the time. The commission told Nikanor Ivanovich that they would remove the deceased's papers in order to sort them out, that the deceased's living space, that is to say, his three rooms (the study, living room, and dining room that had once belonged to the jeweller's widow) would revert to the house committee, and that the deceased's belongings would be kept where they were under seal until notification of the heirs.

News of Berlioz's death spread throughout the building with supernatural speed, and Bosoi started getting calls at seven o'clock Thursday morning. Then people began showing up in person to submit claims for the vacated rooms. Within two hours Nikanor Ivanovich had received thirty-two such claims.

They contained pleas, threats, slanderous gossip, denunciations, offers to undertake renovations at their own expense, references to unbearable overcrowding, and the impossibility of sharing an apartment with bandits. Included too was an artistically powerful and gripping account of someone stealing *pelmeni* from apartment No. 31 and stuffing them into a jacket pocket, plus two threats of suicide and one confession of a secret pregnancy.

Nikanor Ivanovich was constantly being called out into the hall of his apartment, grabbed by the sleeve, whispered to, winked at, and promised a little something for his efforts.

This torment lasted until noontime when Nikanor Ivanovich simply fled from his apartment and went to the office at the main entrance, but when he saw people were on the lookout for him there as well, he took off again. After managing somehow to escape the people who chased him across the asphalt courtyard, he took refuge in entranceway No. 6 and then climbed upstairs to the fifth floor and that vile apartment No. 50.

After catching his breath on the landing, the corpulent Nikanor Ivanovich rang the bell, but no one came to the door. He rang a second time, and a third, and began grumbling and cursing under his breath. Even then no one answered. Finally he lost his patience, took a bunch of duplicate keys belonging to the housing administration out of his pocket, opened the door authoritatively, and walked in.

"Hey there, maid!" Nikanor Ivanovich shouted in the semidark hallway. "What's your name? Grunya, is it? Are you there?"

No one replied.

Then Nikanor Ivanovich took a folding ruler out of his briefcase, removed the seal from the study door, and stepped inside the room. Or, rather, he was just starting to step inside when he stopped in amazement in the doorway, and even gave a shudder.

Sitting at the deceased's desk was a stranger, tall and emaciated and wearing a checked jacket, jockey cap, and pince-nez... well, in short, you know who.

"And who might you be, citizen?" asked Nikanor Ivanovich in a frightened voice.

"Hullo! Nikanor Ivanovich," the unexpected citizen called out in a quavering tenor, and leaping to his feet, he greeted the chairman with an abrupt and forceful handshake. Nikanor Ivanovich was hardly enthralled by this welcome.

"Excuse me," he began suspiciously, "but who exactly are you? Are you here in an official capacity?"

"Ah, Nikanor Ivanovich!" the stranger exclaimed confidingly. "How do you define official and unofficial? All that depends on your point of view. All that is arbitrary and relative. Today I'm unofficial, but tomorrow I might be official! And vice versa, of course, or even something worse."

This kind of reasoning gave no satisfaction whatsoever to the chairman of the house committee. A suspicious person by nature, he decided that the bombastic citizen was certainly unofficial, and maybe even superfluous.

"So who are you? What's your name?" the chairman asked with increasing severity, and even began to bear down on the stranger.

"My name is," replied the citizen, unperturbed by the severity of tone, "...well, let's say, Korovyov. And wouldn't you like a bite to eat, Nikanor Ivanovich? No need for ceremony! Huh?"

"I beg your pardon," began Nikanor Ivanovich, by now indignant, "but what in hell does a bite to eat have to do with this!" (However unpleasant it may be, one must admit that Nikanor Ivanovich was by nature somewhat rude.) "You have no right to be in the deceased's quarters! What are you doing here?"

"And won't you sit down, Nikanor Ivanovich," cried the citizen, without losing his composure, and making a great display of offering the chairman a seat.

Absolutely enraged, Nikanor Ivanovich refused to sit down and shouted, "Who are you anyway?"

"I serve, if you please, as an interpreter for the foreign visitor currently residing in this apartment," explained the fellow who called himself Korovyov, as he clicked the heel of his scuffed, red shoe.

Nikanor Ivanovich's mouth fell open. The presence of a foreigner in the apartment, and with an interpreter no less, came as a complete surprise to him, and he demanded an explanation.

The interpreter was happy to oblige. The foreign artiste, Mr. Woland, had been graciously invited by the director of the Variety Theater, Stepan Bogdanovich Likhodeyev, to stay in his apartment for the duration of his tour, approximately a week, and yesterday Stepan Bogdanovich had written to Nikanor Ivanovich to that effect with a request that he issue the foreigner a temporary residence permit since he, Likhodeyev, was going to Yalta.

"He didn't write me anything," said the astonished chairman.

"Just take a look in your briefcase, Nikanor Ivanovich," Korovyov suggested sweetly.

Nikanor Ivanovich shrugged and opened his briefcase and immediately found Likhodeyev's letter inside.

"How could I have forgotten?" mumbled Nikanor Ivanovich, gazing dully at the already opened envelope.

"It happens sometimes, it happens sometimes," cackled Korovyov. "Absentmindedness, absentmindedness and over-exhaustion, and high blood pressure, my dear friend Nikanor Ivanovich! I am horribly absentminded myself. We'll have a drink sometime, and I'll tell you a few facts from my life story, you'll die laughing!"

"When precisely is Likhodeyev going to Yalta?"

"Why he's already gone, gone," shrieked the interpreter. "He's already rolling along, yes indeed! He's already the devil knows where!" and here the interpreter waved his arms like a windmill.

Nikanor Ivanovich said that he had to see the foreigner in person, but the interpreter denied him that request. It was impossible. He was too busy. Training the cat. "I can show you the cat, if you wish," offered Korovyov.

Nikanor Ivanovich, in turn, declined this offer. The interpreter then made him an unexpected, but most intriguing proposition.

In view of the fact that Mr. Woland did not wish to live in a hotel, and since he was used to having a lot of room, wouldn't it be possible for the house committee to rent him the entire apartment, including the rooms that belonged to the deceased, for the week of Woland's performance in Moscow?

"After all, it's hardly a matter of concern to him, to the deceased," hissed Korovyov in a whisper. "You will agree, won't you, Nikanor Ivanovich, that he has no further use for this apartment?"

Somewhat confused, Nikanor Ivanovich protested that foreigners were supposed to stay at the Metropole and not in private apartments...

"I tell you, he's fussy as the devil!" whispered Korovyov. "He just doesn't want to! Doesn't like hotels! I've had it up to here with these foreign visitors!" Korovyov complained confidentially, poking a finger at his veiny neck. "Believe me, they run you ragged! They come here, and they either snoop around like a son of a bitch, or they wear you out with their whims: this isn't right, that isn't right... Besides, Nikanor Ivanovich, your committee has everything to gain and nothing to lose. He doesn't begrudge any expense." Korovyov glanced around, and then whispered in the chairman's ear, "He's a millionaire!"

The interpreter's proposition made a lot of practical sense. It was a very solid proposal, but there was something decidedly unsolid about his manner of speaking, his attire, and that sickening, totally useless pince-nez. As a result, a vague sense of uneasiness troubled the chairman's soul, but he decided to accept the offer anyway. The fact of the matter was that the house committee had incurred, alas, an enormous deficit. They had to buy heating oil for the fall, and where the money would come from was a mystery. Maybe the foreign visitor's money would get them out of the hole. Even so, the businesslike and cautious Nikanor Ivanovich said that he would first have to clear the matter with the Intourist Office.

"I understand!" screeched Korovyov. "How could you not sort things out! It's essential! Here's the telephone, Nikanor Ivanovich, why don't you sort them out right away. And don't be embarrassed to ask for money," he added in a whisper, as he drew the chairman toward the phone in the hall. "Who can you get money from if not from him! If you could only see the villa he has in Nice! Next summer when you go abroad, make sure you go and have a look—you'll faint!"

All the arrangements with the Intourist Office were made over the phone with a swiftness that amazed the chairman. It turned out that they already knew about Mr. Woland's plans to stay in Likhodeyev's private apartment, and they had no objections whatsoever.

"Marvelous!" cried Korovyov.

A bit dazed by his constant chatter, the chairman said that the house committee agreed to rent apartment No. 50 for a week to the artiste Woland at the rate of... Nikanor Ivanovich stammered somewhat and said, "Five hundred rubles a day."

At this point Korovyov really bowled the chairman over. Winking roguishly in the direction of the bedroom, where the cushioned leaps of a heavy cat could be heard, he hissed, "That comes to thirty-five hundred for the week, right?"

Nikanor Ivanovich quite expected him to add, "You've got quite an appetite, don't you, Nikanor Ivanovich!" but again Korovyov surprised him. "You call that money! Ask for five thou, he'll pay it."

Nikanor Ivanovich gave a confused grin and failed to notice that he was standing next to the deceased's writing desk, where Korovyov was drawing up two copies of a contract with great speed and agility. Next, he whisked them into the bedroom and returned with both copies signed in the foreigner's scrawling hand. The chairman signed the contract too. Here Korovyov asked for a receipt for the five thousand...

"Write it out, Nikanor Ivanovich, write it out! Five thousand rubles..." And then, in a manner ill-suited to the seriousness of the occasion, he said, *"eins, zwei, drei!"* as he counted out five stacks of fresh banknotes for the chairman.

This was done to the accompaniment of Korovyov's little jokes and quips, such as, "A penny saved is a penny earned," "A fool and his money are soon parted," and other things of that sort.

After re-counting the money, the chairman took the foreigner's passport from Korovyov in order to make out a temporary residence permit, and then put it, along with the contract and the money, into his briefcase. Unable to control himself, he bashfully asked for a free pass to the show...

"Why, of course!" bellowed Korovyov. "How many tickets would you like, Nikanor Ivanovich, twelve, fifteen?"

The dumbfounded chairman explained that he needed only two tickets, for himself and his wife, Pelageya Antonovna.

Korovyov grabbed a notepad and jauntily wrote out a pass for two in the front row. As the interpreter thrust the free pass at Nikanor Ivanovich with his left hand, he used his right to press a fat wad of crisp bills into the chairman's other hand. The latter took one look at them, blushed hard, and tried to push them away.

"We're not supposed to..." he muttered.

"I won't take no for an answer," Korovyov whispered in his ear. "We're not supposed to, but foreigners are. You'll offend him, Nikanor Ivanovich, and that would be unfortunate. After all the trouble you went to..."

"It's strictly enforced," the chairman whispered in the softest of tones and looked furtively around.

"But where are the witnesses?" Korovyov whispered in his other ear. "I ask you, where are they? What's your problem?"

And it was then, as the chairman insisted afterwards, that the miracle took place: the wad of bills crawled into his briefcase all on its own.

Then, in a weakened and even disoriented state, the chairman found himself on the staircase. A jumble of thoughts whirled around in his head: the villa in Nice, the trained cat, the thought that there had indeed been no witnesses and that Pelageya Antonovna would be thrilled about the free pass. They were disjointed thoughts, but pleasant on the whole. And still, the chairman felt a pinprick somewhere in the depths of his soul. A pinprick of disquietude. A thought hit him like a blow on the head, right there on the staircase, "How did the interpreter get into the study if there was a seal on the door?!" And why hadn't he, Nikanor Ivanovich, asked about that? For a while the chairman gazed goggle-eyed at the stairs like a sheep, but then he decided to forget the whole thing and not to torture himself over something so complicated...

No sooner had the chairman left the apartment, than a low voice came from the bedroom, "I didn't like that Nikanor Ivanovich. He's a skinflint and a swindler. Can't we make sure he doesn't come round here again?"

"Messire, your wish is my command!" Korovyov replied from somewhere, but in a pure and resonant voice, not a quavering one.

And immediately the accursed interpreter appeared in the hall, dialed a number, and began to whine into the phone, "Hello! I consider it my duty to inform you that our house committee chairman here at 302B Sadovaya Street, Nikanor Ivanovich Bosoi, is speculating in foreign currency. At the present moment there are four hundred dollars wrapped in newspaper in the ventilator shaft of his toilet in apartment No. 35. My name is Timofei Kvastsov, and I live in apartment No. 11 in the same building. But I ask that you not reveal my name. I am afraid that the aforementioned chairman will try to get even."

Then he hung up, the scoundrel!

What happened next in apartment No. 50 is unknown, but what happened next in Nikanor Ivanovich's apartment is known. The chairman locked himself in the toilet and took out of his briefcase the packet of bills that had been forced on him by the interpreter, and checked to make sure that it contained four hundred rubles. He then wrapped the packet in a piece of newspaper and stuffed it into the ventilator shaft.

Five minutes later the chairman was sitting at the table in his small dining room. From the kitchen his wife brought him a plate of neatly sliced herring smothered with chopped scallions. Nikanor Ivanovich poured himself a small carafe of vodka, drank it down, poured another, drank that down, speared three pieces of herring on his fork... and at that moment the doorbell rang. Pelageya Antonovna had just brought in a steaming saucepan, one glance at which was enough to guess that the pan contained, in the very thick of the piping hot borshch, the most delicious thing in the world, a marrow bone.

His mouth watering, Nikanor Ivanovich began howling like a dog, "Damn you to hell! They won't even let you eat. Don't let anyone in, I'm not here, I'm not here. If it's about the apartment, tell them to stop hounding me. There'll be a meeting in a week..."

His wife ran into the entry hall, while Nikanor Ivanovich dipped a ladle into the fire-breathing lake and fished out the bone, which was cracked lengthwise. At that moment two men walked into the dining room, accompanied by a very pale Pelageya Antonovna. One look at the men and Nikanor Ivanovich turned pale too, and got up from the table.

"Where's the toilet?" asked the first man with an air of concern. He was wearing a white Russian-style shirt.

Something knocked against the dining table (it was Nikanor Ivanovich who had dropped his spoon on the oilcloth).

"Over here, here," babbled Pelageya Antonovna.

And the visitors headed straight into the hall.

"What's this all about?" asked Nikanor Ivanovich, trailing behind the men. "Nothing like that could be in our apartment... And can I see your ID... excuse me..."

The first man handed Nikanor Ivanovich his ID, and the second one proceeded to stand up on a stool in the toilet and thrust his hand into the ventilator shaft. Nikanor Ivanovich's eyes grew dim. They removed the newspaper, but the package turned out to contain not rubles, but some unknown currency that was blue-green in color and had a picture on it of an old man. Nikanor Ivanovich saw all this in a haze, however— spots were swimming in front of his eyes.

"There are dollars in the ventilator shaft," said the first man thoughtfully. In a soft and polite voice he asked Nikanor Ivanovich, "Does this packet belong to you?"

"No!" replied Nikanor Ivanovich in a terrified voice. "My enemies planted it there."

"That does sometimes happen," agreed the first man and added, again softly, "But you'll have to hand over the rest of it too."

"I don't have any! Nothing at all! I swear to God, I've never even touched the stuff!" screamed the chairman in desperation.

He rushed over to the bureau, pulled out a creaky drawer and took out his briefcase, all the while crying out disconnected phrases, "Here's the contract... that filthy interpreter planted it there... Korovyov... the guy with the pince-nez!"

He opened the briefcase, looked inside, and thrust his hand in. His face turned blue and he dropped the briefcase into the borshch. There was nothing in the briefcase: neither Styopa's letter, nor the contract, nor the foreigner's passport, nor the money, nor the free pass. In short, nothing but the folding ruler.

"Comrades!" shouted the chairman in a fury. "Take them into custody! There are evil powers in this building!"

No one knows what came over Pelageya Antonovna at that point, but she waved her arms and shouted, "Confess, Ivanovich! You'll get off easier!"

Nikanor Ivanovich's eyes became bloodshot, and he raised his fists over his wife's head, shouting hoarsely, "Oh, you damned fool!" Then he felt weak and sank into a chair, evidently deciding to bow to the inevitable.

In the meantime, out on the landing, Timofei Kondratyevich Kvastsov was putting first his ear and then his eye to the keyhole of the chairman's apartment, dying of curiosity.

Five minutes later the residents of the building who were in the courtyard at the time saw the chairman being led to the entrance-gates by two men. It was reported that Nikanor Ivanovich looked terrible, tottered like a drunk as he passed by, and was mumbling something.

An hour later an unknown man appeared in apartment No. 11 just as Timofei Kondratyevich was choking with glee and telling the other residents how the chairman had been carted off to jail. The stranger beckoned with his finger for Timofei Kondratyevich to come out of the kitchen and into the hall. He said something to him, and then they both vanished.

News from Yalta

A T the same time as disaster struck Nikanor Ivanovich, not far from 302B, on that same Sadovaya Street, two men sat in the office of the financial director of the Variety Theater: Rimsky himself and Varenukha, the theater manager.

Two windows of the large second-floor office looked out on Sadovaya Street, and another, behind the financial director, who was sitting at his desk, looked out on the Variety's summer garden, where there were soft-drink stands, a shooting gallery, and an open-air stage. Apart from the desk, the office furnishings included a bunch of old theater bills hanging on the wall, a small table with a carafe of water, four armchairs, and a dusty, time-worn scale model of some stage revue set up on a stand in the corner. Well, it goes without saying that the office also contained a small fireproof safe, battered and chipped, which stood on Rimsky's left, next to the desk.

Rimsky, who was sitting at the desk, had been in a foul mood since morning. Varenukha, on the other hand, was very animated and somehow especially restless and energetic. For the time being he had no outlet for his nervous energy.

Varenukha had taken refuge in the financial director's office in order to escape from the free-ticket hounds who poisoned his existence, especially on days when there was a change of program. And today was just such a day.

As soon as the phone began to ring, Varenukha picked up the receiver and lied into it, "Who? Varenukha? He's not here. He's left the theater."

"Call Likhodeyev again, please," said Rimsky in irritation.

"He's not home. I already sent Karpov over. There's no one in his apartment."

"The devil knows what's going on," hissed Rimsky, clicking his adding machine.

The door opened, and an usher came in dragging a thick stack of additional theater bills hot off the press. Printed in large red letters on green sheets of paper was:

TODAY AND EVERY DAY AT THE VARIETY THEATER
AN ADDED ATTRACTION:
PROFESSOR WOLAND
PERFORMS BLACK MAGIC WITH
AN EXPOSÉ IN FULL

Varenukha stepped back from the playbill, which he had draped over the scale model, admired it, and ordered the usher to paste them up everywhere.

"It looks good, eye-catching," noted Varenukha as the usher was leaving.

"Well, I don't like this venture at all," grumbled Rimsky, gazing angrily at the playbill through his horn-rimmed glasses. "And, I'm amazed they've allowed him to perform at all!"

"No, Grigory Danilovich, don't say that, it was a very shrewd move. The whole point of it is the exposé."

"I don't know, I don't know, it has no point at all, as far as I'm concerned, and besides, Styopa's always dreaming up things like this! If only he'd let us have a look at the magician. Have you seen him? Where the hell did they dig him up?"

It was obvious that neither Varenukha nor Rimsky had seen the magician. Yesterday Styopa ("like a madman," to quote Rimsky) had run in to see the financial director with the draft of a contract, ordered him to draw it up and to authorize payment. And, the magician had disappeared, and no one had seen him except Styopa.

Rimsky took out his watch, saw it was five after two, and became positively enraged. This was the limit! Likhodeyev had called around eleven and said that he would be there in half an hour. Not only had he not come, he had disappeared from his apartment!

"I've got work to do!" snarled Rimsky, poking his finger at a pile of unsigned papers.

"Maybe he's fallen under a streetcar, like Berlioz?" said Varenukha, holding the receiver to his ear and listening to the deep, prolonged, and utterly hopeless ringing.

"Wouldn't be so bad," said Rimsky through his teeth, in barely audible tones.

At that very moment a woman walked into the office, wearing a uniform jacket, a cap, a black skirt, and sneakers. She removed a small white square and a notebook from her waist-pouch and asked, "Is this the Variety? Express telegram for you. Sign please."

Varenukha left a scrawl in the woman's notebook, and as soon as the door closed behind her, he opened the square.

After reading the telegram, he blinked, and handed it to Rimsky.

The telegram read as follows, "Yalta–Moscow. Variety. Today eleven-thirty Criminal Investigation Department appeared nightshirt-trouser-clad brown-haired psycho allegedly Likhodeyev Director Variety Wire Yalta CID whereabouts Director Likhodeyev."

"Yeah, sure, and I'm your Aunt Mary!" exclaimed Rimsky, and added, "One more surprise!"

"A False Dmitri," said Varenukha and he began speaking into the phone, "Telegraph office? Charge to Variety. Take a telegram... Are you listening? 'Yalta Criminal Investigation Department... Director Likhodeyev Moscow Financial Director Rimsky.' "

Taking no heed of the communiqué about the Yalta impostor, Varenukha again picked up the phone to try to find out where Styopa was and, naturally, he could not locate him anywhere.

Just as he was holding the receiver in his hand, trying to figure out where to call next, the same woman who had brought the first telegram reappeared and handed him a new envelope. Varenukha opened it in haste, read what was written, and whistled.

"What now?" asked Rimsky, twitching nervously.

Varenukha handed him the telegram in silence, and the financial director read the following words: "Please believe transported Yalta Woland's hypnosis wire CID confirmation identity Likhodeyev."

Rimsky and Varenukha, their heads touching, reread the telegram, and when they finished, they stared at each other in silence.

"Citizens!" said the woman angrily. "Sign for it and then you can be quiet for as long as you want! I've got telegrams to deliver."

Varenukha, still staring at the telegram, scribbled something in the notebook, and the woman disappeared.

"Weren't you talking to him on the phone just after eleven?" asked the director in complete bewilderment.

"Oddly enough, yes!" cried Rimsky in piercing tones. "But whether I talked to him or not is irrelevant, he can't possibly be in Yalta now! That's absurd!"

"He's drunk," said Varenukha.

"Who's drunk?" asked Rimsky, and again they both stared at each other.

That an impostor or lunatic had sent a telegram from Yalta was beyond doubt. What was odd, though, was how the Yalta jokester could have known about Woland, who had arrived in Moscow only yesterday. How could he know about the connection between Likhodeyev and Woland?

"Hypnosis..." said Varenukha, repeating the word in the telegram. "How did he hear about Woland?" He crinkled up his eyes and suddenly announced decisively, "No, this is nonsense, nonsense, nonsense!"

"Where the devil is this Woland staying?" asked Rimsky.

Varenukha got in touch with the Intourist Office immediately and reported, to Rimsky's complete surprise, that Woland was staying in Likhodeyev's apartment. He then dialed Likhodeyev's apartment and listened to the phone ring repeatedly and insistently. In between rings he could hear from somewhere far away a deep, somber voice singing, "the cliffs, my refuge..." and Varenukha decided that a voice from some radio station had somehow cut into the telephone circuit.

"There's no answer at the apartment," said Varenukha, hanging up the phone. "Perhaps I should try again..."

He didn't finish his sentence. The same woman appeared in the door again, and both Rimsky and Varenukha got up to meet her, but this time it was a dark sheet of paper that she removed from her bag, rather than a small white square.

"This is beginning to get interesting," said Varenukha through his teeth, staring after the woman as she made a quick exit. Rimsky was the first to get hold of the sheet.

Against the dark background of the photographic paper, one could clearly make out black, handwritten lines: "Proof my handwriting my signature Wire confirmation put Woland under secret surveillance. Likhodeyev."

During his twenty years in the theater Varenukha had seen a lot of things, but now he felt as if a shroud were covering his brain, and he was unable to say anything except the trite and, moreover, utterly absurd phrase, "This can't be!"

Rimsky, on the other hand, reacted differently. He got up, opened the door, and roared at the messenger girl sitting on the stool outside, "Don't let anyone in unless they have mail to deliver!"—and locked the door.

Then he took a pile of papers out of his desk and began a careful comparison of the bold, backward-slanting letters in the photogram and the letters in Styopa's memoranda and in his signatures, which were embellished with a spiral flourish. Varenukha leaned over the desk and breathed hotly on Rimsky's cheek.

"It's his handwriting, all right," the financial director finally pronounced, and Varenukha echoed him, "His, indeed."

When Varenukha looked into Rimsky's face, he was amazed by the change that had taken place. The already thin financial director seemed to have gotten even thinner and to have aged, and the eyes behind his horn-rimmed glasses had lost their customary sharpness, and expressed not only alarm, but sorrow as well.

Varenukha did everything you expect someone to do who is in a state of shock: he ran around the office and raised his arms up twice, like someone crucified, drank a whole glass of yellowish water from the carafe, and exclaimed, "I don't understand! I don't understand! I do not under-stand!"

Rimsky stared out the window, thinking intensely about something. The financial director was in a very difficult position: he had to devise, right on the spot, an ordinary explanation for out-of-the-ordinary happenings.

The financial director narrowed his eyes and tried to imagine Styopa, shoeless and in a nightshirt, getting on some unheard-of, super-fast plane at around 11:30 in the morning and then, also at 11:30, the same Styopa standing in his socks at the airport in Yalta... The devil knew how!

Maybe it wasn't Styopa who called him from his apartment? No, it was Styopa! As if he didn't know Styopa's voice! And even if it hadn't been Styopa on the phone that morning, it was certainly Styopa who appeared in his office as recently as yesterday evening, bringing that foolish contract and annoying the financial director with his thoughtlessness. How could he have left town or taken a plane without telling the theater? And even if he had taken a plane last night, he couldn't have gotten there by noon today. Or could he?

"How many kilometers is it to Yalta?" asked Rimsky.

Varenukha stopped his running about and shouted, "I thought of that! I already thought of that! By train to Sevastopol it's about 1500 kilometers. And it's another eighty kilometers from there to Yalta. But, by air, of course, it's less."

Hm... Yes... Trains were out of the question. But what then? A fighter plane? Who would let Styopa on a fighter plane without shoes? Why? Maybe he took off his shoes when he arrived in Yalta. Again: why? Besides, they wouldn't have let him on a fighter plane even with shoes! And what did a fighter plane have to do with it? Still, they had it in writing that he appeared at the Criminal Investigation Department at 11:30 in the morning, but he was talking on the phone in Moscow... wait a minute... at that point the face of Rimsky's watch suddenly appeared before his eyes... He remembered where the hands had been. God! It had been 11:20. So where does that leave us? If we assume that Styopa left for the airport right after our conversation and got there in, say, five minutes, which, by the way, is also inconceivable, then we are left to conclude that the plane took off right on the spot and covered more than 1000 kilometers in just five minutes?! Meaning that it traveled at more than 1200 kilometers per hour!! That's impossible, so he can't be in Yalta.

What other explanation was there? Hypnosis? There was no hypnosis in the world that could propel someone more than 1000 kilometers! So is he only imagining that he's in Yalta? He's imagining it, perhaps, and the Yalta CID is imagining it too?! No, you'll have to excuse me, but things like that don't happen. But hadn't they sent a wire from there?

The financial director's face looked literally horror-struck. Meanwhile, the doorknob was being pulled and twisted from the outside, and the messenger girl was heard shouting desperately, "You can't go in! I won't let you! Even if you kill me! There's a meeting!"

Rimsky did his utmost to control himself, picked up the phone, and said, "Connect me with Yalta, it's urgent."

"Smart!" Varenukha exclaimed to himself.

But the call to Yalta did not go through. Rimsky hung up the phone and said, "The line's out of order, as if out of spite."

It was obvious that the faulty line had a particularly devastating effect on Rimsky and even made him reflective. After musing for a while, he again picked up the receiver with one hand and with the other began writing down what he was saying into the phone.

"Take an express telegram. Variety. Yes. Yalta. Criminal Investigation Department. Yes. 'Today around 11:30 Likhodeyev phoned me in Moscow. Stop. After that missed work and cannot be located by phone. Stop. Handwriting confirmed. Stop. Steps taken to put said artiste under surveillance. Financial Director Rimsky.'"

"Very smart!" thought Varenukha, but before he could think it properly these words echoed in his head, "It's stupid! He can't be in Yalta!"

Meanwhile, Rimsky did the following: he neatly folded all the telegrams that had been received, put them in a packet along with a copy of the telegram he had sent, put the packet into an envelope, sealed it, wrote something on it, and then handed it to Varenukha saying, "Ivan Savelyevich, take this over in person right away. Let them figure it out."

"Now that's really smart!" thought Varenukha, and he stuffed the envelope into his briefcase. Then, just in case, he dialed Styopa's apartment again, listened, winked joyously and mysteriously, and smirked. Rimsky stretched his neck to listen.

"May I speak to the artiste Woland?" Varenukha asked sweetly.

"They're busy," a crackling voice replied, "Who may I say is calling?"

"The manager of the Variety Theater, Varenukha."

"Ivan Savelyevich?" the receiver exclaimed joyously. "I'm terribly happy to hear your voice! How's your health?"

"*Merci,*" the astonished Varenukha replied. "And who am I speaking to?"

"The assistant, his assistant and interpreter, Korovyov," crackled the receiver. "I'm at your service, my dear Ivan Savelyevich! Tell me how I can be of help to you. Well?"

"Excuse me, but is Stepan Bogdanovich Likhodeyev not at home?"

"Alas, no! He's not!" shouted the receiver. "He's gone."

"Where to?"

"He went for a drive outside of town."

"Wha... what's that? A dr... drive? And when will he be back?"

"He said, I'm just going out for some fresh air and I'll be right back!"

"I see..." said Varenukha, completely at a loss. "*Merci.* Be so kind as to tell Monsieur Woland that he will be appearing today in the third part of the program."

"I will indeed. But of course. Without fail. Right away. To be sure. I'll tell him," tapped out the receiver abruptly.

"All the best," said the astonished Varenukha.

"Please accept," said the receiver, "my best, my warmest wishes and regards! I wish you success! Good luck! Complete happiness. Everything!"

"Well, of course! It's just what I said!" cried the manager excitedly. "He didn't go to any Yalta, he just went for a ride in the country!"

"If that's the case," said the financial director, turning pale with rage, "words can't describe what a swine he is!"

Here the manager jumped up and let out such a shout that Rimsky shuddered.

"I just remembered! I just remembered! There's a Crimean restaurant just opened up in Pushkino called the 'Yalta.' That solves everything! He must have gone there, had too much to drink, and started sending us telegrams!"

"This is really too much," replied Rimsky, his cheek twitching and his eyes blazing with real fury. "Well, he'll pay a heavy price for this little jaunt!..." He suddenly broke off and added hesitantly, "But what about the Criminal Investigation Department..."

"That's absurd! More of his little games," interjected the affable Varenukha, who then asked, "So should I take this packet over anyway?"

"Absolutely," answered Rimsky.

Again the door opened, and in walked the same woman... "She's back!" thought Rimsky with inexplicable anguish. And both of them stood up to meet her.

This time the telegram read as follows, "Thanks confirmation send me ASAP 500 rubles CID flying Moscow tomorrow Likhodeyev."

"He's lost his mind," said Varenukha weakly.

But Rimsky jingled his key, took some money out of the safe, counted out 500 rubles, rang for the messenger, gave him the money and sent him off to the telegraph office.

"Good heavens, Grigory Danilovich," said Varenukha, not believing his eyes. "If you ask my opinion, you're throwing the money away."

"It'll come back," Rimsky replied softly, "and that little outing will cost him plenty." Then he added, pointing to Varenukha's briefcase, "Get going, Ivan Savelyevich, don't delay."

And Varenukha ran out of the office with the briefcase.

When he went downstairs, he saw an extremely long line at the box office and learned from the cashier that she expected to be sold out within the hour because the public had come in droves after seeing the additional playbills. Varenukha told the cashier to set aside thirty of the best seats in the orchestra and loges and then rushed out of the box office. After fighting off the obnoxious free-pass seekers, he ducked into his office to grab his cap. At that moment the phone rang.

"Yes!" shouted Varenukha.

"Ivan Savelyevich?" inquired the receiver in a loathsome nasal twang.

"He's not in the theater!" Varenukha was about to shout back, but the receiver immediately cut him off, "Don't play the fool, Ivan Savelyevich, just listen. Don't take those telegrams anywhere, and don't show them to anyone."

"Who is this speaking?" roared Varenukha. "Stop playing games, citizen! You'll be exposed! What's your number?"

"Varenukha," sounded the same loathsome voice. "Do you understand Russian? Do not take those telegrams anywhere."

"So, you're not going to stop?" shouted the manager in a frenzy. "Well, you better watch out! You'll pay for this!" He shouted yet another threat, but then stopped because he sensed that there was no longer anyone listening to him on the line.

At this point, the office somehow suddenly began to get dark. Varenukha ran out, slammed the door behind him, and hurried out to the summer garden through the side door.

The manager was agitated and full of energy. After the impudent phone call he was convinced that a band of hooligans was playing nasty tricks, and that the tricks had something to do with Likhodeyev's disappearance. A desire to unmask the villains overcame the manager and, strange as it may seem, he began to experience a sense of pleasant anticipation. This happens when someone is seeking to be the center of attention, the bearer of sensational news.

In the garden the wind blew in the manager's face and got sand in his eyes, as if it were trying to bar his way or give him a warning. A window on the second floor banged so hard that the glass almost flew out, the tops of the maples and lindens rustled uneasily. It got dark and turned cooler. The manager rubbed his eyes and saw a yellowbellied thundercloud crawling low over Moscow. A muffled growl was heard in the distance.

Although Varenukha was in a hurry, an irresistible urge compelled him to run into the outside toilet for a second to check if the electrician had put netting over the light.

He ran past the shooting gallery and into the thick clump of lilac bushes which sheltered the pale-blue lavatory facility. The electrician turned out to have been efficient, for the lamp under the eaves of the men's room was already encased in wire mesh, but the manager was upset to see that even in the pre-storm darkness, pencil and charcoal graffiti were visible on the walls.

"What is this..." began the manager, when suddenly a voice behind him purred, "Is that you, Ivan Savelyevich?"

Varenukha shuddered, turned around and saw a short, fat fellow with what seemed to be a cat's face.

"It is," came Varenukha's hostile reply.

"How very, very nice," said the catlike fat man in a squeaky voice, and then he suddenly whirled around and gave the manager such a smack on the ear that his cap flew off his head and disappeared into the toilet without a trace.

The blow flooded the whole lavatory with tremulous light for an instant, and a clap of thunder sounded overhead. Then the light flashed again, and another figure appeared before the manager—he was short and had fiery-red hair, the shoulders of an athlete, a walleye, and a fang.

This second fellow, apparently a lefty, landed a blow to the manager's other ear. The sky thundered again in reply, and a downpour hit the wooden roof of the lavatory.

"What are you doing, com..." whispered the half-crazed manager, only then realizing that the word "comrades" was hardly appropriate for thugs attacking a man in a public restroom. After croaking out "citiz...," he realized they didn't deserve that name either and received a third horrible blow, he didn't know who from, which made his nose bleed and spattered the fat man.

"What have you got in the briefcase, you parasite?" screamed the cat-like figure in a piercing voice. "Telegrams? Weren't you warned over the phone not to take them anywhere? I'm asking you, weren't you?"

"I was war... war... warned," spluttered the manager, gasping for breath.

"But you ran off anyway? Hand over the briefcase, scum!" shrieked the other one in the same nasal twang that had been heard over the phone, whereupon he pulled the briefcase out of Varenukha's trembling hands.

And the two of them grabbed the manager under the arms, dragged him out of the garden and hauled him down Sadovaya Street. The thunderstorm was raging with full fury, water groaned and droned and gushed into the sewers, bubbled and swelled in waves, lashed down from the roofs past the drainpipes, poured through the gateways in foaming streams. Every living being had been washed away from Sadovaya Street, and there was no one to save Ivan Savelyevich. It took the thugs only a second to leap through the turbid waters in the glare of the lightning and drag the manager to No. 302B. As they flew in the gateway with him, two barefoot women were huddled against the wall, clutching their shoes and stockings in their hands. The thugs then headed for entrance No. 6, and Varenukha, close to madness, was hauled up to the fifth floor and tossed into the familiar semidark hallway of Styopa Likhodeyev's apartment.

Here the two hoodlums vanished, and in their place appeared a girl who was stark naked. She had red hair and burning phosphorescent eyes.

Realizing that this was the worst thing to have happened to him, Varenukha let out a groan and backed into the wall. But the girl walked right up to the manager and laid the palms of her hands on his shoulders. The manager's hair stood on end because he could sense, even through the cold, soaking fabric of his peasant shirt, that those palms were colder still, cold as ice.

"Come let me give you a kiss," said the girl tenderly, her shining eyes coming right up to his. Varenukha lost consciousness and did not feel the kiss.

XI

Ivan is Split in Two

THE wood on the opposite shore of the river which, just an hour ago, had been shining in the May sun, now grew blurry and dim and then dissolved.

A veil of water hung outside the window. Threads of lightning kept flashing in the sky, the heavens split open, and a fearsome, flickering light flooded the sick man's room.

Ivan cried softly as he sat on his bed and looked out at the turbid, frothing, bubbling river. With every clap of thunder he let out a piteous cry and covered his face in his hands. Sheets of paper covered with Ivan's writing lay on the floor. They had been blown about by the wind, which had swept through the room before the storm began.

The poet's attempts to compose a report on the terrible consultant had come to nothing. As soon as he received a pencil stub and some paper from the stout nurse, whose name was Praskovya Fyodorovna, he had rubbed his hands together in a businesslike fashion and hastily set to work at the bedside table. He had dashed off a smart beginning, "To the police. From Ivan Nikolayevich Bezdomny, member of MASSOLIT. Report. Yesterday evening I arrived at Patriarch's Ponds with the deceased Berlioz..."

And the poet immediately became confused, largely due to the word "deceased." It made everything sound absurd from the start: how could he have arrived somewhere with the deceased? Dead men don't walk! They really will think I'm a madman!

Such thoughts made him start revising. The second version came out as follows, "...with Berlioz, later deceased..." That didn't satisfy the author either. He had to write a third version, and that came out even worse than the other two, "...with Berlioz, who fell under a streetcar..." What was irksome here was the obscure composer who was Berlioz's namesake; he felt compelled to add, "...not the composer..."

Tormented by these two Berliozes, Ivan crossed everything out and decided to begin with a strong opening that would immediately get the reader's attention. He began with a description of the cat boarding the streetcar, and then went back to the episode of the severed head. The head and the consultant's prediction made him think of Pontius Pilate, and in order to make the report more convincing, he decided to include the whole story about the procurator, starting with the moment when he came out onto the colonnade of Herod's palace dressed in a white robe with a blood-red lining.

Ivan worked hard, crossing out what he had written and adding new words. He even tried to do drawings of Pontius Pilate, and of the cat on its hind legs. But the drawings didn't help either, and the more the poet worked, the more confused and incomprehensible his report became.

By the time an ominous stormcloud with smoking edges had appeared from the distance and enveloped the woods, and the wind had blown the papers off the table, Ivan felt drained of energy and unable to cope with the report. Making no effort at all to pick up the scattered pages, he burst into silent and bitter tears.

The kind-hearted nurse, Praskovya Fyodorovna, came by to check on Ivan during the storm and was upset to see him crying. She closed the blinds so that the lightning would not frighten him, picked up the papers from the floor, and ran off with them to get the doctor.

The doctor appeared, gave Ivan an injection in his arm and assured him that he would stop crying, that now everything would pass, everything would change and all would be forgotten.

The doctor turned out to be right. The wood across the river started to look as it had before. It stood out sharply, down to the last tree, beneath the sky which had been restored to its former perfect blueness, and the river grew calm. Ivan's anguish began to diminish right after the injection, and now the poet lay peacefully, gazing at the rainbow spread across the sky.

Things stayed this way until evening, and he never even noticed when the rainbow evaporated, the sky faded and grew sad, and the wood turned black.

Ivan drank some hot milk, lay down again, and was himself surprised at how his thoughts had changed. The image of the demonic, accursed cat had somehow softened in his memory, the severed head no longer frightened him, and when Ivan stopped thinking about the head, he began to reflect on how the clinic wasn't so bad, everything considered, and how Stravinsky was a clever fellow and a celebrity and extremely pleasant to have dealings with. And, besides, the evening air was sweet and fresh after the storm.

The asylum was falling asleep. The frosted white lights in the quiet corridors went out, and in accordance with regulations, the faint blue night-lights came on, and the cautious steps of the nurses were heard less frequently on the rubber matting in the corridor outside the door.

Now Ivan lay in a state of sweet lethargy, gazing now at the shaded lamp, which cast a mellow light down from the ceiling, now at the moon, which was emerging from the black wood. He was talking to himself.

"Why did I get so upset over Berlioz falling under a streetcar?" the poet reasoned. "In the final analysis, let him rot! What am I to him, anyway, kith or kin? If we examine the question properly, it turns out that I, essentially, didn't really know the deceased. What did I actually know about him? Nothing, except that he was bald and horribly eloquent. And so, citizens," continued Ivan, addressing an invisible audience, "let us examine the following: explain, if you will, why I got so furious at that mysterious consultant, magician, and professor with the black, vacant eye? What was the point of that whole absurd chase, with me in my underwear, carrying a candle? And what about that grotesque scene in the restaurant?"

"But, but, but..." said the old Ivan to the new Ivan, addressing him in a stern voice from somewhere inside his head or behind his ear, "but didn't he know in advance that Berlioz's head would be cut off? How could you not get upset?"

"What is there to discuss, comrades!" retorted the new Ivan to the broken-down old Ivan. "Even a child can see that there is something sinister about all this. He is, no doubt about it, a mysterious and exceptional personality. But that's what makes it so interesting! The fellow was personally acquainted with Pontius Pilate, what could be more interesting than that? And instead of making that ridiculous scene at Patriarch's Ponds, wouldn't it have been better to have asked him politely about what happened next to Pilate and the prisoner Ha-Notsri? But instead, I got obsessed with the devil knows what! Is it such an earth-shattering event—that an editor got run over! Does it mean the magazine will have to close down? So, what can you do? Man is mortal and, as was said so fittingly, sometimes suddenly so. Well, God rest his soul! There'll be a new editor, and maybe he'll be even more eloquent than the last one."

After dozing off for awhile, the new Ivan asked the old Ivan spitefully, "So how do I look in all this?"

"Like a fool!" a bass voice pronounced distinctly, a voice which did not come from either one of the Ivans and was amazingly reminiscent of the consultant's bass.

For some reason Ivan did not take offense at the word "fool," but was pleasantly surprised by it, smiled, and fell into a half-sleep. Sleep was creeping up on Ivan, and he could already see a palm tree on an elephantlike trunk, and a cat went by—not a fearsome one, but a jolly one, and, in short, sleep was about to engulf him when suddenly the window grille moved aside noiselessly, and a mysterious figure, who was trying to hide from the moonlight, appeared on the balcony, and shook a warning finger at Ivan.

Not feeling the least bit afraid, Ivan raised himself in bed and saw that there was a man on the balcony. And this man pressed his finger to his lips and whispered, "Shh!"

XII

Black Magic and Its Exposé

A little man with a pear-shaped, raspberry-colored nose, wearing checked trousers, patent-leather shoes, and a yellow bowler hat full of holes, rode out onto the stage of the Variety Theater on an ordinary two-wheeled bicycle. He made a circle to the accompaniment of a foxtrot, and then let out a triumphant hoot as he made his bicycle stand up on end. While riding on just the back wheel, the man turned upside down and managed, at the same time, to unscrew the front wheel and send it offstage. He then continued his ride on the one wheel, pedalling with his hands.

Next appeared a buxom blonde in tights and a short skirt speckled with silver stars, who circled around on a unicycle, perched on top of a long metal pole. As they passed each other, the man shouted out greetings and tipped his hat to her with his foot.

The last to come out was a child of about eight with an old man's face, who darted in between the two adults on a tiny two-wheeler outfitted with a huge automobile horn.

After making several loops, the entire company pedalled up to the very edge of the stage to the accompaniment of an anxious drumroll from the orchestra. The spectators seated in the front rows gasped and pulled back in their seats, for it seemed as if all three performers were about to come crashing down into the orchestra with their cycles.

But the bicycles stopped short, just as their front wheels threatened to skid off into the orchestra pit and onto the musicians' heads. With a loud cry of "Oop," the cyclists jumped off their bikes and bowed, and the blonde threw kisses to the audience, while the child made a funny noise on his horn.

The theater shook with applause, and the pale-blue curtain drew together from both sides, hiding the cyclists from view. The green lights of the exit signs went out, and in the web of the trapezes under the dome, the white globes of the house lights began to blaze like the sun. It was the intermission before the final part of the program.

The only person to have no interest whatsoever in the wonders of the Giulli family's cycling technique was Grigory Danilovich Rimsky. He was sitting all alone in his office, biting his thin lips, and his face kept twitching convulsively. Likhodeyev's strange disappearance was now compounded by the utterly unforeseen disappearance of the manager Varenukha.

Rimsky knew where he had gone, but he had gone there and... not come back! Rimsky hunched his shoulders and whispered to himself, "But why?"

And what is odd is that it would have been simpler than anything for a man as businesslike as the financial director to call the place where Varenukha had gone and find out what had happened to him. However, ten o'clock was approaching, and he still couldn't bring himself to do it.

At ten Rimsky took himself firmly in hand and picked up the receiver, only then to discover that his phone was dead. The messenger boy reported that the other phones in the building were also out of order. This admittedly unpleasant but hardly supernatural occurrence completely unnerved the financial director and yet delighted him as well: he wouldn't have to make the call.

Just as the red light signalling the start of intermission began to flicker above the financial director's head, the messenger boy came in and announced that the foreign artiste had arrived. For some reason this made the financial director wince with pain. Turning darker than a stormcloud, he headed backstage to receive the guest artiste, there being no one left but him to do so.

Those who were curious were using various pretexts to peer into the large dressing room off the corridor where the bells signalling the end of intermission were already ringing. Among them were conjurers in bright robes and turbans, a roller skater in a white knitted jacket, a storyteller whose face was pale with powder, and a make-up man.

The visiting celebrity astounded everyone with his unusually long and splendidly cut tailcoat, and by the fact that he was wearing a black eye mask. But even more amazing were the black magician's two companions: a tall fellow in checks with a broken pince-nez and a fat black cat, who walked into the dressing room on his hind paws and then proceeded to make himself comfortable on the couch, squinting at the naked bulbs on the makeup mirror.

Trying to put a smile on his face, which only made it look sour and mean, Rimsky bowed to the silent magician, who was sitting on the couch next to the cat. No one shook hands, but the overly familiar fellow in checks introduced himself as "their assistant." This surprised the financial director and unpleasantly so, since there had been absolutely nothing in the contract about any assistant.

Dryly and very tensely, Grigory Danilovich asked the fellow in checks, who had fallen on him out of the blue, where the artiste's equipment was.

"Why, our most precious Director, our diamond from heaven, how quaint you are," answered the magician's assistant in a quavering voice. "Our equipment is always with us. Here it is! *Eins, zwei, drei!*" He then wiggled his gnarled fingers in front of Rimsky's eyes and suddenly pulled out Rimsky's gold watch and chain from behind the cat's ear. Up until now it had been in the financial director's vest pocket, underneath his buttoned jacket, with its chain looped through the buttonhole.

Rimsky grabbed his stomach involuntarily, the onlookers gasped, and the makeup man, who was peering in through the door, clucked approvingly.

"Could this be your watch? Please take it," said the fellow in checks, smiling in an overly familiar way as he handed the flustered Rimsky his property on a grubby palm.

"You wouldn't want to get on a streetcar with the likes of him," whispered the storyteller gaily to the makeup man.

But then the cat pulled a trick that was even more skillful than the one with Rimsky's watch. Suddenly rising from the couch, he walked on his hind paws to the table under the mirror, pulled the stopper out of the carafe, poured some vodka into a glass, drank it, put the stopper back in place, and then wiped his whiskers off with a makeup rag.

This time no one even gasped, mouths simply opened wide, and the makeup man whispered ecstatically, "Now, that's first-class!"

At this point the third bell rang, and everyone, keyed up and anticipating an exciting act, rushed out of the dressing room.

A minute later the lights dimmed in the auditorium, and the footlights came on, casting a reddish glow on the bottom of the curtain. A stout fellow, clean-shaven and cheerful as a baby, wearing rumpled tails and soiled linen, appeared through the brightly lit opening in the curtain and stood before the audience. This was the master of ceremonies, George Bengalsky, well known to all of Moscow.

"And so, citizens," began Bengalsky, smiling a babylike grin, "now I would like to present..." Here he interrupted himself and began speaking in a different tone, "I see that our audience has increased for the third part of the program. Half the city is here with us today! Just recently I met a friend and said to him, 'Why don't you come and see us? Yesterday half the city was here.' And he says, 'But I live in the other half!' Bengalsky paused, expecting a burst of laughter, but when none came, he continued, "And so, I would like to present the famous foreign artiste, Monsieur Woland, in a performance of black magic! Of course, you and I know," here Bengalsky smiled a knowing smile, "that there is no such thing in the world as black magic, and it is nothing other than superstition and that Maestro Woland is simply a master of conjuring technique, a fact which will become obvious in the most interesting part of his performance, that is, when he reveals the secrets behind his technical skill. And so, since we all applaud both expertise and its exposé, let us welcome Mr. Woland!"

After delivering this whole spiel, Bengalsky pressed his palms together and waved them in welcoming fashion at the opening in the curtain, whereupon it drew apart with a soft rustle.

The entrance of the magician with his tall assistant and his cat, who came out on stage on his hind paws, made a big hit with the audience.

"An armchair, if you will," Woland commanded softly, and that very second an armchair appeared on stage out of nowhere, and the magician sat down. "Tell me, dear Fagot," inquired Woland of the buffoon in checks, who obviously had another name besides Korovyov, "have the Muscovites changed, in your opinion, in any significant way?"

The magician looked out over the hushed audience, which was still stunned by the chair's sudden appearance out of thin air.

"Indeed they have, Messire," was Fagot-Korovyov's soft reply.

"You are right. They have changed a great deal... on the outside, I mean, as has the city, by the way. Apart from the obvious changes in dress, there are now these... what are they called... streetcars, automobiles..."

"Buses," Fagot chimed in, respectfully.

The audience listened attentively to this conversation, thinking it was the prelude to the magic tricks. In the crowd of performers and stage hands backstage, Rimsky's pale, tense face could be seen.

Bengalsky, who had moved to the side of the stage, began to look bewildered. He raised his eyebrows slightly and, taking advantage of the pause, said, "The foreign artiste is expressing his delight with Moscow, which has advanced technologically, and with its inhabitants as well." Here Bengalsky smiled twice, first at the orchestra, and then at the gallery.

Woland, Fagot, and the cat turned their heads toward the master of ceremonies.

"Did I really express delight?" the magician asked Fagot.

"No, indeed, Messire, you expressed no delight whatsoever," was Fagot's reply.

"So what is this man talking about?"

"He simply lied!" pronounced the assistant in checks, booming out his words to the entire theater, and turning to Bengalsky, he added, "My compliments, citizen, on your lies."

Laughter broke out in the gallery, and Bengalsky shuddered, his eyes bulging.

"But I, of course, am not so much interested in buses, telephones, and such..."

"Apparatus!" prompted the fellow in checks.

"Exactly so, thank you," said the magician slowly, in a deep bass. "A much more important question is: have the Muscovites changed on the inside?"

"Indeed, sir, that is a most important question."

Backstage, people began exchanging looks and shrugging their shoulders; Bengalsky stood red-faced, and Rimsky was pale. But at this point the magician seemed to sense the growing alarm and said, "However, we've gotten carried away, dear Fagot, and the audience is beginning to get bored. Show us something simple for starters."

The audience stirred with relief. Fagot and the cat walked along the footlights to opposite ends of the stage. Fagot snapped his fingers and shouted cavalierly, "Three, four!" He then pulled a deck of cards out of thin air, shuffled it, and tossed it like a ribbon to the cat. The latter caught the ribbon of cards and threw it back. The satin snake gave a snort, Fagot opened his mouth wide, like a fledgling, and swallowed all of it, card after card.

After that the cat made a bow, shuffled his right hind paw, and received thunderous applause.

"First-class! First-class!" people cried rapturously from backstage.

Fagot pointed his finger at the orchestra section and announced, "The deck of cards is now, my esteemed citizens, in row seven in citizen Parchevsky's possession, that is, lodged just in between a three-ruble note and a summons to appear in court for non-payment of alimony to citizeness Zelkova."

People in the orchestra began to stir and rise from their seats, and finally a man, whose name was, in fact, Parchevsky, and who had turned red with astonishment, retrieved the deck of cards from his wallet and, not knowing what else to do with it, began poking it in the air.

"Keep it as a souvenir!" yelled Fagot. "You weren't kidding yesterday when you said at supper that if it weren't for poker, your life in Moscow would be totally unbearable."

"That's an old trick," shouted someone from the balcony. "The guy in the orchestra is part of the act."

"You think so?" bellowed Fagot, narrowing his eyes at the balcony. "In that case, you're part of the act too, because now the deck is in your pocket!"

There was a stir in the balcony, and a joyous voice rang out, "It's true! He does have it! Here, here... but wait! They're ten-ruble notes!"

The spectators in the orchestra turned their heads. In the balcony a perplexed citizen had found a packet of bills in his pocket, wrapped the way they are at the bank, with the words "One Thousand Rubles" written on top.

His neighbors descended upon him, while he, flabbergasted, picked at the wrapper with his nail, trying to ascertain whether the notes were real or make-believe.

"By God, they're real! Ten-ruble notes!" came joyous shouts from the balcony.

"Play me a game with a pack like that," said a fat man merrily, who was seated in the center of the orchestra.

"*Avec plaisir!*" replied Fagot, "but why just you? Everyone will take part!" And he gave a command, "Everybody look up please!" "One!" A pistol appeared in his hand. "Two," he shouted. The pistol jerked upwards. "Three!" he shouted. There was a flash, a bang, and suddenly white pieces of paper began to rain down onto the hall, falling from the dome ceiling, and diving in between the trapezes.

They whirled all around, scattered off to the sides, pelted the balcony, piled into the orchestra pit and onto the stage. Within seconds, growing thicker as it fell, the rain of bills had reached the seats, and the audience began catching them.

Hundreds of hands went up, people held the bills up to the light from the stage and found watermarks that were perfectly genuine and authentic. The smell of the bills also left no room for doubt: it was the incomparably delectable smell of newly minted money. First merriment and then astonishment swept the theater. It was all abuzz with the words "ten-ruble notes," "ten-ruble notes," and happy laughter was heard and shouts of "ah, ah!" Some people were already crawling in the aisles, looking under the seats, and many were standing on top of their seats, trying to catch the capriciously twirling bills.

The faces of the policemen began to look more and more bewildered, and performers piled out from backstage.

In the dress circle a voice was heard saying, "What's that you're grabbing? That's mine! It was coming toward me!" Another voice yelled, "Don't push me or I'll push you back!" And suddenly a slap was heard, whereupon a policeman's helmet appeared in the dress circle and someone was taken away.

The general excitement grew in intensity, and no one knows how it all would have ended if Fagot had not put a stop to the shower of rubles by suddenly blowing into the air.

Two young men exchanged a happy and meaningful glance, got up from their seats and headed straight for the buffet. The theater was abuzz, and all eyes gleamed with excitement. Yes, yes, who knows how it all would have ended if Bengalsky had not summoned up the strength to do something. Making an effort to regain his composure, he rubbed his hands together in his customary way, and his voice resonated loudly, "Citizens, we have just witnessed an example of so-called mass hypnosis. A purely scientific experiment, designed to prove beyond a doubt that there are no miracles and that magic does not exist. Let's ask Maestro Woland to show us how the experiment was done. Now, citizens, you shall see how these paper bills that seem to be money will disappear as suddenly as they appeared."

Here he began to clap, but no one joined in. As he clapped, a confident smile played on his face, but that same confidence was not reflected in his eyes. They, on the contrary, were full of entreaty.

The audience did not like Bengalsky's speech. A total silence ensued which was then broken by the checked Fagot.

"Yet another example of what we call balderdash," he announced in a loud braying tenor. "The paper bills, citizens, are real money!"

"Bravo!" a bass bellowed out from somewhere on high.

"And by the way," said Fagot, pointing at Bengalsky, "this fellow is getting to be a bore. He keeps butting in when nobody asks him to and spoiling the performance with his bogus comments! What should we do with him?"

"Tear off his head!" came a stern voice from the balcony.

"What did you say? What was that?" said Fagot, responding to the ugly suggestion. "Tear off his head? Now that's an idea! Behemoth!" he screamed to the cat, "Do it! *Eins, zwei, drei!!*"

Then an incredible thing happened. The cat's black fur stood on end, and he let out a spine-tingling "meow." Then he shrunk into a ball, and like a panther, lunged straight at Bengalsky's chest, and from there leapt onto his head. With a low growl, the cat stuck his chubby paws into the emcee's greasy hair, and with a savage howl, tore the head off its thick neck in two twists.

The two and a half thousand people in the theater screamed in unison. Fountains of blood spurted from the severed arteries in the neck and poured down the emcee's shirt front and tailcoat. The headless body's legs buckled absurdly, and it plopped onto the floor. The hysterical screams of women were heard. The cat handed the head to Fagot, who lifted it up by the hair and showed it to the audience, and the head cried out desperately to the whole theater, "Get a doctor!"

"Are you going to keep on talking rubbish?" Fagot inquired of the weeping head in threatening tones.

"I won't anymore!" rasped the head.

"Stop torturing him, for God's sake!" shouted a woman in the loge. The magician turned in her direction.

"So, ladies and gentlemen, should we forgive him?" asked Fagot, addressing the audience.

"Yes, forgive him, forgive him!" shouted individual and, for the most part, female voices which then joined with male voices to form a single chorus.

"What is your command, Messire?" asked Fagot of the man in the mask.

"Well," the latter replied pensively, "they are like people anywhere. They love money, but that has always been true... People love money, no matter what it is made of, leather, paper, bronze, or gold. And they are thoughtless... but, then again, sometimes mercy enters their hearts... they are ordinary people... On the whole, they remind me of their predecessors... only the housing shortage has had a bad effect on them..." And in a loud voice he commanded, "Put his head back on."

Taking care to make sure it was on right, the cat plopped the head back in place, and it sat on the neck as if it had never left. And, most important, not even a scar was left on the neck. The cat swept his paws over Bengalsky's shirtfront and tailcoat, and the bloodstains vanished. Fagot lifted the seated Bengalsky to his feet, stuck a packet of ten-ruble bills into his coat pocket and directed him off stage with the words, "Get lost! It's more fun without you."

Swaying and looking around in a daze, the emcee made it only as far as the fire extinguisher, and there he got sick. He cried in woe, "My head, my head!"

Rimsky was among those who rushed over to him. The emcee cried, grabbed at the air with his hands, and mumbled, "Give me back my head! Give me back my head! Take my apartment, take my pictures, only give me back my head!"

A messenger ran for a doctor. People urged Bengalsky to lie down on a couch in the dressing room, but he fought them off and got rowdy. An ambulance had to be called. When the unfortunate emcee had been carted off, Rimsky ran back to the stage, only to find new miracles in progress. And, by the way, it was either then, or a short time before that, that the magician and his faded armchair disappeared from the stage—something which the audience failed to notice, totally absorbed as it was in the extraordinary things Fagot was doing on stage.

After dispatching the ailing emcee, Fagot made the following announcement, "Now that we've gotten rid of that bore, let's open a store for the ladies!"

Suddenly the stage floor was covered with Persian rugs, huge mirrors appeared, illuminated along the sides by elongated green bulbs, and between the mirrors were glass display cases where the audience, in a state of happy bedazzlement, beheld Parisian frocks in various colors and styles. These were in some of the cases, and in others were hundreds of hats, with feathers and without, and hundreds of shoes, with buckles and without—black, white, yellow, leather, satin, suede, shoes with straps and shoes with gems. Containers of perfume appeared among the shoes, as well as mountains of chamois, satin, and silk handbags with piles of elongated, embossed gold lipstick cases scattered in between them.

The devil only knows where the red-haired girl in the black evening dress came from, who was standing by the display cases with a proprietary smile, her beauty marred only by a strange scar on her neck.

With a saccharine smile, Fagot announced to the women in the audience that the store would exchange their old clothes and shoes for Parisian styles and Parisian shoes. He added that the same sort of exchange would apply to handbags and the like.

The cat scraped his hind paw and, simultaneously, gestured with his front paw, the way doormen do upon opening the door.

Sweetly, albeit with a touch of throatiness, the redhead began to recite words which were baffling but seductive, judging by the women's faces in the orchestra, *"Guerlain, Chanel No. 5, Mitsouko, Narcisse Noir,* evening gowns, cocktail dresses..."

Fagot twisted and squirmed, the cat bowed, and the girl opened the glass cases.

"Be our guests!" bellowed Fagot. "No need to be shy or stand on ceremony!"

The audience was excited, but no one, as yet, made any move to go up on stage. Finally, a brunette stepped out of the tenth row of the orchestra and, smiling as if to say she had nothing better to do, came down the aisle and walked up the side stairs to the stage.

"Bravo!" cried Fagot. "Greetings to our first customer! Behemoth, bring the lady a chair! Shall we begin with shoes, Madame!"

The brunette sat down in the chair, whereupon Fagot laid out a whole pile of shoes on the carpet in front of her. She took off her right shoe, tried on a lilac one, tapped her foot on the carpet, and examined the heel.

"Won't they pinch?" she asked thoughtfully.

"Madame, Madame!" exclaimed Fagot in offended tones, and the cat gave an insulted meow.

"I'll take this pair, Monsieur," said the brunette with dignity as she put on the other shoe.

The brunette's old shoes were thrown behind the curtain, and she herself headed in that direction, accompanied by the redhead and Fagot, who was carrying hangers draped with an assortment of dresses in different styles. The cat fussed about, offered assistance, and hung a tape measure around his neck in order to look more important.

A minute later the brunette came out from behind the curtain wearing a dress that made the entire orchestra section gasp. The brave woman, whose appearance had improved amazingly, stopped in front of the mirror, straightened her bare shoulders, touched the hair at the back of her neck, and twisted around, trying to get a look at herself from the rear.

"The firm asks you to accept this as a memento," said Fagot, handing her an open box with a bottle of perfume inside.

"*Merci,*" the brunette answered haughtily, and she went back down to her seat. As she walked up the aisle, people jumped up, trying to touch the box.

And at this point all hell broke loose, women came onto the stage from all directions. Above the general din of excited chatter, laughter and sighs, a man's voice was heard saying, "I won't let you!" and a woman's voice reposting, "Tyrant, philistine! Don't break my arm!" Women disappeared behind the curtain, left their dresses there and came out wearing new ones. An entire row of ladies sat on gilt-legged stools, energetically tapping the carpet with their newly shod feet. Fagot was down on his knees, assisting with a metal shoehorn; the cat was wearing himself out, trudging back and forth between the display cases and the stools, weighted down with piles of handbags and shoes; the redhead with the disfigured neck would appear and disappear, and it got to the point where she was chattering away exclusively in French, and amazingly, the women understood everything she said, even those who did not know a word of French.

There was general astonishment when a man made his way onto the stage and announced that his wife had influenza, and that he was there to ask for something on her behalf. To prove that he was married, the man was ready to show his passport. The declaration of the concerned husband provoked laughter, Fagot yelled that he believed him completely, even without a passport, and handed him two pairs of silk stockings. The cat, for his part, threw in a lipstick case.

The women who were latecomers rushed onto the stage, while the lucky ones poured off it dressed in ball gowns, lounging pajamas with dragons, severely cut suits, and hats tilted over the eyebrow.

Then Fagot announced that due to the late hour, in exactly one minute the store would be closing until tomorrow evening. There was an incredible uproar on stage. Women snatched up shoes in haste, without even trying them on. One woman swept behind the curtain like a tempest, tore off her clothes and grabbed the first thing in sight—a silk robe with a huge floral design, and for good measure, she grabbed two bottles of perfume too.

Exactly a minute later a shot rang out, the mirrors disappeared, the display cases and stools vanished, and the carpet melted into thin air along with the curtain. The last thing to disappear was the mountain of old dresses and shoes, and the stage again became stark, empty and bare.

And then a new character got involved in the act.

A pleasant, resonant, and very persistent baritone was heard coming from Box No. 2.

"Just the same, citizen artiste, it would be much appreciated if you would reveal to the audience the techniques you use in your magic, especially the trick with the paper bills. The return of the emcee to the stage would also be appreciated. The audience is worried about his fate."

The baritone belonged to none other than Arkady Apollonovich Sempleyarov, a guest of honor at that evening's performance, and the chairman of the Acoustics Commission for Moscow Theaters.

Arkady Apollonovich was seated in a box with two ladies: one older, expensively and stylishly dressed, and the other young, pretty, and dressed more simply. The former was Arkady Apollonovich's wife, as the official report of the proceedings would later reveal, and the latter was a distant relative of his, an aspiring young actress, who had arrived from Saratov, and was staying with Arkady Apollonovich and his wife in their apartment.

"*Pardon!*" retorted Fagot. "I beg your pardon, but there is nothing to reveal here. Everything is clear."

"No, I'm sorry! An exposé is absolutely imperative. Otherwise your brilliant act will leave a painful impression. The audience demands an explanation."

"The audience," said the impudent buffoon, interrupting Sempleyarov, "seems to have said nothing, right? But in deference to your wishes, I shall begin the exposé in a moment. However, for that purpose will you allow me to present one final little number?"

"Why not," replied Arkady Apollonovich in a condescending tone, "but make sure it comes with an exposé!"

"Of course, of course. Well then, Arkady Apollonovich, may I ask you where you were yesterday evening?"

Upon hearing this inappropriate and, possibly, even rude question, Arkady Apollonovich's face changed dramatically.

"Yesterday evening Arkady Apollonovich was at a meeting of the Acoustics Commission," declared Arkady Apollonovich's wife very haughtily, "but I don't understand what this has to do with magic."

"*Oui, madame!*" confirmed Fagot. "Naturally, you don't! As for the meeting, you're completely mistaken. Arkady Apollonovich left for the alleged meeting, which, to set the record straight, was not scheduled for yesterday, and then when he got to Chistye Prudy, where the Acoustics Commission meets, he let his driver go (the whole audience grew hushed) and went by bus to Yelokhovsky Street to pay a visit to Militsa Andreyevna Pokobatko, an actress in a touring regional company, and he stayed there for about four hours."

"Oh!" came an anguished cry in the hushed silence.

Arkady Apollonovich's young relative suddenly let out a low-pitched, terrifying laugh.

"That explains everything!" she exclaimed. "And I've had my suspicions for a long time. Now I know why that third-rater got the part of Luisa!"

And then she suddenly waved her short, stubby, lilac umbrella and hit Arkady Apollonovich over the head.

The vile Fagot, alias Korovyov, cried out, "Here you have, respected citizens, the kind of exposé which Arkady Apollonovich so persistently asked for!"

"You wretched woman, how dare you lay a hand on Arkady Apollonovich!" threatened his spouse, rising up to her full height in the box.

The young relative was seized with another fit of satanic laughter.

"If anyone can lay a hand on him, I certainly can," she answered through her laughter, and again her umbrella was heard, cracking Arkady Apollonovich over the head.

"Police! Arrest her!" shrieked Madame Sempleyarov in such a terrifying voice that it made many people's blood run cold.

And at this point the cat leapt up to the footlights and roared out to the theater in a human voice, "The show is over! Maestro! Hack out a march!!"

The half-crazed conductor, only dimly aware of what he was doing, waved his baton, and the orchestra did not so much start to play, burst out in, or even strike up, but rather, to use the cat's repulsive expression, it hacked out an improbable march, so sloppily played that it did not resemble a march at all.

For a moment it seemed as if the half-clear, semi-distinct, yet provocative words of the march had been heard, once upon a time, in a *café-chantant* somewhere under southern skies:

> *His Excellency*
> *Had a taste for domestic fowl*
> *And was always on the prowl*
> *For good-looking chicks!!!*

Or maybe those were not the words, and there were other ones to the same music which were also highly indecent. That's not important, what is important is that after this, something like the fall of the Tower of Babel broke out in the Variety Theater. The police rushed to the Sempleyarovs' box, curiosity-seekers climbed onto the railing, hellish bursts of laughter and mad shrieks were heard, which were drowned out by the golden crash of cymbals coming from the orchestra pit.

And the stage was suddenly empty, and both the trickster Fagot and the huge brazen cat Behemoth had melted into thin air and vanished, just as the magician and his faded armchair had vanished before them.

XIII

Enter the Hero

A ND SO, the stranger pressed a warning finger to his lips and whispered "Shh!" to Ivan.

Ivan lowered his feet over the side of the bed and stared. Peering cautiously into the room from the balcony was a clean-shaven, dark-haired man of about thirty-eight; he had anxious eyes, a sharp nose, and a shock of hair hanging over his forehead.

After making certain that Ivan was alone, the mysterious visitor listened intently, then mustered his courage and entered the room. Ivan noticed that he was wearing hospital clothes: underwear, slippers on bare feet, and a dark brown robe thrown over his shoulders.

The newcomer winked at Ivan, stuck a bunch of keys in his pocket and asked in a whisper, "May I sit down?" When he received a nod of assent, he settled into the armchair.

"How did you get in here?" said Ivan in a whisper, obeying his guest's warning gesture. "Aren't the window grilles locked?"

"They are locked," confirmed the guest, "but Praskovya Fyodorovna is an extremely nice, if, alas, absentminded person. I pinched her keys a month ago, which allows me to go out onto the balcony that encircles the entire floor and thus visit a neighbor on occasion."

"But if you can go out onto the balcony, you can get out of here. Or is it too high up?" queried Ivan.

"No," was the guest's firm reply. "It's not because it's too high that I can't get out, but because there's nowhere for me to get out to." After a pause he added, "So, we're stuck sitting here?"

"Yes, stuck," replied Ivan, gazing into the newcomer's anxious-looking brown eyes.

"Yes..."—here the guest suddenly became agitated. "I hope you're not violent, are you? Because, you see, I can't tolerate noise, rows, violence, or anything of that sort. And I especially can't stand people screaming, whether in suffering, rage, or for any other reason. Reassure me, tell me—you're not violent, are you?"

"Yesterday in a restaurant I smashed some guy in the puss," confessed the transformed poet manfully.

"The reason?" the guest asked sternly.

"None really, I admit," answered Ivan, becoming embarrassed.

"Disgraceful," the guest scolded and added, "And besides, why do you say things like 'smash some guy in the puss'? After all, nobody knows exactly what it is that a man has, a face or a puss. Most likely, it's still a face. So, when it comes to fists... No, you should stop doing that sort of thing once and for all."

After giving Ivan this lecture, the guest inquired, "Your profession?"

"Poet," Ivan acknowledged somewhat unwillingly.

The newcomer became distressed.

"Oh, how unlucky I am!" he exclaimed, but then caught himself, apologized, and asked, "And what is your name?"

"Bezdomny."

"Uh-oh," said the guest with a frown.

"What's the matter, don't you like my poetry?" asked Ivan with curiosity.

"Emphatically not."

"And what have you read?"

"I haven't read any of your poetry!" retorted the visitor irritably.

"Then how can you tell?"

"Well," replied the guest, "it's not as if I haven't read other things like it, now is it? But maybe, by some miracle, yours is different? All right, I'm ready to take it on faith. Tell me yourself, are your poems any good?"

"Horrible!" Ivan blurted out boldly and frankly.

"Don't write any more!" the newcomer implored.

"I promise you, I swear I won't!" was Ivan's solemn reply.

They sealed the vow with a handshake, and then the sounds of soft footsteps and voices were heard from the corridor.

"Shh," whispered the guest, jumping out onto the balcony and closing the grille behind him.

Praskovya Fyodorovna looked in and asked how Ivan was feeling and whether he wanted to sleep in the dark or with a light. Ivan asked her to leave the light on, and Praskovya Fyodorovna exited after wishing the patient good night. And when everything had quieted down, the guest came back again.

He told Ivan in a whisper that a new patient had just been brought into Room 119, a fat fellow with a purple face who kept muttering something about foreign currency in the ventilator shaft, and who swore that evil powers had settled into his building on Sadovaya Street.

"He's cursing out Pushkin for all he's worth and shouting, 'Kurolesov, encore, encore!'" said the guest, twitching anxiously. When he calmed down, he took a seat and said, "But, never mind about him," and continued his conversation with Ivan, "So how did you end up here?"

"Because of Pontius Pilate," Ivan replied, looking sullenly down at the floor.

"What?!" shouted the guest, abandoning caution, and then clamping his hand over his mouth. "A striking coincidence! I beg you, I beg you, tell me all about it!"

Feeling for some reason that he could trust the stranger, Ivan began telling him about yesterday's happenings at Patriarch's Ponds, starting out haltingly and timidly, but then growing bolder as he went along. And indeed, Ivan Nikolayevich found a sympathetic listener in this mysterious key thief! The guest did not treat Ivan as if he were a madman, showed the greatest interest in what he was saying, and became ecstatic as the story progressed. He kept interrupting Ivan with exclamations, "Well, well, go on, go on, I beg you! Only in the name of all that's holy, don't leave anything out!"

Ivan left nothing out, for he himself found it easier to tell the story that way, and gradually he got to the point where Pontius Pilate came out on the balcony in his white cloak with the blood-red lining.

The guest then folded his hands as if in prayer and whispered, "Oh, I guessed right! I guessed everything right!"

Following the description of Berlioz's horrible death the listener made a puzzling remark, and his eyes flashed with hatred, "I'm just sorry that it wasn't Latunsky, the critic, or that hack Mstislav Lavrovich instead of Berlioz." And in a frenzy, but noiselessly, he exclaimed, "Go on!"

The cat who paid his fare was a big hit with the guest, and he choked with silent laughter as he watched Ivan, excited by the success of his storytelling, jump down on his haunches and pantomime the cat holding a coin up to his whiskers.

"And so," Ivan concluded, after telling about the events at Griboyedov and again becoming gloomy and sad, "that's how I wound up here."

The guest laid a sympathetic hand on the poor poet's shoulder and said, "Unhappy poet! But you, dear fellow, brought it all on yourself! You shouldn't have acted so carelessly, even rudely, with him. Now you're paying the price. Why, you should be grateful you got off relatively cheaply."

"But who was he anyway?" asked Ivan, shaking his fists in agitation.

The guest stared at Ivan and answered with a question "You're not going to get all upset now, are you? All of us here are unstable... There won't be any calls for the doctor, or injections, or other stuff like that, will there?"

"No, no!" exclaimed Ivan, "just tell me who he is."

"All right then," replied the guest, weighing his words and speaking distinctly, "Yesterday at Patriarch's Ponds you had a meeting with Satan."

As he had promised, Ivan did not go berserk, but he was nevertheless totally flabbergasted.

"That can't be! He doesn't exist!"

"I beg your pardon! You're the last person in the world who should say such a thing. You were obviously one of the first ones to suffer at his hands. And here you are, as you very well know, in a mental hospital, and yet you still claim that he doesn't exist. I find that really rather strange!"

Completely befuddled, Ivan fell silent.

"As soon as you began describing him," the guest continued, "I guessed who it was you had the pleasure of conversing with yesterday. And I'm really surprised at Berlioz! You, of course, are still an innocent," here the guest again apologized, "but he, at least, from what I've heard, had read a thing or two! The very first words the professor spoke confirmed all my suspicions. It's impossible not to recognize him, my friend! And besides, you're... forgive me for saying so, you're, if I'm not mistaken, an ignorant man, are you not?"

"Absolutely," agreed the now unrecognizable Ivan.

"So there you see... why even the face you described... the dissimilar eyes, the eyebrows! By the way, forgive me, but you probably haven't even heard the opera *Faust*, have you?"

Ivan became terribly strangely embarrassed for some reason, and with a flushed face started mumbling something about a trip to a sanitarium in Yalta.

"There you are, there you are... it's not surprising! But Berlioz, I repeat, amazes me... He's not only very well-read, he's also very shrewd. Although I must say in his defense that Woland could certainly pull the wool over the eyes of someone far shrewder than he."

"What?!" Ivan shouted out in return.

"Quiet!"

Ivan slapped himself on the forehead and said in a croak, "Now I understand, now I understand. He had the letter 'W' on his visiting card. Well I'll be, so that's how it is!" He fell into a state of befuddled silence for awhile, gazing out at the moon floating beyond the window grille, and then he said, "So that means he really could have been with Pontius Pilate, doesn't it? Since he was already born then, right? And they call me a madman!" Ivan added, pointing in outrage at the door.

A bitter grimace distorted the guest's mouth.

"Let's look truth straight in the eye," said the guest, turning his face toward the nocturnal orb passing through the clouds beyond the window grille. "You and I are both mad, there's no denying it! You see, he shook you up—and you lost your mind because you obviously had tendencies in that direction to begin with. But there's no doubt at all that what you told me really did happen. But it's so bizarre that even a psychiatrist of genius like Stravinsky naturally didn't believe you. Was he the one who examined you?" (Ivan nodded). "The man you conversed with was at Pilate's, and he was also at Kant's for breakfast, and now he's paying a visit to Moscow."

"Yes, and the devil only knows what mischief he'll do here! Shouldn't we try and catch him?" said the not-entirely suppressed old Ivan, rearing his head from inside the new one, although without much confidence.

"You already tried and look where it got you," was the guest's ironic response. "I wouldn't advise others to try it either. But rest assured that he'll cause more trouble. Oh, how annoying it is that you were the one to meet him, and not I. Even though I'm all burnt-out and the coals have turned to ash, I swear, I would have given up Praskovya Fyodorovna's keys for a meeting like that, and they're all I have to give up. I'm a poor man!"

"But what do you need him for?"

The guest was sad for a long time, and his face twitched, but finally he said, "You see, strangely enough, I'm in here for the same reason you are, namely, because of Pontius Pilate." Here the guest looked around anxiously and said, "The fact is that a year ago I wrote a novel about Pilate."

"You're a writer?" asked the poet with interest.

The guest's face darkened, and he shook his fist at Ivan and then said, "I am the Master." He became stern, reached into the pocket of his robe and took out a grimy black cap that had the letter "M" embroidered on it in yellow silk. He put the cap on and modeled it for Ivan in profile and full face, in order to prove that he was the Master. "She sewed this for me with her own hands," he added mysteriously.

"What's your name?"

"I no longer have a name," the strange guest replied with gloomy disdain. "I gave it up, just as I've given up everything else in life. Let's drop the subject."

"Well, then at least tell me about your novel," requested Ivan tactfully.

"By all means. My life has turned out to be anything but ordinary, if I do say so myself," the guest began.

...A historian by training, he had worked until two years ago at one of the Moscow museums and had also done translations...

"From what language?" Ivan inquired with interest.

"I know five languages besides my own," answered the guest, "English, French, German, Latin, and Greek. And I also read a little Italian."

"Wow!" whispered Ivan with envy.

The historian had lived a solitary life. He had no family anywhere and virtually no friends in Moscow. And then, imagine, one day he won 100,000 rubles.

"You can imagine my surprise," whispered the guest in the black cap, "when I rummaged around in the dirty laundry basket and found out I had the same number that was printed in the paper! A ticket given me at the museum," he explained.

After winning 100,000, Ivan's mysterious guest did the following: he bought some books, moved out of his room on Myasnitskaya Street... "Ugh, what a damned hole that was!" snarled the guest.

...He rented two rooms from a private home builder in the basement of a small house in a garden on a small street near the Arbat. He quit his job at the museum and began to write a novel about Pontius Pilate.

"Ah, that was a golden age!" the narrator whispered, his eyes shining. "It was a completely private apartment, with its own entrance and a sink with running water," he emphasized with particular pride, for some reason, "and small windows looking out over the path leading to the gate. Just opposite, in front of the fence, not more than four steps away, there were lilac bushes, a linden tree, and a maple. Ah! Ah! Ah! Once in a while in winter I'd see someone's black feet through the window and I'd hear the snow crunching as they walked by. And there was always a fire burning in my stove! But then spring came suddenly, and through the dim glass I saw the lilac branches, which had first been bare, now dressed in green. And then, last spring something happened that was far more entrancing than winning 100,000 rubles. And that, you will agree, is a huge sum of money!"

"Yes it is," agreed Ivan, who was listening attentively.

"I had opened the window and was sitting in the second and tinier of the two rooms,"—the guest used his hands to illustrate—"a couch and across from it, another couch, and between them a small table with a beautiful night lamp on it, and closer to the window, books. Here, a small desk, and in the first room—an enormous room, fourteen square meters—books, more books, and a stove. Ah, what a great place I had! The smell of the lilacs was extraordinary! And I was becoming lightheaded from exhaustion, and Pilate was flying to an end..."

"White cloak, blood-red lining! I understand!" exclaimed Ivan.

"Exactly! Pilate was flying to an end, an end, and I already knew that the last words of the novel would be: '...The fifth procurator of Judea, the knight Pontius Pilate.' Well, naturally, I'd go for walks. 100,000 is a huge sum, and I had a handsome suit. Or I'd dine at some inexpensive restaurant. There was a marvelous restaurant on the Arbat, I don't know if it's still there."

Here the guest's eyes opened wide, and he continued whispering as he gazed at the moon, "She was carrying some hideous, disturbing yellow flowers. The devil only knows what they're called, but for some reason they're the first ones to bloom in Moscow. And those flowers stood out very distinctly against her black spring coat. She was carrying yellow flowers! A bad color. She turned off Tverskaya into a side street and then looked back. Do you know Tverskaya? Thousands of people were walking along Tverskaya, but I assure you, she saw only me and she gave me a look that was not merely anxious, but even pained. And I was struck not so much by her beauty as by the extraordinary, incomparable loneliness in her eyes!

"Obeying that yellow sign, I, too, turned into the side street and followed her. We walked silently along the dull winding lane, I on one side, and she on the other. And, imagine, there wasn't a soul in the street. I was in torment because I felt that I had to talk to her, and I was afraid I wouldn't be able to utter a word, and she would go away, and I would never see her again.

"And then, imagine, she said unexpectedly, 'Do you like my flowers?'

"I distinctly remember the sound of her voice, rather low, but halting, and however silly this may seem, I felt that an echo sounded in the lane and reverberated off the dirty yellow wall. I quickly crossed over to her side of the street and, walking up to her, replied, 'No.'

"She looked at me with surprise, and I suddenly and completely unexpectedly realized that this was the woman I had loved my whole life! Amazing, isn't it? Naturally, you'll say I'm a madman, right?"

"I'm not saying anything," Ivan exclaimed, adding, "Please, go on!"

And the guest continued, "Yes, she gave me a look of surprise, and then she asked, 'Is it that you just don't like flowers?'

"I thought I detected hostility in her voice. I walked alongside her, trying to keep in step with her, and to my surprise, I felt no constraint whatsoever.

"'No, I like flowers, but not those,' I said.

"'What kind do you like?'

"'I like roses.'

"Then I regretted having said that because she smiled guiltily and threw her flowers into the gutter. A bit flustered, I retrieved them nonetheless, and handed them back to her, but she pushed them away with a smile, and I ended up carrying them.

"Thus we walked in silence for awhile until she took the flowers out of my hand and threw them on the pavement. Then she put her hand, in a flared black glove, through my arm, and we walked off together."

"Go on," said Ivan, "and please don't leave anything out."

"Go on?" the guest echoed. "Well, you yourself can guess what happened next." Suddenly he wiped away an unexpected tear with his right sleeve and continued, "Just like a murderer jumps out of nowhere in an alley, love jumped out in front of us and struck us both at once! The way lightning strikes, or a Finnish knife! She, by the way, would later say that it wasn't like that, that we had, of course, loved each other for a very long time, without knowing or ever having seen each other, and that she was living with another man... and I was then... with that... what's her name..."

"With whom?" asked Bezdomny.

"With that... well... with that... well..." the guest answered, snapping his fingers.

"You were married?"

"Well, yes, that's why I'm snapping my fingers... To that Varenka... Manechka... no, Varenka... with the striped dress, at the museum... But I can't remember.

"And so she used to say that she had gone out that day carrying the yellow flowers so that I would at last find her, and that if it hadn't happened, she would have poisoned herself because her life was empty.

"Yes, love struck us instantly. I knew it that very day, an hour later, when we lost track of where we were and found ourselves on the embankment by the Kremlin wall.

"We talked as if we had parted only the day before, as if we had known each other for many years. We agreed to meet the next day on the same spot by the Moscow River, and we did. The May sun was shining for us. And very, very soon afterwards, that woman became my secret wife.

"She would come to me every day, and from morning on I'd start waiting for her. My impatience expressed itself in the way I endlessly rearranged the things on my table. Ten minutes before she arrived I would sit by the window and start listening for the creaking sound of the decrepit gate. And, oddly, before I met her, hardly anyone—in fact, no one—ever visited our little yard, but now it seemed that the whole city was beating a path to our door. The gate would creak, my heart would jump, and, imagine, I'd look through the window and there, level with my head, I'd see a pair of dirty boots. A knife grinder. Who in my house would need a knife grinder? What was there to sharpen? What sort of knives?

"She would come through the gate only once, but until that happened, my heart would suffer at least ten palpitations, I'm not lying. And then, when it was time for her arrival and the hands were pointing to noon, my heart wouldn't stop pounding until her shoes, noiselessly, without tapping, with their black suede bows and steel buckles, drew level with the window.

"Sometimes she'd play games and stop at the second window and tap her toe against the glass. I'd be at the window in a second, only to find that the shoes had disappeared along with the black silk dress that blocked the sun, and I'd go and let her in.

"Nobody knew about our affair, I can swear to that, although that rarely happens. Her husband didn't know and neither did her friends. Of course, the people in the old house where my basement apartment was knew, they could see a woman was coming to visit me, but they did not know her name."

"And what was her name?" asked Ivan, who was totally mesmerized by the love story.

The guest made a gesture indicating that he would never tell anyone her name, and went on with his story.

Ivan learned that the Master and the unknown woman fell in love so intensely that they became absolutely inseparable. Ivan could clearly visualize the two rooms in the basement apartment, where it was always twilight because of the lilacs and the fence. The shabby red furniture, the writing desk with the clock on it that chimed every half hour, and the books, books that went from the painted floor to the soot-covered ceiling, and the stove.

Ivan learned that his guest and his secret wife had decided, from the very beginning of their intimacy, that it was fate which had brought them together on the corner of Tverskaya and that side street, and that they were meant to be together forever.

Ivan learned from his guest's story how the lovers spent their days. She would arrive, and the first thing she would do was put on an apron and light the oil-stove on the wooden table in the narrow entryway, which also contained the sink that for some reason the poor patient was so proud of. Then she would prepare lunch and serve it on the oval table in the first room. When the May thunderstorms came, and water rushed past the blurred windows and through the gateway, threatening to inundate the lovers' last refuge, they would light the stove and bake potatoes. Steam poured off the potatoes, the charred potato skins made their fingers black. There was laughter in the basement, and after the rain the trees in the garden would shed broken twigs and clusters of white flowers.

When the storms were over and steamy summer arrived, the long-awaited roses they both loved appeared in the vase. The man who called himself the Master worked feverishly on his novel, and the novel also enthralled the unknown woman.

"Really, at times her fascination with it would make me jealous," whispered Ivan's nocturnal guest who had come from the moonlit balcony.

Running her slender fingers and pointed nails through her hair, she endlessly reread what he had written, and then she sewed the very cap he had shown Ivan. Sometimes she would squat down next to the lower shelves or stand up on a chair next to the upper ones and dust the hundreds of books. She predicted fame, urged him on, and started calling him Master. She waited eagerly for the promised final words about the fifth procurator of Judea, recited the parts she especially liked in a loud sing-song voice, and said that the novel was her life.

It was finished in August and given to an obscure typist who typed up five copies. And, finally, the time came when they had to leave their secret refuge and go out into the world.

"And I went out into the world, with the novel in my hands, and then my life ended," whispered the Master, dropping his head—and his sad black cap with the yellow "M" shook for a long time. He went on with his story, but it became somewhat disjointed. The only thing that was clear was that some kind of catastrophe had befallen Ivan's guest.

"It was my first venture into the literary world, but now that it's all over and my ruin is at hand, I think back on it with horror!" said the

Master in a solemn whisper, raising his hand. "Yes, he dealt me a staggering blow, a staggering blow!"

"Who?" asked Ivan in a barely audible whisper, afraid of interrupting the distraught narrator.

"The editor, I tell you, the editor. Yes, well, he read it. He kept looking at me as if an abscess had blown up my cheek, looked off into the corner, and even giggled with embarrassment. He wheezed and crumpled the manuscript unnecessarily. The questions he asked me seemed insane. He said nothing about the novel itself but asked me who I was, where I came from, whether I'd been writing for a long time, and why nothing had been heard of me before. And then he asked what I thought was a totally idiotic question: who had given me the idea of writing a novel on such a strange subject?

"Finally, I got sick and tired of him, and I asked him straight out whether he was going to publish the novel or not.

"He got flustered at this point, began mumbling something and declared that he could not decide the matter alone and that the other members of the editorial board, namely, the critics Latunsky and Ariman and the writer Mstislav Lavrovich, would have to see my work as well. He asked me to come back in two weeks.

"So I went back in two weeks and was greeted by some spinster whose eyes had a cross-eyed squint from chronic lying."

"That's Lapshyonnikova, the editor's secretary," said Ivan, smiling, only too familiar with the world his guest was describing with such anger.

"Maybe so," cut in the guest. "In any event, she returned my novel, which was now really tattered and soiled. Trying not to look me in the eye, Lapshyonnikova informed me that they had enough material to last them for two more years and therefore, the question of their publishing my novel was, as she put it, 'not relevant.'

"What do I remember after that?" mumbled the Master, wiping his brow. "Oh yes, the red petals scattered on the title page and my beloved's eyes. Yes, I remember those eyes."

The story of Ivan's guest was becoming more and more muddled and full of gaps. He said something about slanting rain and despair in their basement refuge, and about taking the novel somewhere else. He cried out in a whisper that he didn't blame her for pushing him into the fray, not one bit, oh no, he didn't blame her!

"I remember it, I remember that damned insert page in the newspaper," muttered the guest, drawing a newspaper page in the air with two fingers, and Ivan guessed from further confused phrases that some other editor had published a large fragment from the novel by the man who called himself the Master.

In his words, not two days passed before an article written by the critic Ariman, entitled "An Enemy under the Editor's Wing," appeared in another paper, which said that Ivan's guest, taking advantage of the editor's carelessness and ignorance, had tried to sneak into print an apologia for Jesus Christ.

"Ah, I remember," cried Ivan, "but I forget your name!"

"Let's leave my name out of it," replied the guest. "I repeat, it does not exist anymore. That's not what's important. The next day another article appeared in another paper signed by Mstislav Lavrovich, in which the author proposed striking a blow, and a strong one at that, against Pilatism and against that religious freak who had tried to sneak (that damned word again) it into print.

"Stunned by that unheard-of word 'Pilatism,' I opened a third newspaper. There I saw two articles: one by Latunsky, and the other signed with the initials M. Z. Believe me, Ariman's and Lavrovich's writings seemed like child's play compared with Latunsky's. Suffice it to say, his article was called 'A Militant Old Believer.' I was so absorbed in reading about myself that I didn't even notice her standing in front of me (I'd forgotten to shut the door), holding a wet umbrella and wet newspapers. Her eyes flashed with fire, her hands trembled and were cold. First she rushed over to kiss me, then, pounding her fist on the table, she told me in a hoarse voice that she was going to poison Latunsky."

Ivan gave an embarrassed grunt but said nothing.

"Completely joyless autumn days followed. The novel was written, there was nothing more to be done, and our life consisted of sitting on the rug next to the stove, staring at the fire. Besides, we started spending more time apart than we had before. She began going out for walks. And something strange happened, as had often been the case in my life... I suddenly made a friend. Yes, yes, imagine, I don't make friends easily as a rule, due to a devilish peculiarity of mine: it's a strain for me to be with people, and I'm distrustful and suspicious. But—imagine, despite all that, some unlikely, unexpected fellow, who looks like the devil knows what, will unfailingly make his way into my heart, and he'll be the one I like more than anyone else.

"So, one day during that accursed time the gate to our garden opened. It was, as I recall, a pleasant fall day. She was out. And a man came through the gate who had some sort of business to discuss with my landlord. After it was over, he came down into the garden and quickly introduced himself to me. He said he was a journalist. I took such a liking to him that, imagine, I sometimes think of him even now and miss him. So we got to be friends, and he started to visit me. I found out he was a bachelor and lived next door, in an apartment very like mine, but that he felt cramped there, and so on. He never invited me over. My wife took an extreme dislike to him. But I stood up for him. She told me, 'Do as you like, but that man strikes me as repulsive.'

"That made me laugh. Yes, but strictly speaking, what was it about him that made him so appealing to me? The fact is that a man who has no surprises inside, up his sleeve, is uninteresting. But Aloisy (oh, I forgot to say that my new acquaintance was named Aloisy Mogarych) did have a surprise up his sleeve. Namely, that up until then I had never met, nor did I think I ever would meet, someone with a mind like his. If I didn't understand the meaning of some remark in the paper, Aloisy explained it to me in literally a minute. And it was obvious that such explanations came easily to him. It was the same with things and issues in everyday life. But that was the least of it. Aloisy won my heart because of his passion for literature. He didn't rest until he had persuaded me to let him read my novel from cover to cover. Moreover, his response was very flattering, but he said everything the editor had said to me about the novel, with striking precision, just as if he'd been there himself. He hit the mark ten times out of ten. He even explained to me, and I suspect faultlessly, why my novel couldn't be published. He didn't mince words either: such and such a chapter will not do...

"The articles, take note, did not cease. The first ones made me laugh, but the more of them there were, the more my attitude to them changed. The next stage was amazement. There was something uncommonly fake and uncertain in every line of these articles, despite their threatening and self-assured tone. I kept thinking—and I couldn't rid myself of the thought—that the authors of these articles weren't saying what they wanted to say, and that that was why they were so furious. And then, imagine, a third stage set in: fear. No, not fear of the articles, mind you, but fear of things totally unrelated to either the articles or the novel. For example, I started being afraid of the dark. In short, the stage of mental illness had set in. It seemed to me, especially when I was going to sleep, that some octopus with supple and cold tentacles was stealing up to me, coming straight for my heart. So I had to sleep with the light on.

"My beloved had changed greatly (naturally, I didn't say a word to her about the octopus, but she could see that something was wrong with me): she had become thin and pale, had stopped laughing, and was always asking me to forgive her for advising me to publish the excerpt from the novel. She said that I should give everything up and spend what remained of the 100,000 on a trip south to the Black Sea.

"She was very insistent, and so as to avoid a quarrel with her (something told me that I wouldn't make it to the Black Sea), I promised to do it right away. But she said she would get me the ticket herself. Then I took out all my money, that is, around 10,000 rubles, and gave it to her.

"'Why so much?' she asked me in amazement.

"I told her something about my being afraid of thieves and wanting her to take care of the money for me until my departure. She took it, put it in her bag, and began kissing me, saying that she would rather die than leave me alone in the condition I was in, but that she was expected at home, was bowing to necessity, and would be back the next day. She begged me not to be afraid of anything.

"That was at dusk, in mid-October. And she left. I lay down on the couch and fell asleep without turning on the light. I woke up with the feeling that the octopus was nearby. Fumbling around in the dark, I barely managed to put on the light. My pocket watch said it was 2 a.m. When I went to bed, I felt as if I was getting sick, and when I woke up, I was sick. It suddenly seemed to me as if the autumn darkness would break through the windowpanes and pour into the room, and that I would drown in it as in ink. When I got out of bed, I was no longer in control of myself. I let out a scream and thought of running to someone for help, if only to my landlord upstairs. I struggled with myself the way a madman does. I had just enough strength to crawl over to the stove and light the wood. When the logs began to crackle, and the stove door began to knock, I seemed to feel a little better... I ran out into the hallway and turned on the light. Then I found a bottle of white wine, uncorked it and started drinking it straight out of the bottle. That helped my fear abate somewhat, enough, at least, to stop me from running off to my landlord and to return to the stove instead. I opened the stovedoor so that the heat began to warm my face and hands, and I whispered, 'Guess that something awful has happened to me... Come to me, come, come!!'

"But nobody came. The fire roared in the stove, and the rain beat against the windows. Then came the final blow. I took the heavy typescripts and notebook drafts of the novel out of the desk drawer and started to burn them. It's a fiendishly difficult thing to do because paper that has been written on doesn't burn easily. I broke my nails tearing the notebooks apart, then I stood the pages upright between the logs and jabbed at them with the poker. At times the ashes would get the best of me and choke out the fire, but I fought back, and the novel, despite stubborn resistance, was perishing. Familiar words flashed before me, and a yellowness crept relentlessly up the pages, but you could still make out the words. They disappeared only when the paper turned black and I beat them viciously with the poker.

"It was then that someone began scratching softly at the window. My heart gave a leap, I hurled the last notebook into the flames and rushed to open the door. Brick steps led up from the basement to the door into the yard. I stumbled up to the door and asked quietly, 'Who's there?'

"And a voice, her voice, answered me, 'It's me...'

"I don't remember how I managed the key and chain. The minute she stepped inside, she fell against me, completely soaked, shivering, with wet cheeks and tousled hair. The only thing I could say was, 'Is it you?' and then my voice broke, and we ran downstairs. She left her coat in the hall, and we went quickly into the first room. She let out a soft cry, and with her bare hands threw what was left in the stove onto the floor, a packet of sheets burning on the bottom. Smoke immediately filled the room. I stamped out the flames and she threw herself on the couch and started to cry convulsively and uncontrollably.

"When she calmed down, I said, 'I came to hate that novel, and I'm afraid. I'm sick. I'm terrified.'

"She got up and started to speak. 'My God, you are sick. Why did you do it, why? But I'll save you. I'll save you. What's this all about?'

"I saw her eyes, swollen from smoke and tears, and I felt her cold hands stroking my forehead.

"'I'll cure you, I'll cure you,' she murmured, clutching me by the shoulders. 'You'll reconstruct it. Why, oh why didn't I keep a copy myself!'

"She bared her teeth in fury and said something else that I couldn't make out. Then, with her lips pursed, she started gathering and sorting the burnt pages. It was a chapter from the middle of the novel, I don't remember which. She stacked the pages neatly, wrapped them in paper and tied them with a ribbon. All her movements showed decisiveness and self-control. She asked for some wine and after drinking it, began to speak more calmly.

"'This is what we get for lying,' she said, 'and I don't want to lie anymore. I'd stay with you right now, but that's not the way I want to do it. I don't want to leave him with the memory of my running off at night. He never did me any harm... He was called out suddenly, there was a fire at his factory. But he'll be back soon. I'll tell him everything in the morning, I'll tell him that I love someone else, and then I'll come back to you forever. Tell me, though, perhaps that isn't what you want?'

"'My poor thing, my poor dear,' I said to her. 'I won't let you do that. Things will go badly for me, and I don't want you to perish with me.'

"'Is that the only reason?' she asked, drawing her eyes close to mine.

"'The only one.'

"She became terribly animated, pressed herself against me, wrapped her arms around my neck and said, 'I will perish with you. And I'll be back with you in the morning.'

"The last thing that I remember in my life is the strip of light coming from the entryway, and in that light a loosened curl, her beret, and her eyes, full of determination. I also remember a black silhouette in the outer doorway and a white package.

"'I'd see you home, but I don't have the strength to come back here alone, I'm afraid.'

"'Don't be afraid. Just be patient for a few hours. I'll be back with you in the morning.'

"Those were her last words in my life... Shh!" the sick man interrupted himself suddenly and raised his finger. "This moonlit night is restless."

He disappeared out onto the balcony. Ivan heard the sound of wheels in the corridor and a faint cry or sob.

When everything had quieted down, the guest came back and told Ivan that Room 120 had a new occupant. Someone had been brought in who kept asking to have his head returned. An anxious silence passed between the interlocutors, but once they calmed down, they returned to the story that had been interrupted. The guest was about to open his mouth, but the night was indeed a restless one. Voices could still be heard in the corridor, and the guest whispered in Ivan's ear so quietly that what he was saying was heard only by the poet, with the exception of the opening sentence, "Fifteen minutes after she left me, there was a knock at the window..."

What the sick man was whispering into Ivan's ear obviously made the sick man very upset. Convulsive spasms kept contorting his face. Fear and fury swam and raged in his eyes. The storyteller pointed toward the moon which had long since disappeared from the balcony. Only after all the outside noises ceased did the guest move away from Ivan and start speaking a little more loudly.

"Yes, so there I was in my yard in the middle of January, at night, wearing the same coat, but with the buttons torn off, shivering from the cold. Behind me were snow drifts, covering the lilac bushes, and in front of me and down below—my feebly lit, blind-covered windows. I leaned over and listened at the first window: a phonograph was playing inside my apartment. That was all I could hear, and I couldn't see anything. After standing there for awhile, I went out through the gate into the lane. The snow was falling heavily. A dog dashed under my feet and frightened me, and I ran across the street to get away from it. The cold and the fear, which had become my constant companion, had brought me to the breaking point. I had nowhere to go, and the simplest thing for me to do, of course, would have been to throw myself under one of the streetcars that passed along the main street at the end of my lane. I could see those light-filled, iced-over boxes in the distance and could hear the ghastly grating sound that they made on the frost and ice. But, my dear neighbor, the whole point was that fear had invaded every cell in my body. And I was as afraid of the streetcar as I had been of the dog. Yes, my illness is the worst in the building, I assure you."

"But you could have let her know," said Ivan, sympathizing with the poor patient. "Besides, didn't she have your money? Naturally, she kept it, didn't she?"

"Don't worry, of course she kept it. But you don't seem to understand me. Either that, or I've lost the facility I once had for describing things. However, I don't miss it very much, since I have no further use for it. If I had let her know," the guest stared reverently into the darkness of the night, "the letter she received would have come from an insane asylum. How can you send letters with an address like that ? A mental patient? Surely you're joking, my friend! Make her unhappy? No, I'm not capable of that."

Ivan could offer no objection to that, but he sympathized with his guest in silence and felt compassion for him. And the latter, feeling the pain of his memories, nodded his black-capped head and said, "Poor woman... But I'm hoping that she's forgotten me..."

"But you may get well..." said Ivan timidly.

"I'm incurable," the guest replied calmly. "When Stravinsky says that he'll bring me back to life, I don't believe him. He's humane and simply wants to comfort me. I don't deny, by the way, that I'm much better now. But where was I? Oh, yes, the ice and cold, the speeding streetcars. I knew that this clinic had already opened, and I set out for it on foot across the whole city. What madness! I would certainly have frozen to death when I got outside the city if a chance occurrence hadn't saved me. A truck had broken down about four kilometers outside the city, and I went over to speak to the driver. To my surprise, he took pity on me. He was on his way here, and he gave me a lift. The worst thing that happened to me was that I got frostbite on the toes of my left foot. But they fixed that. And this is my fourth month here. And, you know, I don't find it so bad here, not bad at all. One really shouldn't make big plans for oneself, dear neighbor. Take me, for example, I wanted to travel around the globe. Well, it turned out that wasn't meant to be. I can see only an insignificant little piece of it. I don't think it's the best piece of it either, but, as I said, it's not so bad. Summer will be here soon, and the balcony will be covered with ivy, just as Praskovya Fyodorovna promises. Having her keys has given me new possibilities. There'll be a moon at night. Ah, it's gone! The air is fresher. It's getting on past midnight. It's time for me to go."

"Tell me," asked Ivan, "what happened next to Yeshua and Pilate. Please, I want to know."

"Oh, no, no," the guest answered, twitching painfully, "I can't think of my novel without a shudder. Your friend from Patriarch's Ponds could have done it better than I. Thanks for the conversation. Good-bye."

And before Ivan could realize what was happening, the window grille shut softly, and the guest was gone.

XIV

Praise Be to the Rooster

H IS nerves couldn't take it, as they say, and Rimsky ran off to his office without waiting for the police to finish their report of what had happened. He sat at his desk and stared with swollen eyes at the magic ten-ruble bills that lay before him. The financial director was at his wit's end. A steady roar rose from the street as the public streamed out of the theater. The financial director's overly sensitive ears suddenly heard the sharp trill of a police whistle, which is hardly ever a good omen. When that sound was repeated and then accompanied by another more imperious and prolonged one, only then to be joined by loud cackles of laughter and hoots, the financial director knew immediately that something scandalous and nasty had happened outside, and that, however much he wanted to brush it aside, it was intimately connected with the disgusting show put on by the black magician and his assistants. The quickwitted financial director was not mistaken.

No sooner had he looked out the window onto Sadovaya Street, than his face became distorted, and he said in a hiss rather than a whisper, "I knew it!"

In the bright light of the high-intensity streetlamps, he saw on the sidewalk below a woman wearing nothing but a chemise and violet drawers. True, there was a hat on her head and an umbrella in her hands.

Milling around the woman, who was completely distraught and alternately crouching down or trying to run away, was an excited crowd, cackling in a way that sent shivers down the director's spine. Hovering next to the woman was a man struggling to get out of his summer coat, who was so upset that he was unable to extricate his arm from the sleeve.

Cries and screams of laughter also came from another direction—from the motor entrance on the left, and when he turned to look, Grigory Danilovich saw another woman, this time in pink underwear. She jumped from the pavement to the sidewalk, in an effort to hide herself in the entranceway, but her way was barred by people streaming out of the theater. Victimized by her own frivolity and her mania for clothes, and deceived by Fagot and his vile company, the poor creature dreamed of only one thing: falling through the earth. A policeman was headed in her direction, drilling the air with his whistle, and behind the policeman came a pack of cheery young men wearing caps. They were the ones cackling and hooting.

A thin mustachioed cabbie drove up to the first naked woman and reined in his bony, broken-down nag with a flourish. The cabbie's whiskered face was plastered with a grin.

Rimsky hit his head with his fist, spat, and moved away from the window.

He sat at the desk for awhile, listening to the noise from the street. The whistling reached full pitch at various points and then started to subside. To Rimsky's surprise, the scandal came to an unexpectedly speedy conclusion.

The time to act was approaching, he would have to drink the bitter cup of responsibility. The telephones had been repaired during the third part of the program, and he had to make calls, report what had happened, ask for help, lie himself out of any responsibility, blame everything on Likhodeyev, get himself off the hook, and so forth. Confound you, devil!

Twice the flustered director put his hand on the receiver and twice he picked it up. And suddenly the deadly silence of the office was shattered by the sound of the telephone itself, blasting in the financial director's face. He shuddered and grew cold. "Boy, my nerves are really shot," he thought and picked up the receiver, whereupon he recoiled and turned white as a sheet. A soft but at the same time insinuating and depraved female voice whispered into the phone, "Don't make any calls, Rimsky, or you'll be sorry..."

The phone then went dead. Feeling his flesh crawl, the financial director put down the receiver and glanced for some reason at the window behind his back. Through the sparse and barely green branches of the maple tree outside the window he glimpsed the moon slipping behind a translucent cloud. Inexplicably transfixed by the branches, Rimsky stared at them, and the more he did, the more strongly he felt the grip of fear.

Making an effort to regain his composure, the financial director finally turned away from the moon-filled window and got up. To call anyone was now out of the question, and the financial director had only one thought on his mind—to get away from the theater as fast as possible.

He listened: the building was silent. Rimsky realized that he had been all alone on the second floor for some time, and the thought filled him with an uncontrollable childlike dread. When he thought of having to walk down the empty corridors and go down the staircase alone, he shuddered. He feverishly grabbed the hypnotist's ten-ruble bills off the desk, stuffed them into his briefcase and coughed, in order to build up his courage. The cough came out sounding hoarse and feeble.

And here it seemed to him that a smell of damp decay had suddenly seeped under the office door. A shudder ran down the financial director's spine. And a clock chimed suddenly and began to strike midnight. Even that made the financial director shudder. But his heart really sank when he heard a key turning softly in the lock. The financial director clutched his briefcase with cold damp hands and felt that he would not be able to contain himself and would burst out screaming if the scraping in the keyhole lasted one more minute.

Finally the door yielded to someone's push, opened, and who stepped quietly into the office but Varenukha. Rimsky's legs buckled beneath him and he plopped down into his chair. Sucking air into his lungs, he smiled a kind of ingratiating smile and said softly, "God, what a fright you gave me..."

Indeed, that sudden appearance could have frightened anyone, and yet, at the same time, it came as a great joy: at least one small thread in this tangled business had unraveled.

"Well, get it out! Tell me! Well!" rasped Rimsky, pulling at the thread. "What's the meaning of all this?!"

"Please, forgive me," the man who had come in replied in a hollow voice, closing the door. "I thought you had already left."

Without taking off his cap Varenukha went over to the armchair and sat down opposite Rimsky at the desk.

It must be said there was something slightly odd about Varenukha's reply which was immediately picked up by the financial director, who was as sensitive to vibrations as any seismograph in the world. What was going on? Why had Varenukha come into the financial director's office if he had assumed he wasn't there? After all, he had his own office. That was for starters. And second, no matter which entrance Varenukha had used, he would have bumped into one of the night watchmen, all of whom had been told that Grigory Danilovich would be in his office for some time.

But the financial director did not dwell on this oddity for very long. He didn't feel up to it.

"Why didn't you call? What was all that nonsense about Yalta?"

"Well, it's just as I said," the manager answered, and he made a smacking sound with his lips as if he had a toothache. "They found him in a tavern in Pushkino."

"What do you mean Pushkino?! Isn't that right near Moscow? And didn't the telegrams come from Yalta?!"

"Yalta like hell! He got the Pushkino telegrapher drunk, they started fooling around and that meant, among other things, sending telegrams marked 'Yalta.'"

"I see, I see... Well, OK, OK..." said Rimsky, crooning rather than speaking. A yellowish light shone in his eyes. A festive vision of Styopa having to leave work in disgrace formed in his head. He'd be free! Free at least of that disaster known as Likhodeyev! And maybe Stepan Bogdanovich was in for more than just getting fired... "Give me the details," said Rimsky, tapping the paperweight against the desk.

And Varenukha began to recount the details. As soon as he had arrived at the place where the financial director had sent him, he had
been received right away and listened to with great attention. No one,
of course, had ever seriously believed that Styopa was in Yalta.
Everyone now agreed with Varenukha that Likhodeyev had obviously
been at the Yalta restaurant in Pushkino.

"Where is he now?" asked the agitated financial director, interrupting the manager's account.

"Well, where could he be?" replied the manager with a crooked
smile. "Naturally, in a drunk tank!"

"Of course, of course! Where else!"

And Varenukha continued his story. And the more he talked, the
more vivid an impression the financial director formed of Likhodeyev's
long chain of outrageous and disgraceful misdeeds. And each succes-
sive link in the chain was worse than the last. Take, for example, the
drunken dance with the telegraph clerk on the lawn outside the Pushkino telegraph office to the strains of some idler's accordion! The chase
after some women who were screeching in terror! The attempt to start
a fight with the bartender at the Yalta! Throwing green onions all over
the floor of that same Yalta. Smashing eight bottles of dry white "Ai-
Danil" wine. Breaking the meter of a cab when the driver refused to
take him as a passenger. Threatening to arrest the citizens who were trying to end his spree... In short, holy terror!

Styopa was well known in Moscow theater circles, and everyone
knew that he was hardly—a gift to humanity. But what the manager was
saying about him now was too much, even for Styopa. Yes, too much. In
fact, much too much...

Rimsky's piercing eyes bore into the manager's face from across the
desk, and the more the manager talked, the gloomier Rimsky looked.
The manager embellished his story with various vile details, and the
more vivid and piquant they became, the less Rimsky believed him.
When Varenukha reported that Styopa had gone so far as to resist those
who had come to take him back to Moscow, the financial director knew
for sure that everything the manager was saying—the manager who had
returned at midnight—everything was a lie! A lie from beginning to end.

Varenukha had not gone to Pushkino, nor had Styopa himself been
in Pushkino. There was no drunken telegraph clerk, no broken glass in
the bar, Styopa had not been tied up... none of it had happened.

Once the financial director became convinced that the manager was
lying to him, fear crept over his body, starting with his feet, and for the
second time it seemed to the financial director that a putrid malarial
dampness had spread over the floor. Without ever taking his eyes off
the manager—who was sitting in the armchair in an oddly contorted
way, trying always to stay within the bluish shadow cast by the desk
lamp and rather peculiarly shielding his eyes from the lamp light with a

newspaper—the financial director thought of only one thing: what did it all mean? Why would the manager, who had returned too late to see him, be lying to him so blatantly in an empty and quiet building? And a sense of danger, unidentified but imminent, began to take hold of Rimsky's heart. While pretending not to notice the manager's maneuvers and his tricks with the newspaper, the financial director examined his face, hardly listening any more to the tale Varenukha was spinning. There was something that seemed even more inexplicable than the slanderous story of Styopa's escapades in Pushkino, fabricated for no discernible reason whatsoever, and that something was the change in the manager's appearance and manners.

Despite the manager's efforts to keep his face in shadow by pulling the visor of his cap down over his eyes, and despite his maneuvers with the newspaper as well, the financial director did manage to observe a huge bruise that began at his nose and extended across his right cheek. In addition, the manager's customarily ruddy complexion had taken on an unhealthy chalky pallor, and, despite the sultriness of the night, his neck was wrapped in an old striped muffler. If one added to this the manager's new habit, evidently acquired during his absence, of making disgusting sucking and smacking sounds with his lips, the sharp change in his voice, which had become rough and hollow, and the furtive and cowardly look in his eyes, then one could say without hesitation that Ivan Savelyevich Varenukha had become unrecognizable.

Something even more disturbing gnawed at the financial director, but however much he strained his already inflamed brain, however much he stared at Varenukha, he couldn't figure out what it was. He was sure of only one thing: there was something weird and unnatural about this combination of the manager and the familiar chair.

"Well, eventually he was subdued and shoved into a car," droned on Varenukha, peering out from behind the newspaper and covering his bruise with his palm.

Rimsky suddenly stretched out his hand and started drumming his fingers on the table, while at the same time nonchalantly pressing his palm down on the buzzer of an electric bell. Then he froze. A loud alarm should have gone off in the empty building. But the alarm did not go off, and the buzzer sank lifelessly into the desktop. The buzzer was dead and the bell was broken.

The financial director's maneuver did not escape Varenukha, who winced and asked with a malicious gleam in his eye, "Why did you press the alarm?"

"Habit," was the financial director's hollow reply as he moved his hand away. Then he asked in a shaky voice, "What's that on your face?"

"The car braked, and I hit my face against the door handle," answered Varenukha, turning his eyes away.

"He's lying!" the financial director exclaimed to himself. Then his eyes widened and bulged crazily as he fixated on the back of Varenukha's chair.

On the floor behind the chair there were two intersecting shadows, one blacker and denser, the other faint and gray. The armchair's back and pointed legs cast a clear shadow on the floor, but there was no shadow from Varenukha's head above the chair back, nor was there any shadow from his feet beneath its legs.

"He doesn't cast a shadow!" cried Rimsky to himself in desperation. He started to tremble.

Varenukha glanced furtively behind the chair, following Rimsky's crazed eyes, and realized that he had been found out.

He stood up (as did the financial director) and stepped away from the desk, his briefcase clutched in his hands.

"You guessed it, damn you! You always were smart," said Varenukha, smirking maliciously in Rimsky's face. Suddenly he sprang to the door and quickly lowered the bolt. The financial director looked around in desperation as he moved over to the window that looked out onto the garden. There in the moonlight he saw the face of a naked girl pressed against the glass, her bare arm stuck through the *fortochka*, trying to open the latch on the lower part of the window. The upper part was already open.

It seemed to Rimsky that the light in the desk lamp was going out and the desk was tilting sideways. An icy wave swept over Rimsky, but fortunately he found the strength to resist it and didn't fall. He had enough strength left to whisper, but not shout, "Help..."

As he guarded the door, Varenukha jumped up and down beside it, staying suspended in the air for a long time and swaying back and forth. Hissing and smacking his lips, he winked at the girl in the window and pointed at Rimsky.

The girl then doubled her efforts and stuck her red head through the *fortochka*, stretching her hand out as far as it would go. She scratched at the lower window latch with her nails and shook the window frame. Her hand began to stretch as if it were made of elastic and became covered with a corpselike greenness. Finally the corpse's green fingers grabbed hold of the tip of the window latch, turned it, and the casement began to open. Rimsky gave a faint cry, pressed against the wall, and held out his briefcase in front of him as if it were a shield. He knew his end had come.

The casement window swung wide open, but it was not fresh night air and the fragrance of the linden trees that wafted into the room, it was the smell of the grave. The dead girl stepped onto the windowsill, and Rimsky could clearly see patches of decay on her breast.

And at that moment the unexpected and joyous crowing of a rooster was heard coming from the garden, from the low building behind the shooting gallery where the performing birds were kept. The trained rooster was raucously trumpeting the news that dawn was advancing on Moscow from the east.

Savage fury distorted the girl's face, and she rasped out a curse. Over by the door Varenukha let out a screech and fell down from the air onto the floor.

The rooster crowed again, the girl grated her teeth, and her red hair stood on end. At the third cockcrow she turned and flew out of the room. And right behind her came Varenukha, who jumped up in the air, assumed a horizontal position, like a flying Cupid, and floated slowly over the desk and out the window.

His head as white as snow, with not one black hair left, an old man, who not long before had been Rimsky, ran over to the door, undid the lock, opened the door, and started running down the dark corridor. Stricken with terror and moaning, he felt for the switch at the top of the staircase and turned on the light. Trembling and shaking, the old man fell on the stairs because it seemed to him that Varenukha was softly collapsing on him from above.

When he got to the bottom of the stairs, Rimsky saw the night watchman asleep on a chair by the box office in the lobby. He tiptoed past him and slipped out through the main door. Once he was outside he felt a little better. He was sufficiently in command of his senses to realize, when he clutched his head, that he had left his hat behind in the office.

Needless to say, he did not go back for it, but ran across the wide street, gasping for breath, to the movie theater on the opposite corner where nearby, a dim red light could be seen. A minute later he was at the taxi, before any one else could intercept it.

"To the Leningrad Express, you'll get a tip," said the old man, breathing heavily and clutching his heart.

"I'm on my way to the garage," said the driver with loathing and turned away.

Then Rimsky unfastened his briefcase, pulled out fifty rubles, and thrust them at the driver through the open window.

Minutes later the rattling car was rushing like a whirlwind along the Sadovaya Ring. The passenger was jounced about on the seat, and when he looked into the rearview mirror, he caught glimpses of the joyous look in the driver's eyes and the crazed look in his own.

Rimsky jumped out of the car in front of the station and shouted at the first person he saw, who was wearing a white apron and a badge, "One first-class ticket, here's thirty rubles," whereupon he crumpled and pulled the ten-ruble notes out of his briefcase. "If there's no first-class, then second, and if not that, then third."

The man with the badge turned to look at the clock and grabbed the rubles out of Rimsky's hands.

Five minutes later the express train pulled out of the glass-domed station and vanished into the darkness. And along with it vanished Rimsky.

XV

Nikanor Ivanovich's Dream

I T'S not hard to guess that the fat man with the purple face who had been put into Room No. 119 at the clinic was Nikanor Ivanovich Bosoi.

Before coming to Professor Stravinsky, however, he had spent some time in another place.

Very little of that other place remained in Nikanor Ivanovich's memory. All he could remember was a desk, a bookcase, and a couch.

The people there had tried to engage Nikanor Ivanovich in conversation, but since his head was spinning from an influx of blood and from extreme emotional distress, the conversation had been strange and muddled. In fact, it had not really been a conversation at all.

The first question Nikanor Ivanovich had been asked was, "Are you Nikanor Ivanovich Bosoi, chairman of the house committee at 302B Sadovaya Street?"

Which made Nikanor Ivanovich burst out into a horrible cackle and answer, "Of course I'm Nikanor Ivanovich! But what the devil kind of a chairman am I!"

"Meaning what?" they asked Nikanor Ivanovich with narrowed eyes.

"Meaning," he replied, "that if I were a real chairman, I would have seen immediately that he was an evil power! How else can you explain it? The cracked pince-nez, his being dressed in rags... What kind of a foreign interpreter looks like that!"

"Who are you talking about?" they asked Nikanor Ivanovich.

"Korovyov!" cried Nikanor Ivanovich. "The one who's moved into apartment No. 50 in our building! Write it down: Korovyov! You have to catch him right away! Write it down: entrance No. 6. That's where he is."

"Where did you get the foreign currency?" they asked Nikanor Ivanovich in cordial tones.

"Almighty God," Nikanor Ivanovich began, "sees everything and that is the path I should take. I never touched any foreign currency or had the slightest idea what it looked like! The Lord is punishing me for my sins," Nikanor Ivanovich went on heatedly, buttoning and unbuttoning his shirt, and crossing himself. "I took bribes! I did, but I took them in our own Soviet money! I took money for registering people in the apartment house, I won't deny it, it happened. Our secretary Prolezhnyov is a fine one too, that he is! Let's face it, everyone in the house management office is a crook. But I didn't take any foreign currency!"

When they told Nikanor Ivanovich to stop playing games and explain how the dollars got into the ventilation shaft, he got down on his knees and rocked back and forth with his mouth open wide, as if he wanted to swallow one of the parquet panels.

"Do you want me" he wailed, "to eat the floor to prove I didn't take it? But that Korovyov, he's a devil."

There is a limit to everyone's patience, and a voice was raised behind the desk, hinting to the effect that it was time for Nikanor Ivanovich to start speaking in a human tongue.

At this point Nikanor Ivanovich jumped to his feet, and the room with the couch resounded with his roar, "There he is! There he is behind the bookcase! Look at him smirk! And his pince-nez... Grab him! Sprinkle the room with holy water!"

The blood drained from Nikanor Ivanovich's face, shaking, he kept making the sign of the cross in the air, rushed over to the door and then back again, started to recite some prayer, and then finally started spouting complete gibberish.

It was quite clear that Nikanor Ivanovich was unfit for any kind of conversation. They led him out and put him in a separate room, where he calmed down somewhat and merely sobbed and prayed.

Naturally, they made a trip to Sadovaya Street and paid a visit to apartment No. 50. But they did not find any Korovyov there, nor had anyone in the building ever seen or heard of any such person. The apartment, which had been occupied by the deceased Berlioz and by Likhodeyev who had gone to Yalta, was empty, and the wax seals hung peacefully and undisturbed on the cabinets in the study. When they left Sadovaya Street, they took with them the disoriented and dispirited secretary of the house management committee, Prolezhnyov.

In the evening Nikanor Ivanovich was taken to Stravinsky's clinic. There his behavior became so violent that they had to give him an injection prescribed by Stravinsky, and it wasn't until after midnight that Nikanor Ivanovich finally fell asleep in Room 119, occasionally emitting a deep, anguished moan.

But the longer he slept, the calmer his sleep became. He stopped tossing and moaning, his breathing became easier and more even, and he was left alone.

Then Nikanor Ivanovich had a dream which doubtlessly had its source in the day's experiences. The dream began with some people with golden trumpets leading Nikanor Ivanovich most solemnly over to a pair of huge polished doors. When they got there, his companions saluted him with a kind of fanfare, and then a booming bass was heard coming from on high, saying merrily, "Welcome, Nikanor Ivanovich! Hand over your foreign currency."

Taken totally by surprise, Nikanor Ivanovich noticed a black loud-speaker above his head.

Then he found himself inside a theater with a gilt ceiling, crystal chandeliers, and sconces on the walls. Everything was as one would expect in a small but richly appointed theater. There was a stage draped with a deep-cerise velvet curtain with depictions of enlarged ten-ruble gold pieces scattered across it like stars, a prompter's box, and even an audience.

What amazed Nikanor Ivanovich was that the audience consisted of men only, and for some reason, they all had beards. No less striking was the fact that there were no chairs in the theater, and the entire audience was sitting on the slippery, magnificently polished floor.

Feeling out of place in this large and unfamiliar company, Nikanor Ivanovich hesitated for awhile and then followed everyone's example and sat down Turkish-style on the parquet floor, in between a robust, red-bearded fellow and a pale hairy one. Neither of the two paid much attention to the new arrival.

At this point the soft sound of a bell was heard, the lights went out in the theater, the curtains parted, and an illuminated stage came into view with an armchair and a small table topped by a golden bell. The back of the stage was draped in thick black velvet.

An actor wearing a dinner jacket came out on stage. He was young, clean-shaven, very good-looking, and wore his hair parted down the middle. The audience stirred, and everyone turned their eyes to the stage. The actor walked over to the prompter's box and rubbed his hands.

"Are you all seated?" he asked in a soft baritone and smiled at the audience.

"Yes, yes," the audience of tenors and basses replied in unison.

"Hm..." the actor began thoughtfully. "And how is it you're not bored, that's what puzzles me? Real people are outside on the streets right now, enjoying the spring sun and the warmth, and you're stuck here on the floor in a stuffy theater! Is the program really that interesting? However, to each his own," the actor concluded philosophically.

Then he changed the timbre and intonation of his voice and boomed out merrily, "And so, the next act on our program is Nikanor Ivanovich Bosoi, the chairman of a house committee and the head of a special-diet cafeteria. Please come up on stage, Nikanor Ivanovich!"

The audience responded with friendly applause. Nikanor Ivanovich's eyes bulged with astonishment, and the emcee, shielding his eyes from the glare of the footlights, spotted him in the audience and coaxed him tenderly up on stage. And then, without knowing how, Nikanor Ivanovich found himself on the stage. The glare of the colored lights hit his eyes from in front and below, plunging the theater and audience beyond into darkness.

"Well, Nikanor Ivanovich, set a good example," began the young actor sincerely, "and hand over your foreign currency."

Silence ensued. Nikanor Ivanovich took a deep breath and began quietly, "I swear to God that..."

But before he could finish, the whole theater broke out in disgruntled cries. Nikanor Ivanovich was disconcerted and fell silent.

"If I understand you correctly," began the man in charge of the program, "you wish to swear to God that you have no foreign currency?" He shot Nikanor Ivanovich a sympathetic look.

"That's exactly right. I don't have any," replied Nikanor Ivanovich.

"Of course," said the actor, "but forgive my indiscretion: how, then, did four hundred dollars end up in the bathroom of the apartment of which you and your wife are the sole residents?"

"By magic!" said someone in the darkened hall with obvious irony.

"Precisely so, by magic," Nikanor Ivanovich replied timidly, not to anyone in particular, neither the actor nor the invisible audience, and he went on to elaborate, "An evil power, the interpreter in checks, planted them there."

And again the audience roared in disapproval. When quiet had been restored, the actor said, "That fairy tale puts La Fontaine to shame! Four hundred dollars were planted in your bathroom! You, audience, are all foreign-currency speculators, I ask you, as specialists, does this case make sense?"

"We are not speculators," shouted various offended parties from the floor, "but it doesn't make any sense."

"I agree with you completely," said the actor firmly. "And I ask you, what sorts of things are planted on people?"

"Babies!" shouted someone from the floor.

"Absolutely right," affirmed the emcee. "Babies, anonymous letters, proclamations, time bombs, and a lot of other things, but four hundred dollars isn't one of them because nobody's that stupid." And turning to Nikanor Ivanovich, the actor added mournfully and reproachfully, "You're a disappointment to me, Nikanor Ivanovich! I had such faith in you. So then, this particular act has not been a success."

The audience began to hiss and boo at Nikanor Ivanovich.

"He's the foreign-currency speculator!" the audience screamed. "It's guys like that who make us innocent folk suffer!"

"Don't chastise him," said the emcee softly. "He'll repent." He then turned his blue eyes, brimming with tears, to Nikanor Ivanovich and added, "Well, Nikanor Ivanovich, go back to your place!"

After this the actor rang the bell and announced loudly, "Intermission, you scoundrels!"

A shaken Nikanor Ivanovich, who, to his surprise, had somehow become part of a theatrical program, again found himself in his place on the floor. Then he dreamed that the theater plunged into total darkness, and the walls were lit up with bright red lights, flashing the words, "Hand over your foreign currency!" Then the curtains parted again, and the emcee said invitingly, "Would Sergei Gerardovich Dunchil please come up on stage."

Dunchil turned out to be a good-looking, but very stout man of about fifty.

"Sergei Gerardovich," said the emcee. "You've been sitting here for more than a month now, and yet you still refuse to hand over the rest of your foreign currency; now, when your country is in need of it, and it's of absolutely no use to you, you still refuse to comply. You're an intelligent fellow and understand all this perfectly, and yet you still don't want to meet me halfway."

"Unfortunately, I can't do anything, since I don't have any more foreign currency," Dunchil replied calmly.

"Don't you have any diamonds at least?" asked the actor.

"No diamonds either."

The actor hung his head and looked pensive, and then he clapped his hands. A middle-aged woman emerged from the wings and came out on stage. She was fashionably dressed, that is, in a tiny hat and a coat with no collar. She had an anxious air, and Dunchil stared at her without moving a muscle.

"Who is this woman?" the man in charge of the program asked Dunchil.

"She's my wife," Dunchil answered with dignity, as he looked at the woman's long neck with a flicker of disgust.

"We have disturbed you, Madame Dunchil, for the following reason: we wished to ask you if your husband still has any foreign currency?"

"He's already handed over everything he had," was her nervous reply.

"Indeed," said the actor. "Well, if you say so. And if he's handed everything over, then we shouldn't keep him any longer, should we! You may leave the theater, if you wish, Sergei Gerardovich," said the actor with an imperious wave of his hand.

Calmly and with dignity, Dunchil turned and walked toward the wings.

"Just one minute!" the emcee stopped him. "As a farewell, let me show you one last number from our program." Again he clapped his hands.

The black curtains at the back of the stage parted, and out came a beautiful young woman in a ball gown carrying a gold tray on which there was a thick package tied with striped ribbon and a diamond necklace which gave off blue, yellow, and red sparkles.

Dunchil stepped backward, and his face blanched. The audience fell silent.

"Eighteen thousand dollars and a necklace worth forty thousand gold rubles," announced the actor solemnly, "has been kept by Sergei

Gerardovich in Kharkov in the apartment of his mistress, Ida Gerkulanovna Vors, who is honoring us with her presence here, and who graciously helped us to locate these treasures, which, though priceless, are worthless when in private hands. Many thanks to you, Ida Gerkulanovna."

The beauty flashed a toothsome smile and fluttered her thick eyelashes.

"And hiding behind your mask of dignity," said the actor, now addressing Dunchil, "is a bloodthirsty spider, an astounding liar, and a cheat. Your six weeks of dogged stubbornness has exhausted us all. Go on home now, and may the hell that your wife is preparing for you be your punishment."

Dunchil swayed and seemed about to collapse, but a pair of sympathetic hands reached out and steadied him. The curtain then fell and blocked everyone on stage from view.

Wild applause so shook the hall that it seemed to Nikanor Ivanovich that the light bulbs in the chandeliers were jumping out of their sockets. And when the curtain went up, there was no one left on stage except the actor. He cut off a second burst of applause, bowed and said, "The Dunchil who appeared before you in our program represents a typical ass. Why just yesterday I had the pleasure of telling you how senseless it is to try and keep a secret cache of foreign currency. There are, I assure you, absolutely no circumstances in which you can use it. Take that same Dunchil, for example. He earns a splendid salary and has everything he needs. A beautiful apartment, a wife, and a beautiful mistress. But no! Instead of living a peaceful, quiet life free of unpleasantness, after handing over his foreign currency and precious stones, he, greedy blockhead that he is, ended up being publicly exposed and earned himself a major family crisis as well. This being the case, who will come forward? Nobody wants to? In that case, the next number in our program is that well-known dramatic talent, the actor Savva Potapovich Kurolesov, who has been invited to perform excerpts from *The Covetous Knight* by the poet Pushkin."

Kurolesov appeared on stage immediately and turned out to be a tall, beefy, clean-shaven fellow in a white tie and tails.

With no preamble whatsoever, he assumed a gloomy-looking expression, raised his eyebrows, and while looking at the gold bell out of the corner of his eye, began reciting in an unnatural voice:

"While awaiting a tryst with a sly temptress, the young rake..."

And Kurolesov told a lot of bad things about himself. Nikanor Ivanovich heard Kurolesov confess how an unhappy widow, moaning, had gone down on her knees before him in the rain, but had failed to touch the actor's hard heart.

Up until his dream Nikanor Ivanovich had not known the works of Pushkin at all, although he had been well acquainted with Pushkin himself, since he made daily use of such expressions as, "Will Pushkin be paying for the apartment?" or "I suppose it was Pushkin who unscrewed the bulb on the staircase?" or "So Pushkin will be buying the oil, right?"

Now that Nikanor Ivanovich had been introduced to one of Pushkin's works, he felt sad and imagined the woman down on her knees in the rain with her orphans, and he found himself thinking, "That Kurolesov must be a real bastard!"

Meanwhile, Kurolesov, his voice getting higher and higher, continued to repent, and he befuddled Nikanor Ivanovich completely when he suddenly began to address someone who wasn't there and then answered for this invisible person, calling himself, in turn, "lord," "baron," "father," "son," and addressing himself with both the formal and intimate forms of "you."

Nikanor Ivanovich was sure of only one thing: the actor died a horrible death, screaming, "My keys! My keys!" whereupon he fell wheezing onto the floor, while carefully removing his necktie.

After he had died, Kurolesov got up from the floor, shook the dust off his dress trousers, smiled a fake smile, and withdrew to lukewarm applause. The emcee then began to speak, "We have just heard Savva Potapovich's remarkable performance of *The Covetous Knight*. That knight had high hopes that frolicsome nymphs would flock around him and that he would enjoy many similar delights. But as you can see, nothing of the sort came to pass. No nymphs flocked around him, the muses paid him no tribute, he did not erect any castles. On the contrary, he ended up in disgrace and died from a damned stroke while sitting on top of a chest full of foreign currency and precious stones. May this be a warning to you: something similar will happen to you, maybe even worse, if you don't hand over your foreign currency!"

It is difficult to say whether it was Pushkin's poetry or the emcee's prose that made the greatest impression, but suddenly a timid voice was heard in the audience, "I'll hand mine over."

"By all means, please come up on stage," invited the emcee, staring out at the dark auditorium.

On stage there appeared a short, fair-haired fellow who, by the looks of him, hadn't shaved for about three weeks.

"I'm sorry, what is your name?" queried the emcee.

"Kanavkin, Nikolai," answered the shy newcomer.

"Ah! Pleased to meet you, Citizen Kanavkin, and what would you like to tell us?"

"I'll hand mine over," was Kanavkin's timid reply.

"How much?"

"A thousand dollars and twenty gold ten-ruble coins."

"Bravo! Is that all there is?"

The man in charge of the program stared straight into Kanavkin's eyes, and in so doing, seemed to be bombarding him with rays. The audience held its breath.

"I believe you!" exclaimed the actor at last, lowering his eyes. "I believe you! Those eyes aren't lying. After all, how many times have I told you that your biggest mistake is underestimating the significance of people's eyes. The tongue can conceal the truth, but the eyes never! You're asked an unexpected question, you don't even flinch, it takes just a second to get yourself under control, you know just what you have to say to hide the truth, and you speak very convincingly, and nothing in your face twitches to give you away. But the truth, alas, has been disturbed by the question, and it rises up from the depths of your soul to flicker in your eyes and all is lost. The truth is detected and you are caught!"

After delivering this very convincing speech, the actor cordially questioned Kanavkin, "So where is it hidden?"

"At Porokhovnikova's, my aunt's, on Prechistenka..."

"Ah! That's... just a minute... that's Klavdiya Ilinichna's place, is that right?"

"Yes."

"Ah yes, yes, yes, yes! A small private residence? With the gardens across the street? Well of course! I know the place, I know it well! And where did you put the money?"

"In the cellar, in an Einem candy box..."

The actor clapped his hands.

"Have you ever seen anything like it?" he cried out in exasperation! "Where it's certain to get moldy and rot! Can you imagine entrusting people like this with foreign currency? Huh? By God, they're as innocent as children!"

Kanavkin himself realized that he had ruined things and was completely at fault, and he hung his tufted head.

"Money," continued the actor, "should be kept in the State Bank, in special, moisture-free safe-deposit boxes, and not in your aunty's cellar where the rats can get at it! Shame on you, Kanavkin! You're a grown man."

Not having any hole to drop through, Kanavkin settled for fingering the hem of his jacket.

"Well, all right then," said the actor in less harsh tones, "no point in rubbing it in..." Then suddenly he added, "Oh, by the way, while we're at it... let's kill two birds with one stone... Doesn't your aunty have some foreign currency too? Huh?"

Kanavkin, who had not expected things to take such a turn, shuddered and the theater fell silent.

"Oh, Kanavkin," said the emcee in a mildly reproachful tone, "and I was just singing his praises! And he had to go and spoil everything! That was not smart, Kanavkin! After what I just said about eyes. It's obvious your aunty has some foreign currency too. So why go on torturing us for no reason?"

"She does have some!" Kanavkin shouted brashly.

"Bravo!" cried the emcee.

"Bravo!" roared the audience.

When the roar subsided, the emcee congratulated Kanavkin, shook his hand, offered to have a car drive him home and then ordered someone in the wings to pick up the aunt in the same car and invite her to attend a performance at the women's theater.

"Oh, by the way, your aunt didn't say where she hid hers, did she?" inquired the emcee, as he kindly offered Kanavkin a cigarette and a lighted match. Kanavkin lit up and managed a woebegone grin.

"I believe you, I do," sighed the actor. "That old skinflint wouldn't tell the devil where she put it, so why would she tell her nephew. Well, never mind, we'll try and arouse her finer feelings. Perhaps not all the strings in her usurious heart have rotted away. All the best, Kanavkin!"

And a happy Kanavkin departed. The actor then inquired if anyone else wanted to hand over any foreign currency, and he was answered by silence.

"Peculiar birds, I swear!" he said, shrugging his shoulders, and the curtains closed.

The lights went out, it was dark for awhile, and then a nervous tenor could be heard singing from afar, "There are piles of gold there and they all belong to me!"

Then came two bursts of muffled applause from somewhere.

"Somebody's handing over her money in the women's theater," burst out Nikanor Ivanovich's red-bearded neighbor. He heaved a sigh and added, "Oh, if it weren't for my geese!... You see, I keep some fighting-geese out at Lianozovo... I'm afraid they'll die without me. A fighting-bird is delicate and needs a lot of attention... Oh, if it weren't for my geese! Pushkin can't catch me off guard!" And he heaved another sigh.

At this point bright lights came on in the hall, and Nikanor Ivanovich began to dream that cooks in white hats carrying ladles in their hands came streaming through all the doors into the theater. The cooks were dragging in a vat of soup and a tray filled with slices of black bread. The audience came to life. The merry cooks pushed through the rows of spectators, ladling the soup into bowls and doling out bread.

"Eat up, guys," cried the cooks, "and hand over your foreign currency! Why sit here for nothing? Who wants to eat this filthy gruel! Go home and have a real drink and some hors d'oeuvres, and feel good!"

"Let's take you, dad, what are you in for?" asked a fat, red-necked cook, addressing Nikanor Ivanovich and passing him a bowl of soup with one lone cabbage leaf floating on top.

"I haven't got any! I haven't got any!" screamed Nikanor Ivanovich in a terrible voice. "Can't you understand? I haven't got any!"

"You don't?" roared the cook in a threatening bass, "You don't?" he crooned tenderly like a woman. "You don't, you don't," he murmured soothingly, as he metamorphosed into the nurse Praskovya Fyodorovna.

She was softly shaking Nikanor Ivanovich by the shoulder as he moaned in his sleep. Then the cooks melted away and the theater with the curtains fell to pieces. Through his tears Nikanor Ivanovich could make out his room in the clinic and two people in white coats, but they were nothing like the smarmy cooks who had dished out unwanted advice. They were doctors, and with them was Praskovya Fyodorovna, who was holding a gauze-covered dish with a syringe instead of a soup bowl.

"But what's this for," said Nikanor Ivanovich bitterly as they gave him the injection. "I don't have any! None! Let Pushkin hand over his foreign currency. I don't have any!"

"Of course you don't," said the kindhearted Praskovya Fyodorovna soothingly, "and no one can blame you for it."

Nikanor Ivanovich felt better after the injection and then fell into a dreamless sleep.

But thanks to his cries, his anxiety communicated itself, first to Room 120, where the patient woke up and started to look for his head, and then to Room 118, where the unknown Master became upset and started wringing his hands in anguish, while gazing at the moon and recalling that bitter autumn night, the last in his life, and the strip of light coming from under the door to his basement, and her loosened hair.

From Room 118 anxiety spread along the balcony to Ivan, and he woke up and burst into tears.

But the doctor quickly calmed all his distraught and afflicted patients, and they began to doze off. Oblivion came to Ivan last of all, just as dawn was breaking over the river. After the medicine had filtered through his entire body, peace and calm engulfed him like a wave. His body felt lighter, and the warm breeze of sleep caressed his head. The last thing he heard before he fell asleep was the pre-dawn twittering of the birds in the wood. But they soon fell silent, and he began to dream that the sun was already sinking behind Bald Mountain, and the mountain was encircled by a double cordon...

XVI

The Execution

T HE sun was already sinking behind Bald Mountain, and the mountain was encircled by a double cordon.

The cavalry ala that had crossed the procurator's path around noontime had set out at a trot, moving toward the city's Hebron Gate. A path had already been cleared for it. The infantry of the Cappadocian cohort had pushed the crowds of people, camels, and mules over to the sides of the road, and the ala, raising white columns of dust skyward as it moved along, trotted out to the intersection of two roads: one heading south to Bethlehem, the other northwest to Jaffa. The ala took the northwest road. The same Cappadocians were deployed along the sides of the road, having been successful in their efforts to clear the various caravans hurrying to Yershalaim for the holiday out of the way in a timely fashion. Crowds of pilgrims had left their striped tents, which were pitched temporarily on the grass, and were standing behind the Cappadocians. After traveling about a kilometer, the ala overtook the second cohort of the Lightning Legion, and after travelling another kilometer, the ala was the first to arrive at the foot of Bald Mountain. There the men dismounted. The commander divided them into platoons, and they cordoned off the base of the small hill so that it was accessible only from the Jaffa road.

A short time later the ala was joined by the second cohort, which set up another cordon higher up the mountain.

The last to arrive was the century under the command of Mark Ratkiller. It advanced in two columns, one on either side of the road, and in the middle of the columns, escorted by the secret guard, came the cart carrying the three condemned prisoners. They wore white boards around their necks which said, in both Aramaic and Greek, "Outlaw and Rebel."

Behind their cart came other carts, loaded with freshly hewn crossbeamed posts, ropes, shovels, buckets, and axes. Riding in these carts were the six executioners. Following them on horseback were the centurion Mark, the head of the temple guard of Yershalaim, and the man in the hood with whom Pilate had had a brief exchange in the darkened room inside the palace.

A column of soldiers brought up the rear of the procession, and it was followed by a crowd of about two thousand curiosity-seekers, unfazed by the hellish heat and intent on attending an interesting spectacle.

Joining them were the curious pilgrims, who were not deterred from tagging along at the tail of the procession. The column wound its way up Bald Mountain as the thin voices of the accompanying heralds shouted out the words spoken by Pilate at noontime.

The ala allowed everyone to go up as far as the second cordon, but the second century permitted only those connected with the execution to ascend any higher. Then it maneuvered quickly to disperse the crowd around the entire hill, so that the crowd was contained by the cordon of infantry above and the cordon of cavalry below. Now the crowd could see the execution through the thin chain of foot soldiers.

And so, more than three hours had passed since the procession had ascended the mountain, and the sun was already sinking over Bald Mountain, but the heat was still unbearable. The soldiers in both cordons were suffering from the heat, languishing from boredom, and cursing the three outlaws in their hearts, sincerely wishing them all a speedy death.

The short commander of the ala, his forehead damp and his white tunic dark with sweat, stationed himself at the bottom of the hill near the open part of the ascent. He kept walking over to the leather bucket of the first platoon, scooping out handfuls of water, drinking, and then wetting down his turban. After getting a little relief from this, he would walk back and again begin pacing back and forth along the dusty road leading to the summit. His long sword knocked against his laced leather boot. The cavalry commander wanted to be a model of endurance for his men, but he took pity on them and allowed them to stand under the pyramid-shaped tents they had fashioned by sticking their lances into the ground and draping them with their white cloaks. These tents provided the Syrians some shelter from the merciless sun. The water buckets were emptied quickly, and the cavalrymen from the different platoons took turns going for water to the gully at the foot of the hill, where in the infernal heat and sparse shade of some emaciated mulberry trees, a muddy stream lived out its remaining days. The grooms stood there with the now rested horses, and, worn down by boredom, were trying to stay inside the shifting shade.

The soldiers' tedium and the curses they directed at the outlaws were understandable. The procurator's fears that the execution would provoke riots in his hated city of Yershalaim had fortunately proved groundless. And contrary to all expectations, when the execution entered its fourth hour, there was not one person left in between the double cordon formed by the infantry up above and the cavalry down below. The crowd had been scorched by the sun and driven back to Yershalaim. All that was left beyond the line of the two Roman centuries were two dogs. No one knew who they belonged to and how they had ended up on the hill. But the heat had prostrated them as well, and they lay panting with their tongues out, oblivious to the green-backed lizards scurrying between the red-hot stones, the only creatures unafraid of the sun, and the prickly plants curling over the ground.

No one had attempted to free the prisoners, either in Yershalaim, which had been inundated with troops, or here on the cordoned-off hill, and the crowd had gone back to the city because there was, really, nothing interesting about this execution, and back in the city preparations were already under way for the great feast of Passover, which would begin that evening.

The Roman infantry in the second cordon was suffering more than the cavalry in the first. The only respite the centurion Ratkiller allowed his men was to remove their helmets and replace them with wetted-down headbands, but he kept his soldiers standing, with their spears in their hands. Wearing the same kind of headband around his head, only dry, not wetted-down, he paced back and forth not far from the group of executioners, without having removed the silver lions' heads from his tunic, or his scabbard, sword, or knife. The sun beat down on the centurion without causing him any distress, and it was impossible to look at the lions' heads on his tunic, so blinding was the glare of the silver, which seemed to be boiling in the sun.

Ratkiller's disfigured face showed no sign of exhaustion or discontent, and it seemed that the giant centurion had the strength to go on pacing like that all day and all night, and the next day as well—in short, for as long as he had to. To keep walking with his hands on his heavy, bronze-studded belt, to gaze sternly now at the posts with the men being executed, now at the soldiers in the cordon, and to kick the toe of his shaggy boot indifferently at the bleached human bones or bits of flint that lay in his path.

The man in the hood had settled himself on a three-legged stool not far from the posts and sat in placid immobility, only occasionally poking at the sand with a twig out of boredom.

That there was not a single person behind the line of legionaries is not completely true. There was one man there, but he was simply not visible to everyone. The spot he had chosen was not on the side where there was an open ascent up the mountain and where the most comfortable view of the execution could be had, but on the northern side of the hill where the ascent was not sloping and accessible, but uneven, with crevices and cracks, and where in one of the crevices, clinging to the heaven-cursed waterless soil, trying to survive, was a sickly fig tree.

It was precisely under this tree which gave no shade at all that this single spectator, who was not a participant in the execution, had ensconced himself, and he had been sitting there on a rock from the very beginning, that is, for more than three hours. Yes, the place he had chosen was the worst rather than the best place to view the execution. Nevertheless, from that vantage point the posts were visible, and visible as well, beyond the cordon, were the two shiny spots on the centurion's chest, and that was evidently, more than sufficient for this man who obviously wanted to remain unobserved and undisturbed by anyone.

Four hours before, however, when the execution was just beginning, this man had acted very differently and had been very noticeable indeed—no doubt that was why he had changed his behavior and had sequestered himself.

It was when the procession had passed the second cordon and reached the top of the hill, that he had made his first appearance, acting like an obvious latecomer. Breathing heavily, he did not walk, but ran up the hill, pushing others aside, and when he saw that the line had closed in front of him as well as everyone else, he acted as if he did not understand the angry shouts being directed at him and made a naive attempt to break through the cordon to the place of execution where the condemned men were already being taken off the cart. For his efforts he received a heavy blow on the chest with the dull end of a spear, and he jumped back from the soldiers with a cry not of pain, but of despair. He gave the legionary who had struck him a dull and totally indifferent look, as if he were impervious to physical pain.

Coughing and gasping for breath, clutching his chest, he ran around the circumference of the hill, trying to find some break in the line on the northern side where he might be able to slip through. But it was too late. The ring had closed. And the man, his face contorted with grief, was forced to abandon his attempts to break through to the carts, from which the posts had already been removed. Such attempts would only have led to his capture, and being arrested on that particular day was certainly not part of his plan.

And so he had gone over to a crevice on the side of the hill, where it was more peaceful and no one would bother him.

This black-bearded man, his eyes suppurating from the sun and from lack of sleep, was now sitting on a rock, consumed with anguish. With a sigh, he would periodically open his tallith, once light-blue, but now ragged and dirty-gray from a life of wandering, and bare his chest, which had been bruised by the spear and was dirty with sweat. Then, in a state of unbearable torment, he would raise his eyes to the sky, following the flight of three vultures who, for some time now, had been tracing broad circles high in the sky in anticipation of the feast to come. Or he would fix his hopeless gaze on the yellow earth and see there the remains of a dog's skull, with lizards running all over it.

The man's suffering was so great that from time to time he would start talking to himself, "Oh, what a fool I am," he mumbled, swaying back and forth on his rock in a state of mental anguish, digging his nails into his swarthy chest. "Fool, stupid woman, coward! I'm carrion, and not a man!"

He would fall silent, drop his head, and then after taking a drink of warm water from his wooden flask, he would become animated again and grab for the knife hidden on his chest under his tallith, or for the piece of parchment in front of him on the rock, beside a small stick and a bladder of ink.

The parchment already had some scattered jottings:

The minutes go by, and I, Levi Matvei, am here on Bald Mountain, and still death does not come!

And further on:

The sun is sinking, and still, no death.

Now, in a hopeless state, Levi Matvei had used his sharp stick to record the following:

God! Why art thou angry at him? Send him death.

When he had written that, he burst into tearless sobs and again dug his nails into his chest.

The reason for Levi's despair was the terrible misfortune that had befallen Yeshua and himself, and also the mistake that he felt he, Levi, had made. Two days before, Yeshua and Levi had been in Bethany outside Yershalaim, where they had been visiting a vegetable gardener who had been most favorably impressed by Yeshua's preachings. Both guests had worked in the garden all morning, helping their host, and they were planning to go into Yershalaim in the evening when it was cooler. But for some reason Yeshua had suddenly started to hurry, said he had urgent business in the city and left by himself around noontime. That had been Levi Matvei's first mistake. Why, oh why had he let him go alone?

In the evening Matvei had not been able to go to Yershalaim. He was hit by a sudden and terrible illness. He shook all over, his body was on fire, his teeth chattered, and he constantly had to ask for water. He was unfit to go anywhere. He collapsed on a horse-blanket in the gardener's barn and lay there until dawn on Friday, when Levi's illness left him as suddenly as it had come. Although he was still weak and his legs trembled beneath him, he was tormented by forebodings of disaster, and so he said good-bye to his host and set out for Yershalaim. There he learned that his forebodings had not deceived him. Disaster had taken place. Levi was in the crowd and heard the procurator pronounce the sentence.

When the condemned men had been taken out to the mountain,

Levi Matvei ran alongside the column in the crowd of curiosity-seekers, trying, at least, to find some inconspicuous way to let Yeshua know that he, Levi, was there, that he would not forsake him on his final journey, and that he was praying that Yeshua would have a speedy death. But Yeshua had been looking up ahead to where they were taking him and had not seen Levi.

And then, when the procession had gone a short distance, Matvei had a simple and ingenious idea as he was being jostled by the crowd pressing in upon the column. And being as hotheaded as he was, he immediately cursed himself for not having thought of it sooner. The cordon of soldiers was not impenetrable. There were gaps in it. If one were quick and timed it right, it might be possible to bend down, slip between two of the legionaries, get to the cart and jump up on it. Then Yeshua would be saved from suffering.

A single instant would be enough to plunge a knife into Yeshua's back and shout, "Yeshua! I am saving you and am going with you! I, Matvei, your true and only disciple!"

And if God would grant him yet another instant of freedom, then he might be able to stab himself as well and avoid death on the post. But the latter was of little concern to Levi, the former collector of taxes. He did not care how he died. The only thing he wanted was for Yeshua, who had never done anyone any harm in his whole life, to escape being tortured.

The plan was a very good one, but it had one flaw: Levi had no knife. Nor did he have any money to buy one.

Enraged at himself, Levi broke away from the crowd and ran back to the city. Only one thought burned in his fevered brain and that was to get hold of a knife there right away, by whatever means, and then to catch up with the procession once again.

He reached the city gates, maneuvering his way through the crush of caravans pouring into the city, and over to his left he saw the open door of a bread shop. Breathing heavily after his run down the blistering street, Levi regained control of himself and walked sedately into the shop. He greeted the woman behind the counter and asked for a loaf from the top of the shelf, saying it appealed to him more than the others. When the woman turned around to get it, he silently and quickly grabbed from the counter a long, razor-sharp bread knife, ideal for his purposes, and bolted out of the shop.

A few minutes later he was again on the Jaffa road. But the procession was nowhere in sight. He started to run. Occasionally he would have to fall down on the dusty road and lie still in order to catch his breath. And so he would lie, startling those passing by on mules and on foot, enroute to Yershalaim. He lay, listening to his heart pounding in his head, ears, and chest. After he had gotten some of his breath back, he jumped up and started running again, but at a slower and slower pace. When he could finally see the dust in the distance raised by the long procession, it had already reached the foot of the mountain.

"Oh, God!" groaned Levi as he realized that he would be late. And he did come too late.

As the fourth hour of the execution was ending, Levi's suffering reached its peak, and he flew into a rage. He got up from his rock and threw away the knife which, as it seemed to him now, he had stolen in vain. He stamped on his flask, thus depriving himself of water, tore the kaffiyeh off his head, clutched at his straggly hair and began cursing himself.

He cursed and yelled out meaningless words, he roared and spat, reviling his mother and father for bringing such a fool into the world.

Seeing that his cursing and swearing had no effect, and had caused no change in the blazing sun, he narrowed his eyes, clenched his dry fists, raised them up to the sky, to the sun that was creeping lower and lower as it lengthened the shadows and neared its fall into the Mediterranean Sea, and he demanded that God send a miracle right away. He demanded that God send death to Yeshua then and there.

When he opened his eyes, he realized that everything on the hill had stayed the same, with the exception of the shiny spots on the centurion's chest which had gotten dimmer. The sun's rays were falling on the backs of those being executed, who were facing toward Yershalaim. Then Levi cried out, "I curse you, God!"

In a hoarse voice he shouted that he had become convinced of God's injustice and no longer had any intention of believing in Him.

"You're deaf!" bellowed Levi. "If you weren't deaf, you would have heard me and killed him on the spot."

Narrowing his eyes, Levi waited for fire to fall from the sky and strike him down. That failed to happen, and without opening his eyelids, Levi went on shouting out caustic, offensive remarks to the sky. He screamed about his utter disenchantment and about the fact that there were other gods and religions. Yes, another god would not have allowed, would never have allowed, someone like Yeshua to be strung up on a post and burned by the sun.

"I was mistaken!" cried the now completely hoarse Levi. "You are the God of evil! Or has the smoke from the temple censers blinded your eyes, and are your ears deaf to everything but the trumpet calls of the priests? You are not an omnipotent God. You are a black God. I curse you, God of outlaws, their protector and their soul!"

At this point something blew in the face of the former tax collector and something stirred beneath his feet. There was another gust, and when Levi opened his eyes, he saw that everything around him had changed, either because of his curses or for some other reason. The sun had disappeared without reaching the sea it sank into every evening. After swallowing the sun, a menacing thundercloud was rising relentlessly on the western horizon. White foam bubbled around its edges, and its smoky black belly was fringed with yellow. The cloud rumbled from time to time and emitted streaks of fire. The wind that had suddenly blown up chased spirals of dust down the Jaffa road, across the sparse Valley of Gion, and over the pilgrims' tents.

Levi fell silent and wondered whether the thunderstorm about to envelop Yershalaim would have any effect on poor Yeshua's fate. And as he gazed at the streaks of fire that were splitting open the stormcloud, he begged for the lightning to strike Yeshua's post. Levi looked repentantly at the clear part of the sky not yet devoured by the stormcloud, where the vultures had flown in order to escape the thunder and lightning, and he thought that he had been much too hasty with his curses. Now God would not listen to him.

Levi turned his gaze to the foot of the hill where the cavalry regiment was deployed, and saw that significant changes had taken place there. He had a good view from above and could see the soldiers bustling about, pulling their lances out of the ground and throwing on their capes, and the grooms running out to the road, leading raven-black horses by the reins. It was obvious that the regiment was preparing to move out. Shielding his face from the blowing dust with his hand and spitting the sand out of his mouth, Levi tried to figure out the significance of the cavalry's imminent departure. When he turned his glance upward, he could make out a small figure in a crimson-colored military chlamys, who was making his way up to the execution site. Sensing that the joyous end was at hand, the former tax collector felt a chill in his heart.

The man ascending the mountain in the fifth hour of the outlaws' suffering was the commander of the cohort, who had ridden out from Yershalaim along with his orderly. At a wave of Ratkiller's hand, the cordon of soldiers opened up, and the centurion saluted the tribune. The latter drew Ratkiller aside and whispered something to him. The centurion saluted a second time and moved over to the group of executioners who were sitting on rocks at the foot of the posts. The tribune walked over to the man sitting on the three-legged stool, and he got up politely to meet him. The tribune said something to him in a low voice, and they both walked over to the posts. They were joined by the chief of the temple guard.

Ratkiller cast a squeamish glance at the dirty rags piled on the ground by the posts, rags that had once been the criminals' clothing and had been rejected by the executioners. He summoned two of them and ordered, "Follow me!"

A crazed, raspy-sounding song could be heard coming from the nearest post. On it was Gestas, who had been driven mad by the flies and the sun when the execution was nearing the end of its third hour, and who was now quietly singing something about grapes. He would, however, occasionally shake his turbaned head, and when he did, flies would lazily swirl off his face, only to return and light on it again.

Dismas, who was on the second post, was suffering more than the other two because he had not lost consciousness, and he shook his head right and left frequently and systematically, so that he could strike an ear against each shoulder.

Yeshua had been more fortunate than the other two. In the first hour he had had intermittent fainting spells, and then he lost consciousness. His head, in its straggly turban, hung on his chest and he was, therefore, so covered with flies that his face had disappeared beneath a black, heaving mask. Fat horseflies clung to his groin, stomach, and armpits, sucking on his naked yellow body.

In response to a sign made by the man in the hood, one of the executioners took a spear, and another brought a bucket and sponge over to the post. The one with the spear raised it and ran it along each of Yeshua's arms, which were stretched out along the crossbeam of the post and fastened to it with ropes. The body with its protruding ribs gave a shudder. The executioner ran the end of the spear over his stomach. Then Yeshua raised his head and the flies took off with a buzzing sound, thus revealing the hanged man's face. Bloated from bites, and with swollen eyelids, his face was unrecognizable.

Unglueing his eyelids, Ha-Notsri glanced down. His usually bright eyes were now dulled.

"Ha-Notsri!" said the executioner.

Ha-Notsri's swollen lips moved slightly and in a hoarse outlaw's voice he asked, "What do you want? Why have you come?"

"Drink!" said the executioner, lifting the water-soaked sponge to Yeshua's lips on the end of the spear. His eyes flashing with joy, Yeshua pressed his lips to the sponge and greedily drew in the moisture. Dismas's voice was heard from the neighboring post, "That's unfair! He's as much of an outlaw as I am."

Dismas strained his body, but could not move. His arms were tied to the crossbeam in three places with rings of rope. He pulled in his stomach, dug his nails into the ends of the crossbeam, and turned his head toward Yeshua's post. His eyes burned with malice.

A cloud of dust enveloped the place of execution. It got very dark. When the dust lifted, the centurion shouted, "Silence on the second post!"

Dismas fell silent. Yeshua pulled away from the sponge, and trying unsuccessfully to make his voice sound gentle and convincing, he hoarsely implored the executioner, "Give him a drink."

It was getting darker and darker. The stormcloud rushing toward Yershalaim already filled half the sky. Turbulent white clouds swept by in front of the thundercloud, which was bursting with black water and fire. Lightning flashed and thunder clapped right above the hill. The executioner removed the sponge from the spear.

"Praise the merciful Hegemon!" he whispered solemnly and quietly pierced Yeshua through the heart. Yeshua shuddered and whispered, "Hegemon..."

Blood ran down his stomach, his lower jaw trembled convulsively, and his head dropped down.

As the thunder clapped a second time, the executioner let Dismas drink, and with the same words, "Praise the Hegemon!" killed him too.

Gestas, who had lost his reason, cried out in fright as soon as the executioner appeared beside him, but when the sponge touched his lips, he growled something and took hold of it with his teeth. Seconds later, his body also hung limply, straining against the ropes.

The man in the hood walked behind the executioner and the centurion, and behind him came the head of the temple guard. After stopping at the first post, the man in the hood looked closely at the bloodied Yeshua, touched the sole of his foot with his white hand and said to his companions, "He's dead."

The same ritual was repeated at the other posts.

Following this, the tribune signalled to the centurion, turned around, and began walking down the hill together with the head of the temple guard and the man in the hood. Dusk had fallen, and lightning ripped through the black sky. Suddenly there was a burst of fire and the centurion's shout, "Break ranks!" was drowned out by the thunder. The happy soldiers ran off down the hill, putting on their helmets.

Darkness covered Yershalaim.

The sudden downpour hit the centuries as they were halfway down the hill. The water poured down so ferociously that churning streams nipped at the soldiers' heels as they ran down the hill. They slipped and fell on the wet clay as they hurried to reach the level road on which—barely visible through the veil of water—the cavalry, soaked to the bone, was heading back to Yershalaim. A few minutes later, in the churning brew of thunder, fire, and water, there was only one man left on the hill.

Brandishing the knife, which had not been stolen in vain, scaling the slippery ledges, grabbing hold of anything he could, crawling at times on his hands and knees, he headed straight for the posts. He would at times disappear in complete darkness, only then to be suddenly lit up by flickering light.

When he reached the posts, standing ankle-deep in water, he ripped off his heavy, soaked tallith, and wearing only his shirt, threw himself at Yeshua's feet. He cut the ropes around his shins, climbed up on the lower cross beam, embraced Yeshua, and released his arms from their restraints. Yeshua's wet, naked body fell on top of Levi and knocked him to the ground. Levi was about to hoist him up on his shoulder, but something stopped him. He left the body in a pool of water on the ground with its head thrown back and its arms flung out and ran, slipping on the wet clay, over to the other posts. He cut the ropes on them too, and the two bodies fell to the ground.

Minutes later, all that was left on the top of the hill were those two bodies and three empty posts. The water beat down on the bodies and turned them over.

By that time both Levi and Yeshua's body had vanished from the top of the hill.

XVII

An Upsetting Day

O N Friday morning, that is, the day after the accursed performance, the entire staff of the Variety Theater—the bookkeeper Vasily Stepanovich Lastochkin, two clerks, three typists, both cashiers, the messenger boys, ushers, and cleaning women—in short, everyone at the theater, were not at their posts. Instead, they were all sitting on the sills of the windows above Sadovaya Street, looking down at what was happening outside the theater. Stretched along the wall in a double line that reached as far as Kudrinsky Square were thousands of people. At the front of the line stood twenty or more of the most prominent scalpers in the Moscow theatrical world.

The people in line were very agitated and kept attracting the attention of passersby with their inflammatory stories of the previous day's extraordinary performance of black magic. These stories had particularly distressed the bookkeeper, Vasily Stepanovich, who had not attended the performance. The ushers were saying all sorts of preposterous things, for example, that after the performance some ladies ran down the street indecently clad and other things of that sort. The modest and quiet Vasily Stepanovich merely blinked his eyes as he listened to all their wondrous tales. He had no idea what he should do, even though something did have to be done, and by him in particular, since he was now first in command at the Variety Theater.

By ten in the morning the line of ticket seekers had swelled to such proportions that the police had gotten wind of it. Mounted and on foot they descended on the scene with astonishing speed and managed to restore some order. However, even an orderly line a mile long was a source of distraction and amazement for the people on Sadovaya Street.

That was the situation outside the theater, and inside things weren't going very well either. The phones in the offices of Likhodeyev, Rimsky, and Varenukha, as well as those in the ticket office and the bookkeeping department, had been ringing nonstop since early morning. At first Vasily Stepanovich had made some sort of response to callers, as had the cashier and the ushers, who mumbled something into the phone, but after a while they stopped answering altogether because they had absolutely no answer to give to questions about the whereabouts of Likhodeyev, Varenukha, or Rimsky. At first they had tried to get off with lines like, "Likhodeyev is in his apartment," but this only made the callers say that they had called there and been told that he was at the Variety.

An agitated lady had called, demanding to speak with Rimsky. After she had been advised to call his wife, the receiver burst into tears, saying that she was his wife and that Rimsky was nowhere to be found. It was the beginning of a kind of nonsensical farce. The cleaning woman had already told everyone that when she came to clean the financial director's office, she found the door wide open, the lights on, the window overlooking the garden smashed, the chair overturned on the floor, and no one there.

Just after ten Madame Rimsky charged into the Variety, wringing her hands and sobbing. Vasily Stepanovich was totally at a loss and had no idea what to advise her. Then at ten-thirty the police showed up. Their first, completely reasonable, question was, "What's going on here, citizens? What's this all about?"

The theater staff pushed a pale and flustered Vasily Stepanovich forward and then stepped back. He had no choice but to call a spade a spade and admit that the administration of the Variety Theater, to wit, the director, financial director, and manager, had vanished and their whereabouts were unknown, that after last night's performance the emcee had been removed to a psychiatric hospital, and that, briefly put, last night's show had been nothing short of scandalous.

After consoling the sobbing Madame Rimsky as much as they could and sending her home, they seemed most interested in the cleaning woman's account of the state of the financial director's office. The staff was asked to get back to work, and a short time later an investigative unit arrived, accompanied by a muscular dog the color of cigarette ash, with highly intelligent eyes and pointed ears. The theater staff was immediately abuzz with the rumor that the dog was none other than the famous Ace of Diamonds. And, it was, in fact, he. His behavior astounded everyone. As soon as Ace of Diamonds ran into the financial director's office, he started to growl and bared his monstrous yellow fangs, then he lay down on his belly, his expression a blend of anguish and fury, and started to crawl over to the broken window. Having overcome his fear, he suddenly jumped up on the windowsill, stuck his pointed muzzle up in the air, and let out a wild and vicious howl. Not wanting to come down from the window, he growled and trembled and tried to jump out.

The dog was led out of the office and let go in the lobby, and from there he went out the front entrance into the street, leading those who were following him over to the taxi stand. There he lost the scent. After that, Ace of Diamonds was taken away.

The investigative unit settled into Varenukha's office and began summoning, one by one, all members of the Variety staff who had witnessed everything that had gone on at yesterday's performance. It must be said that the investigators encountered unforeseen difficulties every step of the way. The thread kept breaking in their hands.

Had there been any posters? Yes, there had. But during the night they had been pasted over with new ones, and now for the life of them, they could not find a single one! And where had the magician come from? Who knows? Wouldn't there have been a contract?

"One would assume so," replied a distraught Vasily Stepanovich.

"And if there had been a contract, would it have gone through book-keeping?"

"Absolutely," answered Vasily Stepanovich in distress.

"So where is it?"

"It's not here," replied the bookkeeper, growing paler by the minute and spreading his hands helplessly. And indeed, there was no trace of any contract, not in bookkeeping's files, nor in those of the financial director, Likhodeyev, or Varenukha.

And what was this magician's name? Vasily Stepanovich didn't know, he hadn't been at the show. The ushers didn't know, the ticket-office cashier crinkled her brow and thought and thought, and finally said, "Wo...Woland, I think."

And are you sure it was Woland? Well, maybe not. Maybe it was Faland.

The Bureau of Foreigners had never heard of any magician named Woland or Faland.

Karpov, the messenger boy, reported that he thought that the magician had been staying at Likhodeyev's apartment. Naturally they went there right away. And no magician was to be found. Nor was Likhodeyev. Grunya the maid wasn't there either, and no one knew where she had gone. Missing too was the chairman of the house committee, Nikanor Ivanovich, and Prolezhnyov!

Something utterly unimaginable had occurred: the entire administrative staff of the theater had disappeared. A strange and scandalous performance had taken place yesterday, but who had staged it and at whose instigation was not known.

And meanwhile, it was getting on toward noon, the time when the box office was supposed to open. Under the circumstances, however, that was out of the question! A huge piece of cardboard was hung on the doors of the theater, saying, "Today's performance cancelled." There was a commotion, starting at the head of the line, but once it was over, the line nevertheless began to break up, and in an hour there was no trace of it left on Sadovaya Street. The team of investigators left to continue their work elsewhere, the theater staff was dismissed, except for the watchmen, and the doors of the Variety were locked.

The bookkeeper Vasily Stepanovich still had two things to do right away: first, go to the Entertainment Commission to report on yesterday's events, and second, visit the commission's finance office to turn over the proceeds from yesterday's performance—21,711 rubles.

The meticulous and efficient Vasily Stepanovich wrapped the money in a newspaper, tied it with twine, put it in his briefcase, and, knowing the procedure well, set off for the taxi stand, rather than the bus or trolley stop.

As soon as the drivers of three separate cabs spotted the prospective passenger heading toward them with a bulging briefcase, they all took off from under his nose, looking back at him, for some reason, with loathing.

Dumbfounded, the bookkeeper stood stock-still for some time, trying to figure out what it all meant.

A few minutes passed and an empty cab pulled up, but as soon as the driver took a look at the passenger, he made a face.

"Are you free?" asked Vasily Stepanovich, coughing with surprise.

"Show me your money," the cabbie replied angrily, without looking at him.

Becoming more and more dumbfounded, the bookkeeper pressed the precious briefcase under his arm, removed a ten-ruble bill from his wallet, and showed it to the driver.

"I won't take you," was his curt reply.

"I beg your pardon..." began the bookkeeper, but the cabbie interrupted him, "Do you have any threes?"

The completely baffled bookkeeper took two threes out of his wallet and showed them to the driver.

"Get in," he shouted, banging the meter so hard that he almost broke it. And off they went.

"Are you short on change?" the bookkeeper asked timidly.

"I've got loads of change!" roared the driver, his eyes, bloodshot with rage, blazing in the rearview mirror. "This is the third time today. And others are having the same problem. Some son of a bitch gives me a ten-ruble bill, I give him change—four-fifty... He's gone, the bastard! Five minutes later I look and what have I got: a label from a bottle of mineral water instead of a ten-ruble bill!" Here the cabbie let loose some unprintable words. "The next guy I pick up beyond Zubovskaya Street. Another ten. I give him three rubles change. He walks off! I rummage in the change purse, and out flies a bee and stings me on the finger! The bastard!" the cabbie again let go a stream of unprintable words. "But the ten is gone. Yesterday at the Variety (unprintable words) some sort of slimy magician did an act with ten-ruble bills (unprintable words)..."

The bookkeeper was stunned. He shrunk back in his seat and acted as if he were hearing the word "Variety" for the first time, but meanwhile he thought, "Boy, oh boy!"

Having reached his destination, the bookkeeper paid the driver without any problem. He entered the building, and as he headed down the corridor to the director's office, he saw that he had come too late. The office of the Entertainment Commission was in chaos. A messenger girl ran past the bookkeeper with her eyes bulging and her kerchief askew.

"He's not there, not there, not there, my dears!" she was screaming, to no one knows whom. "His jacket and trousers are there, but there's nothing in the jacket!"

She disappeared behind a door and immediately afterwards, sounds of breaking dishes were heard. The head of the first section, whom the bookkeeper knew, ran out of the secretaries' room, but he was in such a state that he didn't recognize the bookkeeper and disappeared somewhere without a trace.

Shaken by all this, the bookkeeper reached the secretaries' room, which served as an anteroom to the chairman's office, and here he was utterly thunderstruck.

A menacing voice could be heard coming through the closed door of the office, a voice that unmistakably belonged to Prokhor Petrovich, the chairman of the commission. "Who is he raking over the coals now, I wonder?" thought the flustered bookkeeper, and as he looked around, he saw something else that was unnerving: there in a leather armchair, sobbing uncontrollably and clutching a wet handkerchief, her head thrown back and her legs stretched out into the middle of the room was Prokhor Petrovich's personal secretary, the beautiful Anna Richardovna.

She had lipstick all over her chin, and black streams of mascara ran down her eyelashes, and over her peachlike cheeks.

When she saw who had come in, Anna Richardovna jumped up and threw herself at the bookkeeper. Grabbing his lapels, she shook him and screamed, "Thank God! At least there's one brave soul! They all ran off, they all betrayed him! Come with me and see him, I don't know what to do!" And still sobbing, she dragged the bookkeeper into the office.

Once there, the first thing the bookkeeper did was drop his briefcase. Everything in his head went topsy-turvy. And, it must be said, with good reason.

Behind the huge desk with its massive inkwell sat an empty suit, moving a pen with no ink in it over a sheet of paper. The suit was wearing a tie, and had a fountain pen sticking out of its breastpocket, but there was no neck and no head above the collar, nor were there any wrists poking out of the sleeves. The suit was hard at work and completely oblivious to the confusion raging all around. Hearing someone come in, the suit leaned back in its chair, and from above its collar came the voice of Prokhor Petrovich, so familiar to the bookkeeper, "What is it?

The sign on the door says that I'm not seeing anyone!"

The beautiful secretary let out a shriek, wrung her hands, and screamed, "See? Do you see?! He isn't there! He's not! Bring him back, bring him back!"

Just then someone poked his head in the door, groaned, and then left. The bookkeeper felt his legs start to tremble and sat down on the edge of a chair, but he didn't forget to pick up his briefcase. Anna Richardovna kept jumping around him, grabbing at his suit, and yelling, "I always tried to stop him when he used devil oaths! And now he's bedeviled himself!" At this point she ran over to the desk and in a soft musical voice that was slightly nasal-sounding from so much crying, she exclaimed, "Prosha! Where are you?"

"Who are you calling 'Prosha?'" the suit asked haughtily, sinking deeper in the chair.

"He doesn't recognize me! He doesn't! Don't you see?" sobbed the secretary.

"Please don't sob in the office!" said the irascible striped suit, already angry, extending its sleeve for a fresh stack of papers, obviously intending to attach memos to them.

"No, I can't look at this, no, I can't!" cried Anna Richardovna and ran out into the anteroom, followed like a shot by the bookkeeper.

"Just imagine, I was sitting here," began Anna Richardovna, trembling with agitation, and once again grabbing the bookkeeper by his sleeve, "and in walks a cat. Black, big as a hippopotamus. I, naturally, screamed 'Scat!' He takes off, and a fat man with a kind of catlike mug comes in instead. He says to me, 'Are you the one who screams "Scat" to visitors?' And he goes right in to Prokhor Petrovich. Naturally, I follow him and yell, 'Have you gone crazy?' But the brazen fellow goes right up to Prokhor Petrovich and sits down in the chair opposite! Well, Prokhor Petrovich, he's the nicest man you'll ever meet, but he's highstrung. He just blew up. I don't deny it. He's irritable, works like a horse—and he blew up. 'How dare you,' he says, 'burst in unannounced?' And, just imagine, that smart aleck sank back in his chair and said, smiling, 'But I've come,' he says, 'on a little matter of business.' Prokhor Petrovich blew up again, 'I'm busy!' And the other one, can you believe it, says back, 'You're not busy with anything at all...' How do you like that? Well, naturally, at that point Prokhor Petrovich's patience ran out, and he shouted, 'What the hell is this? Get him out of here, the devil take me!' And then, just imagine, the other one flashes a grin and says, 'You want the devil to take you? That can be arranged!' And, bang, before I can let out a scream, I see that the guy with the catlike mug is gone, and sit... sitting there is the suit... Ooooh!" howled Anna Richardovna, her mouth stretched so wide that it lost its shape.

She choked back her sobs and took a deep breath, but then she said something completely nonsensical, "And it writes, writes, writes! Drives you crazy! Talks on the phone! A suit! Everyone's run off like scared rabbits!"

The bookkeeper merely stood there, shaking. But at that point fate came to his rescue. Striding into the anteroom in a calm and businesslike way came the militia, that is, two policemen. When she saw them, the beautiful secretary began sobbing even harder and pointed to the office door.

"Come now, citizeness, let's not have any crying," said the first policeman calmly. The bookkeeper, feeling his presence to be completely superfluous, left the anteroom, and a minute later, was out in the fresh air. There seemed to be a draft blowing inside his head, like wind ringing in a pipe, and in this ringing he could hear bits and pieces of the ushers' tales about the cat that took part in yesterday's performance. "Aha! Could our cat-friend be making a return appearance?"

Having made no progress at all at the Commission, the conscientious Vasily Stepanovich decided to visit the branch office located on Vagankovsky Lane. To calm himself down a bit, he made the trip on foot.

The Moscow branch office of the Entertainment Commission was located in an old house, peeling from age, set far back in a courtyard, and was famous for the porphyry columns in its vestibule.

On that particular day, however, visitors were less struck by the columns than they were by what was going on beneath them.

Several visitors stood frozen to the spot, staring at the young lady who was sitting and weeping at the table where all the entertainment literature was displayed and sold. At the moment in question she was not engaged in salesmanship of any kind and was instead waving off all sympathetic questions with a flick of her wrist. Meanwhile, from upstairs and downstairs, from every side and every department of the building came the clanging of at least twenty phones.

After crying for a bit, the young lady suddenly shuddered and shouted out hysterically, "Here we go again!" and then broke out in a quavering soprano:

A glorious sea, our sacred Baikal...

A messenger who appeared on the staircase threatened someone with his fist and then joined the young woman, singing in a dull, toneless baritone:

Glorious the ship, the barrel of salmon! . . .

The messenger's voice was joined by others coming from farther away, the chorus swelled, and soon the song echoed from every corner of the branch office. In Room No. 6, the closest by, where the accounting department was, a powerful, slightly hoarse, deep bass rang out above the other voices. Accompanying the choir, was the intensified clanging of the telephones.

Hey, northeast wind... roll out the breakers!...

roared the messenger on the staircase.

Tears streamed down the young woman's face, she tried to clench her teeth, but her mouth opened of its own accord, and at an octave higher than the messenger, she sang:

The fine fellow hasn't far to go!

The speechless visitors were struck by the fact that although the choristers were scattered throughout different rooms, they sang very harmoniously, as if the whole chorus were standing in one place with its eyes glued to an invisible conductor.

Pedestrians on Vagankovsky Lane stopped by the courtyard gates and marveled at the gaiety that reigned in the branch office.

As soon as the first verse came to an end, the singing stopped abruptly, as if it were again obeying a conductor's baton. The messenger swore under his breath and ran off somewhere.

Here the front doors opened, and a man appeared in a summer overcoat, a white robe showing below the hem. He was in the company of a policeman.

"Do something, Doctor, I beg you!" The young woman cried hysterically.

The secretary of the branch office ran out onto the staircase, obviously ashamed and embarrassed. He started stammering, "Don't you see, Doctor, we have a case here of mass hypnosis of some kind... So, it's essential that..." He didn't finish his sentence, began to choke on his words, and suddenly sang out in a tenor:

Shilka and Nerchinsk...

"Fool," the young woman managed to yell, but rather than explain whom she was calling a fool, she broke into a forced roulade and started singing about Shilka and Nerchinsk herself.

"Get a hold of yourself! Stop singing!" said the doctor to the secretary.

It was obvious that the secretary would have given anything in the world to be able to stop singing, but he could not. And together with the chorus, his voice rang out with the news, heard by pedestrians out on the street, that in the wilds he was untouched by voracious beasts and unscathed by marksmen's bullets!

At the end of the verse the young woman was the first to receive a dose of valerian from the doctor, who then ran after the secretary and the others so that he could do the same for them.

"Excuse me, my young citizeness," said Vasily Stepanovich suddenly, addressing the young woman, "but has a black cat been here by any chance?"

"What cat?" she screamed angrily. "It's an ass we've got in this office, a real ass!" and then she added, "Let him hear! I'll tell the whole story," and she did, in fact, go on to relate what had happened.

It turned out that the director of the Moscow branch office, "who had made a complete mess of the leisure activities program" (the young woman's words exactly), had a mania for organizing all kinds of clubs and circles.

"He was trying to butter up his superiors!" yelled the young woman.

In just a year's time the director had managed to organize a Lermontov study group, a chess-and-checkers club, a ping-pong club, and a horseback-riding club. And he threatened to have two additional clubs in place by summer: one for fresh-water rowing and the other for mountain climbing.

And then today, during the lunch break, the director walks in and...

"And he's leading some son-of-a-bitch by the hand," related the young woman, "who comes from nobody knows where, and who's wearing tight checked trousers and a cracked pince-nez... with an unbelievable mug on him!"

And then, according to the young woman, he introduced him to everyone in the cafeteria as a noted specialist in the organization of choral groups.

The faces of the would-be mountain climbers clouded over, but the director encouraged everyone to be enthusiastic, and the specialist cracked jokes and showed off his wit, and gave his solemn word that the singing would take up hardly any time and would, incidentally, be extremely advantageous for everyone.

Well, naturally, as the young woman reported, the first to jump up were Fanov and Kosarchuk, notorious office toadies, who announced that they were going to join the chorus. The rest of the staff then realized that there was no way to escape it; so they said they would join too. It was decided that the singing would take place during the lunch break since the rest of the time was taken up with Lermontov and checkers. The director, in order to set a good example, announced that he was a tenor, and that was the beginning of the nightmare. The choirmaster-specialist in checks intoned, "Do-mi-sol-do!" He dragged the shy ones out of the closets where they were hiding to avoid singing, and told Kosarchuk that he had absolute pitch. Then he started to whine and bare his teeth, asked everyone to humor an old choirmaster, struck a tuning fork, and begged them to strike up a chorus of "Glorious Sea."

They did. And gloriously. The fellow in checks really did know his business. When they had finished the first verse, the choirmaster excused himself and said, "I'll be back in a minute!"—and... disappeared. They thought he really would return in a minute. But then ten minutes passed, and he still wasn't back. They were overcome with joy—he'd run away.

And suddenly they started singing the second verse as if of their own accord, following the lead of Kosarchuk, whose pitch may not have been perfect, but who did have quite a pleasant high tenor. They finished the second verse. Still no choirmaster! They went back to their places, but before they could manage to sit down, they started singing against their will. It was beyond their power to stop. They would be quiet for three minutes or so, and then start up again. At this point they realized that something bad had happened. Mortified, the director locked himself in his office.

It was here that the young woman's story broke off. The valerian had been no help at all.

Fifteen minutes later three trucks drove up to the gates on Vagankovsky Lane and the director of the branch office and the rest of his staff got in.

Just as the first truck came to a pitching halt at the gates, and then pulled out into the lane, the office staff, who were standing in the back, their arms around each other, opened their mouths and filled the street with song. The second truck followed suit, and then the third. And they all drove off. Pedestrians going about their business cast only a fleeting glance at the trucks, manifesting no curiosity whatsoever and assuming that they were going on an excursion outside the city. And they were, in fact, going outside the city, only not on an excursion. They were going to Professor Stravinsky's clinic.

Half an hour later the bookkeeper arrived at the finance office in a completely befuddled state, with hopes of finally divesting himself of yesterday's receipts. Having learned from experience, he peered cautiously into the oblong office where the clerks sat behind frosted glass windows with gold lettering. The bookkeeper could see no signs of upset or disarray. Everything was quiet, just as one would expect in a proper establishment.

Vasily Stepanovich stuck his head in the window which had a sign above it saying, "Deposits," said hello to the clerk, whom he did not know, and politely asked for a deposit slip.

"Why do you need one?" asked the clerk behind the window.

The bookkeeper was perplexed.

"I want to hand over my cash receipts. I'm from the Variety."

"Just a minute," replied the clerk and then proceeded to put a screen over the hole in his window.

"That's odd," thought the bookkeeper. His perplexity was natural under the circumstances. It was the first time he had ever encountered such a thing. Everyone knows how hard it is to acquire money; obstacles to that can always be found. But not once in his thirty years of experience had the bookkeeper ever found anyone, whether an official or a private citizen, who had difficulty accepting money.

But at last the screen was moved aside, and the bookkeeper again leaned up to the window.

"Do you have a lot?" asked the clerk.

"21,711 rubles."

"Wow!" replied the clerk with inexplicable irony and handed him a green slip of paper.

Having seen the form a hundred times, the bookkeeper filled it out instantly and began untying his package. When he removed the wrapping, his eyes glazed over, and he let out an agonizing groan.

Foreign currency flashed before his eyes. Packets of Canadian dollars, English pounds, Dutch guilders, Latvian lats, and Estonian crowns...

"Here he is, one of those tricksters from the Variety," boomed an intimidating voice at the stunned bookkeeper's back. And Vasily Stepanovich was then taken into custody.

XVIII

Unlucky Visitors

A T the same time as the conscientious bookkeeper was in the taxi enroute to his encounter with the writing suit, a respectably dressed man with a small imitation-leather suitcase was getting off the reserved-seat first-class car of the No. 9 train from Kiev. This passenger was none other than Maximilian Andreyevich Poplavsky, the uncle of the late Berlioz, an economic planner who lived in Kiev on what was formerly Institute Street. The reason for his trip to Moscow was a telegram received late in the evening two days before. It said, "I have just been cut in half by a streetcar at Patriarch's. Funeral Friday 3 PM. Come. Berlioz."

Maximilian Andreyevich was considered one of the smartest men in Kiev and justifiably so. But even the smartest man would be befuddled by a telegram like that. If a man can wire that he has been cut in half, it's obvious it wasn't a fatal accident. But then why mention a funeral? Or, could it be that he's in very bad shape and foresees that he is going to die? That was a distinct possibility, but the preciseness of the information was odd nonetheless. How could he know that his funeral was going to be at precisely 3 p.m. on Friday? An amazing telegram!

But what are smart people smart for, if not to untangle tangled things? It was very simple. There had been a mistake, and the message had been transmitted in garbled form. The word "I" had obviously come from another telegram and been put where "Berlioz" should have been, at the beginning of the telegram, instead of at the end where it ended up. After such a correction the telegram became intelligible, albeit, of course, tragic.

After the attack of grief which struck his wife had subsided, Maximilian Andreyevich began to make plans to go to Moscow.

Maximilian Andreyevich had a secret that must be revealed. Although he did indeed feel sorry for his wife's nephew, who had died in the prime of his life, he was a practical man and saw that there was no particular need for him to attend the funeral. Nevertheless, Maximilian Andreyevich had been in a great hurry to get to Moscow. What made him do it? Only one thing—the apartment. An apartment in Moscow! That's serious business! No one knows why, but Maximilian Andreyevich didn't like Kiev, and the thought of moving to Moscow had gnawed at him so persistently recently that he had begun to lose sleep over it.

He got no pleasure from the Dnieper overflowing in spring, when the islands on the lower shore became flooded, and the water merged with the horizon. He got no pleasure from the striking beauty of the view from the base of the Prince Vladimir statue. The patches of sunlight that played on the brick paths of Vladimir Hill in spring gave him no joy. He wanted none of that, he wanted just one thing—to move to Moscow.

The ads he placed in the papers, offering to exchange his Institute Street apartment in Kiev for a smaller flat in Moscow, had produced no results. There were no takers, and if someone did turn up once in a while, the offer was made in bad faith.

The telegram had given Maximilian Andreyevich a shock. It would be a sin to pass up such an opportunity. Practical people know that opportunity doesn't knock twice.

In a word, come hell or high water, he had to make sure he inherited his nephew's apartment on Sadovaya Street. True, it would be difficult, very difficult, but the difficulties had to be overcome, no matter what. As an experienced man of the world, Maximilian Andreyevich knew the first thing he had to do to accomplish this goal was to get registered, if only on a temporary basis, in his late nephew's three-room apartment.

On Friday afternoon Maximilian Andreyevich walked into the office of the housing committee of No. 302B Sadovaya Street in Moscow.

In a narrow room, where there was an old poster on the wall showing in several drawings ways of reviving someone drowned in the river, an unshaven middle-aged man with frightened-looking eyes sat behind a wooden desk all by himself.

"May I see the chairman of the housing committee?" the economic planner inquired politely, taking off his hat and putting his suitcase on the chair by the doorway.

This, it would seem, simplest of questions so unnerved the man at the desk that a change came over his face. Squinting with alarm, he mumbled incomprehensibly that the chairman was not there.

"Is he in his apartment?" asked Poplavsky. "I'm here on a very urgent matter."

The seated man's reply was again incoherent. But even so, the implication was that the chairman was not in his apartment either.

"When will he be back?"

The seated man said nothing in reply, and looked out the window with a kind of anguish.

"Aha!" said the smart Poplavsky to himself and inquired after the secretary.

The strange man at the desk turned purple from the strain and, again incomprehensibly, said that the secretary wasn't there either... that he was ill... and that no one knew when he'd be back...

"Aha!" said Poplavsky to himself, "But is there anyone here from the housing committee?"

"Me," the man answered in a weak voice.

"You see," Poplavsky began impressively, "I am the sole heir of the deceased Berlioz, my nephew, who, as you know, died at Patriarch's Ponds, and I am bound by the law to assume the inheritance that consists of our apartment, No. 50..."

"I don't know anything about it, comrade," interrupted the man glumly.

"But, see here," said Poplavsky in resonant tones. "You are a member of the committee and are obliged to..."

At this point a man walked into the room. The man at the desk took one look at him and turned pale.

"Committee member Pyatnazhko?" asked the new arrival.

"Yes," answered the man at the desk in barely audible tones.

The newcomer whispered something to him, and the latter became completely flustered, got up from the desk, and seconds later, Poplavsky was left alone in the empty housing committee office.

"Oh, what a complication! All I needed was to have them all suddenly be...," thought Poplavsky with annoyance, as he crossed the asphalt courtyard and hurried to apartment No. 50.

As soon as the economic planner rang the bell, the door opened. Maximilian Andreyevich entered the darkened hallway. He was a little surprised that he couldn't tell who had opened the door. There was no one in the hallway except a huge black cat who was sitting on a chair.

Maximilian Andreyevich coughed, stamped his feet, and then the study door opened, and out walked Korovyov into the hallway. Maximilian Andreyevich bowed politely to him, but said with dignity, "My name is Poplavsky. I am the uncle..."

But before he could finish, Korovyov pulled a dirty handkerchief out of his pocket, buried his nose in it, and burst into tears.

"...of the deceased Berlioz..."

"I know, I know," interrupted Korovyov, removing the handkerchief from his face. "The minute I laid eyes on you, I guessed it was you!" Then he was convulsed with tears and cried out, "What a tragedy, huh? How could such a thing happen, huh?"

"Run over by a streetcar?" asked Poplavsky in a whisper.

"Killed instantly," shouted Korovyov, and the tears started streaming from under his pince-nez. "Instantly! I was there and saw it. Believe me, it happened in a flash! Off went the head! Then the right leg—crunch, right in two! Then the left—crunch, right in two! That's what you get with streetcars!" Apparently unable to control himself, Korovyov turned his face to the wall next to the mirror and began shaking with sobs.

Berlioz's uncle was genuinely struck by the stranger's behavior. "And they say people aren't sensitive nowadays!" he thought, feeling his own eyes begin to smart. However, at just that moment a bothersome little cloud settled over his soul and a reptilian thought flickered: Could this sincere and sensitive fellow already have registered himself in the deceased's apartment? Such things have been known to happen, after all.

"Excuse me, but were you a friend of my dear departed Misha?" he asked, wiping his dry left eye with his sleeve and studying the grief-stricken Korovyov with his right. But the latter was in such a paroxysm of tears that nothing he said was intelligible except for "crunch, right in two!" which he kept repeating. After he had cried himself out, Korovyov finally unglued himself from the wall and said, "No, I can't take it anymore! I'm going to take 300 drops of valerian!..." and turning his utterly tear-drenched face to Poplavsky, he added, "Those damned streetcars!"

"Pardon me, but was it you who sent me the telegram?" asked Maximilian Andreyevich, agonizing over who this amazing crybaby could be.

"He did!" answered Korovyov, pointing to the cat.

Poplavsky, his eyes bulging, thought he had misheard.

"No, I can't go on, I haven't the strength," Korovyov went on, sniffling. "When I think of the wheel going over his leg... one wheel alone weighs about 360 pounds... Crunch! I'll go lie down and lose myself in sleep," at which point he vanished from the hallway.

The cat stirred, jumped down from the chair, stood on its hind legs, spread its forepaws, opened its jaws and said, "Well, I sent the telegram. Now what?"

Maximilian Andreyevich's head started spinning, his arms and legs became paralyzed, he dropped his suitcase and sat down on a chair opposite the cat.

"I believe I asked you in Russian," the cat said sternly. "Now what?"

But Poplavsky gave no reply.

"Passport!" snapped the cat and stretched out a chubby paw.

Completely at a loss and unable to see anything but the sparks burning in the cat's eyes, Poplavsky pulled his passport out of his pocket as if it were a dagger. The cat removed a pair of black thick-rimmed glasses from the table under the mirror, put them on his snout, which made it look even more impressive, and took the passport from Poplavsky's trembling hand.

"I wonder: will I faint or not?" thought Poplavsky. Korovyov's sobbing could be heard in the distance, and the smells of ether, valerian, and some other nauseating abomination filled the entire hallway.

"Which department issued this document?" asked the cat, staring at it intently. No answer was forthcoming.

"Department 412," replied the cat himself, tracing his paw over the passport, which he held upside down. "But, of course! I know that department very well! They give passports to anyone who walks in! But I, on the other hand, wouldn't give a passport to someone like you! Not on your life! One look at you and I'd refuse on the spot!" At this point the cat became so enraged that he threw the passport on the floor. "Permission to attend the funeral is hereby revoked," the cat continued in an official-sounding voice. "Be so kind as to return to your place of residence." He then bellowed through the door, "Azazello!"

In answer to his call a short little man ran out into the hallway—he walked with a limp, wore black tights, had a knife stuck inside his leather belt, was red-haired, had a yellow fang, and a cataract clouding his left eye.

Poplavsky felt he was suffocating, got up from his chair and staggered backwards, his hand clutching his heart.

"Azazello, show him out!" ordered the cat and walked out.

"Poplavsky," the recent arrival said softly, with a nasal twang, "I hope by now everything is completely clear?"

Poplavsky nodded.

"Return to Kiev immediately," Azazello continued. "Stay quiet as a mouse and stop dreaming about apartments in Moscow, is that clear?"

This short little man, who scared Poplavsky to death with his fang, his knife, and his cataract, only came up to the economist's shoulders, but his actions were smooth, efficient, and forceful.

First he picked up the passport and handed it to Maximilian Andreyevich, and the latter took it with a lifeless hand. Then the one called Azazello picked up the suitcase with one hand, and threw open the door with the other. Taking Berlioz's uncle by the arm, he escorted him out to the landing. Poplavsky leaned against the wall. Azazello opened the suitcase without benefit of a key, took out a huge roast chicken with only one drumstick, wrapped in greasy newspaper, and put it down on the top of the stairs. Then he pulled out two pair of underwear, a razor strop, a book, and a case and kicked everything except the chicken down the stairs. The empty suitcase was also sent flying. Judging by the sound it made when it crashed below, its top had come off.

Next the red-haired thug grabbed the chicken by its leg and slammed it so roughly and savagely across Poplavsky's neck that the carcass flew apart, leaving Azazello with only the drumstick in his hand. "Everything was in a state of confusion in the Oblonsky household," as the famous writer Lev Tolstoy so justly put it. He would have said the same thing here, too. Indeed! Everything in Poplavsky's vision became jumbled. A long spark flashed before his eyes which then converted into a black serpent, which for an instant blotted out the May sun. Poplavsky then went flying down the stairs, passport in hand. When he reached the turn on the stairs, he smashed in the windowpane with his foot and sat down on the step. The legless chicken tumbled past him and fell into the stairwell. Azazello, still at the top of the stairs, devoured the drumstick in a flash and stuck the bone in the side pocket of his tights, after which he went back to the apartment and shut the door with a bang.

It was then that the cautious footsteps of someone coming up the stairs were heard.

After running down another flight, Poplavsky sat down on a small wooden bench on the landing to catch his breath.

A diminutive elderly gentleman with an unusually sad face, wearing an old-fashioned tussore-silk suit and a stiff straw hat with a green band, was coming up the stairs. He stopped near Poplavsky.

"May I ask you, citizen," the man in tussore-silk inquired sadly, "where is apartment No. 50?"

"Upstairs," was Poplavsky's abrupt reply.

"My humble thanks, sir," the man replied, equally as sadly, and proceeded up the stairs, while Poplavsky got up from the bench and ran downstairs.

The question arises: did Maximilian Andreyevich rush off to the police station to lodge a complaint against the thugs who had brutalized him so savagely in broad daylight? Emphatically no, not at all, that can be said with confidence. To go to the police and say that a cat wearing glasses had just examined your passport, and that a man in tights, with a knife had... No citizens, Maximilian Andreyevich was far too smart for that!

When he got to the bottom of the stairs, he saw a door off the exit leading to a closetlike room. The window on the door had been knocked out. Poplavsky put his passport away in his pocket and looked around, hoping to spot his scattered belongings. But there was no trace of them. Poplavsky himself was surprised at how little that upset him. There was something else on his mind, an intriguing and tempting thought: to use the little man to test the apartment again. He had asked where it was, which meant it was his first visit. This, in turn, meant that he would fall into the clutches of the gang who had taken over apartment No. 50. Something told Poplavsky that the little man would be exiting the apartment momentarily. Naturally Maximilian Andreyevich no longer had any plans to attend his nephew's funeral, but there was still time before his train departed for Kiev. The economist looked around and slipped into the closet.

At this moment a door banged far upstairs. "That's him going in..." thought Poplavsky, his heart sinking. It was cool in the closet, and it smelled of mice and boots. Maximilian Andreyevich sat down on some kind of wood stump and decided to wait. From the closet he had a good view of the door of main entrance No. 6.

The Kievan had to wait longer than he expected, however. For some reason the staircase remained deserted. He could hear well, and finally a door banged on the fifth floor. Poplavsky froze. Yes, those were his footsteps. "He's coming down." A door opened on the floor below. The footsteps halted. A woman's voice. A sad voice in reply... yes, it was his voice... It said something like, "Leave me alone, for Christ's sake..."

Poplavsky's ear was pressed close to the broken window. It caught the sound of a woman laughing. Brisk and determined steps came down the stairs; then a woman's back flashed by. The woman was carrying a green oilcloth bag and she went out the entrance into the courtyard. The footsteps of the little man started up again. "That's strange! He's going back up to the apartment! Could he himself be one of the gang? Yes, he's going back. That's the door opening again upstairs. Oh well, we'll wait a little longer."

This time he did not have long to wait. The sounds of a door. Steps. Steps halting. A desperate cry. The meowing of a cat. Quick rapid footsteps coming down, down, down!

Poplavsky got what he had waited for. The sad little man flew by, crossing himself and muttering something. He was hatless, looked crazed, his bald head was scratched, and his trousers were soaking wet. He began pulling at the doorknob, so traumatized that he could not tell whether the door opened in or out. He finally managed to get it right and flew out into the sunshine of the courtyard.

His test of the apartment concluded, Poplavsky lost all interest in both his deceased nephew and the apartment. Trembling at the thought of the danger to which he had subjected himself, Maximilian Andreyevich ran out into the courtyard, mumbling just three words, "It's all clear! It's all clear!" Minutes later a trolley was carrying the economic planner in the direction of Kiev Station.

While the economist was sitting downstairs in the closetlike room, the little old man was having a most unpleasant experience upstairs. He was the bartender at the Variety Theater, and his name was Andrei Fokich Sokov. While the investigation was in progress at the theater, Andrei Fokich had kept apart from the proceedings, and the only thing noticeable about him was that he seemed sadder than usual, and, in addition, that he had tried to find out from Karpov, the messenger, where the visiting magician was staying.

And so, after leaving the economist on the landing, the bartender had gone up to the fifth floor and rung the bell of apartment No. 50.

The door was opened immediately, but the bartender shuddered, stumbled back, and did not go in immediately. An understandable reaction: the door had been opened by a girl wearing nothing but a white maid's cap and a coquettish lace apron. She did, however, have gold slippers on her feet. The girl's figure was superb, and the only thing wrong with her otherwise flawless exterior was the purplish scar on her neck.

"Well, come in, since you rang!" said the girl, fixing her lecherous green eyes on the bartender.

Andrei Fokich gulped, blinked, and took off his hat as he stepped into the entrance hall. Just then the telephone in the entrance hall started to ring. The shameless maid put one leg up on a chair, picked up the receiver and said, "Hello!"

Not knowing where to put his eyes, the bartender shifted from one foot to the other and thought, "That's some maid the foreigner's got! Phew! What filth!" And to save himself from such filth, he looked off to the side.

The entire large, semidark entrance hall was crammed with unusual objects and articles of clothing. A funereal cape with a fiery-red lining was slung over the back of a chair, and on the table under the mirror there was a long sword with a shiny gold hilt. Standing in the corner as nonchalantly as canes or umbrellas, were three swords with silver hilts. And hanging on deer antlers were berets with eagle feathers.

"Yes," the maid was saying into the phone, "Who is it? Baron Maigel? Hullo. Yes! The artiste is at home today. Yes, he'll be happy to see you. Yes, there'll be guests... Tails or a black dinner jacket. What? Before midnight." After finishing her conversation, the maid put back the receiver and turned to the bartender, "What can I do for you?"

"I have to see the citizen artiste."

"Is that so? In person?"

"Yes," answered the bartender sadly.

"I'll ask," said the maid, evidently hesitating, and barely opening the door into the late Berlioz's study, she announced, "Sir, there's a little man out here who says he needs to see Messire."

"Show him in," came Korovyov's cracked voice from the study.

"Go into the parlor," the girl said simply, as if she were dressed like a normal person, and she opened the door to the parlor and left the entrance hall.

When he entered the room he had been invited into, the bartender was so struck by the furnishings that he forgot why he had come. Streaming through the large stained-glass windows (the whim of the jeweller's wife who had vanished without a trace) was an extraordinary light, similar to the light in a church. Wood was burning in the huge old-fashioned fireplace despite the hot spring day. Yet it was not the least bit hot in the room; in fact, quite the opposite. A cellarlike dampness enveloped the man entering the room. Sitting on a tiger skin in front of the fireplace was a huge black cat, squinting contentedly at the fire. There was a table that made the God-fearing bartender shudder when he saw it: the table was covered with a brocaded altar cloth. On the altar cloth numerous bottles were arranged—potbellied, dusty, and moldy. Amidst the bottles a plate gleamed, and it was immediately obvious that the plate was made of pure gold. By the fireplace a short red-headed man with a knife in his belt was roasting pieces of meat skewered on a long steel sword, and the juice from the meat dripped in the fire, and the smoke went up the chimney. It smelled not only of roast meat, but of very strong perfume and incense, which made the bartender, who had learned of Berlioz's death and his place of residence from the newspapers, wonder if they weren't performing some kind of requiem mass for him. However, that notion was so preposterous that he dismissed it out of hand.

The stunned bartender suddenly heard a deep bass say, "Well, sir, how can I help you?"

There in the shadows was the one whom the bartender needed to see.

The black magician lay sprawled on an immense couch that was low to the floor and strewn with pillows. It seemed to the bartender that the artiste was wearing nothing but black underwear and black pointed slippers.

"I," the bartender began bitterly, "am the chief bartender and buffet manager of the Variety Theater..."

The artiste stretched out a hand sparkling with precious stones, as if to seal the bartender's lips, and began speaking heatedly, "No, no, no! Not another word! Not in any circumstances, never! I wouldn't put a thing from that buffet of yours into my mouth! I, most venerable sir, passed your counter yesterday, and I still can't forget the sturgeon and the brynza cheese. My good man! Brynza isn't supposed to be green, someone must have deceived you. It's supposed to be white. And that tea? It's dishwater! With my own eyes I saw some sloppy girl pour unboiled water out of a pail into your huge samovar, yet they continued pouring tea from it anyway. No, my dear fellow, that's not the way to do things."

"Excuse me," began Andrei Fokich, stunned by this sudden attack, "but I didn't come about that, the sturgeon's not the issue."

"How can it not be the issue if it's spoiled?"

"They sent us sturgeon that's second-grade fresh," said the bartender.

"Dear fellow, that's absurd!"

"What's absurd?"

"Second-grade fresh—that's absurd! Freshness comes in only one grade—first-grade, and that's it. And if the sturgeon's second-grade fresh, that means it's rotten!"

"Excuse me," the bartender said once again, not knowing how to escape the artiste's tongue lashing.

"I cannot excuse you," the latter said firmly.

"But I didn't come about that," said the bartender, now completely at a loss.

"You didn't?" the foreign magician asked in amazement. "What was it, then, that brought you here? If my memory doesn't deceive me, I've known only one other person in your line of work, and that was a lady sutler, but that was long before you were even born. However, I'm glad you've come. Azazello! A stool for the bar manager."

The one roasting the meat turned around, terrifying the bartender with his fangs, and deftly handed him one of the low, dark oak stools. There was nothing else in the room to sit on.

"Thank you very much," said the bartender, lowering himself onto the stool, the back leg of which then caved in with a crash. The bartender let out a groan and hit his rump painfully against the floor. As he fell, his leg upset another stool nearby, spilling a full glass of red wine all over his trousers.

The artiste exclaimed, "Oops! Did you hurt yourself?"

Azazello helped the bartender get up and offered him another seat. In a grief-stricken voice the bartender refused his host's suggestion that he remove his trousers and dry them in front of the fire. Feeling extremely uncomfortable in his wet underwear and clothes, he sat down gingerly on the other stool.

"I love sitting low to the ground," said the artiste, "because then falling off isn't so dangerous. Now then, we were talking about the sturgeon, were we not? My dear fellow! Freshness, freshness, and more freshness—that should be every buffet manager's motto. Yes, well, wouldn't you like to have a taste..."

Here, in the crimson glow of the fireplace a sword flashed in front of the bartender, and Azazello put a sizzling piece of meat on a gold platter. He sprinkled it with lemon juice and handed the bartender a two-pronged gold fork.

"Thank you very much... but I..."

"No, no, try it!"

Out of politeness the bartender put a piece in his mouth and realized immediately that he was eating something that was truly very fresh and, what's more, unusually tasty. But even so, as the bartender chewed the fragrant, succulent meat, he almost choked and fell a second time. A large dark bird flew in from the adjoining room, softly brushing its wing against the bartender's bald head. Alighting on the mantelpiece, next to the clock, it turned out to be an owl. "Oh, my God!" thought Andrei Fokich, who, like all bartenders, was nervous and edgy. "This is some apartment!"

"A glass of wine? White? Red? Which imported wine do you prefer at this hour?"

"Thank you... but I don't drink..."

"How unfortunate! How about a game of dice? Or do you like some other games? Dominoes? Cards?"

"I don't play," replied the already weary bartender.

"That's the limit," concluded the host. "There is, if you don't mind my saying so, something sinister about men who avoid wine, games, the company of charming women, and good dinner-table conversation. People like that are either seriously ill or they secretly disdain their fellow men. True, there are exceptions. Among those who have feasted with me there have sometimes been extraordinary cads! And so, tell me what brings you here."

"Yesterday you had occasion to perform some tricks..."

"I?" the magician exclaimed in amazement. "I beg your pardon. That isn't my sort of thing!"

"Sorry," said the bartender, taken aback. "But what about the performance of black magic..."

"Oh that, well, of course! My dear man! I'll tell you a secret: I'm not a stage performer at all. I just wanted to see the citizens of Moscow en masse, and the easiest way to do it was in a theater. So my retinue here," he nodded at the cat, "arranged the performance, while I merely sat and watched the Muscovites. But don't look like that. Just tell me what it was about the performance that brought you here."

"If you recall, among other things, paper money flew down from the ceiling..." the bartender lowered his voice and looked around in embarrassment. "Well, everybody started grabbing the bills. And a young man comes up to me at the bar and gives me a ten-ruble bill, and I give him eight-fifty in change... Then someone else..."

"Also a young man?"

"No, an older man. Then a third came, a fourth... I give them all change. And today when I went to check the cash register, I look and what do I see but strips of paper instead of money. The bar was a hundred and nine rubles short."

"Dear oh dear!" exclaimed the artiste. "Can they truly have thought it was real money? I can't believe they did it on purpose."

The bartender looked around wryly and miserably, but said nothing.

"Can they really have been swindlers?" the magician asked his guest anxiously. "Can there really be swindlers in Moscow?"

The bartender smiled so bitterly in reply that no doubts remained: there were indeed swindlers in Moscow!

"That's beneath contempt!" said Woland in outrage. "You're a poor man... you are a poor man—aren't you?"

The bartender drew his head into his shoulders, so that it would become obvious that he was a poor man.

"How much do you have in savings?"

Although the question was asked sympathetically, it was impossible not to view a question like that as indelicate. The bartender squirmed.

"Two hundred and forty-nine thousand rubles in five separate savings accounts," came a cracked voice from the next room. "And two hundred ten-ruble gold pieces under the floor at home."

The bartender seemed to be riveted to his stool.

"Well, that isn't so large a sum, of course," said Woland indulgently to his guest. "Although, strictly speaking, it is of no use to you. When will you die?"

Here the bartender became indignant.

"Nobody knows that and it's nobody's business," he replied.

"True, nobody knows," came the same noxious voice from the study, "but it's hardly Newton's binomial theorem! He'll die in nine months, that is, next February, from cancer of the liver, in the First Moscow State University Clinic, Ward No. 4."

The bartender's face turned yellow.

"Nine months," Woland calculated thoughtfully. "249,000... In round numbers that comes out to 27,000 a month, isn't that right? Not a lot, but enough if one lives modestly... And there's still the gold rubles..."

"He won't manage to cash those in," broke in the same voice, sending a chill through the bartender's heart. "After Andrei Fokich dies, they'll tear down the house right away and the gold rubles will be sent to the State Bank."

"And I wouldn't advise you to go to the clinic either," the artiste continued. "What point is there in dying in a ward, listening to the moans and rasps of the terminally ill? Wouldn't it be better to spend the twenty-seven thousand on a banquet, then, after taking poison, depart for the other world to the sound of violins, surrounded by intoxicated beautiful women and dashing friends?"

The bartender sat motionless, and seemed to have gotten much older. His eyes had dark circles around them, his cheeks drooped, and his lower jaw sagged.

"But we've gotten off the track," exclaimed the host. "Back to business. Show me your strips of paper."

Shaken, the bartender pulled a package out of his pocket, untied it and froze. Wrapped in the newspaper were ten-ruble bills.

"My dear fellow, you really are ill," said Woland, shrugging his shoulders.

The bartender got up from the stool, a strange smile on his face.

"But," he said, stuttering, "but what if they try to... again..."

"Hmm..." the artiste grew pensive. "Well, then, come back and see us again. By all means! Happy to have made your acquaintance."

Here Korovyov popped out of the study, grabbed the bartender's hand and started shaking it, begging Andrei Fokich to give everyone, everyone his regards. Completely befuddled, the bartender headed for the entrance hall.

"Hella, show him out!" shouted Korovyov.

Again the naked redhead appeared in the hall! The bartender squeezed through the door, squeaked out a "good-bye," and staggered on his way like a drunk. After going down a few steps, he stopped and sat down on the stairs. He pulled out the package to check the contents: the ten-ruble bills were still there. At that point a woman with a green bag came out of the apartment facing the landing. Seeing a man sitting on the step, staring dully at ten-ruble bills, she smiled and said pensively, "What a building we have... Only morning and this guy's already drunk. The window on the stairs is smashed again!" She studied the bartender more carefully and added, "Hey citizen, you're up to your ears in ten-ruble bills. How about throwing some my way! Huh?"

"Leave me alone, for Christ's sake," said the bartender fearfully and quickly hid the money. The woman laughed, "Go to hell, you old skinflint! I was just joking..." and she started down the stairs.

The bartender got up slowly, raised his hand to adjust his hat, and found that it wasn't on his head. The thought of going back was horrible, but he regretted the loss of his hat. He hesitated for a moment, but then went back and rang the bell.

"What do you want now?" asked the hellish Hella.

"I forgot my hat," whispered the bartender, poking at his bald head. Hella turned away, the bartender mentally spat and closed his eyes. When he opened them, Hella was handing him his hat and a sword with a dark hilt.

"That's not mine," whispered the bartender, pushing the sword aside and quickly putting on his hat.

"Did you really come without a sword?" marveled Hella.

The bartender mumbled something and started swiftly down the stairs. For some reason his head felt hot and uncomfortable in the hat; he took it off and jumping with fright, let out a soft yelp. In his hands was a velvet beret with a rumpled cock's feather. The bartender crossed himself. At that very moment the beret meowed and turned into a black kitten, which then leapt back onto Andrei Fokich's head and dug its claws into his bald spot. Letting out a desperate scream, the bartender plunged down the stairs, and the kitten fell off his head and scooted back up the stairs.

Bursting out into the open air, the bartender ran over to the gates at a trot and left devils' den No. 302B forever.

What happened to him next is well known. After bursting through the gateway, the bartender looked around wildly, as if searching for something. A minute later he was in a drugstore across the street. Just as he uttered the words, "Tell me, please..." the woman behind the counter yelled out, "Citizen! Your head is all cut up!"

Five minutes later the bartender, wearing a gauze bandage, found out that the leading specialists in liver disease were considered to be Professors Bernadsky and Kuzmin. When he asked which one was closer, he lit up with joy when he learned that Kuzmin lived literally across the yard in a little white house. Two minutes later he was there.

The house was old, but very comfortable, very cozy. Thinking about it later, the bartender recalled that the first person to greet him was an elderly nurse, who wanted to take his hat, but since he did not have one, she shuffled off somewhere, chewing on her toothless gums.

Next came a middle-aged woman, who materialized next to a mirror and under what appeared to be an archway. She told him that the earliest appointment she could give him was the nineteenth, no sooner. The bartender realized immediately how he could get around that. After glancing with a fading eye through the archway, where three men were sitting in what was manifestly a waiting room, he whispered, "I'm terminally ill..."

The woman looked perplexedly at his bandaged head, hesitated, and said, "Well, then..." and let the bartender pass through the arch.

At that moment the door across the way opened, a gold pince-nez sparkled, and a woman in a white coat said, "Citizens, this patient has priority."

Before he could turn his head, the bartender found himself in Doctor Kuzmin's office. The room was rather long, and there was nothing frightening, medical, or solemn about it.

"What seems to be the problem?" inquired Doctor Kuzmin in a pleasant voice, looking a bit apprehensively at the bandaged head.

"I've just learned from a reliable source," the bartender replied, staring wildly at a framed group photograph, "that I'm going to die of cancer of the liver next February. Please stop that from happening."

Professor Kuzmin arched himself against the high back of his Gothic leather chair.

"Excuse me, but I don't understand... you mean you've been to a doctor? Why is your head bandaged?"

"What doctor? You should have seen this doctor!" replied the bartender and suddenly his teeth began to chatter. "Don't bother about my head, it has nothing to do with this. The hell with my head, it's beside the point. It's the liver cancer I want you to stop."

"But who was it who told you?"

"You better believe him!" the bartender implored impassionedly. "Because he knows!"

"I don't understand any of this," said the doctor, shrugging his shoulders and moving his chair back from the desk. "How can he know when you're going to die? Especially when he's not even a doctor!"

"In Ward No. 4," the bartender replied.

The doctor then stared at his patient, at his head, at his damp trousers, and thought, "That's all I need! A madman!" He asked, "Do you drink vodka?"

"Never touch the stuff," the bartender replied.

A minute later he was undressed, lying on a cold oilskin couch, and the doctor was kneading his stomach. Here it must be said, the bartender cheered up considerably. The doctor stated categorically that the bartender showed absolutely no signs, at least at the present time, of liver cancer. But that since... since he was afraid, and some charlatan had scared him to death, he should have all the necessary tests...

The doctor wrote out instructions for him, explaining where he was to go and what he was to bring. In addition, he gave him a referral slip for a neuropathologist, Doctor Burye, saying that his nerves were completely shot.

"How much do I owe you, Doctor?" the bartender asked in a soft, trembling voice as he pulled out a thick wallet.

"Whatever you wish," the doctor replied dryly and brusquely.

The bartender took out thirty rubles and put them on the desk, and then, with unexpected softness, as if with a cat's paw, he placed a jingling stack of gold coins, wrapped in newspaper, on top of them.

"And what is that?" asked Kuzmin, twirling his mustache.

"Don't turn your nose up at it, Doctor," the bartender whispered. "I beg you—stop the cancer."

"Take back your gold," said the professor, feeling proud of himself. "You'd do better to look after your nerves. Bring in a urine sample tomorrow, don't drink a lot of tea, and don't use any salt on your food."

"Not even in my soup?" asked the bartender.

"Don't put salt on anything," ordered Kuzmin.

"Oh!" the bartender exclaimed dejectedly, looking entreatingly at the doctor as he gathered up his coins and backed away toward the door.

The doctor had only a few patients that evening, and by dusk the last one had left. As he was taking off his robe, he glanced at the place where the bartender had left the three ten-ruble notes, and instead of rubles, he saw three Abrau-Dyurso champagne labels.

"Well, I'll be damned!" muttered Kuzmin, trailing his robe over the floor and fingering the pieces of paper. "Not only was he a schizophrenic, he was a swindler too! But I still can't understand what he wanted from me? All that for a urine analysis? Oh! I bet he stole my coat!" And the doctor rushed into the entrance hall, dragging his robe by one sleeve. "Ksenya Nikitishna!" he shouted shrilly in the doorway, "Check and see, are the coats still there?"

As it turned out, they all were. But when the doctor returned to his office and finally took off his robe, he stood rooted to the parquet floor, his eyes trained on the desk. There where the labels had been sat a stray black kitten, looking very forlorn and meowing over a saucer of milk.

"What is this, pray tell?! This is really too..." Kuzmin felt a chill at the back of his neck.

Ksenya Nikitishna rushed in when she heard the doctor's whimpering cry and calmed him down completely by telling him that one of the patients had obviously left the kitten there, and that such things often happen to doctors.

"They're probably poor," explained Ksenya Nikitishna, "whereas we, of course..."

They tried to figure out who had left the kitten surreptitiously. Suspicion fell on an old woman with stomach ulcers.

"Of course, she's the one," said Ksenya Nikitishna. "She probably thought: I don't care if I live or die, but I feel sorry for the poor kitten."

"But really!" cried Kuzmin. "And what about the milk?! Did she bring that too? And the saucer as well?"

"She brought it in a bottle and poured it into a saucer here," volunteered Ksenya Nikitishna.

"No matter, take the kitten and the saucer away," said Kuzmin, escorting Ksenya Nikitishna to the door. When he went back, the situation had changed.

As he was hanging up his robe, the doctor heard laughter in the courtyard. He looked out and was naturally struck dumb. A woman wearing only a chemise was running across the yard to the building opposite. The doctor even knew who it was: Marya Alexandrovna. A boy was giggling.

"What's going on?" said Kuzmin contemptuously.

Just then, on the other side of the wall in his daughter's room, the foxtrot "Hallelujah" started playing on the phonograph, and at the same moment a sparrow started chirping behind Kuzmin's back. He turned around and saw a huge sparrow hopping on top of his desk.

"Hmm... just keep calm...," the doctor said to himself. "It must have flown in when I had my back to the window. Everything's OK!" the doctor told himself, feeling in his heart that everything was not OK, and mainly, of course, because of the sparrow. When he looked at it more closely, the doctor realized immediately that it was not exactly an ordinary sparrow. The filthy bird was lame in its left foot and was behaving in an obviously affected way, dragging the foot in syncopated rhythm. In a word, the sparrow was doing a foxtrot to the music playing on the phonograph, like a drunk at a bar. The bird acted as rudely as it knew how, staring insolently at the doctor.

Kuzmin reached for the phone, thinking that he would call his old classmate and colleague Burye, to ask him what it meant when you started seeing sparrows like that at age sixty, and when your head was spinning to boot.

Meanwhile the sparrow landed on the inkstand, which had been given to the doctor as a gift, befouled it (I'm not kidding!), flew up in the air, hovered briefly, and then with a steely beak pecked furiously at the glass on the graduation photo of the class of 1894, shattering it to bits. After that, it flew out the window.

Instead of calling Burye, the professor decided to call the Bureau of Leeches, saying that he, Doctor Kuzmin, wanted them to send him over some leeches right away.

After putting down the receiver, the doctor turned back to his desk, and immediately let out a wail. Sitting at his desk, wearing a nurse's kerchief, was a woman with a bag that said "Leeches." The doctor screamed when he saw her mouth. It was a man's mouth, crooked, open to the ears, with one fang sticking out. The nurse's eyes were dead.

"I'll take the money," said the nurse in a man's bass voice. "No point in it lying around here." She raked up the champagne labels with a bird's claw and melted into thin air.

Two hours went by. Doctor Kuzmin was sitting in bed in his room, with leeches stuck to his temples, his neck, and behind his ears. On the silk quilt at his feet sat the gray-whiskered Doctor Burye, looking at him with sympathy and trying to reassure him that it was all nonsense. Outside the window, it was already night.

We have no idea whether there were any other strange occurrences in Moscow that night, and we have no intention of trying to find out, since the time has come for us to proceed to Part Two of this true narrative. Follow me, reader!

Part Two

XIX

Margarita

FOLLOW me, reader! Who ever told you there is no such thing in the world as real, true, everlasting love? May the liar have his despicable tongue cut out!

Follow me, my reader, and only me, and I'll show you that kind of love!

No! The Master was mistaken that night in the hospital when, just after midnight, he told Ivan bitterly that she had forgotten him. That could never be. Of course she hadn't forgotten him.

First, let me tell you the secret the Master didn't want to tell Ivan. His beloved's name was Margarita Nikolayevna. Everything the Master said about her to the poor poet was absolutely true. His description of his beloved was accurate. She was beautiful and intelligent. And one more thing: it can be said with assurance that many women would have given anything to trade places with Margarita Nikolayevna. The childless, thirty-year-old Margarita was married to an outstanding specialist who had made an extremely important discovery of national significance. Her husband was young, handsome, kind, honest, and adored his wife. Margarita Nikolayevna and her husband occupied the entire upper floor of a beautiful house in a garden on one of the small streets near the Arbat. An enchanting spot! Anyone who wishes to can take a look at the garden and see for himself. Let him ask me and I'll give him the address and show him the way—the house is still standing to this very day.

Margarita Nikolayevna had plenty of money. Margarita Nikolayevna could buy anything that took her fancy. Her husband's circle of friends included some interesting people. Margarita Nikolayevna never touched a primus stove. Margarita Nikolayevna was ignorant of the horrors of life in a communal apartment. In a word... was she happy? Not for a minute! She hadn't been happy since marrying at age nineteen and going to live in her husband's house. Gods, my gods! What did this woman want? What did this woman want, whose eyes always burned with an incomprehensible fire? This witch with a slight squint in one eye, who adorned herself with mimosa in springtime—what did she want? I do not know. I have no idea. Evidently, she spoke the truth when she said it was the Master she needed and not the Gothic-style house, the private garden, or the money. She loved him, she was telling the truth.

Even I, a truthful narrator, but a detached observer nonetheless, feel my heart contract when I think of what Margarita went through the next day when she came to the Master's house and found that he was no longer there. Fortunately, she had not as yet had a talk with her husband, who had not come home when he was supposed to. She did everything she could to find out what had happened to the Master and, of course, had no success whatsoever. She then went back to her house and resumed her former life.

But as soon as the dirty snow disappeared from the sidewalks and pavements, as soon as the damp, restless wind of spring tugged at the *fortochka,* Margarita Nikolayevna began to feel even more miserable than she had during the winter. She often cried in secret, long and bitter tears. She didn't know whether the man she loved was alive or dead. And as the despairing days passed, the thought came to her more and more, especially at twilight, that she was tied to a dead man.

She should either forget him or die herself. It was really impossible to go on with the life she was living. Impossible! Forget him, no matter what it cost—forget him! But he could not be forgotten, that was the trouble.

"Yes, yes, yes, I made the very same mistake!" Margarita would say as she sat by the stove and stared at the fire which had been lit in memory of the fire that burned when he was writing Pontius Pilate. "Why did I leave him that night? Why? I must have been crazy! I came back the next day, just as I said I would, but it was already too late. Yes, like poor Levi Matvei, I came back too late!"

All of this was absurd of course, since how would her staying with the Master that night have made things any different? Could she really have saved him? "Nonsense!" we would have exclaimed, but not in front of a woman who has been driven to despair.

Margarita Nikolayevna lived in this kind of torment throughout the winter and into the spring. On that same day when there was all the commotion caused by the black magician's appearance in Moscow, on Friday, when Berlioz's uncle was sent packing back to Kiev, when the bookkeeper was arrested, and when many other grotesque and baffling things took place, Margarita woke up around noontime in her bedroom, which had a bay window looking out on the tower of the house.

Upon awakening Margarita did not burst into tears as she often did, because she woke up with a premonition that on that day something was finally going to happen. Once she sensed this premonition she nurtured it, wanting it to take root in her soul, and fearing that it would leave her.

"I believe!" Margarita whispered solemnly, "I believe! Something's going to happen! It can't help but happen because why, in fact, have I been made to suffer for life? I admit that I've cheated and lied and lived a secret life hidden from everyone, but even that doesn't deserve such cruel punishment. Something is bound to happen because nothing lasts forever. And besides, the dream I had was prophetic, I swear it was."

This is what Margarita Nikolayevna whispered to herself as she gazed at the crimson shades suffused with sunlight, nervously got dressed, and combed her short curly hair before the triple mirror of her vanity table.

Margarita's dream that night had truly been unusual. The fact was that she had not dreamed about the Master during that whole agonizing winter. At night he would leave her, and it was only during the daytime that she suffered. But now she had dreamed about him.

Margarita had dreamed about an unfamiliar locale—a bleak and dismal place, under an overcast, early-spring sky. Beneath a cover of patchy clouds there was a flock of noiseless rooks. A rough bridge crossed a turbid, swollen stream. Dismal, scrubby, half-bare trees. A lone aspen, and beyond that, amidst trees and past a vegetable garden, was a log hut that could have been an outside kitchen, a bathhouse, or the devil knows what. The whole setting was so dead and dismal that it made you want to hang yourself on the aspen by the bridge. Not a breath of wind, not a cloud moving, not a living soul. A hellish place for a living being!

And then, imagine, the door of the log hut opened and there he was. Quite far away, but clearly visible. He looked tattered and you couldn't tell what he was wearing. His hair was disheveled, he was unshaven. His eyes looked pained and anxious. He was beckoning to her with his hand, calling to her. Choking in the dead air, Margarita started running to him over the furrowed ground, and then she woke up.

"The dream can mean only one of two things," Margarita Nikolayevna reflected. "If he's dead and was beckoning to me, that means he's come for me, and I shall die soon. That's very good, because my suffering will then end. Or, if he's alive, then the dream can only mean that he's reminding me of his existence! He wants to tell me that we'll see each other again. Yes, we'll see each other very soon."

Still excited, Margarita got dressed and tried to convince herself that, in essence, everything was turning out well, and that one had to know how to seize such opportunities and take advantage of them. Her husband had gone away on a business trip for three whole days. She had three whole days to herself, and nobody could stop her from thinking and day-dreaming about whatever she pleased. She had the whole apartment to herself, five rooms on the upper floor of a private house that would be the envy of thousands of Muscovites.

However, despite having the run of the house for three whole days, Margarita chose far from the best spot in that luxurious apartment. After drinking some tea, she went off to the dark, windowless room where the luggage was kept and where there were two large bureaus filled with various old odds and ends. She squatted down in front of the first bureau and opened the bottom drawer. From beneath a pile of silk scraps she took out the one possession she valued most in life: an old brown leather album which contained a photograph of the Master, a savings book with ten thousand deposited in his name, dried rose petals pressed in tissue paper, and part of a typewritten manuscript that was singed at the bottom.

Returning to her bedroom with these treasures, Margarita Nikolayevna set the picture against her triple mirror and sat in front of it for an hour or so, holding the fire-damaged manuscript on her knees, as she leafed through and reread what, after the fire, had neither a beginning nor an end, "...The darkness that had come in from the Mediterranean covered the city so detested by the procurator. The hanging bridges which connected the temple with the fearsome Antonia Tower had disappeared, and an abyss descended from the sky, covering the winged gods above the hippodrome, the Hasmonaean palace and its embrasures, the bazaars, the caravanseries, alleys, and pools... Yershalaim—the great city—vanished as if it had never existed..."

Margarita wanted to read more, but there was nothing more except the charred and tattered fringe.

Wiping away her tears, Margarita Nikolayevna put down the manuscript and leaned her elbows on the vanity table. She sat there in front of the mirror for a long time, not taking her eyes off the Master's picture. Then her tears dried. Margarita put all the things together neatly, and minutes later they were back in their hiding place beneath the silk rags, and the lock on the door to the dark room locked shut.

Margarita Nikolayevna was putting her coat on in the front hall, getting ready to go out for a walk. The beautiful Natasha, her maid, asked her what she wanted for dinner, and when she said she didn't care, for amusement, Natasha began a casual conversation with her mistress, and started relating God knows what, something about a magician at the theater yesterday who had performed astounding tricks, handing out free bottles of imported perfume and stockings, and then how, after the show, when everyone was out on the street, abracadabra—they were all naked! Margarita Nikolayevna collapsed on the chair beneath the hall mirror and burst out laughing.

"Natasha! Shame on you," said Margarita, "a girl like you who knows how to read; people in lines make up the devil knows what, and here you go repeating it!"

Natasha blushed a deep red and protested heatedly that nothing was made up, and that she herself had been in a food store on the Arbat today and had seen a woman come in wearing shoes, but when she went to pay the cashier, her shoes disappeared off her feet and she was left standing in her stockings. Her eyes popped, there was a hole in her heel! And the shoes were the magic ones she had gotten at the show.

"And she left just like that?"

"Just like that!" cried Natasha, blushing even deeper because she wasn't being believed. "And last night, Margarita Nikolayevna, the police picked up about a hundred people. Women who had been at the show were running down Tverskaya in nothing but their drawers."

"Well, naturally you got all this from Darya," said Margarita Nikolayevna. "I've known for a long time that she's a terrible liar."

The amusing conversation ended in a pleasant surprise for Natasha. Margarita Nikolayevna went into her bedroom and came out with a pair of stockings and a bottle of cologne. Saying that she wanted to do a trick too, she gave them to Natasha and asked only one thing in return: that she not run down Tverskaya in just her stockings, and that she not listen to Darya. Mistress and maid then kissed and parted.

Settling back against the soft, comfortable seat of the trolleybus, Margarita rode along the Arbat, thinking about her own affairs and eavesdropping on the hushed conversation of the two men sitting in front of her.

They were whispering some sort of gibberish to each other, turning around now and then, in fear of being overheard. The robust, beefy fellow with sharp piglike eyes, sitting by the window, was softly telling the little man next to him that they had had to cover the coffin with a black cloth...

"Impossible!" the little one whispered in astonishment. "That's preposterous... So what did Zheldybin do?"

Along with the steady drone of the bus, came words from the window, "Criminal investigation... scandal... complete bafflement!"

Margarita Nikolayevna managed to make some sense out of these disconnected bits of conversation. They were whispering about how the head of some corpse—whose, they didn't say—had been stolen out of its coffin that very morning! And that was why the man named Zheldybin was in such a state. The two men whispering also seemed to have some connection with the vandalized corpse.

"Will we have time to buy flowers?" worried the little one. "Didn't you say the cremation was at two?"

In the end Margarita Nikolayevna got fed up listening to the mysterious prattle about a stolen head, and she was glad when it was time for her to get off.

Minutes later Margarita Nikolayevna was sitting on one of the benches beneath the Kremlin wall, having positioned herself so that she had view of the Manège.

Margarita squinted in the bright sunlight, recalled her dream of the previous night, and recalled that exactly one year before, on the same day and at the same time, she had been sitting with him on this same bench. And her black bag was lying beside her on the bench, just as it had then. Although he wasn't with her now, Margarita Nikolayevna was talking to him in her thoughts: "If you've been exiled, why haven't you let me know? People do manage to let others know. Have you fallen out of love with me? No, somehow I can't believe that. That means you were exiled and died... Then I beg you, release me, give me the freedom to live and breathe." Margarita Nikolayevna answered for him: "You are free... Am I stopping you?" Then she protested, "What kind of an answer is that? No, make me forget you, then I'll be free."

People walked past Margarita Nikolayevna. A man gave the well-dressed woman a sidelong glance, attracted by her beauty and the fact that she was alone. He coughed and sat down at the end of the bench where Margarita Nikolayevna was sitting, and after gathering up his courage, said, "Decidedly beautiful weather today..."

But Margarita gave him such a glowering look that he got up and left.

"That's what I mean," said Margarita in her head to the man who possessed her. "Why, really, did I chase that man away? I'm bored, and there was nothing wrong with that Lovelace except, perhaps, for his stupid 'decidedly.' Why am I sitting here alone beneath the wall, like an owl? Why am I cut off from life?"

She became totally sad and depressed. But suddenly that morning's wave of expectation and excitement hit her in the chest. "Yes, something is going to happen!" The wave hit her again, and then she realized it was a wave of sound. The beating of drums and the blaring of trumpets, slightly off-key, could be heard with ever-increasing clarity through the din of the city.

Leading the procession that was passing the park railing was a mounted policeman, followed by three men on foot. Next came the musicians on a slow-moving truck. After that, a brand-new open hearse carrying a wreath-covered coffin and four people—three men and a woman—each of whom was standing on a corner of the platform.

Even from a distance Margarita could tell that the faces of those standing in the hearse accompanying the deceased on his last journey looked strangely perplexed. This was especially true of the woman standing in the left rear corner of the vehicle. Her plump cheeks seemed to be bursting with some kind of juicy secret, and there was an ambiguous sparkle in her puffy little eyes. It seemed as if she couldn't contain herself and was about to wink at the deceased and say, "Have you ever seen anything like it? A real mystery!" Similarly perplexed faces could be seen on the three hundred or so mourners walking slowly behind the hearse.

Margarita watched the procession as it passed, listening to the fading sounds of the mournful bass drum, beating out its ever-constant "boom, boom, boom." "What an odd funeral," she thought. "And how depressing that 'boom' is! Ah, really I'd sell my soul to the devil if I could only find out if he's still alive or not! Who, I wonder, are those amazed-looking people burying?"

"Mikhail Alexandrovich Berlioz," said a somewhat nasal masculine voice beside her, "the chairman of MASSOLIT."

Surprised, Margarita Nikolayevna turned and saw a man at the other end of the bench who must have sat down noiselessly when she was preoccupied with the procession and, presumably, had asked her last question out loud, without knowing it.

Meanwhile the procession had come to a halt, probably because of the traffic lights up ahead.

"Yes," the stranger continued, "their mood is amazing. They're taking someone to be buried and all they can think about is what happened to his head!"

"What head?" asked Margarita, peering at her unexpected neighbor, who turned out to be a short man with fiery red hair and a fang, who was wearing a starched shirt, a fine striped suit, patent-leather shoes, and a bowler hat. His tie was flashy. But the most astonishing thing of all was that sticking out of his breast pocket, where most men carry a handkerchief or a pen, there was a well-gnawed chicken bone.

"Well, you see," the redhead explained, "this morning at Griboyedov the dead man's head was removed from his coffin."

"But how can that be?" Margarita asked involuntarily, recalling the whispers she had overheard on the bus.

"The devil knows how!" the redhead replied casually. "But if you ask me, it might be worth asking Behemoth about that. A terribly clever theft it was too. Caused an unbelievable scandal! And what's more, no one knows who would need the head, or why!"

However preoccupied Margarita Nikolayevna was with her own concerns, she was nonetheless struck by the stranger's bizarre chatter.

"But wait a minute!" she blurted out. "Which Berlioz? Was it the one in today's paper who..."

"Precisely so, precisely so..."

"So, does that mean that the mourners are writers?" asked Margarita, suddenly baring her teeth.

"Yes, naturally!"

"And do you know who they are by sight?"

"Every last one," replied the redhead.

"Tell me," said Margarita, her voice becoming hollow. "Is the critic Latunsky among them by any chance?"

"How could he not be?" answered the redhead. "There he is over there, fourth row from the end."

"The blond one?" asked Margarita, squinting.

"Ash-blond... See, he's got his eyes raised up to heaven."

"The one who looks like a Catholic priest?"

"That's him!"

Studying Latunsky, Margarita asked no more questions.

"And you, I can see," said the redhead, smiling, "hate this Latunsky."

"I also hate a few others," answered Margarita through her teeth. "But it's not worth talking about."

By now the procession had moved on; a line of mostly empty cars stretched out behind the marchers.

"If you say so, Margarita Nikolayevna!"

Margarita was astounded, "Do you know me?"

In place of an answer, the redhead swept the bowler off his head and held it in his outstretched hand.

"Looks like a real thug!" thought Margarita, examining her sidewalk interlocutor.

"But I don't know you," said Margarita dryly.

"How could you know me? But I've been sent to see you regarding a certain small matter."

Margarita turned pale and recoiled.

"You should have said that right away," she began, "instead of spouting the devil knows what about a severed head! Have you come to arrest me?"

"Not at all," exclaimed the redhead. "What is this: as soon as you start talking they think you're going to arrest them! I simply have some business to discuss with you."

"I don't understand at all. What business?"

The redhead looked around and said mysteriously, "I've been sent to give you an invitation for this evening."

"Are you raving? An invitation from whom?"

"A certain distinguished foreigner," said the redhead, narrowing his eyes meaningfully.

Margarita got furious.

"A new breed has appeared: street pimps," she said, getting up to leave.

"That's the thanks I get for taking on assignments like this!" exclaimed the redhead, taking offense, and as Margarita turned to leave, he growled after her, "Fool!"

"Scoundrel!" she retorted, and as she turned, she heard the redhead's voice behind her, "'The darkness that had come in from the Mediterranean covered the city so detested by the procurator. The hanging bridges which connected the temple with the fearsome Antonia Tower had disappeared... Yershalaim—the great city—vanished as if it had never existed...' And you can vanish too, along with your charred manuscript and your dried rose! Sit here on the bench alone, and beg him to set you free so you can breathe and be allowed to forget him!"

Margarita's face blanched, and she turned back to the bench. The redhead looked at her with tightly narrowed eyes.

"I don't understand any of this," said Margarita Nikolayevna softly. "You could have found out about the burnt pages... broken into my house and spied on me... Did you pay off Natasha, is that it? But how could you know my thoughts?" She wrinkled her brow, looking agonized, and added, "Tell me, who are you? What department are you from?"

"What a bore this is," grumbled the redhead and said in a louder voice, "Excuse me, but I already told you I'm not from any department! Please, sit down."

Margarita obeyed without a fuss, but as she sat down, she asked again, "Who are you?"

"Well, if you must know, my name is Azazello, but that won't mean anything to you anyway."

"But won't you tell me how you knew about those pages and about my thoughts?"

"No, I won't," was Azazello's dry reply.

"But do you know anything about him?" whispered Margarita imploringly.

"Well, let's say I do."

"I beg you, just tell me one thing, is he alive? Don't torment me."

"Yes, he's alive, he's alive," Azazello replied unwillingly.

"My God!"

"Please, no fits and no screams," said Azazello with a frown.

"I'm sorry, forgive me," mumbled the now-compliant Margarita. "It's true, I got angry at you. You will admit, though, that when someone on the street invites a woman to go somewhere... I'm not prejudiced, I assure you," Margarita let out a mirthless laugh, "but I never see any foreigners, I have no desire to socialize with them... and besides, my husband... My tragedy is that I live with someone I don't love, but it would be ignoble of me to ruin his life. He's never shown me anything but kindness..."

Azazello listened to her disconnected speech with obvious boredom and said sternly, "Please be quiet for a minute."

Margarita fell into submissive silence.

"My invitation is from a foreigner who is perfectly safe. And not a soul will know about your visit. I can promise you that."

"But what does he need me for?" Margarita asked insinuatingly.

"You'll find that out later."

"I see... I'm supposed to sleep with him," said Margarita reflectively.

Azazello gave a haughty smirk and replied, "That would, I can assure you, be the answer to any woman's dream," a chuckle distorted Azazello's face, "but I must disappoint you, that won't happen."

"But who is this foreigner?!" Margarita cried out loudly in exasperation, causing passersby to turn their heads. "And why should I have any interest in seeing him?"

Azazello leaned over to her and whispered in a gravely significant way, "A great interest indeed... You'll have the opportunity to..."

"To do what?" exclaimed Margarita, her eyes widening. "Am I right, are you suggesting that I can get news of him there?"

Azazello nodded silently.

"Then I'll go!" Margarita exclaimed with vigor, seizing Azazello by the arm. "I'll go anywhere you want!"

Heaving a sigh of relief, Azazello leaned back against the bench, which had the name "Nyura" carved in large letters on it, and observed ironically, "A troublesome race, these women!" He buried his hands in his pockets and stretched his legs out in front of him. "Why did they send me on this job? Behemoth should have gone, he's the one with the charm..."

With a bitterly sad smile, Margarita said, "Stop trying to mystify and torment me with your riddles... I'm an unhappy person, and you're taking advantage of that. I may be getting involved in something strange, but if I am, I swear it's only because you lured me with your talk of him! My head is spinning from all these things I don't understand..."

"No scenes, no scenes," retorted Azazello with a grimace. "You should put yourself in my position. Smacking some bureaucrat in the puss, booting out some old geezer, shooting someone, or anything along those lines, that's my real specialty, but talking with a woman in love—no thanks. I've been trying to talk you into this for half an hour now. So will you go?"

"I'll go," was Margarita Nikolayevna's simple reply.

"Then be so kind as to take this," said Azazello, who pulled a round gold jar out of his pocket, and handed it to Margarita, saying, "Hide it, or people will see. It'll do you good, Margarita Nikolayevna, your grief has really aged you in the past six months." Margarita flared up but said nothing, and Azazello continued, "Tonight, at exactly nine-thirty, be so kind as to take off your clothes and spread this ointment over your face and your whole body. Then you can do as you like, but don't leave the phone. I'll call you at ten and tell you everything you need to know. You don't have to worry about anything, you'll be taken where you have to go, and you won't be caused any upset. Understood?"

After a short silence, Margarita replied, "Understood. This thing is pure gold, I can tell by the weight. Well, what of it, I know perfectly well that I'm being bribed and lured into some shady business, for which I'll have to pay a high price."

"What is this," said Azazello, practically hissing, "are you starting in again?"

"No, wait!"

"Give me back the cream!"

Margarita clutched the jar tighter and continued, "No, wait... I know what I'm getting myself in for. But I'll do anything for his sake, because there's no hope left for me in this world. But if you destroy me, you'll be sorry! Yes, you will! Because I'll be dying for love!"—and, pounding her chest, Margarita gazed at the sun.

"Give it back," Azazello yelled angrily. "Give it back, and to hell with everything! Let them send Behemoth!"

"Oh, no!" exclaimed Margarita, to the astonishment of passersby, "I agree to everything, I agree to play out this whole comedy with the cream, I agree to go to the devil and back! I won't give it back!"

"Bah!" Azazello howled suddenly. His eyes bulging, he began pointing at something over toward the park railing.

Margarita turned to where Azazello was pointing, but didn't notice anything in particular. Then she turned back to him, expecting an explanation for that absurd "Bah!"—but there was no one there to provide it: Margarita Nikolayevna's mysterious interlocutor had vanished.

Margarita quickly thrust her hand into her bag, where, prior to Azazello's howl, she had hidden the jar, and assured herself that it was still there. Then, without further reflection, she ran hurriedly out of Alexandrovsky Park.

XX

Azazello's Cream

THE full moon hung in the clear evening sky, visible through the branches of the maple tree. The lindens and acacias traced an intricate pattern of spots on the garden floor. The triple-casement bay window, wide open but with blinds drawn, shone with a harsh electric light. The lights in Margarita Nikolayevna's bedroom were all turned on, revealing a state of total chaos. Chemises, stockings, and underwear were lying on the blanket on top of the bed, and other undergarments were strewn on the floor, along with a pack of cigarettes that had gotten crushed in the excitement. There were slippers on the night table next to an unfinished cup of coffee and an ashtray that held a smoking cigarette butt. A black evening gown hung on the back of a chair. The room smelled of perfume. And from somewhere came the smell of a red-hot iron.

Margarita Nikolayevna was sitting before her mirror in a bathrobe, which had been thrown over her naked body, and black suede shoes. In front of her lay a gold watch and next to it the small jar she had received from Azazello. Margarita's eyes were glued to the watch. At times it seemed to her as if the watch were broken and the hands weren't moving. But they were moving, albeit very slowly, as if they kept getting stuck, and finally the big hand hit twenty-nine minutes after nine. Margarita's heart gave such a terrible thump that at first she couldn't even pick up the jar. When she pulled herself together and opened the jar, she saw that it contained a greasy, yellowish cream which seemed to smell of swamp mud. With the tip of her finger Margarita scooped up a small glob of the cream and put it in her palm, which made the swampy, woodland smell more noticeable. She then began rubbing the cream into her cheeks and forehead.

The cream spread easily and seemed to be absorbed immediately. After several applications of the cream, Margarita looked in the mirror, and dropped the jar on the face of her watch, cracking the crystal. She closed her eyes, took another look, and burst into wild laughter.

Her eyebrows, which had been plucked thread-thin at the ends, had thickened and now arched evenly over her eyes, which had become green. There was no longer any trace of the tiny vertical line on the bridge of her nose which had first appeared back in October when the Master disappeared. Gone, too, were the yellowish shadows around her temples and the barely noticeable crowsfeet at the outer corners of her eyes. Her cheeks were suffused with a rosy blush, her forehead had become clear and white, and her hair-salon permanent wave had loosened.

There in the mirror, staring back at thirty-year-old Margarita, was a twenty-year-old woman with naturally curly black hair, showing her teeth and laughing unrestrainedly.

Having laughed her fill, Margarita swept off her robe, scooped up a generous glob of the light, greasy cream, and began rubbing it vigorously all over her body, which immediately became rosy and began to glow. Then the throbbing in her temple, which had been bothering her all evening, ever since her meeting with Azazello in Alexandrovsky Park, disappeared in a flash, as if a needle had been removed from her brain. The muscles in her arms and legs got stronger, and then Margarita's body became weightless.

She gave a little jump and stayed suspended in the air, just above the carpet, then she felt a slow downward pull, and was back on the ground.

"Oh, what a cream! What a cream!" cried Margarita, throwing herself into an armchair.

The cream had transformed more than her appearance. Now her whole body, every part of it, surged with joy, and she felt as if tiny bubbles were prickling her all over. Margarita felt free, free of everything. In addition, she realized with utter clarity that her premonition of the morning had come true and she was leaving her house and her former life forever. But one thought from that former life still persisted, namely, that there was one last thing she had to do before embarking on the new and extraordinary something that was pulling her upwards, into the air. So, naked as she was, flying intermittently, she ran out of the bedroom into her husband's study, turned on the lights, and rushed to the desk. On a sheet of paper torn off a pad, she wrote in pencil, quickly and boldly and without any corrections, the following note:

> Forgive me and forget me as quickly as you can. I'm leaving you forever. Don't try to find me, it's useless. I've become a witch because of the grief and the misfortunes that have befallen me. It is time for me to go. Farewell.
>
> *Margarita*

Her soul relieved of every care, Margarita flew back into her bedroom, and Natasha ran in after her, loaded down with all sorts of things. And suddenly everything—a dress on a wooden hanger, lace shawls, dark-blue silk shoes on shoe trees, and a belt—fell to the floor, and Natasha clasped her now free hands.

"Well, do I look good?" cried Margarita loudly in a husky voice.

"How did it happen?" whispered Natasha, reeling backwards. "How did you do it, Margarita Nikolayevna?"

"It's the cream! The cream, the cream!" replied Margarita, pointing to the gleaming gold jar and doing a turn in front of the mirror.

Forgetting about the crumpled dress on the floor, Natasha ran over to the mirror and stared with voracious burning eyes at what was left of the cream. Her lips whispered something. She turned again to Margarita and said with a kind of reverence, "What skin! What skin! Why, Margarita Nikolayevna, your skin is glowing!" But then she remembered herself, ran over and picked up the dress, and began smoothing it out.

"Put it down! Put it down!" Margarita shouted at her. "The devil with it, throw everything out! Or, rather, keep it as a memento. To remember me by. You can take everything in the room."

Natasha stood for awhile, as if in a daze, staring at Margarita, then she fell on her neck, kissing her and shouting, "Like satin! It glows! Like satin! And your eyebrows, what eyebrows!"

"Take all this stuff, and the perfume, too, and put it in your trunk and hide it," shouted Margarita. "But don't take the jewelry, or they'll accuse you of stealing."

Natasha put whatever came to hand into a bundle, dresses, shoes, stockings, and underwear, and ran out of the bedroom.

Just then the sounds of a virtuoso waltz came blaring through an open window across the street, and a car was heard spluttering as it pulled up to the gates.

"Azazello will call any minute!" exclaimed Margarita, listening to the waltz streaming in from outside. "Yes, he will! And the foreigner is harmless. Yes, I can see that now, he's harmless!"

The car roared and pulled away from the gates. The gate banged and steps were heard coming down the path.

"That's Nikolai Ivanovich, I can tell by his footsteps," thought Margarita. "I'll have to do something interesting and amusing as a way of saying good-bye."

Margarita pulled the shade aside and sat sideways on the windowsill, her hands clasped on her knee. The moonlight caressed her right side. Margarita raised her head toward the moon and assumed a pensive and poetic expression. Footsteps were heard once or twice again and then they suddenly stopped. After admiring the moon a little longer, Margarita sighed for the sake of appearances, and turned to look down at the garden where she did, in fact, see Nikolai Ivanovich, who lived on the floor below her. Bathed in bright moonlight, he was sitting on a bench, and it was obvious that he had sat down suddenly. His pince-nez was askew, and he was clutching his briefcase to his chest.

"Well, hello, Nikolai Ivanovich," said Margarita in a sad voice. "Good evening! Have you come from a meeting?"

Nikolai Ivanovich made no reply.

"I, as you can see," Margarita continued, leaning further out into the garden, "have been sitting here alone, bored, looking at the moon, and listening to the waltz."

Margarita passed her left hand across her forehead, adjusting a stray curl, then said angrily, "That's not polite, Nikolai Ivanovich! I am a lady, after all! It's rude not to answer when someone is talking to you!"

Nikolai Ivanovich, visible in the moonlight down to the last button on his gray waistcoat, the last hair on his blond goatee, suddenly grinned a wild grin, got up from the bench, and obviously beside himself with embarrassment, did not remove his hat, as one would have expected, but, rather, waved his briefcase to the side and got into a crouching position, as if he were about to do a Russian dance.

"Oh, what a bore you are, Nikolai Ivanovich," continued Margarita. "I can't tell you how sick and tired I am of all of you, and how happy I am to be leaving you! To the devil's mother with all of you!"

Just then Margarita heard the phone ring in the bedroom behind her. She jumped off the windowsill and, forgetting about Nikolai Ivanovich, grabbed the receiver.

"It's Azazello," said the voice in her ear.

"Dear, dear Azazello!" exclaimed Margarita.

"It's time to fly away," said Azazello, and it was clear from his tone that he was pleased with Margarita's genuine display of joy. "When you fly over the gates, shout, 'I'm invisible!' Then fly around over the city for awhile, to get used to it, and after that, head south, away from the city, and go straight to the river. They're expecting you!"

Margarita hung up the phone, at which point something wooden-sounding started bumping around in the next room and began knocking at the door. Margarita opened the door, and in flew a dancing broom, brush-end up. It tapped a few beats on the floor with its handle, gave a kick, and strained toward the window. Margarita squealed with delight and jumped astride the broomstick. Only then did she remember that in all the confusion she had forgotten to get dressed. She galloped over to the bed and grabbed the first thing she saw, a light-blue chemise. Waving it like a banner, she flew out the window. And the sound of the waltz over the garden intensified.

Margarita slipped down from the window and saw Nikolai Ivanovich on the bench. He seemed to be frozen to it and was listening in a stupefied state to the banging and shouting coming from the lighted bedroom of his upstairs neighbors.

"Farewell, Nikolai Ivanovich!" cried Margarita, dancing about in front of him.

He groaned and began edging down the bench, feeling his way with his hands and knocking his briefcase to the ground.

"Good-bye forever! I'm flying away," shouted Margarita, drowning out the waltz. She then decided that she had no need of the chemise and with an ominous chuckle she threw it over Nikolai Ivanovich's head. Blinded, he tumbled off the bench onto the bricks of the path.

Margarita turned to take one last look at the house where she had suffered so long, and in the lighted window she saw Natasha gaping with astonishment.

"Farewell, Natasha!" Margarita shouted and urged her broom upward. "Invisible! I'm invisible!" she shouted even more loudly, and with the branches of the maple tree brushing against her face, she flew out over the gates and into the street. And the totally crazed waltz followed her aloft.

XXI

Flight

INVISIBLE and free! Invisible and free! After flying down her own street, Margarita came to another one which crossed it at a right angle. In an instant she cut across this long and crooked, patched and mended side street with its oil shop with the rickety door which sold kerosene by the jugful and pesticide in bottles, and it was here that she learned that however enjoyable her freedom and invisibility were, she still had to be somewhat careful. It was only by some miracle that she avoided a fatal collision with the rickety old lamppost down at the corner. After dodging it successfully, Margarita took a firmer hold of her broomstick and checked her speed, keeping a watchful eye out for electric wires and signs hanging over the sidewalk.

The third street on her route led directly to the Arbat. It was here that Margarita gained full mastery of her broom and realized how sensitive it was to the slightest touch of her hands or feet, and that she would have to be very careful flying over the city and not be too reckless. In addition, it was obvious to her, even before she got to the Arbat, that people on the street could not see her flying. Nobody craned his head, or shouted "look, look!" or jumped out of the way, or screamed or fainted or broke out in wild laughter.

Margarita flew along noiselessly, at very slow speed and not too high up, at about second-storey level. But even at slow speed, just as she was about to come out onto the blindingly lit Arbat, she made a slight miscalculation and hit her shoulder against an illuminated circular sign with an arrow painted on it. This made her angry. She reined in her obedient broom, flew over to the side, and then made a sudden charge at the sign, smashing it to smithereens with the end of her broom handle. Splinters crashed, pedestrians jumped out of the way, a whistle blew, and Margarita, the perpetrator of this gratuitous prank, burst out into gales of laughter. "I should be more careful on the Arbat," she thought. "Everything is so mixed up here that you get confused." She began diving between the various wires. The tops of cars, trolleybuses, and buses floated by beneath her, and rivers of hats flowed along the sidewalks, or so it seemed from up high. Streams branched off these rivers and flowed into the fiery maws of the stores open at night.

"What a mess this is!" thought Margarita in exasperation. "It's impossible to make a turn." She crossed the Arbat, flew higher, up to fourth-storey level, floated past the blinding lights of the theater marquee on the corner and into a narrow street with tall buildings. All their windows were wide open, and everywhere music could be heard playing on the radios. Out of curiosity Margarita peered into one of the windows. She saw a kitchen. Two primus stoves were roaring on top of the counter, and two women were standing next to it with spoons in their hands, squabbling.

"I told you to turn off the light when you come out of the toilet, Pelageya Petrovna," said the woman standing in front of a saucepan steaming with food, "or we'll have you evicted!"

"You're a fine one to talk," the other replied.

"You're two of a kind," said Margarita loudly and clearly, as she rolled over the windowsill into the kitchen. The two squabblers turned toward the voice and froze, dirty spoons in hand. Reaching carefully between them, Margarita twisted the knobs on both stoves and turned them off. The women groaned and gasped. But Margarita had already become bored in the kitchen and had flown out into the street.

At the end of the street her attention was drawn to the lavish hulk of a newly constructed eight-storey building. Margarita flew down and landed, and she saw that it had a black marble facade, wide doors, through whose glass one could see a doorman's gold-braided cap and the buttons on his uniform, and a sign in gold lettering over the entrance which said, "DRAMLIT HOUSE."

Margarita squinted her eyes at the sign, trying to figure out what "DRAMLIT" might mean. Tucking her broom under her arm, she walked into the entrance and opened the door, knocking against the astonished doorman in the process. On the wall next to the elevator she saw a huge, black board that listed the names and apartment numbers of all the residents written on it in white letters. When she took one look at what was written at the top of the list—"Writers' and Dramatists' House"—she let out a stifled, predatory howl. Raising herself higher in the air, she began reading the names voraciously: Khustov, Dvubratsky, Kvant, Beskudnikov, Latunsky...

"Latunsky!" screeched Margarita. "Latunsky! Why, that's him... He's the one who ruined the Master."

The doorman jumped in amazement and his eyes bulged as he stared at the black board and tried to comprehend the miracle of the directory of residents suddenly letting out a scream. Margarita had, in the meantime, made a beeline upstairs, and was repeating over and over in a kind of rapture, "Latunsky—84... Latunsky—84...

"Here's 82—on the left, 83—on the right, higher up, on the left—84. Here! And here's the namecard—'O. Latunsky.' "

Margarita jumped off her broom, and the stone landing felt pleasantly cool against the soles of her inflamed feet. She rang the bell once, twice. But no one came to the door. As Margarita pressed the bell even harder, she could hear it ringing inside Latunsky's apartment. Yes, the resident of apartment No. 84 on the eighth floor should be grateful to the deceased Berlioz for the rest of his days, grateful that the chairman of MASSOLIT had fallen under a streetcar, and grateful that a memorial meeting had been set up for that very evening. The critic Latunsky was born under a lucky star. It saved him from an encounter with Margarita, who had become a witch on that Friday.

No one answered the door. Then Margarita flew downwards at full speed, counting off the floors as she went, reached the bottom, tore out onto the street and, looking up, counted off the floors on the outside of the building, trying to figure out which were the windows of Latunsky's apartment. They had to be the five dark ones at the corner of the building on the eighth floor. Sure that that was the case, Margarita rose up in the air and a few seconds later she was entering an open window into a room that was dark except for a narrow, silver strip of moonlight. Margarita followed it and fumbled for the light switch. A minute later, the lights were on in the whole apartment. Her broom was standing in a corner. Making sure that no one was home, Margarita opened the front door and checked the nameplate. It was the right one, Margarita had arrived at her destination.

Yes, they say to this very day the critic Latunsky turns pale when he recalls that terrible evening, and that he still pronounces Berlioz's name with reverence. No one knows what dark and foul crime might have marked that evening—when Margarita returned from the kitchen, she had a heavy hammer in her hands.

The naked and invisible aeronaut tried to restrain and control herself, but her hands shook with impatience. Taking careful aim, Margarita struck the piano keys, and a first plaintive wail echoed throughout the apartment. The totally innocent Becker baby grand cried out in frenzy. Its keys were smashed, and the ivory inlays flew in all directions. The instrument droned, howled, wheezed, and clinked. The polished upper sounding board cracked like a pistol shot and broke under the hammer. Breathing hard, Margarita tore at the strings and pounded them with her hammer. Finally, exhausted, she backed off and plopped into an armchair to catch her breath.

A sound of rushing water came from the bathroom and also from the kitchen. "I guess it's already overflowed onto the floor," thought Margarita, and then added aloud, "But there's no point in sitting around here."

A stream of water was already pouring out of the kitchen into the hall. Tramping through the water in her bare feet, Margarita carried buckets of water from the kitchen to Latunsky's study and emptied them into the drawers of his desk. Then, after shattering the doors of the bookcase in the study with her hammer, Margarita descended upon the bedroom. After smashing the mirror on the wardrobe door, she pulled out one of the critic's suits, and submerged it in the bathtub. She poured an inkwell full of ink, taken from the study, onto the luxuriously fluffed-up double bed in Latunsky's bedroom. The destruction she was causing gave Margarita intense pleasure, but the whole time it seemed to her that the damage she was causing was too slight. Therefore, she began striking out at random. She broke the pots of ficus plants in the room where the piano was. Before finishing that, she went back to the bedroom, slashed the sheets with a kitchen knife, and broke the glass-covered photographs. She did not feel in the least bit tired, and the sweat poured off her in streams.

Meanwhile, in No. 82, the apartment right below Latunsky's, the playwright Kvant's maid was drinking tea in the kitchen, thoroughly baffled by the various crashing, clanging, and running sounds coming from up above. When she raised her head toward the ceiling, she suddenly saw that before her very eyes its white color was changing to a kind of deathly blue. As she was staring at it the stain kept getting bigger and bigger, and suddenly it was oozing drops of water. The maid sat transfixed for a minute or two, amazed at what was happening, until finally a veritable shower poured down from the ceiling and splashed onto the floor. At this point she jumped up, put a basin under the stream of water, which didn't help at all since the shower was spreading and had begun to pour down on the gas stove and the table with the dishes. Kvant's maid then shrieked and ran out of the apartment onto the stairs, just as the doorbell started ringing in Latunsky's apartment.

"Well, the ringing has started... It's time to get going," said Margarita. As she mounted her broom, she listened to a woman's voice shouting through the keyhole, "Open up, open up! Dusya, open the door! Isn't something overflowing in there? We're flooded down below."

Margarita rose a few feet in the air and took a swipe at the chandelier. Two bulbs broke, and glass splintered in every direction. The shouting outside the door had stopped, and tramping feet were heard on the stairs. Margarita floated through the window and once outside, swung her hammer and gave the glass a light blow. It sobbed, and shards of glass cascaded down the marble facade. Margarita moved on to the next window. Down below people were running along the sidewalk, and one of the two cars standing at the entrance to the building blew its horn and pulled away.

After finishing with Latunsky's windows, Margarita floated on to the neighboring apartment. The blows fell more frequently, and crashing and tinkling sounds filled the street. The doorman ran out the first entrance, looked up, hesitated for a minute, evidently not yet sure what to do, stuck his whistle in his mouth, and started blowing it like crazy. Accompanied by the whistle, Margarita finished off the last window on the eighth floor with particular relish, then descended to the seventh floor and began smashing the windows there.

Tired by his long period of idleness behind the glass doors of the entranceway, the doorman put his whole soul into blowing his whistle, following the beat of Margarita's hammer, as it were, as if he were playing an accompaniment. During the pauses, when Margarita was flying from one window to the next, he would take a breath, and with every blow of Margarita's hammer he puffed out his cheeks and blew for all he was worth, blasting the night to high heaven.

His efforts, combined with those of the infuriated Margarita, produced major results. The building went into a panic. Windows that were still intact were thrown open and heads appeared for just a second, windows that were already open were shut. In the lighted windows of the buildings across the street dark silhouettes appeared, trying to figure out why the windows of the new Dramlit House were breaking for no apparent reason.

Down on the street people were running toward Dramlit House, and inside it people were tramping up and down all the staircases without rhyme or reason. Kvant's maid kept yelling to the people on the stairs that Kvant's apartment was flooded, and she was soon joined by Khustov's maid from apartment No. 80, the one right below Kvant's. The Khustovs had water streaming from the ceiling both in the kitchen and in the toilet. Finally, a huge piece of plaster broke off the ceiling in Kvant's kitchen and smashed all the dirty dishes. A major downpour followed: bucketsfull of water gushed down from the seeping, sagging squares of sodden plaster. Then screaming began on the stairs of the first entrance. As Margarita was flying past the next-to-last window on the fourth floor, she looked inside and saw a man putting on a gas mask in a state of panic. She tapped his window with her hammer and gave him a fright, and he disappeared from the room.

And suddenly the wild devastation came to an end. Margarita slipped down to the third floor and looked in the corner window, which was covered with a flimsy dark blind. The room was lit by a faint night-light. Sitting in a small bed with netting on the sides was a little boy of about four who was listening fearfully to what was going on. There were no grown-ups in the room. They had apparently all fled from the apartment.

"Windows are breaking," said the boy, calling out, "Mama!"

No one responded, and then he said, "Mama, I'm scared."

Margarita pushed the blind aside and flew into the room.

"I'm scared," the boy repeated, and started to tremble.

"Now, now, don't be frightened, little one," said Margarita, trying to soften her criminal's voice, which had been made hoarse by the wind.

"It's just some boys breaking windows."

"With slingshots?" asked the boy, no longer trembling.

"Yes, yes, with slingshots," affirmed Margarita. "And now go back to sleep!"

"It must be Sitnik," said the boy, "He's got a slingshot."

"That's right, it's him!"

The boy glanced slyly sideways and queried, "But where are you, auntie?"

"I'm nowhere," Margarita replied, "You're having a dream."

"That's what I thought," said the boy.

"Just lie down," instructed Margarita, "and put your hand under your cheek, and you'll see me in your dream."

"Yes, yes," agreed the boy, and he lay down at once with his hand under his cheek.

"I'll tell you a fairy tale," said Margarita, and put her burning hand on top of the boy's close-cropped head. "Once upon a time there was a lady. She had no children, and no happiness either. And at first she cried for a long time, but then she became wicked..." Margarita fell silent, and took her hand away—the boy was sleeping.

Margarita lay the hammer down gently on the windowsill and flew out the window. There was a huge commotion outside the building. People were running up and down the glass-strewn sidewalk, shouting things. Policemen were already on the scene. Suddenly a bell started clanging, and a red fire engine with a ladder rolled into the street from the Arbat...

But what happened next no longer interested Margarita. Taking care not to get entangled in any wires, she grasped her broom more firmly and in a flash she was high above the ill-fated building. The street below slanted off to the side and receded into the depths. Taking its place beneath her feet was a whole tangle of rooftops, crisscrossed by gleaming paths of light. Suddenly the whole mass moved off to the side, and the chains of light blurred and blended.

Margarita gave the broom another upward prod, and the mass of rooftops fell away, replaced by a lake of quivering electric lights. Suddenly this lake rose up vertically, and then appeared above Margarita's head, while the moon shone beneath her feet. Realizing that she had turned a somersault, she resumed her normal position, and when she turned to look, she saw that the lake was no longer there and that in the distance behind her there remained only a rosy glow on the horizon. A second later and it, too, had vanished, and Margarita saw that she was alone with the moon, which was flying above her to her left. Margarita's hair continued to stand up like a haystack, and the moonlight whistled as it washed over her body. Judging by how two rows of widely spaced lights below had merged into two unbroken fiery lines, and by how rapidly they vanished behind her, Margarita surmised that she was traveling at monstrous speed and was amazed that she was not gasping for breath.

After several seconds had passed, a new lake of electric light flared up in the inky blackness of the earth, far below, and it surged up beneath the flying woman's feet, only then to turn into a spinning vortex and disappear into the earth. Seconds later—the same thing happened again.

"Cities! Cities!" shouted Margarita.

After that she saw what looked like two or three dully gleaming swords displayed in open black cases, and realized they must be rivers.

As she flew along, Margarita looked up at the moon over to her left and marveled at how it seemed to be rushing back to Moscow like a madwoman, while at the same time staying strangely in place, so that its surface was clearly visible. There she could see a dark, mysterious shape, which looked something like a dragon or a humpbacked horse, its sharp muzzle pointed back toward the city left behind.

Margarita was now seized by the thought that there was no need for her to drive her broom at such a frenzied speed, that she was depriving herself of the opportunity to look at things properly and enjoy the flight to the fullest. Something told her that they would wait for her at her destination and that there was no reason for her to be bored by such senseless speed and altitude.

Margarita bent the bristle end of her broom downward, so that the tail end rose toward the rear, and after drastically reducing her speed, she headed down to the ground. This downward slide, as if on an airborne toboggan, gave Margarita an intense thrill. The earth rose up to meet her, and out of the formless, once black mass emerged the mysteries and charm of the earth during a moonlit night. The earth was moving toward her, and Margarita was already bathed in the scent of the greening forests. She was flying over the very mists of a dewy meadow, then over a pond. A chorus of frogs sang beneath Margarita, and from somewhere in the distance came the inexplicably heart-rending wail of a train. Soon Margarita glimpsed it. It was crawling along slowly, like a caterpillar, throwing a shower of sparks up in the air. After overtaking it, Margarita passed over another watery mirror, in which a second moon floated by beneath her feet. Descending even lower, she flew along with her feet nearly grazing the the tops of enormous pines.

Behind her Margarita heard the harsh sound of something ripping the air. Gradually this sound of something flying through the air like a missile was joined by a woman's laughter, audible for miles around. Margarita turned around and saw that she was being pursued by a complex black object. As it drew close, it became more clearly defined, and she could see it was a mounted rider. And finally the object completely revealed itself: slowing down and drawing up beside Margarita was Natasha.

Completely naked, her tousled hair flying in the wind, she was flying astride a fat hog, who was clutching a briefcase in his front hooves and beating the air furiously with his back ones. A pince-nez, which had fallen off the hog's nose, gleamed off and on in the moonlight as it dangled from a string at the hog's side, and a hat kept falling over the hog's eyes. After taking a good look, Margarita realized that the hog was Nikolai Ivanovich, and then her laughter, blending with Natasha's, rang out over the forest.

"Natashka!" came Margarita's piercing cry. "Did you use the cream?"

"Darling!" shrieked Natasha, waking the slumbering pines. "My French queen! I smeared it on his bald head too!"

"Princess!" wailed the hog pathetically, carrying his rider at a gallop.

"Darling! Margarita Nikolayevna!" shouted Natasha, galloping along beside her. "I confess I took the cream! But we want to live and fly too! Forgive me, mistress, but I'm not going back, not for anything! Ah, it's good, Margarita Nikolayevna! He proposed to me," at which point Natasha began tweaking the hog, who was puffing with embarrassment, on the neck. "Proposed! What was it you called me, huh?" she shouted, leaning over his ear.

"Goddess!" howled the hog, "I can't fly so fast! I could lose some important papers. Natalya Prokofyevna, I protest."

"To the devil with your papers!" yelled Natasha with an impudent laugh.

"What are you saying, Natalya Prokofyevna! Someone might hear us!" howled the hog in pleading tones.

Galloping alongside Margarita, Natasha laughingly related what had happened after Margarita flew away over the gates.

Natasha confessed that, without touching any of the things Margarita had given her, she had thrown off all her clothes, rushed straight for the cream, and anointed herself with it. And the same thing happened to her that had happened to her mistress. While Natasha was admiring her magical beauty in front of the mirror and laughing with delight, the door opened and in walked Nikolai Ivanovich! He was excited, and was holding Margarita Nikolayevna's chemise, along with his hat and briefcase. Nikolai Ivanovich took one look at Natasha and was stupefied. Red as a lobster, he managed to regain his composure somewhat, and announced that he felt it was his duty to pick up the chemise and return it in person...

"The things he said, the rascal!" said Natasha in squeals of laughter. "The things he said, the propositions he made! The money he promised! He said Klavdiya Petrovna wouldn't find out. Well, am I lying?" yelled Natasha to the hog, who merely lowered his snout in embarrassment.

When they started fooling around in the bedroom, Natasha smeared some cream on Nikolai Ivanovich, and then it was her turn to be struck dumb. The face of the respectable downstairs neighbor had squeezed into a pig's snout, and his arms and legs had acquired hooves. When he looked at himself in the mirror, Nikolai Ivanovich gave a wild and despairing wail, but it was too late. Seconds later he was saddled and mounted, flying the devil knows where out of Moscow, and sobbing with grief.

"I demand the return of my normal appearance!" wheezed and grunted the hog, in a frenzied-pleading sort of way. "I have no intention of flying to an illegal assemblage! Margarita Nikolayevna, it's your duty to get your maid off my back!"

"Ah, so now I'm just a maid? A maid, huh?" cried Natasha, tweaking the hog's ear. "Didn't I used to be a goddess? What was it you called me?"

"Venus!" whined the hog, flying over a roaring, rocky stream, and brushing against a hazel grove with his hooves.

"Venus! Venus!" shouted Natasha triumphantly, with one hand on her hip and extending the other toward the moon. "Margarita! Queen! Ask them to let me stay a witch! They'll do anything you ask, you have the power!"

And Margarita replied, "All right, I promise!"

"Thanks!" yelled Natasha, who suddenly shouted sharply, and somehow dispiritedly, "Giddyap! Giddyap! Faster! Faster! Let's get a move on!" She dug her heels into the hog's flanks, thinned out by the mad gallop, and he bolted ahead so furiously that the air ripped apart again. In an instant Natasha was just a black speck in the distance, and then she disappeared completely, the noise of her flight melting away.

Margarita flew slowly, as before, in a deserted and unfamiliar locale, over hills dotted with occasional boulders and isolated giant firs. As she flew, Margarita reflected on the fact that Moscow was probably far, far away. Her broom was no longer flying above the tall firs but between their trunks, silvered on one side by the moonlight. Margarita's light shadow slithered over the ground in front of her—the moon was now at her back.

Margarita could sense the proximity of water and guessed that she was near her destination. The fir trees parted, and Margarita floated quietly toward a chalky cliff. Just beyond it, down in the shadows, was a river. Patches of mist clung to the bushes at the bottom of the cliff, but the bank opposite was low and flat. There, under a solitary cluster of leafy trees, the light of a campfire flickered and some moving figures could be seen. It seemed to Margarita that she heard a humming, cheerful music coming from there. Beyond it, as far as the eye could see, there were no signs of human life or habitation.

Margarita leaped down off the cliff and descended quickly to the water. It looked tempting to her after her aerial sprint. Tossing her broom aside, she ran and threw herself headfirst into the water. Her light body pierced the water like an arrow and sent a column of water skywards to the moon. The water was as warm as in a bathhouse, and when she surfaced Margarita basked in the pleasures of a solitary night swim in the river.

There was no one in Margarita's immediate vicinity, but splashing and snorting were heard coming from behind some bushes not far away. Someone else was taking a swim, too.

Margarita ran up on shore. Her body tingled after her swim. Feeling no fatigue whatsoever, she danced about joyfully on the wet grass. Suddenly she stopped and listened. The snorting sounds came closer, and a naked fat man with a black silk top hat perched on the back of his head came out from behind some broom bushes. The bather's feet were covered with mud so it looked as if he were wearing black shoes. Judging by his panting breath and hiccups, he had had quite a bit to drink, a fact confirmed by the brandy fumes starting to rise from the river.

The fat man saw Margarita and stared, then he let out a joyous whoop, "Well, what do we have here? Is it her I see? Claudine, it's really you, the merry widow! Are you here, too?"—here he came forward to say hello.

Margarita stepped back and said with dignity, "Go to the devil's mother. What do you mean, Claudine? Mind who you're talking to," and, after a second's thought, she added a long, unprintable oath. All this had a sobering effect on the thoughtless fat man.

"Oh my!" he exclaimed softly with a shudder. "Please forgive me, radiant Queen Margot! I mistook you for someone else. The brandy's to blame, a curse upon it!" The fat man then got down on one knee, swept off his top hat, bowed, and started mumbling some nonsense—half in Russian, half in French—about his friend Guessard's bloody wedding in Paris, and about brandy, and about how crushed he was by his grievous mistake.

"You should have put your trousers on, you son of a bitch," said Margarita, softening.

The fat man broke out in a happy grin when he saw that Margarita wasn't angry, and he announced rapturously that his trouserless state was due simply to his having absentmindedly left them on the banks of the Yenisei River where he had been bathing before coming there, and that he would fly back there at once, seeing it was only a stone's throw away. Then, after commending himself to her good favor and protection, he began edging backwards, until he slipped and fell on his back in the water. But even as he fell, he kept a smile of rapture and devotion on his whisker-framed face.

Margarita summoned her broom with a piercing whistle, mounted it, and was carried over the river to the opposite shore. The shadow cast by the chalk cliff did not reach that far, and the riverbank was flooded in moonlight.

As soon as Margarita touched down on the wet grass, the music under the willows grew louder, and the sparks from the campfire cascaded more merrily into the air. Under the willow branches, studded with soft, fluffy catkins visible in the moonlight, sat two rows of fat-faced frogs, their cheeks distended like rubber, playing a spirited march on wooden pipes. Glowing pieces of rotten wood hung on willow twigs in front of the musicians, to illuminate their music, and the flickering light from the campfire played on the frogs' faces.

The march was being played in Margarita's honor. She was given the most gala reception. Diaphanous mermaids stopped their round dance over the river and waved to Margarita with seaweed. Their moaning salutations carried out over the deserted, greenish shore and could be heard from far away. Naked witches jumped out from behind the willows, formed a line, and began to bow and curtsy in courtly fashion. A goat-legged creature rushed up to Margarita and kissed her hand. Spreading silk on the grass, he inquired whether the queen had enjoyed her swim, and suggested that she lie down and have a rest.

And that's exactly what Margarita did. The creature brought her a goblet of champagne, she drank it, and her heart was suffused with warmth. When she enquired after Natasha, she was told that Natasha had already taken her swim, and had flown on ahead to Moscow, on her hog, to announce that Margarita would be arriving soon, and to help in the preparation of her attire.

Margarita's brief sojourn under the willows was notable for one episode. A whistling sound cut through the air, and a black body, obviously way off target, crash-landed in the water. Seconds later Margarita found herself face to face with the same side-whiskered fat man who had introduced himself so infelicitously on the opposite shore. Evidently he had managed to dash back to the Yenisei, since he was now in full evening dress, albeit soaked from head to toe. Judging by his crash landing in the water, he had obviously had a second go at the brandy. But even this mishap had not wiped the smile off his face. And the amused Margarita, laughing, allowed him to kiss her hand.

Then everyone began preparing to leave. The mermaids concluded their dance and melted into the moonlight. The goat-legged fellow respectfully inquired how Margarita had gotten to the river, and when he learned she had come on a broom, he said, "Oh, whatever for, that's so uncomfortable." In the blink of an eye he devised a rather dubious-looking phone out of two twigs and demanded that a car be sent over on the spot. And, indeed, a minute later there dropped on the island a dun-colored open car, only sitting in the driver's seat instead of the routine chauffeur was a black, long-beaked rook wearing an oilskin cap and long driving gloves. The small island was clearing out. The witches flew away and dissolved in the moonlight. The campfire burned out, and the coals became covered with gray ash.

The man with side whiskers and the goat-legged fellow helped Margarita into the car, and she settled into the wide back seat. The car roared, gave a jump and soared almost as high as the moon, the island vanished, the river vanished, and Margarita was carried off to Moscow.

XXII

By Candlelight

THE steady hum of the car as it flew high above the earth soothed Margarita like a lullaby, and the moonlight warmed her pleasantly. Closing her eyes, she turned her face to the wind and thought with a certain sadness of the unknown river bank she had left behind, which she felt she would never see again. After all that evening's marvels and enchantments, she had already guessed who they were taking her to visit, but that didn't frighten her. The hope that there she would succeed in regaining her happiness made her fearless. However, she had very little time in the car to dream of that happiness. Due either to the rook's expertise, or the car's superior quality, soon after Margarita opened her eyes, she saw below her the shimmering lake of Moscow's lights rather than the darkness of the forest. The black bird-chauffeur unscrewed the right front wheel while they were still in flight, and then landed the vehicle in an utterly deserted cemetery in the Dorogomilov district.

After depositing the unquestioning Margarita and her broom next to one of the gravestones, the rook sent the car rolling straight into the ravine behind the cemetery. It fell with a crash and was destroyed. The rook gave a respectful salute, mounted the wheel and flew off.

A black cloak appeared at once from behind one of the monuments. A fang gleamed in the moonlight, and Margarita recognized Azazello. After motioning to her to get on her broom, he himself jumped astride a long rapier, the two of them soared aloft, and seconds later, unseen by anyone, they set down near 302B Sadovaya Street.

As the two companions, carrying broom and rapier under their arms, passed through the gateway, Margarita noticed a man in a cap and high boots who was loitering there, probably waiting for someone. As light as Azazello's and Margarita's footsteps were, the solitary man heard them and twitched nervously, unable to figure out who was producing them.

At entranceway No. 6 they encountered a second man who looked amazingly like the first. And the same thing happened again. Footsteps... The man turned nervously and frowned. When the door opened and closed, he charged after the invisible intruders, scanned the entranceway, but failed to see anything, of course.

A third man, who was an exact replica of the second, and, therefore, of the first as well, was standing guard on the third-floor landing. He was smoking strong cigarettes, and Margarita coughed as she walked past him. The smoker jumped up from the bench on which he'd been sitting as if he had been jabbed by a needle, began looking nervously about, walked over to the bannister and looked down. By this time Margarita and her escort had already reached the door of apartment No. 50. They did not ring, Azazello opened the door noiselessly with his key.

The first thing that struck Margarita was the total darkness in which she found herself. It was as dark as a dungeon, and, afraid of stumbling, she instinctively grabbed hold of Azazello's cloak. But at that moment a small lamp flickered up above in the distance and began drawing closer. As they were walking, Azazello took Margarita's broom from under her arm, and it disappeared in the darkness without making a sound. They then began ascending broad steps which Margarita started to think would go on forever. It amazed her that the front hall of an ordinary Moscow apartment could contain such an extraordinary, and invisible, but very palpable, endless staircase. But their ascent did come to an end, and Margarita realized that she was on a landing. The light moved up close, and Margarita could see the illuminated face of the tall, black man who was holding the lamp in his hand. Anyone who had had the misfortune of crossing his path in recent days would have recognized him at once, even in that feebly flickering light. It was Korovyov, alias Fagot.

True, Korovyov's appearance was greatly changed. The flickering light was reflected not in the cracked pince-nez, which should have been thrown in the trash long ago, but in a monocle which was, admittedly, also cracked. The wispy mustache on his insolent face was now curled and pomaded, and there was a simple explanation for Korovyov's apparent blackness: he was in evening dress. Only his chest was white.

Magician, choirmaster, wizard, interpreter, or the devil knows what—in a word, Korovyov—bowed, and gesturing to Margarita with a broad sweep of the lamp, he invited her to follow him. Azazello vanished.

"An amazingly bizarre evening," thought Margarita, "I was ready for anything except this! Has their electricity gone out, or what? But most amazing of all is the size of this place. How can all this be crammed into a Moscow apartment? It's simply not possible."

However meager the light from Korovyov's lamp, Margarita nevertheless realized that she was in an absolutely immense room, what is more, a room with a colonnade, which was dark and at first glance, endless. Korovyov stopped beside a small couch, placed his lamp on a little pedestal, gestured to Margarita to sit down and situated himself beside her in a picturesque pose, leaning with his elbow on the pedestal.

"Allow me to introduce myself," said Korovyov in a creaky voice.

"I'm Korovyov. Are you surprised there's no light? We're economizing, is that what you thought? No-no-no, not at all! And if I'm lying, then let the first executioner who comes by—say, one of those who will shortly have the honor of kissing your knee—chop my head off on this very pedestal. It's simply that Messire doesn't like electric light, and we turn it on only at the last moment. And then, believe me, there'll be no shortage of light. It would probably be better if there were less, in fact."

Margarita liked Korovyov, and his high-flown chatter had a calming effect on her.

"No," replied Margarita, "what surprises me the most is where you found all this space." With a sweep of her arm she indicated the immensity of the room.

Korovyov smirked sweetly, so that the shadows stirred in the wrinkles around his nose.

"The simplest thing of all!" he replied. "Anyone familiar with the fifth dimension has no trouble whatsoever expanding his residence to whatever size he wishes. I might add, esteemed lady, to the devil knows what size! However," Korovyov rattled on, "I have known people who haven't the faintest conception of the fifth dimension, or of anything else for that matter, but who have still worked wonders when it came to expanding their residence. Take, for example, the city-dweller I heard about, who got a three-room apartment on Zemlyany Embankment and then turned it into four rooms in a flash without recourse to the fifth dimension or to anything else that goes beyond human reason, namely, by dividing one of the rooms in two with a partition.

"He then proceeded to exchange his one apartment for two separate apartments in different sections of Moscow—one with three rooms, the other with two. That, you'll agree, makes five rooms in all. Then he exchanged the three-room apartment for two separate two-room apartments, and thus, as you can see, became the possessor of six rooms, though, it's true, they were scattered all over Moscow. He put an ad in the paper and announced his desire to exchange six rooms in various parts of Moscow for one five-room apartment on the Zemlyany Embankment and was thus on the verge of executing his last and most brilliant move, when something beyond his control put an end to his activities. It's possible that he still has a room somewhere even now, but, I dare say, it's not in Moscow. Now there's an operator for you, and you were pleased to talk of the fifth dimension!"

Although it was Korovyov himself and not Margarita who had brought up the subject of the fifth dimension, she laughed heartily when she heard his story about the apartment wizard. Korovyov continued, "But to business, to business, Margarita Nikolayevna. You are a very intelligent woman and have, naturally, already guessed who our host is."

Margarita's heart skipped a beat and she nodded.

"Well then, well then," said Korovyov. "We abhor mystery and innuendo of any kind. Every year Messire gives one ball. It is called the Spring Ball of the Full Moon, or the Ball of a Hundred Kings. A huge crowd attends!..."—Here Korovyov clutched his cheek, as if a tooth had started to ache. "But I hope, you'll soon see that for yourself. And so: Messire is a bachelor, as you yourself, of course, understand. But he needs a hostess." Spreading his arms, Korovyov said, "You will agree that without a hostess..."

Margarita listened to Korovyov, trying not to utter a word. She felt a chill beneath her heart, the hope of happiness was making her head spin.

"According to tradition," Korovyov continued, "the hostess of the ball has, first of all, to be named Margarita, and second, she has to be a native of the place where the ball is held. And we, as you can see, are travelling and find ourselves at the present time in Moscow. We found one hundred and twenty-one Margaritas in Moscow, and, would you believe it," here Korovyov slapped himself on the thigh in despair, "not one of them was suitable. And then, at long last, a stroke of luck..."

Korovyov gave an expressive grin, bowing from the waist, and again Margarita felt a chill in her heart.

"To be brief" cried Korovyov. "As brief as can be: you won't refuse to assume this obligation, will you?"

"No, I won't," was Margarita's firm reply.

"We're finished!" said Korovyov, and picking up the lamp, he added, "Please follow me."

They walked between the columns and finally made their way to another room, which for some reason smelled strongly of lemon, where rustling sounds were heard, and where something brushed against Margarita's head. She shuddered.

"Don't be frightened," soothed Korovyov sweetly, taking Margarita by the arm. "It's only Behemoth showing off his ball tricks, nothing more. And, in general, may I be so bold as to offer you some advice, Margarita Nikolayevna, never ever be afraid of anything. That's unwise. The ball will be lavish, that I won't try to hide from you. We'll see some people who wielded vast power in their day. But, truly, when one thinks how microscopically small their resources are compared with the resources of the one in whose retinue I have the honor to serve, then it becomes ridiculous and, I would even say, pathetic... And besides, you yourself are of royal blood."

"Royal blood?" whispered Margarita fearfully, pressing against Korovyov.

"Ah, Queen," cackled Korovyov playfully, "questions of blood are the most complicated in the world! And if you were to ask certain great-grandmothers, especially those renowned for their meekness, some most astonishing secrets would be revealed, esteemed Margarita Nikolayevna. I would not be remiss if in speaking about this subject, I were to draw an analogy to a capriciously shuffled deck of cards. There are things in which neither class distinctions nor national boundaries have any validity whatsoever. I'll give you a hint: a certain sixteenth-century French queen would have been astounded, one must suppose, if someone had told her that many, many years in the future I would be walking arm in arm through a ballroom in Moscow with her charming great-great-great-great-granddaughter. But we have arrived!"

At this point Korovyov blew out his lamp and it disappeared from his hands, and Margarita saw a strip of light on the floor in front of her under a dark door. And Korovyov rapped gently on that door. Here Margarita became so excited that her teeth began to chatter and a shiver ran down her spine.

The door opened. The room turned out to be quite small. Margarita could see a wide oak bed covered with dirty, wrinkled, and crumpled sheets and pillows. In front of the bed stood an oak table with carved legs, on top of which was a candelabrum with sockets shaped like bird claws. Burning in the seven gold claws were thick wax candles. There was also a large chessboard on the table with unusually skillfully crafted chessmen. A low stool stood on a small, threadbare carpet. On still another table there was a gold cup and a second candelabrum whose branches were fashioned like a snake's. The room smelled of sulphur and pitch. The shadows from the candelabra crisscrossed over the floor.

Among those present Margarita immediately recognized Azazello, who was now dressed in tails and standing by the head of the bed. Now that he was all dolled up, Azazello no longer resembled the ruffian in whose identity he had appeared to Margarita in Alexandrovsky Park, and he gave Margarita a particularly gallant bow.

A naked witch, the same Hella who had so embarrassed the respectable bartender at the Variety, and, alas, the same one who, to Rimsky's great good fortune, had been scared off by the rooster on the night of the famous performance, was sitting on the rug by the bed, stirring something in a pan that gave off sulphurous fumes.

In addition to the others there was a huge black cat who was sitting on a tall stool in front of the chess table, holding a knight in his right paw.

Hella got up and bowed to Margarita. The cat did likewise after jumping off its stool. Clicking its right hind paw, it dropped the knight and crawled under the bed to retrieve it.

Dying from terror, Margarita somehow managed to see all this in the deceptive shadows of the candlelight. Her gaze was drawn to the bed, on which sat the one whom poor Ivan, at Patriarch's Ponds, had recently tried to convince of the devil's non-existence. This non-existent being was, in fact, sitting on the bed.

Two eyes bore into Margarita's face. The right eye had a gold spark deep in its center and could pierce anyone's soul to its depths; the left eye was vacant and black, like the narrow eye of a needle, like the entrance to a bottomless well of darkness and shadow. Woland's face was lopsided, the right corner of his mouth stretched downwards, and his high, balding forehead was etched with deep wrinkles which ran parallel to his sharp eyebrows. An eternal suntan seemed to have been burned into Woland's face.

Woland lay sprawled on the bed, dressed only in a long nightshirt, which was dirty and patched on the left shoulder. One naked leg was folded beneath him and the other was stretched out on the stool. Hella was massaging the knee of this dark leg with a smoking salve.

On Woland's bare, hairless chest Margarita also noted a gold chain with a finely carved scarab of dark stone that had some kind of writing engraved on the back. Next to Woland on the bed, on a heavy base, stood a strange globe that seemed to be alive and was lit up on one side by a sun.

The silence lasted for several seconds. "He's studying me," thought Margarita, making an effort to control the trembling in her legs.

After smiling, which seemed to ignite the sparkle in his eye, Woland at last began to speak, "I welcome you, Queen, and beg you to excuse my at-home attire."

Woland's voice was so low that on certain syllables it drawled out into a wheeze.

He picked up a long sword that was lying on top of the bedclothes, bent down, and poked it under the bed, saying, "Come out of there! The game is over. Our guest has arrived."

"Not on my account," whistled Korovyov anxiously in Margarita's ear, playing the role of prompter.

"Not on my account..." began Margarita.

"Messire..." Korovyov breathed into her ear.

"Don't stop on my account, Messire," said Margarita softly but clearly, after regaining control of herself, and smiling, she added, "Please don't interrupt the game on my account. I imagine the chess magazines would pay a tidy sum for the chance to print it."

Azazello cackled softly and approvingly, while Woland looked at Margarita attentively, and then remarked, as if to himself, "Yes, Korovyov's right. How capriciously the deck is shuffled! Blood tells!"

He extended his hand and beckoned Margarita to come closer. She did so without feeling the floor beneath her bare feet. Woland placed his hand, heavy as stone, yet, at the same time, hot as fire, on Margarita's shoulder, turned her towards him, and seated her on the bed next to him.

"Well, since you are so enchantingly kind," he said, "and I never expected otherwise, we'll dispense with formalities." Again he leaned over to the edge of the bed and shouted, "How long is this farce under the bed going to continue? Come out of there, accursed Gans!"

"I can't find the knight," replied the cat in an affected and muffled voice from under the bed. "He galloped off somewhere and a frog's turned up instead."

"What do you think this is, a fairground?" asked Woland, pretending to sound angry. "There was no frog under the bed! Save those cheap tricks for the Variety. If you don't come out this minute, we'll consider that you've forfeited the game, you damned quitter."

"Not at all, Messire!" howled the cat, and he crawled out that second, holding the knight in his paw.

"I'd like you to meet..." began Woland, and then interrupted himself, "No, I can't stand the sight of this clowning fool. Look what he did to himself under the bed."

In the meantime, the cat, covered in dust and standing on his hind paws, was bowing to Margarita. He had a white bow tie around his neck, and a pair of ladies' mother-of-pearl opera glasses hanging from a cord on his chest. In addition, the cat's whiskers were gilded.

"Well, what's all this!" exclaimed Woland. "What did you gild your whiskers for? And why the devil do you need a tie, if you're not wearing trousers?"

"Cats aren't supposed to wear trousers, Messire," replied the cat with great dignity. "Will you tell me next that I have to wear boots? It's only in fairy tales that you see a cat in boots, Messire. But have you ever seen anyone at a ball without a tie? It is not my intention to look ridiculous and risk getting kicked out! Everyone adorns himself as best he can. Keep in mind, Messire, that this applies to my opera glasses as well!"

"But whiskers?..."

"I don't understand," retorted the cat dryly, "why Azazello and Korovyov could sprinkle themselves with white powder when shaving today and why is that preferable to gold? All I did was powder my whiskers! It would be a different matter if I had shaved! A shaved cat—now that really would be an abomination, I couldn't agree more. But I can see..."—here the cat's voice trembled with hurt feelings—"that I'm being picked on, and that I'm facing a serious dilemma—should I even go to the ball? What do you say to that, Messire?"

The cat was so puffed up with hurt feelings that it looked like he would burst in a second.

"Oh, what a rogue he is, what a rogue," said Woland, shaking his head, "and every time the game isn't going his way and he's about to lose, he starts putting up smoke screens, like the worst charlatan on the bridge. Sit down this minute and stop talking drivel."

"I'll sit down," said the cat, seating himself, "but I object to what you just said. My remarks are far from being drivel, as you so nicely put it in the lady's presence; rather, they are a series of neatly packaged syllogisms which would win the respect and admiration of such connoisseurs of the genre as Sextus Empiricus, Martianus Capella, or, who knows, even Aristotle himself."

"Checkmate," said Woland.

"Please, please, let me see," rejoined the cat, starting to survey the board with his opera glasses.

"And so," said Woland, addressing himself to Margarita, "I present to you, Donna, my retinue. This fellow who likes to play the fool is the cat Behemoth. You're already acquainted with Azazello and Korovyov, and this is my maid, Hella. She's quick and efficient, and there is no service which she cannot provide."

The beautiful Hella smiled and turned her green-hued eyes to Margarita while continuing to scoop out gobs of salve which she rubbed on Woland's knee.

"Well, that's that," concluded Woland with a grimace, as Hella pressed his knee with particular force. "As you can see, it's a small, diverse, and ingenuous group." He fell silent and began spinning the globe in front of him. It was so artfully constructed that the deep blue oceans on it moved, and its polar cap looked real, snowy and icy.

Meanwhile, the chessboard was in chaos. An utterly distraught king in a white cape stamped on his square, his arms raised in despair. Three white lansquenet pawns with halberds stared in confusion at a bishop who was waving his crozier and pointing ahead to where Woland's black knights could be seen on adjacent black and white squares, mounted on two mettlesome steeds, who were pawing the squares with their hooves.

Margarita was fascinated and astounded that the chess pieces were alive.

The cat, lowering his opera glasses, quietly poked his king over in the back. The latter covered his face in despair.

"It doesn't look good, dear Behemoth," said Korovyov with quiet venom.

"The situation is serious, but by no means hopeless," retorted Behemoth. "Moreover, I'm completely confident of ultimate victory. A careful analysis of the situation is all that is required."

He began this careful analysis in rather a strange way, namely, by making faces and winking at his king.

"Nothing will help," observed Korovyov.

"Oh!" shouted Behemoth. "The parrots have flown away, just as I predicted!"

And, in fact, from the distance came the sound of many flapping wings. Korovyov and Azazello rushed out.

"To hell with your ball practical jokes!" muttered Woland, without taking his eyes from his globe.

As soon as Korovyov and Azazello were gone, Behemoth's winking intensified. Finally, the white king caught on to what was expected of him. He abruptly pulled off his cape, threw it down on the square and ran off the board. The bishop donned the king's cast-off attire and took the king's place.

Korovyov and Azazello returned.

"False alarm, as always," grumbled Azazello, looking askance at Behemoth.

"I thought I heard something," replied the cat.

"Well, how long is this going to go on?" asked Woland. "Checkmate."

"Perhaps I misheard you, my *maître*, but my king is not in check, nor could he be."

"I repeat, checkmate."

"Messire," responded the cat in a fake-anxious voice. "You must be overtired; my king is not in check."

"Your king is on square G2," said Woland, without looking at the board.

"Messire, I'm horrified!" wailed the cat, faking a look of horror. "There is no king on that square."

"What are you saying?" asked Woland in disbelief as he looked at the board and saw the bishop on the king's square turn away and cover his face with his hand.

"Oh, you scoundrel," said Woland pensively.

"Messire! I must again appeal to logic," began the cat, pressing his paws to his chest. "If a player says checkmate, and there is no trace of the king on the board, then the checkmate is null and void."

"Do you concede or not?" shouted Woland in a terrible voice.

"Let me think for a bit," answered the cat meekly. He then put his elbows on the table, covered his ears with his paws, and began to think. He thought for a long time and finally said, "I concede."

"Kill the stubborn beast," whispered Azazello.

"Yes, I concede," said the cat, "but only because I can't play when I'm being badgered by envious bystanders!" He got up and the chessmen clambered into the box.

"Hella," said Woland, "it's time," and she disappeared from the room. "My leg has flared up again, and now there's this ball..." continued Woland.

"Allow me," said Margarita softly.

Woland stared at her intently and then moved his knee over to her.

The salve was as hot as lava and burned Margarita's hands, but she did not flinch and rubbed it into his knee, trying not to cause him any pain.

"My close friends insist that it's rheumatism," said Woland, keeping his eyes fixed on Margarita, "but I strongly suspect that the pain in my knee is a memento of my intimacy with a certain enchanting witch, whom I met in the Brocken Mountains, on the Devil's Pulpit, in 1571."

"Oh, how can that be!" said Margarita.

"It's nothing! It'll pass in three hundred years' time. A multitude of medications have been recommended to me, but I'm a traditionalist and remain partial to granny's remedies. My grandmother, the vile old hag, left me some incredible herbs! Is there perhaps some sadness or anguish that is poisoning your soul?"

"No, Messire, there's nothing like that," was Margarita's shrewd reply, "and now that I'm here with you, I feel completely fine."

"Blood is what counts," said Woland merrily to no one in particular, and added, "I see my globe interests you."

"Oh yes, I've never seen anything like it."

"Yes, it is nice. To be frank, I don't like listening to the news on the radio. The announcers are usually young women who can't pronounce place names properly. And, what's more, at least a third of them seem to have speech defects, as if that were a job requirement. My globe is much more convenient, especially since I have to know exactly what's going on. For instance, look here. Do you see that piece of land washed on one side by the ocean? Look how it's bursting into flame. A war has broken out there. If you look closer, you'll see it in detail."

Margarita bent toward the globe and saw that a square of earth had grown wider, had assumed vivid colors and had turned into a kind of relief map. And then she saw a strip of river and next to it a village. A house the size of a pea got as big as a matchbox. Suddenly and noise-lessly the roof of the house blew off into the air with a puff of black smoke, the walls of the house caved in, so that nothing was left of the two-storey matchbox except piles of rubble spewing black smoke. When she looked even closer, Margarita could see a tiny female figure lying on the ground, and next to her was a baby, lying in a pool of blood with its arms stretched out.

"So that's that," said Woland, smiling. "He had no time to sin. Abaddon's work is flawless."

"I wouldn't want to be on the side fighting against this Abaddon," said Margarita. "Whose side is he on?"

"The more I talk with you," Woland replied pleasantly, "the more convinced I am that you're very intelligent. Let me put your mind at ease. He is totally neutral and sympathizes equally with both contend-ing sides. As a result, the outcome is always the same for both of them. Abaddon!" called Woland in a soft voice, and out of the wall appeared a thin figure in dark glasses. The glasses made such a strong impression on Margarita that she let out a soft scream and buried her face in Woland's leg. "Stop that!" yelled Woland. "How nervous people are nowadays!" He slapped Margarita's back so hard that her whole body reverberated with the sound. "Can't you see he's got his glasses on? Moreover, he never has appeared, nor will he ever appear, before any-one's time has come. And, besides, I'm here. You're my guest! I just wanted to show him to you."

Abaddon stood motionless.

"Do you think he could take off his glasses for just a second?" asked Margarita, pressing close to Woland and trembling, but only out of cu-riosity.

"No, that is impossible," Woland replied in a grave voice, waving his arm at Abaddon, who then disappeared. "What do you wish to say, Azazello?"

"Messire," answered Azazello, "permit me to speak. Two outsiders have appeared: a beautiful woman who keeps whimpering and begs permission to stay with her mistress, and also her, pardon my expression, hog."

"Beautiful women have strange ways," remarked Woland.

"It's Natasha, Natasha!" exclaimed Margarita.

"Well, let her stay with her mistress. And send the hog—to the cooks!"

"To be butchered?" cried Margarita in fright. "Have mercy, Messire. That's Nikolai Ivanovich, our downstairs neighbor. You see, there's been a mistake here, she rubbed him with that cream..."

"Just a minute," said Woland, "who the hell is going to butcher him and what the devil for? Just let him sit with the cooks for awhile, that's all! You'll agree, I can't very well let him into the ballroom!"

"Well, yes..." added Azazello, and announced, "Midnight is approaching, Messire."

"Ah, good." Woland turned to Margarita, "And so, please come with me... I thank you in advance. Don't get flustered and don't be afraid of anything. Drink nothing but water, or else you'll wilt and it will be hard for you. Time to go!"

Margarita got up from the rug, and then Korovyov appeared in the doorway.

XXIII

Satan's Grand Ball

MIDNIGHT was approaching, they had to hurry. Margarita had only a vague idea of her surroundings. She recalled candles and a pool inlaid with semiprecious stones. Margarita stood on the bottom of the pool while Hella, helped by Natasha, covered her with a hot, thick, red liquid. Margarita tasted salt on her lips and realized she was being washed with blood. The mantle of blood was followed by another—thick, transparent, and pink— and Margarita's head spun from the oil of roses. Next she was laid on a bed of crystal and rubbed with large green leaves until she sparkled. At this point the cat burst in and began to help. He squatted at her feet and started polishing the soles of her feet, as if he were a shoeshine boy polishing shoes on the street.

Margarita cannot remember who sewed her pale rose-petal slippers, or how they got fastened with gold clasps all on their own. Some force lifted Margarita up and stood her in front of a mirror, where she saw a regal diamond tiara sparkling on her head. Korovyov appeared from somewhere and hung on Margarita's breast a heavy, oval-framed picture of a poodle on a heavy chain. This adornment was a great burden to the queen. The chain immediately began chafing her neck, and the weight of the picture caused her to bend forward. But Margarita was rewarded for the discomfort caused by the black poodle and chain. Her reward was the new deference shown her by Korovyov and Behemoth.

"Never mind, never mind, never mind!" mumbled Korovyov in the doorway of the room with the pool. "There's nothing you can do, you just have to wear it, you have to, you have to... Allow me, Your Majesty, to give you one last bit of advice. The guests will be a diverse lot—oh, very diverse—but, Queen Margot, whatever you do, don't show any partiality! Even if you take a dislike to someone... I know that you, of course, will not show this on your face... No, no, don't even think of it! He'll notice it, he'll notice it right away! You have to like him, you have to like him, Your Majesty! The hostess of the ball will be rewarded for that a hundred times over. And another thing: don't ignore anyone! Give a little smile if you don't have time for a word. Even the tiniest nod of your head will do. Anything you wish, but not indifference. That causes them to wither..."

Accompanied by Korovyov and Behemoth, Margarita stepped out of the room with the pool into total darkness.

"I'll do it, I'll do it," whispered the cat. "I'll give the signal!"

"Do it!" Korovyov replied in the darkness.

"Let the ball begin!" yelled the cat shrilly, and Margarita at once let out a scream and shut her eyes for several seconds. The ball descended upon her immediately as light combined with sound and smell. Carried along on Korovyov's arm, Margarita found herself in a tropical forest. Red-breasted, green-tailed parrots clung to liana vines, hopping all about, and shouting deafeningly, "Delighted to see you!" But the forest came to an abrupt end, and its bathhouse humidity was replaced by the coolness of a ballroom with columns made of a sparkling, yellowish stone. The ballroom, like the forest, was completely empty, except for naked negroes in silver headbands, standing motionlessly by the columns. Their faces flushed dark-red with excitement when Margarita flew in with her retinue, which now included Azazello, who had materialized from somewhere. Here Korovyov let go of Margarita's arm and whispered, "Go straight to the tulips!"

A low wall of white tulips rose up in front of Margarita, and beyond it she saw countless shaded lamps and in front of them the white chests and black shoulders of men in formal dress. Then Margarita realized where the ball music was coming from. A blast of trumpets crashed down on her, and from beneath it a surge of violins broke loose and washed over her body like blood. An orchestra of some one hundred and fifty men was playing a polonaise.

The man in tails on the podium, towering above the orchestra, took one look at Margarita, turned pale, smiled, and with a sudden wave of his hand made the orchestra rise to its feet. Without ceasing to play for an instant, the orchestra, now standing, immersed Margarita in sound. The man towering above the orchestra turned his back to it and bowed low, his arms spread wide, and Margarita, smiling, waved at him.

"No, not enough, not enough," whispered Korovyov, "he won't sleep all night. Shout to him, 'I salute you, Waltz King!'"

Margarita did just that and was amazed to find that her voice, full-throated as a bell, drowned out the sound of the orchestra. The man trembled with happiness and pressed his left hand to his chest, while continuing with his right to conduct the orchestra with a white baton.

"Not enough, not enough," whispered Korovyov. "Look over to your left at the first violins, and nod your head so that each one thinks you've recognized him individually. They're all world-famous. Look at the one in the first chair, that's Vieuxtemps. Good, very good. Now let's move on."

"Who's the conductor?" asked Margarita as she flew away.

"Johann Strauss!" cried the cat. "And may they hang me on a liana vine in the tropical forest if an orchestra like this ever played at any other ball! I was the one who sent out the invitations! And, please note, not one of the musicians took sick or refused to play."

The next ballroom had no columns; instead, on one side were walls of red, pink, and milky-white roses, and on the other a wall of Japanese double camellias. Between these walls, fountains gushed and hissed, and champagne frothed, bubbling, in three pools, the first of which—was clear-violet, the second—ruby-red, and the third—crystal. Negroes in scarlet headbands scurried about, pouring silver ladles of champagne from the pools into shallow goblets. Through an opening in the pink wall, a man in a red swallowtail coat could be seen bouncing about excitedly on a stage. In front of him, a jazz band blasted away at an intolerable volume. As soon as the conductor saw Margarita, he made such a low bow that his hands touched the floor, then he straightened up and let out a piercing yell, "Hallelujah!"

He slapped himself once on one knee, then crossed one hand over the other and slapped his other knee twice, grabbed a cymbal from the musician nearest him, and struck it against a pillar.

As she flew off, Margarita saw only that the jazz virtuoso, competing with the polonaise that was blaring at Margarita's back, was beating his cymbals over his musicians' heads while they cringed in mock terror.

Finally they flew out to the landing where, Margarita realized, Korovyov had first greeted her in the dark with a lamp. Now the landing was flooded with blinding light pouring out of crystal lamps shaped like grape clusters. Margarita was shown to her place, and a low amethyst column appeared beneath her left arm.

"You can rest your hand on it if you get tired," whispered Korovyov.

A black-skinned man tucked a pillow embroidered with a gold poodle under Margarita's feet, and, with someone's hands guiding her, Margarita bent her right knee and put her foot on the cushion.

Margarita tried to look around. Korovyov and Azazello were standing nearby in ceremonial poses. Next to Azazello were three young men who vaguely reminded Margarita of Abaddon. She felt a chill on her back. When Margarita turned around, she saw that wine was bubbling out of the marble wall behind her and flowing into a pool sculpted out of ice. She felt something warm and furry by her left foot. It was Behemoth.

Margarita was standing at a great height, and a vast carpeted staircase descended beneath her feet. Down at the bottom, so far away that Margarita felt she was gazing through the wrong end of binoculars, she could see an enormous foyer with a fireplace so huge that a five-ton truck could drive into its cold, black maw. The foyer and staircase, so brightly lit that they pained the eyes, were empty. The sound of trumpets now reached Margarita from the distance. Thus they stood that way for a minute or so without moving.

"But where are the guests?" Margarita asked Korovyov.

"They'll be here, Your Majesty, they'll be here any minute. There'll be no lack of them. And, to be honest, I'd rather be chopping wood than standing here on this landing to receive them."

"Chopping wood is nothing," interjected the garrulous cat. "I'd rather be a streetcar conductor, and there's no job in the world worse than that."

"Everything has to be ready in advance, Your Majesty," explained Korovyov, his eye gleaming through the cracked monocle. "There's nothing worse than having the first guest roam around without knowing what to do while his lawful shrew of a wife scolds him in a whisper for their being the first to arrive. Balls like that should be done away with entirely, Your Majesty."

"Done away with entirely," affirmed the cat.

"Not more than ten seconds till midnight," added Korovyov. "It's about to start."

Those ten seconds seemed extraordinarily long to Margarita. They appeared to have passed already, yet absolutely nothing had happened. Then, suddenly, there was a loud crash in the enormous fireplace at the bottom of the stairs, and out popped a gallows with a dangling corpse half turned to dust. This dust shook itself off the noose, fell to the ground, and out jumped a handsome black-haired fellow in tails and patent-leather shoes. Out of the fireplace slid a small, semi-rotted coffin, its top flew off, and another clump of dust tumbled out of the coffin. The handsome fellow rushed gallantly over to it and extended a bent arm, the second clump of dust formed itself into a fidgety, naked woman in black evening slippers, with black feathers on her head, and then both the man and the woman began hurrying up the staircase.

"The first guests!" exclaimed Korovyov. "Monsieur Jacques and his wife. May I introduce you, Your Majesty, to a most interesting man! An inveterate counterfeiter and traitor to his country, but a very good alchemist. He won fame," whispered Korovyov in Margarita's ear, "for poisoning the king's mistress. And that's not something that happens to everyone! Look how handsome he is!"

A distinctly pale Margarita, her mouth agape, looked downwards and saw the coffin and gallows disappear through a side door in the foyer.

"Delighted to see you!" howled the cat, right in Monsieur Jacques's face, as he reached the top of the stairs.

Meanwhile, down below, a headless skeleton with one arm torn out of its socket had emerged from the fireplace, hit the floor and turned into a man in tails.

Monsieur Jacques's wife was already down on one knee in front of Margarita, and pale from excitement, she kissed Margarita's knee.

"Your Majesty..." murmured Monsieur Jacques's wife.

"Her Majesty is delighted!" cried Korovyov.

"Your Majesty..." said the handsome Monsieur Jacques softly.

"We're delighted," howled the cat.

The young men, Azazello's companions, smiling lifeless, but polite smiles, guided Monsieur Jacques and his wife over to the side, to the goblets of champagne which the negroes were holding. Coming up the stairs at a run was a solitary man in tails.

"Count Robert," whispered Korovyov to Margarita. "Intriguing as always. Note the humor, Your Majesty—the same case in reverse: he was a queen's lover and poisoned his wife."

"We are happy, Count," cried the cat.

One after the other, three coffins tumbled out of the fireplace, splitting open and breaking apart on impact, then someone in a black cloak appeared, who was then stabbed in the back by the next to follow him out of the black maw. A muffled scream was heard below. Out of the fireplace ran an almost totally decomposed corpse. Margarita grimaced, and somebody's hand held a vial of smelling salts to her nose. It seemed to Margarita that the hand was Natasha's. The staircase began to fill up with people. Now on every step were men in tails, who all looked completely alike from a distance, and naked women who differed from each other only by their shoes and the color of the feathers on their heads.

Approaching Margarita and hobbling in a strange wooden boot on her left foot, came a lady whose eyes were cast down like a nun's. She was thin, humble-looking, and for some reason had a wide, green bandage around her neck.

"Who's the green one?" queried Margarita mechanically.

"A most charming and reputable lady," whispered Korovyov. "May I present to you Signora Tofana. She was extremely popular among the charming young ladies of Naples as well as the female residents of Palermo, especially those who were sick of their husbands. It does happen, Your Majesty, that a woman gets sick of her hus—..."

"Yes," was Margarita's hollow reply as she smiled at two men in tails, who bowed to her, one after the other, kissing her knee and her hand.

"And so," said Korovyov, managing to whisper in Margarita's ear while also shouting to someone, "Duke! A glass of champagne! Delighted to see you!... And so, as I was saying, Signora Tofana sympathized with these poor women's predicament, and sold them vials of some kind of potion. The wife would pour it into her husband's soup, the husband would eat it, thank her for her tender attention, and feel marvelous. True, a few hours later the husband would develop a terrible thirst, then take to his bed, and the day after that the beautiful Neapolitan lady, who had fed her husband the soup, would be as free as the spring breeze."

"And what's that on her foot?" asked Margarita, continuing to greet the guests who had overtaken the hobbling Signora Tofana. "And why is that green thing on her neck? Is her neck withered?"

"Delighted to see you, Prince!" cried Korovyov, while whispering to

Margarita, "She has a splendid neck, but something unpleasant happened to her in prison. That's a Spanish boot on her foot, Your Majesty, and here's how she got the bandage: when the jailers found out that five hundred or so ill-chosen husbands had left Naples and Palermo permanently, they became enraged and strangled Signora Tofana in prison."

"How happy I am, Black Queen, for the great honor that has befallen me," whispered Tofana in a nunlike voice, attempting to get down on her knee. The Spanish boot impeded her. Korovyov and Behemoth helped Tofana to get up.

"I'm glad to see you," replied Margarita to Tofana, while extending her hand to others.

A steady stream of guests was now coming up the stairs. Margarita could no longer see what was going on in the foyer. She raised and lowered her hand mechanically, and baring her teeth monotonously, smiled at the guests. The air on the landing hummed continuously, and the music coming from the ballrooms Margarita had left behind sounded like the sea. "Now that woman there is a bore," said Korovyov not in a whisper but out loud, knowing that he could not be heard above the hum of voices. "She adores balls, yet all she can think of is to complain about her handkerchief."

Margarita scanned the crowd coming up the stairs and found the woman Korovyov was pointing to. She was a young woman of about twenty, with an unusually stunning figure, but with agitated and insistent eyes.

"What handkerchief?" asked Margarita.

"She has a chambermaid assigned to her," explained Korovyov, "and every night for thirty years the maid has laid out a handkerchief for her on her night table. The minute she wakes up she sees it there. She's tried burning it in the stove and drowning it in the river, but nothing helps."

"What kind of handkerchief?" whispered Margarita, raising and lowering her hand.

"A handkerchief with a dark-blue border. The fact is that when she was a waitress in a cafe, her boss lured her into the storeroom one day, and nine months later she gave birth to a baby boy, carried him into the woods, stuffed the handkerchief in his mouth, and then buried him in the ground. At her trial she said she had nothing to feed the child."

"And where's the owner of the cafe?" asked Margarita.

"Your Majesty," squeaked the cat suddenly from below. "Allow me to ask you: what does the owner have to do with this? He wasn't the one who smothered the baby in the woods!"

Margarita, continuing to smile and shake hands with her right hand, sank the sharp nails of her left hand into Behemoth's ear and whispered, "If you dare, you bastard, to butt into the conversation one more time..."

Behemoth let out a highly unceremonious squeal and rasped, "Your Majesty... my ear will swell up... Why spoil the ball for me with a swollen ear?... I was speaking legalistically... from the legal point... I'll be quiet, I'll be quiet... Think of me not as a cat, but a fish, only leave my ear alone."

Margarita let go of his ear, and saw a pair of importunate somber eyes in front of her.

"I am happy, Hostess-Queen, to have been invited to the Grand Ball of the Full Moon."

"And I," replied Margarita, "am glad to see you. Very glad indeed. Do you like champagne?"

"What do you presume to be doing, Your Majesty?" yelled Korovyov in Margarita's ear in mute desperation. "You'll cause a traffic jam!"

"Yes, I do," said the woman imploringly and suddenly began repeating mechanically, "Frieda, Frieda, Frieda! My name is Frieda, Your Majesty."

"Drink as much as you want tonight, Frieda, and don't worry about anything," said Margarita.

Frieda stretched out both her hands to Margarita, but Korovyov and Behemoth, with great finesse, grabbed her under her arms and she was lost in the crowd.

A wall of people was now advancing up the staircase as if about to storm the landing where Margarita stood. Naked female bodies moved up the stairs in between tailcoated men. Their bodies— swarthy, white, coffee-colored or completely black—swept up against Margarita. In their red, black, chestnut, and flaxen hair precious stones sparkled, playing and dancing in the downpour of light. And the advancing column of men looked as if it had been sprayed with droplets of light—light splashed by the diamond studs on their chests. Now every second Margarita felt the touch of lips against her knee, every second she stretched out her hand to be kissed, her face tensed in a mask of welcome.

"I'm delighted to see you," crooned Korovyov in a monotone. "We are delighted... Her Majesty is delighted."

"Her Majesty is delighted..." said Azazello in a nasal twang behind her.

"Delighted," cried the cat.

"The marquise..." mumbled Korovyov, "poisoned her father, two brothers, and two sisters because of an inheritance... Her Majesty is delighted!... Lady Minkina!... Ah, how lovely you look! She's a bit nervous. Why was it necessary to burn the maid's face with a curling iron? Naturally that sort of behavior can get you murdered... Her Majesty is delighted! Your Majesty, a minute of your attention! Emperor Rudolph, wizard and alchemist... Here's another alchemist—he was hanged... Ah, here she is! Ah, what a marvelous brothel she had in Strasbourg!... We're delighted to see you!... A Moscow dressmaker, we all love her for her inexhaustible imagination... she had a salon, and thought up something terribly amusing: she drilled two cute little round holes in the wall..."

"And the ladies didn't know?" asked Margarita.

"Every last one of them knew, Your Majesty," replied Korovyov. "Delighted to see you!... This twenty-year-old rascal, a dreamer and an

eccentric, was remarkable for the strange fantasies he had since childhood. A certain young woman fell in love with him and he went and
sold her to a brothel..."

A river streamed from below. The end of the river was nowhere in
sight. Its source, the huge fireplace, continued to feed it. Thus one
hour passed and the second began. At this point Margarita began to notice that her chain had become heavier than it had been. Something
strange had also happened to her hand. Lifting it made her wince.
Korovyov's interesting remarks ceased to engage Margarita. And the
slant-eyed, Mongol faces, and the white and black faces became indis-
tinguishable from each other, and merged together at times, and the air
between them began, for some reason, to quiver and undulate. A sharp
pain, as from a needle, suddenly pierced Margarita's right hand, and
clenching her teeth, she lay her elbow on the pedestal. A rustling
sound, like wings flapping against a wall, came from the ballroom behind her, and she realized that countless hordes of guests were dancing
there, and it seemed to Margarita that even the massive marble, mosaic,
and crystal floors in that remarkable room were pulsating with rhythm.

Neither Gaius Caesar Caligula, nor Messalina aroused Margarita's interest now, nor did any of the other assorted kings, dukes, cavaliers, sui-
cides, poisoners, gallows birds and procuresses, jailers and cardsharps,
executioners, informers, traitors, madmen, detectives, corrupters of
youth. Their names all got jumbled in her head, their faces melted into
one huge blur, and only one face lingered tormentingly in her memory,
the face of Malyuta Skuratov, framed by a truly fiery-red beard. Margarita's legs were giving way beneath her, and she was afraid of breaking
into tears at any minute. But it was her right knee, the one that kept getting kissed, that caused her the worst suffering. It was swollen, and the
skin had turned blue, despite the fact that Natasha's hand had appeared
to daub the knee with a perfumed sponge. At the end of the third hour
Margarita looked down the staircase with utterly hopeless eyes and then
trembled with joy: the stream of guests was thinning out.

"Patterns of arrival at balls are always the same, Your Majesty," whispered Korovyov. "Now the wave has crested, we're in the last throes of
this torture, I promise you. Aren't those the playboys from Brocken
Peak? They're always the last to arrive. Yes, that's them. Two drunken
vampires... Is that everyone? No, here's one more. No, two!"

The last two guests came up the stairs.

"Well, this is someone new," said Korovyov, squinting through his
monocle. "Ah yes, yes. I seem to recall that Azazello once paid him a
visit and gave him some advice over brandy as to how he could get rid
of a man whose threats of exposure scared him to death. So, he ordered
an acquaintance, who was his subordinate, to spray the walls of the
man's office with poison."

"What's his name?" asked Margarita.

"To tell the truth, I still don't know," replied Korovyov. "You'll have to ask Azazello."

"And who's with him?"

"That's the underling who did his bidding. Delighted!" roared Korovyov to the last two guests.

The stairs were empty. They waited a little bit longer, just to make sure. But no one else emerged from the fireplace.

A second later, without knowing how she got there, Margarita found herself once again in the room with the pool, and once there, burst into tears from the pain in her arm and leg, and collapsed on the floor. But Hella and Natasha comforted her, again gave her a blood shower, again massaged her whole body, and Margarita came back to life.

"There's more to do, more to do, Queen Margot," whispered Korovyov, who had just appeared by her side. "You have to make the rounds of the ballrooms, so our honored guests don't feel ignored."

And again Margarita flew out of the room with the pool. On the stage behind the tulips, where the Waltz King and his orchestra had been playing, a monkey jazz band now ranted and raged. A huge gorilla with shaggy sideburns and a trumpet in his hand was conducting as he danced ponderously to the beat. In one row sat orangutans, blowing shiny trumpets. Perched on their shoulders were merry chimpanzees with accordions. Two baboons with leonine manes were playing grand pianos, and these pianos were drowned out by the thundering, squealing, and banging of saxophones, violins, and drums in the paws of gibbons, mandrills, and marmosets. On the mirror-like floor countless pairs seemed to merge into one in a remarkable display of agility and gracefulness, all whirling in one direction, and moving forward like a wall that threatened to sweep away everything in its path. Live satin butterflies swooped up and down above the dancing hordes, flowers fluttered down from the ceilings. Whenever the electricity went off, myriad glowworms lit up in the tops of the columns, and will-o'-the-wisps floated in the air.

Then Margarita found herself in a monstrously large pool, surrounded by a colonnade. A gigantic black Neptune spewed a broad, pink stream from his maw. The intoxicating smell of champagne came wafting up from the pool. Unconstrained merriment reigned here. The ladies, laughing, threw off their shoes, gave their handbags either to their escorts or to the negroes running around with sheets in their hands, and swan-dived into the pool with shrieks. Columns of spray shot up in the air. The crystal bottom of the pool was lit from below, and the light pierced through the vinous depths, illuminating the silvery swimming bodies. They jumped out of the pool completely drunk. Beneath the columns the sound of laughter rang and thundered as in a bathhouse.

In all the commotion Margarita remembered one totally drunken female face with glazed, yet beseeching eyes, and she recalled one word—"Frieda!"

Margarita's head began to spin from the smell of the wine, and she was about to leave when the cat performed a trick in the pool which detained her. Behemoth cast a spell on something near the maw of Neptune, and hissing and bubbling, the bubbly sea of champagne drained from the pool at once, and Neptune started spewing forth a foamless, bubble-less, dark-amber wave. The ladies shrieked and squealed, "Brandy!"—as they rushed away from the edges of the pool and took refuge behind the columns. The pool was filled in a few seconds, and the cat, after turning three somersaults in the air, landed in the billowing brandy. He crawled out, shaking himself off, his necktie shrunk, his opera glasses, and the gilt on his whiskers gone. Only one woman followed Behemoth's example, namely the practical joke-playing dressmaker, and her escort, an unknown young mulatto. They both dived into the brandy, but at this point Korovyov took Margarita by the arm and they left the bathers behind.

It seemed to Margarita that she flew through a place where she saw mountains of oysters in huge stone ponds. Then she was flying over a glass floor with hellish furnaces blazing beneath it and diabolical white chefs scurrying about tending them. Then somewhere, she was no longer sure where, she saw dark cellars where candelabra were burning, where girls were serving sizzling meat on red-hot coals, and where people were drinking to her health out of large tankards. Then she saw polar bears playing accordions and doing a Russian folk dance on a stage. A salamander-magician who was not burning in the fireplace... And for the second time her strength began to fail her.

"One last entrance," whispered Korovyov anxiously, "and we're free."

Accompanied by Korovyov, Margarita again found herself in the ballroom, but now no one was dancing, and the countless crowds of guests were all clustered between the columns, leaving the center of the room vacant. Margarita did not remember who helped her ascend a platform that had materialized in the middle of the open space. When she got to the top, she was surprised to hear midnight striking somewhere since, according to her calculations, midnight had come and gone long ago. When the clock, its location unknown, struck for the last time, silence fell on the crowds of guests.

Then Margarita again caught sight of Woland. He was walking, surrounded by Abaddon, Azazello, and several others who resembled Abaddon and were young and black. Margarita now noticed that another platform, opposite hers, had been prepared for Woland. But he did not use it. What amazed Margarita was that Woland made his last grand entrance at the ball, looking exactly as he had earlier in the bedroom. The same dirty, patched nightshirt hung from his shoulders, his feet still wore their tattered slippers. Woland carried a sword, but he was using the bare sword as a cane, leaning on it.

Limping, Woland stopped beside his platform, and Azazello immediately appeared before him carrying a dish, and on the dish Margarita saw the severed head of a man whose front teeth had been knocked out. There continued to be absolute silence, which was broken only once by a distant and, under the circumstances, inexplicable ring of what seemed to be a front doorbell.

"Mikhail Alexandrovich," said Woland quietly to the head, and then the eyelids of the slain man opened, and Margarita shuddered when she saw that the eyes on the dead face were alive and full of thought and suffering. "Everything came true, didn't it?" continued Woland, looking into the head's eyes. "Your head was cut off by a woman, the meeting never took place, and I'm living in your apartment. That is a fact. And a fact is the most stubborn thing in the world. But now we're interested in facts-to-be, rather than this already accomplished fact. You were always an avid proponent of the theory that after his head is cut off, a man's life comes to an end, he turns to dust, and departs into non-being. I have the pleasure of informing you in the presence of my guests—although they actually serve as proof of a different theory altogether—that your theory is both incisive and sound. However, one theory is as good as another. There is even a theory that says that to each man it will be given according to his beliefs. May it be so! You are departing into non-being, and, from the goblet into which you are being transformed, I will have the pleasure of drinking a toast to being!"

Woland raised his sword. Here, the skin covering the head darkened and shriveled, then fell off in pieces, the eyes disappeared, and soon Margarita saw on the dish a yellowish, emerald-eyed skull on a gold stem. The top of the skull opened on a hinge.

"This very second, Messire," said Korovyov in response to Woland's questioning gaze, "he shall appear before you. In this tomblike silence I can hear his patent-leather shoes squeaking and his glass tinkling as he puts it down on the table after drinking champagne, the last glass of his life. And here he is now."

A new guest, who was quite alone, entered the ballroom, and headed in Woland's direction. On the outside he was no different from the other male guests, except for one thing: he was so upset he was literally shaking, which was obvious even from far away. Red blotches glowed on his cheeks, and his eyes were darting about with alarm. The guest was flabbergasted, which was completely understandable: everything he saw astounded him, Woland's outfit, in particular.

However, the guest was received with marked affection.

"Ah, my dear Baron Maigel," said Woland with an affable smile as he turned to his guest, whose eyes were popping out of his head. "I am delighted to present to you," said Woland to his guests, "the highly esteemed Baron Maigel, a member of the Theatrical Commission whose job is to acquaint foreigners with the sights of the capital."

Here Margarita froze because she suddenly realized who Maigel was.

He had crossed her path several times in the theaters and restaurants of Moscow. "Wait a minute..." thought Margarita, "does that mean that he's dead, too?" But the matter was soon clarified.

"The kind baron," continued Woland with a joyous smile, "was charming enough to call me as soon as he learned of my arrival in Moscow and offer me his specialized services, that is, as a guide to the sights of the city. It goes without saying that I was happy to invite him for a visit."

Just then Margarita saw Azazello hand Korovyov the dish with the skull-shaped goblet.

"By the way, Baron," said Woland, suddenly lowering his voice and speaking chattily, "rumors are circulating regarding your extraordinary inquisitiveness. They say that this, matched with your no less developed talkativeness, has begun to attract general attention. Moreover, spiteful tongues have dropped the words 'informer,' and 'spy.' And, in addition, there is an assumption that this will lead you to a sorry end in less than a month. And so, to save you the bother of a tiresome wait, we have decided to come to your aid and to take advantage of the fact that you wangled yourself an invitation here with the express purpose of eavesdropping and spying on everything you could."

The baron became even paler than Abaddon, who was exceptionally pale by nature, and then something strange happened. Abaddon appeared before the baron and took his glasses off for just a second. At the same moment something flashed like fire in Azazello's hands, and there was a soft noise, like a hand clap, and the baron started to fall backwards, as scarlet blood spurted from his chest and soaked his starched shirt and vest. Korovyov held the goblet under the pulsing stream, and when it was full, he gave it to Woland. By that time the baron's lifeless body was already on the floor.

"Ladies and gentlemen, I drink to your health," said Woland softly, and raising the goblet, he touched it to his lips.

Then a metamorphosis ensued. The tattered slippers and patched nightshirt disappeared. Woland was now wearing a long, black robe with a steel saber on his hip. He walked quickly over to Margarita, raised the goblet to her lips, and in a commanding voice said, "Drink!"

Margarita's head began to spin, she swayed, but the goblet was already at her lips, and voices, whose she could not tell, whispered in both her ears, "Don't be afraid, Your Majesty... Don't be afraid, Your Majesty, the blood has already seeped down into the earth. And there where it spilled, clusters of grapes are already growing."

Margarita took a swallow without opening her eyes, and a sweet current ran through her veins, and there was a ringing in her ears. It seemed to her that deafening roosters were crowing, that somewhere a march was playing. The crowds of guests began to lose their appearance. The women and the men in tails dissolved into dust. Decay engulfed the ballroom before Margarita's very eyes, a cryptlike smell flowed over it.

The columns dissolved, the lights went out, everything shriveled and shrank until there were no fountains, tulips, or camellias. All that was left was what had been there before—the modest living room of the jeweller's wife, and a stream of light coming through the half-opened door. And Margarita walked through this half-opened door.

XXIV

The Liberation of the Master

I N Woland's bedroom everything was as it had been before the ball.
Woland was sitting in his nightshirt on the bed, only Hella was no
longer massaging his leg, but setting the table, where earlier they
had been playing chess, for supper. Korovyov and Azazello had taken
off their tailcoats and were sitting at the table; nestled in next to them
was, naturally, the cat, who didn't want to part with his tie even though
by now it was an utterly grubby rag. Swaying on her feet, Margarita
walked over to the table and leaned on it. Then, as he had before,
Woland beckoned to her to sit down beside him.

"Well, now, did they wear you out completely?" asked Woland.

"Oh, no, Messire," answered Margarita, but barely audibly.

"Noblesse oblige," remarked the cat, and he poured Margarita some
transparent liquid into an ornate small glass.

"Is that vodka?" asked Margarita weakly.

The cat took offense and jumped up on his chair.

"Excuse me, Your Majesty," he whined, "but how could I offer vodka
to a lady? It's pure spirits!"

Margarita smiled and made an effort to move the glass away.

"Drink up, don't be afraid," said Woland, and Margarita picked up
the glass. "Hella, sit down," ordered Woland, as he explained to Margarita, "The night of the full moon is a festive occasion and I have supper
in the company of my intimate associates and servants. And so, how do
you feel? How did that wearisome ball go?"

"Stupendously!" crackled Korovyov. "Everyone was enchanted, en-
amored, overwhelmed! By her tact, her finesse, her appeal, her charm!"

Woland silently raised his glass and clinked it with Margarita's. Margarita drank up obediently, thinking that the spirits would be the end of
her. But nothing had happened. An enlivening warmth spread through
her stomach, there was a soft thump at the nape of her neck, and her
strength returned as if she had just awakened from a long, refreshing
sleep, and in addition, she felt as hungry as a wolf. Her hunger intensi-

fied when she recalled that she had not eaten anything since the previous morning. She started to devour the caviar greedily.

Behemoth cut off a slice of pineapple, salted and peppered it, ate it, and then downed a second glass of spirits with such dash that everyone broke into applause.

After Margarita's second glass of spirits, the candles in the candelabra burned brighter and the flames in the fireplace grew.

Margarita did not feel the least bit drunk. Sinking her white teeth into some meat, she savored its succulent juices as she watched Behemoth spread mustard on an oyster.

"You ought to put some grapes on top of that," said Hella softly, poking the cat in the side.

"Please don't lecture me," replied Behemoth. "I'm an experienced diner, don't worry, very experienced!"

"Ah, how nice it is to have supper like this, around the fireplace, without any fuss, an intimate group, as it were..." twanged Korovyov.

"I disagree, Fagot," retorted the cat, "A ball has a charm and a sweep all its own."

"It has neither sweep nor charm," said Woland, "and those idiotic bears, and those tigers roaring in the bar nearly gave me a migraine."

"All right, Messire," said the cat, "if it is your opinion that there is no sweep, then I shall immediately subscribe to it."

"Watch your step!" was Woland's reply.

"I was only joking," said the cat meekly. "and as for the tigers, I'll see that they're roasted."

"You can't eat tigers," said Hella.

"Is that what you think?" retorted the cat. "Then let me tell you a little story..." Narrowing his eyes with pleasure, he told a story about the time when he was wandering in the desert for nineteen days, and the only nourishment he had was the meat from a tiger he had killed. Everyone listened to his absorbing narrative with interest, and when Behemoth finished, they all exclaimed in chorus, "All lies!"

"And the most interesting thing about this fabrication," said Woland, "is that it was all lies from start to finish."

"Is that what you think? That I'm lying?" exclaimed the cat, and everyone thought that he would go on to protest, but instead, he said softly, "History will be the judge."

"Tell me," said Margarita, who had revived after the vodka, addressing Azazello, "Did you really shoot him, that former baron?"

"Of course I did," answered Azazello. "How could I not shoot him? He absolutely had to be shot."

"I got so upset!" exclaimed Margarita. "It happened so unexpectedly."

"There was nothing unexpected about it," retorted Azazello, but Korovyov began wailing and moaning, "How could one not get upset? I myself was shaken to the core! Crash! Bang! Over falls the baron!"

"I was practically hysterical," put in the cat, licking a spoonful of caviar.

"But what I don't understand is," said Margarita and gold sparks from the crystal flickered in her eyes, "wouldn't the music and the noise from the ball be audible from outside?"

"Of course not, Your Majesty," explained Korovyov. "It has to be done so that it isn't. It has to be done as carefully as possible."

"Of course, of course. But what about that man on the stairs... When Azazello and I were coming in... And the other one at the entranceway... I think he was watching your apartment..."

"You're right! You're right!" shouted Korovyov. "You're right, dear Margarita Nikolayevna! You've confirmed my suspicions! Yes, he was watching our apartment! At first I thought he might have been an absentminded professor or a lovesick beau mooning on the staircase. But no, no! Something didn't feel right to me! Aha! So he was watching our apartment! And the one at the entranceway too! And same for the one by the gate!"

"Won't it be interesting if they do come and arrest you?" asked Margarita.

"They'll come all right, enchanting Queen, they'll come!" replied Korovyov. "I feel it in my bones. Not now, of course, but in their good time they're sure to come. But I don't imagine they'll find anything interesting."

"Oh, how upset I was when that baron fell," said Margarita, evidently still feeling the aftereffects of the first murder she had ever witnessed. "You're probably a very good shot?"

"Not bad," answered Azazello.

"At what distance?" Margarita asked Azazello rather strangely.

"It depends what I'm shooting at," answered Azazello reasonably. "It's one thing to hit the critic Latunsky's window with a hammer, and quite another to hit him in the heart."

"The heart!" exclaimed Margarita, clutching her own for some reason. "The heart!" she repeated in a hollow voice.

"What's this about a critic named Latunsky?" asked Woland, squinting at Margarita.

Azazello, Korovyov, and Behemoth looked down in seeming embarrassment, and Margarita answered with a blush, "There's a certain critic by that name. This evening I demolished his entire apartment."

"What do you know! But why?"

"He, Messire," explained Margarita, "ruined a certain Master."

"But why did you go to all that trouble yourself?" asked Woland.

"Permit me, Messire," cried the cat joyously, and jumping up.

"You stay put," muttered Azazello, standing up. "I'll go over there right now..."

"No!" exclaimed Margarita. "No, Messire, I beg you, it's not necessary!"

"As you wish, as you wish," replied Woland, and Azazello resumed his place.

"So where did we leave off, precious Queen Margot?" said Korovyov. "Ah, yes, the heart. He can hit the heart." Korovyov pointed his long finger at Azazello. "To order, any auricle or any of the ventricles."

Margarita did not grasp the meaning of this immediately, but once she had understood, she exclaimed in amazement, "But they're hidden from view!"

"Dear lady," twanged Korovyov, "that's the point, that they're hidden! That's the whole point! Anyone can hit a visible target!"

Korovyov took a seven of spades out of the desk drawer, offered it to Margarita, and asked her to mark one of the pips with her finger nail. She marked the one in the upper right-hand corner. Hella hid the card under the pillow and yelled, "Ready!"

Azazello, who was sitting with his back to the pillow, pulled a black automatic pistol out of the pocket of his dress trousers, laid the muzzle on his shoulder, and fired without turning to face the bed, thereby giving Margarita a jolt of pleasant fear. The card was removed from the bullet-pierced pillow. It had been hit where Margarita had marked it.

"I wouldn't want to run into you when you've got a gun in your hands," said Margarita, looking coquettishly at Azazello. She had a passion for anyone who could do anything really well.

"Precious Queen," squeaked Korovyov. "Running into him isn't a good idea even when he doesn't have a gun! I give you my word of honor as a former choirmaster and precentor that a meeting with him is unwelcome under any circumstances."

The cat, who had been sitting with a frown on his face during the shooting demonstration, suddenly declared, "I'm going to try to outdo him with the seven card."

Azazello hooted something in reply. But the cat was stubborn and asked for not one, but two guns. Azazello pulled another gun out of his other back trouser pocket and wearing a disdainful smirk, offered both of them to the braggart. They marked two pips on the seven card. The cat made lengthy preparations after turning his back to the pillow. Margarita sat with her fingers in her ears and looked at the owl dozing on the mantelpiece. The cat shot off both guns, whereupon Hella let out a shriek, the dead owl fell off the mantel, and the shattered clock stopped. Hella, one of whose hands was bloodied, howled and dug her nails into the cat's fur, and he responded by grabbing her hair with his claws. They started rolling around the floor in a tangled heap. A goblet fell off the table and smashed to bits.

"Get this crazed she-devil off me!" wailed the cat, as he tried to fight off Hella, who was sitting on his back. The combatants were separated, Korovyov blew on Hella's wounded finger, and it was healed.

"I can't shoot when people are distracting me by talking!" cried

Behemoth, trying to reattach a large clump of fur that had been torn off his back.

"I bet," said Woland, smiling at Margarita, "that he missed on purpose. He's a good shot."

Hella and the cat made up, and as a token of their reconciliation, they kissed. The card was retrieved from under the pillow and checked. No pip had been touched except the one Azazello shot.

"That's not possible," maintained the cat, peering at the candelabrum through the hole in the card.

The merry supper continued. The candles burned down in the candelabra, and the dry, fragrant warmth coming from the fireplace spread through the room in waves. After eating her fill, Margarita was overcome by a feeling of bliss. She watched the bluish-gray smoke rings from Azazello's cigar float into the fireplace, and the cat try to catch them on the end of his saber. She had no desire to go anywhere, although according to her calculations it was already very late. Everything considered, it seemed to be approaching six in the morning. Taking advantage of the pause, Margarita turned to Woland and said timidly, "I should probably go... It's late."

"Where are you rushing off to?" queried Woland politely, albeit dryly. The others kept their silence, pretending to be entranced by the smoke rings.

"Yes, it's time to go," repeated Margarita, who was somewhat disconcerted by their response, and she turned as if in search of a cape or something to put on. Her nakedness had suddenly begun to embarrass her. She got up from the table. Woland quietly removed his soiled and threadbare robe from the bed, and Korovyov threw it over Margarita's shoulders.

"Thank you, Messire," said Margarita in barely audible tones, and she gave Woland a questioning look. He responded with a polite and noncommittal smile. Black anguish immediately threatened to engulf Margarita's heart. She felt cheated. No one, it seemed, had any intention of rewarding her for her services at the ball, nor did they wish to stop her from leaving. And yet it was perfectly obvious to her that she no longer had any place to go. A fleeting thought that she might have to go back to her house sent a jolt of despair through her. Should she ask for something for herself, as Azazello had so temptingly suggested in the Alexandrovsky Park? "No, not for anything," she said to herself.

"All the best to you, Messire," she said aloud, all the while thinking, "If I can just get out of here, I'll go down to the river and drown myself."

"Do sit down," came Woland's sudden command.

A change came over Margarita's face, and she sat down.

"Perhaps you wish to say something before you go?"

"No, nothing, Messire," replied Margarita proudly. "Except, of course, that if you still have need of me, I'm happy to be of service. I'm not in the least bit tired and I thoroughly enjoyed myself at the ball. So much so that if it had lasted longer, I would have been glad to let thousands more murderers and gallows birds kiss my knee." Her eyes filling with tears, Margarita looked at Woland, as through a veil.

"Bravo! You're absolutely right!" said Woland in a fearsome, booming voice. "That's the way!"

"That's the way!" echoed Woland's retinue.

"We've been testing you," Woland continued. "Never ask for anything! Not ever, not for anything, especially from someone who's more powerful than you are. They will offer and grant everything themselves. Sit down, proud woman." Woland tore the heavy robe from Margarita's shoulders, and again she found herself sitting next to him on the bed. "And so, Margot," continued Woland, softening his voice, "what would you like in return for having served as my hostess today? What do you wish for having gone naked at the ball? What value do you put on your knee? What damages did you incur from my guests, whom you just referred to as gallows birds? Speak! And do so without constraint since it is I who have made the offer."

Margarita's heart began to pound, she heaved a sigh and started to collect her thoughts.

"Come now, show more courage!" prompted Woland. "Arouse your imagination, give it free reign! Just witnessing the murder of that inveterate scoundrel of a baron should earn someone a reward, especially if that someone is—a woman. Well?"

Margarita's breath caught in her throat, and just as she was about to say the cherished words she had prepared in her soul, she suddenly turned pale, her mouth opened, and her eyes bulged. "Frieda! Frieda! Frieda!" cried an insistent, beseeching voice in her ears. "My name is Frieda!" And Margarita, stumbling over her words, began speaking, "So that means then... that I can ask... for one thing?"

"Demand, demand, my Donna," replied Woland with an understanding smile. "Demand one thing!"

Oh, how adroitly and precisely did Woland emphasize—"one thing!" in repeating Margarita's words.

Margarita sighed again and said, "I want them to stop giving Frieda the handkerchief she used to smother her baby."

The cat raised his eyes skyward and sighed noisily, but said nothing, evidently recalling how his ear had been tweaked at the ball.

"Ruling out the possibility," Woland grinned, "that you've taken a bribe from that fool Frieda—which would not be in keeping with your queenly dignity—I really don't know what to do. I suppose there is one thing—get hold of some rags and plug up all the cracks in my bedroom!"

"What are you talking about, Messire?" asked Margarita, perplexed by these truly baffling words.

"I agree with you completely, Messire," interjected the cat, "rags are just what you need." And with that he pounded his paw on the table in irritation.

"I'm talking about mercy," said Woland, explaining his words, his fiery eye still fixed on Margarita. "Sometimes it unexpectedly and insidiously slips through the narrowest of cracks. That's why I mentioned the rags."

"And that's what I was talking about too!" exclaimed the cat, and just to be safe, he turned away from Margarita and covered his pointed ears with paws smeared in pink cream.

"Get out of here," Woland said to him.

"I haven't had my coffee yet," replied the cat, "so how can I leave? Surely, Messire, on a holiday night like this you're not dividing your dinner guests into two categories are you? Some—of first grade, and others of second grade freshness, as that pathetic cheapskate of a bar manager would say?"

"Be quiet," ordered Woland, and turning to Margarita, he asked, "Are you, everything considered, an exceptionally kind person? Highly moral?"

"No," replied Margarita forcefully. "I know one has no choice but to be frank with you, and I'll tell you frankly: I'm a thoughtless person. I asked you on Frieda's behalf only because I was careless enough to give her real hope. She's waiting, Messire, she believes in my power. And if her hope is betrayed, I'll be in an awful position. I'll have no peace for the rest of my life. It can't be helped! It just happened that way."

"Oh," said Woland. "that's understandable."

"So will you do it?" asked Margarita softly.

"No, never," answered Woland. "The fact is, dear Queen, there's been a slight mix-up here. Each department should concern itself with its own business. I don't dispute that our resources are quite extensive, much more extensive, in fact, than certain not very discerning people suppose..."

"Yes, much more extensive," chimed in the cat, unable to restrain himself, evidently priding himself on these resources.

"Be quiet, the devil take you!" said Woland, and continued, turning to Margarita, "But really, what sense is there in doing what is supposed to be the business of another, as I put it, department? And so, I will not do it, but you shall."

"Do I really have the power?"

Azazello gave Margarita an ironical sidelong glance and snorted with an imperceptible shake of his red head.

"So do it then, this is torture," muttered Woland. He gave his globe a turn and began focusing on some detail there, evidently preoccupied with another matter during his conversation with Margarita.

"Well, say Frieda," prompted Korovyov.

"Frieda!" came Margarita's piercing cry.

The door flew open, and a dishevelled, naked woman with frenzied eyes, but no longer showing any signs of intoxication, burst into the room and stretched out her hands to Margarita, who said majestically, "You are forgiven. You will not be given the handkerchief anymore."

Frieda let out a wail, fell prostrate on the floor, stretched out like a cross in front of Margarita. Woland waved his hand, and Frieda vanished from sight.

"Thank you, and farewell," said Margarita, and got up to go.

"Well, Behemoth," began Woland, "let's not take advantage of an impractical person's folly on a holiday night," he turned to Margarita, "And so, that didn't count because after all, I did nothing . What do you want for yourself?"

Silence ensued, and it was broken by Korovyov, who whispered in Margarita's ear, "My diamond Donna, I advise you to be a little more sensible this time! Otherwise, good fortune may pass you by!"

"I want, this very instant, right now, to have my lover, the Master, returned to me," said Margarita, and a spasm contorted her face.

At this point a wind tore into the room with such force that the candles in the candelabra almost blew out, the heavy curtain on the window moved aside, and the window flew open, revealing high up in the distance a full moon, but a midnight moon rather than a morning one. A greenish square of a nocturnal light fell from the windowsill onto the floor, and in it appeared Ivan's night visitor, who called himself the Master. He was in his hospital clothes—a robe, slippers, and the little black cap he never parted with. His unshaven face twitched in a grimace, he looked askance with crazy-fearful eyes at the light from the candles, and a flood of moonlight seethed around him.

Margarita recognized him immediately, she let out a moan, clasped her hands and ran to him. She kissed his forehead, his lips, pressed her face against his prickly cheek, and long pent-up tears streamed freely down her face. She uttered only one word, senselessly repeating it over and over, "You... you... you..."

The Master pushed her away and said in a hollow voice, "Don't cry, Margot, don't torment me. I'm seriously ill." He grabbed hold of the windowsill, as if intending to jump up on it and run, stared, baring his teeth at the seated company, and began to shout, "I'm frightened, Margot! I've started having hallucinations again..."

Sobs stifled Margarita, and she whispered, choking on her words, "No, no, no... don't be afraid of anything... I'm with you... I'm with you..."

Deftly and unobtrusively, Korovyov pushed a chair over to the Master, who sat down on it, and Margarita fell on her knees, pressing herself against the sick man's side and thus grew calm. In all her excitement she had not noticed that her nakedness was suddenly gone and she was now wearing a black silk cloak. The sick man lowered his head and began staring at the floor with sick, sullen eyes.

"Yes," began Woland after a silence, "they've done quite a job on him." He commanded Korovyov, "Knight, give this man a little something to drink."

Margarita coaxed the Master in a trembling voice, "Drink it, drink it! Are you afraid to? No, no, believe me, they'll help you!"

The sick man took the glass and drank what was in it, but his hand shook, and the empty glass smashed at his feet.

"A lucky sign! A lucky sign!" whispered Korovyov to Margarita. "See, he's already getting better."

Indeed, the sick man's gaze no longer seemed so wild and distraught.

"But is it really you, Margot?" asked the moonlight guest.

"Have no doubt, it's me," Margarita replied.

"Give him some more!" ordered Woland.

After the Master had drained a second glass, his eyes looked alive and comprehending.

"Well, now, that's something else entirely," said Woland, narrowing his eyes. "Now let's talk. Who are you?"

"Now I am no one," replied the Master, his mouth twisted in a smile.

"Where did you just come from?"

"From an insane asylum. I'm mentally ill," replied the newcomer.

Margarita could not stand to hear these words, and burst into tears again. Then she wiped her eyes and cried, "Horrible words! Horrible words! He's the Master, Messire, I can assure you of that. Cure him, he deserves it."

"Do you know whom you are speaking to now?" Woland asked the newcomer, "Do you know whose guest you are?"

"Yes," answered the Master. "My neighbor in the madhouse was that boy Ivan Bezdomny. He told me about you."

"Well, well," replied Woland. "I had the pleasure of meeting that young man at Patriarch's Ponds. He nearly drove me out of my mind, trying to prove to me that I don't exist! But you, do you believe that it's really me?"

"I have to believe that," said the newcomer, "although it would, of course, be a lot more soothing to regard you as a product of my hallucinations. Excuse me," added the Master, catching himself.

"Well, if it's more soothing, then by all means do so," replied Woland politely.

"No, no," said Margarita fearfully, shaking the Master by the shoulder. "Come to your senses! It really is him!"

The cat put in a word here as well, "But I really do look like a hallucination. Look at my profile in the moonlight." The cat crawled into a strip of moonlight and wanted to say something else, but was asked to be quiet, so he replied, "All right, all right, I'm ready to be quiet. I'll be a silent hallucination," and fell silent.

"But tell me, why does Margarita call you the Master?" asked Woland.

The newcomer laughed and said, "A pardonable weakness on her part. She has too high an opinion of the novel I wrote."

"What is the novel about?"

"It is about Pontius Pilate."

Here again the tongues of flame on the candles began to flicker and jump, the dishes started rattling on the table, and Woland burst out into thunderous laughter, but no one was frightened or surprised by this. For some reason Behemoth began to applaud.

"About what? About what? About whom?" said Woland, after he stopped laughing. "In these times? Why, that's stupendous! Couldn't you find another subject? Let me have a look at it." Woland stretched out his hand, palm upward.

"Unfortunately, I can't do that," replied the Master, "because I burned it in the stove."

"Forgive me, but I don't believe you," said Woland. "That cannot be. Manuscripts don't burn." He turned to Behemoth and said, "Well now, Behemoth, let's have the novel."

The cat jumped off the chair instantly, and everyone saw that he had been sitting on a thick pile of manuscripts. The cat handed the top one to Woland with a bow. Again almost in tears, Margarita started trembling and shouting, "There it is, the manuscript! There it is!"

She threw herself at Woland and added rapturously, "He's omnipotent! Omnipotent!"

Woland took the copy handed to him, turned it over, put it aside, and stared silently and unsmilingly at the Master. For no apparent reason the latter suddenly became distressed and anxious, got up from his chair, wrung his hands, and turning to the distant moon, began trembling and muttering, "Even at night in the moonlight I have no peace... Why have they disturbed me? O gods, gods..."

Margarita clutched at his hospital robe, pressed close to him, and began muttering in tears and anguish, "My God, why isn't the medicine helping you?"

"Never mind, never mind, never mind," whispered Korovyov, weaving about near the Master. "Never mind, Never mind... Just have another glass, and I'll keep you company..."

And the little glass twinkled and sparkled in the moonlight, and that glass did help. They sat the Master in his place, and the sick man's face became calm.

"Well, now everything is clear," said Woland, drumming on the manuscript with his middle finger.

"Totally clear," confirmed the cat, having forgotten his promise to be a silent hallucination. "The gist of this opus is now completely clear to me. What do you say, Azazello?" he said, turning to the silent Azazello.

"I say," said the latter in a nasal twang, "that it would be a good idea to drown you."

"Have mercy, Azazello," replied the cat, "and don't give my master any ideas. Take my word for it, I'd appear to you every night wearing the same moonlight garb as the poor Master here, and I'd beckon to you and lure you into following me. How would you like that, O Azazello?"

"Well, Margarita," said Woland, joining the conversation once again, "Tell me everything, what do you want?"

Margarita's eyes flashed, and she addressed Woland imploringly, "May I have a word with him?"

Woland nodded, and Margarita leaned over to the Master and whispered something in his ear. One could hear his reply to her, "No, it's too late. I want nothing more in life. Except to see you. But my advice to you is still the same—leave me. If you stay with me, you'll be lost too."

"No, I won't leave you," answered Margarita, and she turned to Woland. "I ask that we be returned to the basement apartment on the side street near the Arbat, and that the lamp be lit and that everything be just as it was."

Here the Master laughed, wrapped his arms around Margarita's long-dishevelled curly head, and said, "Ah, don't listen to the poor woman, Messire. Someone else has been living in that basement for a long time now, and besides, as a rule, things can't go back to what they were." He rested his cheek against his beloved Margarita's head, embraced her and began murmuring, "My poor thing, my poor thing..."

"Can't be as they were, you say?" said Woland. "That's true. But we'll give it a try." And he said, "Azazello!"

Immediately, from the ceiling there fell on the floor a bewildered and nearly deranged citizen clad only in his underwear, who was for some reason wearing a cap and holding a suitcase. The man was shaking and turning gray with fright.

"Are you Mogarych?" Azazello inquired of the one who had fallen from the sky.

"Aloisy Mogarych," the latter replied, trembling.

"Are you the one who read Latunsky's article on this man's novel and then filed a complaint against him, saying that he had illegal literature in his possession?" asked Azazello.

The newly arrived citizen turned blue and burst into repentant tears.

"Was it because you wanted to move into his apartment?" asked Azazello in his most cordial nasal twang.

Heard in the room was the infuriated cat, hissing, and Margarita, howling, "Know the witch, know her!"—as she dug her nails in Aloisy Mogarych's face.

A scuffle ensued.

"What are you doing?" screamed the Master in agony, "Margot, don't disgrace yourself!"

"I protest, this is no disgrace," yelled the cat.

Korovyov pulled Margarita away.

"I had a bathroom put in," cried the bloodied Mogarych, his teeth chattering, and terrified, he started babbling some nonsense, "the whitewashing alone... the sulfuric acid..."

"Well, it's good a bathroom's been added," said Azazello approvingly, "He needs to take a bath." Then he shouted, "Begone!"

Mogarych was then turned head over heels and propelled out of Woland's bedroom through the open window.

The Master's eyes popped, and he said under his breath, "Why, that's even neater than what Ivan said about him!" Utterly shaken, he looked all around and finally said to the cat, "Excuse me... was it thou... er, you, sir..." he corrected himself, not sure whether to use the intimate or polite form of address to the cat, "are you, sir, the same cat who got on the streetcar?"

"I am," confirmed the cat, flattered, and he added, "It's nice to hear you address a cat so politely. For some reason cats are usually addressed with the familiar 'thou,' despite the fact that no cat has ever drunk *Bruderschaft* with anyone."

"It seems to me for some reason that you, sir, are not an ordinary cat...," replied the Master hesitantly. "They'll still notice that I'm gone at the hospital," he added timidly to Woland.

"Well, why would they notice that!" replied Woland reassuringly, and then some books and papers appeared in his hands. "Are these your medical records?"

"Yes."

Korovyov threw them into the fireplace.

"No documents, no person," said Korovyov with satisfaction. "And is this your landlord's tenants' register?"

"Yes..."

"Who's registered in it? Aloisy Mogarych?" Korovyov blew on one of the pages of the tenants' register. There! He's gone! And, please note, never was there. And if your landlord acts surprised, tell him Aloisy was someone he dreamt about. Mogarych? What Mogarych? There was never any Mogarych." Here, the tied and secured register evaporated from Korovyov's hands. "And now it's back on the landlord's desk."

"You were absolutely right," said the Master, impressed by the neatness of Korovyov's work, "when you said: no documents, no person. So that means I don't exist since I don't have any documents."

"I beg your pardon," cried Korovyov, "that really is an hallucination, here are your documents," and Korovyov handed them to the Master. Then he shifted his gaze to Margarita and whispered sweetly to her, "And here is your property, Margarita Nikolayevna," whereupon he handed her a notebook with charred edges, a dried rose, a photograph, and, with special care, a savings book. "Here's the ten thousand ruble deposit you made, Margarita Nikolayevna. We have no need of other people's money."

"I'd rather have my paws wither and fall off than touch what belongs to someone else," exclaimed the cat in puffed-up tones, dancing on top of the suitcase to flatten down all the copies of the ill-starred novel.

"And here are your documents, too," continued Korovyov, handing them to Margarita, and then, turning to Woland, he said respectfully, "That's everything, Messire!"

"No, not everything," replied Woland, turning away from his globe. "What are your orders, my dear lady, regarding the disposition of your retinue? I personally have no need of them."

At this point Natasha, still naked, ran in through the open door. She clasped her hands and shouted to Margarita, "Be happy, Margarita Nikolayevna!" She nodded in the direction of the Master and again turned to Margarita, "You see, I always knew where you were going."

"Maids know everything," noted the cat, raising his paw sagaciously. "It's a mistake to think they're blind."

"What do you want, Natasha?" asked Margarita. "Go back to the house."

"Darling, Margarita Nikolayevna," began Natasha imploringly, getting down on her knees. "Ask them," she looked sideways at Woland, "to let me stay a witch. I don't want to go back to the house! Not for an engineer, not for a technician! Yesterday at the ball Monsieur Jacques made me an offer." Natasha opened her hand, revealing some gold coins.

Margarita cast a questioning glance at Woland. He nodded. Then Natasha threw herself on Margarita's neck, gave her a loud kiss, and flew out the window with a triumphant whoop.

In Natasha's place appeared Nikolai Ivanovich. He had assumed his former human form, but he was extraordinarily glum, and even, perhaps, annoyed.

"Here's someone I shall dismiss with special pleasure," said Woland, looking disgustedly at Nikolai Ivanovich. "With exceptional pleasure, since he's totally superfluous here."

"Please give me a certificate," began Nikolai Ivanovich, looking around wildly, but speaking with great insistence, "stating where I spent last night."

"For what purpose?" asked the cat sternly.

"To give to the police and to my wife," was Nikolai Ivanovich's firm response.

"We usually don't give certificates," said the cat with a frown, "but all right, for you we'll make an exception."

Before Nikolai Ivanovich could realize what was happening, the nude Hella was at the typewriter, taking dictation from the cat, "I hereby certify that the bearer of this note, Nikolai Ivanovich, spent the night in question at Satan's ball, having been lured there in a transportational capacity... Hella, put in parentheses! And write 'hog.' Signed—Behemoth."

"And the date?" squealed Nikolai Ivanovich.

"We won't put in the date, otherwise the document will be null and void," retorted the cat, scribbling his signature. He got a seal from somewhere, breathed on it in the customary fashion, affixed a seal saying "Paid," and handed the paper to Nikolai Ivanovich. After this the latter disappeared without a trace, and in his place appeared another unexpected figure.

"So who's this now?" asked Woland squeamishly, shading his eyes from the glow of the candles.

Varenukha hung his head, sighed, and said softly, "Let me go back. I'm not capable of being a vampire. Hella and I almost left Rimsky a goner! I'm just not bloodthirsty enough. Let me go."

"What's all this raving?" asked Woland with a frown. "Who's this Rimsky? And what's this nonsense all about?"

"You needn't trouble about this, Messire," replied Azazello and he turned to Varenukha, "Don't be rude on the phone. Don't tell lies on the phone. Got it? Will you stop doing that?"

Varenukha's head was spinning from joy, his face began to glow, and without knowing what he was saying, he mumbled, "As God is my... that is, I want to say, your hi... right after dinner..." Varenukha pressed his hands to his chest and looked pleadingly at Azazello.

"All right then, go home," the latter replied, and Varenukha melted away.

"Now everyone leave me alone with them," ordered Woland, indicating the Master and Margarita.

Woland's order was immediately obeyed. After a brief silence Woland addressed the Master, "So, you're going back to the basement apartment off the Arbat, is that it? What about your writing? Your dreams, your inspiration?"

"I no longer have any dreams, or inspiration either, for that matter," replied the Master. "Nothing around me interests me except her." He again put his hands on Margarita's head, "They've broken me, I'm depressed, and I want to go back to my basement."

"What about your novel? What about Pilate?"

"It's hateful to me, that novel," answered the Master. "I suffered too much because of it."

"I implore you," begged Margarita sorrowfully, "don't talk that way. Why are you torturing me? You know that I've put my whole life into your work." And turning to Woland, she added, "Don't listen to him, Messire, he's just worn out."

"But shouldn't you be writing about something?" said Woland. "If you've run out of things to say about the procurator, well, write about somebody else, that fellow Aloisy, for example."

The Master smiled. "Lapshyonnikova wouldn't publish it, and, besides, it's not interesting."

"But what will you live on? You'll be forced to live in poverty, you know."

"Gladly, gladly," replied the Master, drawing Margarita to him once again. With his arms around her shoulders, he added, "She'll come to her senses and leave me..."

"I don't think so," said Woland through his teeth and continued, "And so, the man who wrote the story of Pontius Pilate intends to go off to his basement, and live there in poverty by his lamp, is that right?"

Margarita detached herself from the Master's embrace and began speaking very heatedly, "I did everything I could, and I whispered to him the most tempting thing of all. And he refused it."

"I know what you whispered to him," retorted Woland, "but that isn't the most tempting thing. And to you I'll say," he smiled, turning to the Master, "Your novel has some more surprises for you."

"That's very sad," replied the Master.

"No, no, it isn't sad," said Woland, "nothing terrible will happen. Well then, Margarita Nikolayevna, everything is done. Have you any further claims on me?"

"How can you say that, oh, how can you, Messire!"

"Then take this from me as a memento," said Woland, pulling a small, diamond-studded gold horseshoe from under his pillow.

"No, no, no, whatever for!"

"Do you wish to argue with me?" asked Woland, smiling.

Since she had no pocket in her cape, Margarita put the horseshoe in a napkin, and tied it in a bundle. Here something astonished her. She turned to the window, where the moon was shining, and said, "This is what I don't understand... How can it still be midnight when it should have been morning long ago?"

"It's nice to hold on to a holiday midnight a little longer than usual," answered Woland. "Well, I wish you happiness!"

Margarita extended her hands prayerfully to Woland, but did not dare to get close to him, and she cried out softly, "Farewell! Farewell!"

"Till we meet again," said Woland.

And Margarita in her black cape, the Master in his hospital robe, stepped out into the hallway of the apartment of the jeweller's wife, where a candle was burning, and where Woland's retinue was waiting for them. When they set out down the hall, Hella was carrying the suitcase containing the novel and Margarita Nikolayevna's meager belongings, and the cat was helping Hella. At the door of the apartment Korovyov bowed and disappeared, while the others accompanied them down the stairs. The staircase was deserted. As they were crossing the third-floor landing, they heard a soft thud, but no one paid any attention to it. When they reached the front doors of entranceway No. 6,

Azazello blew upward, and as soon as they stepped into the courtyard, which the moonlight did not reach, they saw a man on the doorstep, wearing boots and a cloth cap, who was seemingly sound asleep, and a large, black car parked by the entrance with its lights off. Dimly visible through the windshield was the rook's silhouette.

As they were about to get in the car, Margarita let out a soft cry of despair, "My God, I've lost the horseshoe!"

"Get in the car," said Azazello, "and wait for me. I'll come right back as soon as I find out what happened." And he went back to the front door.

This is what had happened: shortly before Margarita and the Master left with their entourage, a shriveled woman, holding a bag and a tin can, came out of No. 48, the apartment just below the jeweller's wife's. It was that same Annushka, who, the previous Wednesday, had spilled sunflower oil at the turnstile to Berlioz's great misfortune.

Nobody knew, and probably nobody ever will, what this woman actually did in Moscow or what she lived on. The only thing that was known about Annushka was that she could be seen every day, with the can, with the bag, or with both together—either at the oil shop, the market, outside the gates of the building, on the stairs, or, most frequently of all, in the kitchen of apartment No. 48, which was where she lived. Besides that, the most notorious thing about her was that wherever she was, or wherever she appeared—trouble would start at once, and finally, that her nickname was "The Plague."

For some reason Annushka-the-Plague was in the habit of getting up incredibly early, and on that particular morning something roused her from bed before the crack of dawn, just after midnight. The key turned in the door, Annushka's nose stuck out, and then the whole of her emerged, the door slammed shut behind her and she was about to set off somewhere, when a door banged on the upstairs landing, and someone rushed down the stairs, colliding with Annushka, and knocking her sideways, so that she struck the back of her head against the wall.

"Where's the devil taking you in just your drawers?" screeched Annushka, clutching the back of her head. The man in his underwear, wearing a cap and holding a suitcase, and with his eyes closed, answered Annushka in a strange, sleepy voice, "The water pump! The sulfuric acid! The cost of the whitewash alone." And bursting into tears, he roared, "Go away!"

Then he rushed, not further down the stairs, but back—up the stairs to where the windowpane had been kicked out by the economist, and he flew out that window head over heels into the courtyard. Forgetting about the pain in the back of her head, Annushka groaned and ran to the window herself. She lay flat on her stomach on the landing and stuck her head out into the courtyard, expecting to see the broken body of the man with the suitcase stretched out on the asphalt, lit up by the yard-light. But there was absolutely nothing on the asphalt in the courtyard.

She was left to assume that the strange and sleepy individual had flown out of the house like a bird, leaving no trace of himself. Annushka crossed herself and thought. "That No. 50 really is cursed! No wonder people are talking! That's some apartment, that is!"

No sooner had she thought this, than the door upstairs banged again, and down ran a second someone. Annushka pressed herself to the wall and saw a rather respectable-looking citizen with a beard but with a slightly piglike face, or so it seemed to Annushka, dart past her and, like the preceding individual, leave the house through the window, again with no thought of smashing himself on the asphalt. Annushka had now forgotten the purpose of her outing and she just stayed on the stairs, crossing herself, groaning, and talking to herself.

Shortly after that, a third man, beardless, with a round, clean-shaven face, wearing a peasant blouse, ran out of the apartment upstairs—and flew out the window in similar fashion.

To give Annushka her due, it must be said that she was inquisitive and decided to wait a little longer to see if there would be any new marvels. The door upstairs opened again, and now a whole group of people headed down the stairs, but this time they were walking like normal people, and not running. Annushka ran away from the window, went back down to her own door, opened it hastily, hid behind it, and her eye, in a frenzy of curiosity, glimmered through the crack.

Someone who looked neither sick, nor not sick, a strange, pale man in need of a shave, and wearing a black cap and some kind of robe, was going down the stairs, supported by a lady in a black cassock, or so it appeared to Annushka in the semidarkness. The lady was not exactly barefoot, but was wearing transparent, obviously foreign-made evening slippers that had been torn to shreds. Phoo! Never mind the shoes! Why, the lady's actually naked! Well almost, that cassock's thrown right over her naked body! "That's some apartment, that is!" Annushka's soul sang with anticipation of the stories she would tell her neighbors the next day.

Behind the strangely clad lady came a completely naked one carrying a small suitcase, and prowling nearby was a huge, black cat. Rubbing her eyes, Annushka almost squealed out loud

Bringing up the rear of the procession was a short, limping, walleyed foreigner, jacketless, wearing a white dress vest and black tie. The whole company passed Annushka on its way downstairs. At this point something made a soft thump on the landing.

Hearing the footsteps fade, Annushka slithered out from behind the door like a snake, stood her oil can against the wall, lay down on her stomach and started feeling around on the floor of the landing. Her hands picked up something heavy wrapped in a napkin. Annushka's eyes bulged out of her head when she undid the bundle. She held the jewel up to her eyes, and her eyes burned with a wolfish fire. Thoughts whirled through Annushka's head, "I don't know nothing, I don't know a thing! Should I show it to my nephew? Or break it into pieces?... The stones could be pried out... And sold one at a time: one on the Petrovka, another on Smolensky... But the main thing is—I don't know nothing, and I don't know a thing!"

Annushka hid her find in her bosom, grabbed her oil can, and was about to slither back into her apartment, having decided to postpone her trip to town, when there arose before her, the devil knows from where, that same fellow with the white shirtfront and no jacket, and he whispered quietly, "Give me the horseshoe and the napkin."

"What horseshoe-napkin?" asked Annushka, feigning ignorance very skillfully. "I don't know nothing about no napkin. What are you, citizen, drunk or something?"

Without saying another word, the white-chested man squeezed Annushka's throat with fingers as hard as the handrail on a bus, and just as cold, cutting off the air to her lungs. The oil can dropped out of Annushka's hands and fell onto the floor. After cutting off Annushka's air for some moments, the jacketless foreigner removed his fingers from her neck. Gulping for air, Annushka smiled.

"Oh, you mean the little horseshoe," she began. "Here it is! So it belongs to you? I look, and I see it there in the napkin... I took it on purpose, so that nobody would pick it up, otherwise, you could kiss it good-bye!"

After receiving the horseshoe and napkin, the foreigner began to bow and scrape before Annushka, shaking her hand firmly and thanking her warmly with a very pronounced foreign accent, in expressions like these: "I am deeply grateful to you, madam. I cherish this horseshoe as a keepsake and please allow me to present you with 200 rubles, for keeping it safe." And he took the money out of his vest pocket at once and handed it to Annushka.

She, grinning foolishly, could only blurt out, "Oh, I thank you most humbly! *Merci! Merci!*"

The generous foreigner made it to the bottom of the flight in one fell swoop, but before slipping away completely, he shouted from below, this time without an accent, "You old witch, if you ever find anything else that doesn't belong to you, turn it over to the police, and don't hide it in your bosom!"

Her head agog and abuzz from all these happenings on the staircase, Annushka kept shouting *"Merci! Merci! Merci!"* for a long time out of inertia, but the foreigner was long gone.

The car was also gone from the courtyard. After returning Woland's gift to Margarita, Azazello said good-bye to her, asked if she was comfortably seated, Hella enthusiastically smothered Margarita with kisses, the cat kissed her hand, the group waved to the Master, who, lifeless and inert, had sunk into the corner of his seat, then they waved to the rook and immediately melted into thin air, not considering it worth the trouble to climb back up the stairs. The rook turned on the headlights and rolled the car out through the gates past the man who was fast asleep at the gateway. And the lights of the big black car blended in with the other lights on sleepless and noisy Sadovaya Street.

An hour later, in the basement of the small house on one of the side streets off the Arbat, in the front room, where everything was just as it had been a year ago before that terrible autumn night, at the table covered with the velvet tablecloth, beneath the shaded lamp, near which stood the vase filled with lilies of the valley, Margarita sat, weeping quietly from the shock and happiness she had experienced. The fire-damaged notebook lay before her, and next to it towered a pile of undamaged notebooks. The little house was silent. In the small, adjoining room, sound asleep on the couch, covered by his hospital robe, was the Master. His even breathing could not be heard.

When she had cried her fill, Margarita took up the undamaged notebooks and found the place she had been rereading before her meeting with Azazello beneath the Kremlin wall. Margarita did not feel like sleeping. She stroked the manuscript affectionately, as one would stroke a beloved cat, and turned it over in her hands, looking at it from all sides, now pausing at the title page, now looking at the end. She suddenly had a horrible thought that it was all witchcraft, that the notebooks were about to vanish before her eyes, that she would end up in her bedroom back home, and that when she woke up, she would have to go drown herself. But that was the last horrible thought she had, a vestige of the prolonged suffering she had undergone. Nothing vanished, the omnipotent Woland was indeed omnipotent, and Margarita was free to leaf through the pages of the notebooks for as long as she liked, even till dawn. She examined them closely, kissed them, and reread the words again and again, "'The darkness that had come in from the Mediterranean covered the city so detested by the procurator...' Yes, the darkness..."

XXV

How the Procurator
Tried to Save Judas of Kerioth

T HE darkness that had come in from the Mediterranean covered the city so detested by the procurator. The hanging bridges which connected the temple with the fearsome Antonia Tower had disappeared, an abyss descended from the sky, and covered the winged gods above the hippodrome, the Hasmonaean palace and its embrasures, the bazaars, the caravanseries, the alleys, the ponds... Yershalaim—the great city—vanished as if it had never existed. Everything was devoured by the darkness, which frightened all living creatures in Yershalaim and its surroundings. A strange dark cloud drifted in from the sea towards the end of the afternoon on the fourteenth day of the spring month of Nisan.

The cloud had already spilled its belly onto Bald Skull, where the executioners had hastily pierced the condemned men, it had broken over the temple in Yershalaim, coursed down its hills in steamy rivulets, and flooded the Lower City. The cloud gushed through windows and chased people indoors from the winding streets. It was slow to release its moisture and at first gave off only light. Whenever fire ripped through the steamy black brew, the great hulk of the temple with its glistening scaly roof soared out of the pitch darkness into view. But the fire was extinguished in an instant, and the temple again sank into the dark abyss. It leapt out several times, only to fall back again, and each time its fall was accompanied by the thunder of catastrophe.

Other quivering flashes of light summoned from the abyss the palace of Herod the Great that stood opposite the temple on the western hill, and its fearsome eyeless golden statues soared up into the black sky with their arms extended. But the heavenly fire hid once again, and heavy claps of thunder drove the golden idols back into the darkness.

The downpour broke out unexpectedly, and then the thunderstorm turned into a hurricane. On the very spot near the marble bench in the garden where the procurator had conversed with the high priest around noontime, there was a crack of thunder like a canon shot, and a cypress tree broke in two like a cane. Mingling with watery dust and hail, torn roses, magnolia leaves, small twigs, and sand swept through the colonnade onto the balcony. The hurricane scourged the garden.

At this time there was only one man under the colonnade, and that man was the procurator.

Now he was not sitting in his chair, but was instead reclining on a couch next to a low table set with food and jugs of wine. Another couch, unoccupied, stood on the other side of the table. A red puddle, which looked like blood and had not been cleaned up, was spreading out from under the procurator's feet and in it were pieces of a broken jug. The servant, who had been setting the table before the storm, had become flustered by the procurator's stare and upset that he had displeased him in some way, and the procurator, angry at the servant, had smashed the jug on the mosaic floor, saying, "Why don't you look me in the eye when you serve me? Have you stolen something?"

The African's black face turned gray, mortal terror appeared in his eyes, he began to tremble, and almost broke the other jug; but for some reason the procurator's anger subsided as quickly as it had flared up. Just as the African was about to pick up the broken pieces and wipe up the puddle, the procurator waved him away, and the slave ran off. And the puddle remained.

Now, as the hurricane raged the African huddled near a niche, which held a statue of a white naked woman bowing her head—the African was afraid of showing himself at the wrong moment, yet also fearful lest he miss the procurator's summons.

Reclining on his couch in the semidarkness of the storm, the procurator poured himself some wine, drank it in long gulps, and reached occasionally for the bread, crumbling it, and swallowing it in small pieces. Now and again he would suck on an oyster, chew on a slice of lemon, and then take another drink.

Were it not for the roar of the water, the claps of thunder that threatened to smash in the palace roof, the clatter of hail that pounded against the balcony steps, it might have been possible to hear the procurator mumbling something as he talked to himself. And if the intermittent flickers of heavenly fire had been transformed into a steady light, an observer might have been able to see that the procurator's face, its eyes inflamed by wine and by recent bouts of insomnia, expressed impatience, that the procurator was not only gazing at the two white roses, which had drowned in the red puddle, but was constantly turning his face toward the garden and the onslaught of watery dust and sand, that he was waiting for someone, waiting impatiently.

A short time passed, and the veil of water before the procurator's eyes began to thin. As fierce as the hurricane had been, it was growing weaker. Branches no longer cracked and fell. The claps of thunder and flashes of lightning became less frequent. The violet coverlet with the white trim that had been floating above Yershalaim was gone, and all that remained was an ordinary gray, rear-guard cloud. The thunderstorm was moving out to the Dead Sea.

Now it was possible to hear the separate sounds of the rain and of the water as it streamed through the gutters and down the steps of the staircase which the procurator had traversed earlier that day when he had gone to announce the sentence in the square. And finally the gush of the fountain could be heard, which earlier had been drowned out. It was growing lighter. Dark-blue windows began to appear in the gray veil that was sweeping eastward.

Then from afar, breaking through the patter of the now utterly feeble drizzle, the faint sounds of trumpets and the clatter of several hundred hooves reached the procurator's ears. Hearing those sounds, the procurator shifted position, and his face became animated. The ala was returning from Bald Mountain. Judging by the sound, it was moving across the square where the sentence had been pronounced.

At last the procurator heard both the long-awaited footsteps, and the shuffling on the staircase that led to the garden's upper terrace right in front of the balcony. The procurator craned his neck, and his eyes began to sparkle with joy.

The first thing to appear between the two marble lions was a head in a hood, followed by a drenched man in a cloak that stuck to his body. It was the same man who had had a hushed conversation with the procurator in a darkened room of the palace before the pronouncement of the sentence and who, during the execution, had sat on a three-legged stool, playing with a twig.

Heedless of the puddles, the man in the hood cut across the garden terrace, stepped onto the mosaic floor of the balcony, and, raising his arm, said in a pleasant, high-pitched voice, "Health and happiness to the Procurator!" The newcomer spoke in Latin.

"Gods!" exclaimed Pilate. "You haven't a dry thread on you! What a hurricane! Eh? Please go to my room. Do me the favor of changing into dry clothes."

The visitor threw off his hood, revealing his completely soaked head, his hair plastered to his forehead, and with a polite smile on his clean-shaven face, he began to refuse a change of clothes, assuring the procurator that a little rain would cause him no harm.

"I won't hear of it," replied Pilate. He clapped his hands and summoned the servants, who had been hiding from him, to attend to the visitor's needs, and then to serve hot food at once. The procurator's visitor required very little time to dry his hair, change his clothes and footwear, and tidy up in general, and he soon appeared on the balcony steps in dry sandals, a dry crimson military cloak, and with his hair smoothed down.

By this time the sun had returned to Yershalaim, and before departing to sink into the Mediterranean, it sent its farewell rays to the city detested by the procurator and gilded the balcony steps. The fountain had revived completely and was gurgling at full strength, the pigeons had come out on the sand, and were cooing and hopping over the broken twigs, and pecking at something in the wet sand. The red puddle had been mopped up, the pieces of broken pottery had been cleared away, and meat was steaming on the table.

"I await the Procurator's orders," said the visitor, approaching the table.

"But you will hear none until you sit down and have some wine," replied Pilate courteously, indicating the other couch.

The visitor reclined, and a servant poured deep red wine into his cup. Another servant leaned carefully over Pilate's shoulder and filled the procurator's cup. When this was done, the latter signalled both servants to leave.

While the visitor ate and drank, Pilate, sipping his wine, watched his guest with narrowed eyes. The man who had appeared before Pilate was middle-aged, with a very pleasant, round, well-groomed face with a fleshy nose. His hair was of indeterminate color. Now as it dried, it grew lighter. It would have been hard to guess the visitor's nationality. The main thing that defined his face was probably its good-natured expression, an expression belied, however, by his eyes, or, more precisely, not by the eyes themselves, but by the way the visitor looked at his interlocutor. Usually the visitor concealed his small eyes beneath their somewhat odd, puffy-looking lids. A benign slyness shone in the slits of his eyes when he did this. One had to suppose that the procurator's guest was a man inclined to humor. But the humor gleaming in the slits of his eyes would occasionally be banished, when the present guest of the procurator would open his eyelids wide and stare suddenly and directly at his interlocutor, as if he were trying to locate some imperceptible spot on his nose. This would last only for a moment, after which his eyelids would drop again, the slits would reappear, and they would shine again with the same good will and sly intelligence.

The visitor did not refuse a second cup of wine, swallowed several oysters with obvious pleasure, sampled the boiled vegetables, and ate a piece of meat.

After eating his fill, he praised the wine, "A superb wine, Procurator. Is it a Falernum?"

"A thirty-year-old Cecubum," replied the procurator amiably.

The guest pressed his hand to his heart, declined any more food and said he was full. Then Pilate filled his own cup, and his guest did the same. Both of them poured some of their wine onto a platter with the meat, and, raising his cup, the procurator said in a low voice, "To us, to you, Caesar, father of the Romans, dearest and best of men!"

After this they drank their wine, and the Africans cleared the table of food, leaving just the fruit and the jugs. Once again the procurator signalled the servants to leave, and he and his guest were left alone under the colonnade.

"And so," Pilate began softly, "what can you tell me of the mood in the city?"

Involuntarily, he turned his gaze to the place beyond and below the garden terraces, where the colonnades and flat roofs were being gilded by the sun's last rays.

"I believe, Procurator," replied the guest, "that the mood in Yershalaim is now satisfactory."

"So we can count on there being no more disturbances?"

"We can count," replied the guest, looking affectionately at the procurator, "on only one thing in this world—the power of the mighty Caesar."

"May the gods grant him long life," joined in Pilate immediately, "and universal peace." After a brief silence he continued, "So you think we can have the troops withdrawn?"

"I think that the Lightning Cohort can be withdrawn," replied the guest, adding, "But it would be a good idea if it marched around the city as it left."

"A very good idea," the procurator agreed, "I shall have the Lightning Cohort withdrawn the day after tomorrow, and I myself shall leave—and I swear to you by the Feast of the Twelve Gods, and by the Lares—I would have given a great deal to have been able to leave today!"

"The Procurator does not like Yershalaim?" queried the guest goodhumoredly.

"Have mercy on me," exclaimed the procurator, smiling, "There is no more hopeless place on earth. To say nothing of the climate! I get sick every time I am forced to come here. But that alone would not be so bad. It's these holidays—magicians, sorcerers, wizards, these hoards of pilgrims... Fanatics, fanatics! Look at the trouble caused by this messiah alone, who they've suddenly started waiting for this year! Every minute expecting to have to witness some ghastly bloodbath. Constantly having to transfer troops around, reading accusations and denunciations, half of which are written against you yourself! You will agree, that's tedious. Oh, if weren't for the imperial service!..."

"Yes, the holidays here are difficult," agreed the guest.

"With all my heart I wish them to be over soon," added Pilate vigorously. "Then I shall at last be able to return to Caesarea. Can you believe that this absurd construction of Herod's,"—the procurator waved his hand at the colonnade to show that he was referring to the palace—"is positively driving me out of my mind. I cannot bear to spend the night here. No stranger piece of architecture has ever been seen! But let's get back to business. First of all, is that damned Bar-rabban causing you any concern?"

Here the guest looked at the procurator's cheek with that peculiar stare of his. But the procurator was gazing off into the distance with a bored expression, frowning with distaste and contemplating that part of the city which lay at his feet and was fading into the dusk. The guest's stare also faded, and his eyelids drooped.

"One must assume that Bar is now as harmless as a lamb," began the guest, wrinkles appearing on his round face. "It's awkward for him to rebel now."

"Because he's too famous?" asked Pilate with a laugh.

"As always, the Procurator shows a subtle grasp of the issue!"

"But, in any case," the procurator noted with concern, raising a long, slender finger that bore a ring with a black stone, "it will be necessary to..."

"Oh, the Procurator can rest assured that so long as I am in Judea, Bar will not take a step without me being at his heels."

"Now I am calm, as, by the way, I always am when you are here."

"The Procurator is too kind!"

"And now please tell me about the execution," said the procurator.

"What is it precisely that interests the Procurator?"

"Were there no attempts by the crowd to express their outrage? That's the main thing, of course."

"None," replied the guest.

"Very good. Did you yourself establish that death had occurred?"

"The Procurator can be sure of that."

"And tell me... were they given a drink before being hanged on the posts?"

"Yes. But he," here the guest closed his eyes, "refused to drink anything."

"Whom do you mean?" asked Pilate.

"Forgive me, Hegemon!" exclaimed the guest. "Did I not give his name? Ha-Notsri."

"Madman!" said Pilate, grimacing for some reason. A vein twitched under his left eye. "Dying from exposure to the sun! Why refuse what is allowed by the law? How did he express his refusal?"

"He said," replied the guest, again closing his eyes, "that he was grateful and cast no blame for the taking of his life."

"On whom?" asked Pilate in a hollow voice.

"That he did not say, Hegemon."

"Did he try to preach anything in front of the soldiers?"

"No, Hegemon, he was not talkative on this occasion. The only thing he said was that he considered cowardice one of the worst of all human vices."

"What made him say that?" the guest heard a suddenly cracked voice say.

"There is no way of knowing. His behavior was strange in general, as it always was, I might add."

"What was strange about it?"

"He kept trying to look those around him in the eyes and he kept smiling a distracted kind of smile."

"Nothing else?" asked the hoarse voice.

"Nothing else."

The procurator banged his cup as he poured himself more wine. After draining it to the dregs, he began speaking, "This is the fact of the matter: although we have been unable—at least for the present—to locate any of his disciples or followers, we should not assume that there are none."

The guest listened attentively, his head bowed.

"And so, to avoid surprises of any kind," continued the procurator, "immediately and without any fuss, please make the bodies of all three executed men disappear from the face of the earth and bury them quietly and in secret so that neither hide nor hair of them remains."

"Yes, Hegemon," said the guest, and rose, saying, "In view of the complexity and seriousness of this matter, permit me to leave right away."

"No, sit down for a while longer," said Pilate, gesturing to his guest to stay. "There are two other matters. First—your vast accomplishments in the highly demanding post of chief of the secret service for the procurator of Judea afford me the pleasant opportunity of informing Rome of that fact."

Here the visitor's face turned pink, he got up and bowed to the procurator, saying, "I am merely doing my duty as a member of the imperial service!"

"But I would like to request," continued the Hegemon, "that if you are offered a transfer with a promotion, that you refuse it and stay here. I do not wish to lose you on any account. Let them find some other way to reward you."

"I am happy to serve under you, Hegemon."

"I am very glad to hear that. And so, to turn to the other matter. It concerns that, what's his name... Judas of Kerioth."

Here the guest gave the procurator that stare of his, and then, as usual, extinguished it.

"They say," continued the procurator, lowering his voice, "that he allegedly received money for welcoming that crazy philosopher into his house."

"Will receive," the chief of the secret service gently corrected the procurator.

"And is it a large sum?"

"No one can know that, Hegemon."

"Even you?" asked the Hegemon, his astonishment an expression of praise.

"Alas, even I," calmly replied the guest. "But I do know that he will receive the money this evening. He has been summoned today to Kaifa's palace."

"Ah, that greedy old man from Kerioth," remarked the procurator, smiling. "He is an old man, isn't he?"

"The Procurator is never wrong, but this time he is mistaken," replied the guest amiably. "The man from Kerioth is a young man."

"You don't say! Can you describe him to me? Is he a fanatic?"

"Oh, no, Procurator."

"I see. Anything else?"

"He's very handsome."

"And? Has he perhaps one particular passion?"

"It's hard to have precise knowledge of everyone in this vast city, Procurator..."

"Oh, no, no, Afranius! Don't underestimate your talents."

"He does have one passion, Procurator." The guest paused briefly. "A passion for money."

"And what is his occupation?"

Afranius raised his eyebrows, thought a moment, and replied, "He works in a money-changer's shop that belongs to one of his relatives."

"Ah, yes, yes, yes, yes." Here the procurator fell silent, looked around to make sure there was no one on the balcony, and then said quietly, "The fact is today I received information that he will be murdered tonight."

Here the guest not only fixed the procurator with his gaze, he even held it there for a while, and then replied, "You have given too flattering an account of me, Procurator. In my opinion I do not deserve your recommendation. I have no such information."

"You merit the highest possible reward," replied the procurator, "but such information does exist."

"Dare I inquire who gave you this information?"

"Allow me not to disclose that for the moment, especially since the information is accidental, unclear, and unreliable. But it is my duty to foresee everything. That is my job, and more than anything else, I must trust my own intuition because it has never deceived me. According to the information I have, one of Ha-Notsri's secret friends, outraged by this money-changer's monstrous betrayal, has conspired with accomplices to kill him tonight, and to send the money he received for his betrayal back to the high priest with a note saying: 'I am returning your accursed money.'"

The head of the secret service gave the Hegemon no more of his sudden stares and continued listening to him with narrowed eyes, as Pilate continued, "Do you think the high priest will find it pleasant to receive such a gift on the night of the holiday?"

"Not only will it not be pleasant," replied the guest, smiling, "but I believe it will cause a huge scandal, Procurator."

"And I share your opinion. That is why I want you to take care of this matter, that is, take every measure to insure the safety of Judas of Kerioth."

"The Hegemon's command shall be executed," began Afranius, "but I must reassure the Hegemon: the villains' plot is extraordinarily difficult to carry out. After all, just think,"—as he spoke, the guest turned and continued—"they have to track him down, murder him, find out how much money he received, find a way of returning it to Kaifa, and do it all in one night? Today?"

"All the same, he will be murdered tonight," Pilate repeated stubbornly. "I'm telling you, I have a premonition! And my premonitions have yet to deceive me," whereupon a spasm passed over the procurator's face, and he briefly rubbed his hands.

"Yes, sir," obediently replied the guest, who then rose, stood up straight, and suddenly asked severely, "So, they'll murder him, Hegemon?"

"Yes," replied Pilate, "and our only hope is your astonishing proficiency which so amazes everyone."

The guest adjusted the heavy belt under his cloak and said, "I have the honor of wishing you health and happiness."

"Ah, yes," Pilate exclaimed softly, "I almost forgot! I owe you money!"

The guest showed surprise.

"Really, Procurator, you don't owe me anything."

"Yes I do! Remember the crowd of beggars when I entered Yershalaim... I wanted to throw them money, but I didn't have any, so I borrowed some from you."

"Oh, Procurator, that was such a trifle!"

"Even trifles should be remembered."

Pilate then turned, lifted his cloak, which was lying on the chair behind him, took a leather pouch out from underneath, and handed it to the guest. Bowing, the latter accepted it, and hid it under his cloak.

"I shall expect your report," Pilate began, "on the burial and also on this matter of Judas of Kerioth tonight. You hear me, Afranius, tonight. The escort will be given orders to wake me as soon as you appear. I shall be expecting you."

"It has been an honor," said the chief of the secret service, and he turned and left the balcony. A crunching sound was heard as he walked over the wet sand on the terrace, and then the shuffling of his sandals sounded on the marble surface between the two lions. Then his legs, torso, and finally, his hood disappeared from view. Only then did the procurator see that the sun had already set and twilight had come.

XXVI

The Burial

PERHAPS it was the twilight that made the procurator's appearance change so dramatically. He seemed to have aged on the spot, to have become stooped and to have grown anxious as well. Once he looked around and for some reason shuddered when his gaze fell on the empty chair which had his cloak thrown over its back. The holiday night was approaching, the evening shadows were playing their usual tricks and very likely the weary procurator imagined that someone was sitting in the empty chair. Letting faintheartedness get the best of him, and shifting the cloak, the procurator left it lying there and began pacing around the balcony, first rubbing his hands, then going over to the table to grab the wine-cup, then stopping to stare blankly at the mosaic floor as though trying to decipher something written there.

For the second time that day he was overcome by anguish. Rubbing his brow where there now remained only a dull, faintly nagging trace of the hellish morning pain, he kept straining to understand what was causing his mental torment. And he quickly realized what it was but tried to deceive himself. It was clear to him that he had lost something irretrievably that day, and that now he wanted to make up for the loss with minor, inconsequential, and most importantly, belated measures. His self-deception consisted in his trying to convince himself that the actions taken that evening were no less important than the sentence passed that morning. But the procurator was having very little success in convincing himself.

On one of his turns about the balcony he stopped abruptly and whistled. In reply to his whistle, a low growl sounded in the shadows, and a gigantic gray dog with pointed ears and a gold-studded collar bounded onto the balcony from the garden.

"Banga, Banga," cried the procurator weakly.

The dog stood up on his hind paws, lowered his front paws onto his master's shoulders, almost knocking him to the floor, and licked his cheek. The procurator sat down in his chair, and Banga, his tongue out and panting, lay down at his master's feet. The joy in the dog's eyes signified that the thunderstorm—the only thing in the world the intrepid dog feared—was over, and that he was back next to the man he loved, respected, and considered the most powerful on earth, the ruler of all men, who made the dog himself feel privileged, superior, and special as well. But once he had lain down by his master's feet, the dog sensed immediately, even without looking at him, but at the gathering shadows in the garden, that something bad had happened to him. Therefore, the dog changed position, got up, went around to the side of the chair, and put his front paws and head on the procurator's knees, getting wet sand all over the bottom of his cloak. Banga's actions were probably meant to console his master and to let him know that he was prepared to face misfortune with him. He tried to show this with his eyes, which looked sideways up at his master, and his ears, which were perked and at attention. Thus the two of them, the dog and the man who loved each other, greeted the holiday night on the balcony.

In the meantime the procurator's guest had a great number of things to do. After leaving the upper terrace of the garden in front of the balcony, he went down the stairs to the lower terrace, turned right, and went out to the barracks situated inside the palace grounds. In those barracks were billeted the two centuries which had accompanied the procurator to Yershalaim for the holiday, as well as the procurator's secret guard commanded by the guest himself. The guest spent a short time in the barracks, not more than ten minutes, but at the end of that time three carts set out from the barracks yard loaded with entrenching tools and a barrel of water. Fifteen men on horseback wearing gray cloaks accompanied the carts. The entire procession left the palace grounds through the rear gates, headed west, came out at the city walls, and took the path to the Bethlehem road and then proceeded northward. After reaching the crossroads by the Hebron Gate, they headed down the Jaffa road, taken earlier by the execution procession. By that time it was already dark and the moon was showing on the horizon.

Soon after the carts had left with their escort, the procurator's guest, who had now changed into a shabby, dark chiton, also left the palace compound on horseback. The guest headed straight into the city, rather than out of it. A short time later he could be seen approaching the Antonia Fortress, which was located in the northern part of the city, in close proximity to the great temple. The guest did not spend much time at the fortress either, and later could be spotted in the Lower City, in its winding labyrinthine streets. The guest arrived there by mule.

The guest knew the city well and easily found the street he was looking for. It was called Greek Street because a number of Greek shops were located there, including one that traded in rugs. It was there that the guest stopped his mule, dismounted, and tied it to a ring at the gate. The shop was already closed. The guest walked through a wicket gate next to the shop's entrance and found himself in a small square courtyard lined on three sides with sheds. After turning a corner in the yard, he ended up on the stone terrace of an ivy-covered dwelling where he surveyed his surroundings. The house and sheds were dark, because the lamps had not yet been lit. The guest called softly, "Niza!"

A door creaked in answer to his call, and a young woman without a shawl over her head appeared in the shadows of the terrace. She leaned over the railing, peering anxiously, trying to see who was there. When she recognized who it was, she gave him a welcoming smile, nodded her head, and waved.

"Are you alone?" asked Afranius softly in Greek.

"Yes," whispered the woman on the terrace. "My husband left for Caesarea this morning." Here the woman glanced at the door and added in a whisper, "But the servant woman is here." She made a gesture that meant—"come in." Afranius glanced back and stepped onto the stone stairs. He and the woman then disappeared inside the house.

Afranius spent a very short time at the woman's house—not more than five minutes. After that he left the house and terrace, pulled his hood down lower over his eyes, and went out into the street. By then the lamps were being lit in the houses, the holiday-eve throng was still immense, and Afranius on his mule was lost in the stream of people on foot and on horseback. Where he went after that is not known.

Left alone, the woman whom Afranius had called Niza began changing her clothes in a great hurry. No matter how hard it was for her to find what she needed in the dark room, she did not light the lamp and did not call her servant. Only after she was ready and wearing a dark shawl over her head was her voice heard in the house saying, "If anyone should ask for me, say that I have gone to visit Enanta."

The grumbling of the old servant woman was heard in the darkness, "Enanta? Oh, That awful woman! Your husband forbade you to see her! She's a procuress, your Enanta! I'll tell your husband..."

"There, there, there, hush up," answered Niza, and she slipped out of the house like a shadow. Niza's sandals tapped against the stone slabs of the courtyard. Still grumbling, the servant woman closed the door to the terrace. Niza left her house.

At the same time, from another narrow lane in the Lower City, a winding lane which descended in terraces to one of the municipal ponds, through the gate of an unprepossessing house whose blind side faced the street and whose windows opened onto a courtyard, came a young man with a neatly shaved beard, who was wearing a clean white kaffiyeh that fell down to his shoulders, a new light-blue holiday tallith with dangling tassels, and new sandals that creaked. The hook-nosed, handsome man, dressed up for the great holiday, walked briskly, overtaking those who were hurrying home to their holiday table, and one by one he saw the windows begin to blaze with light. The young man was heading down the road that led past the marketplace to the palace of the high priest Kaifa, located at the foot of the temple hill.

A short time later he could be seen entering the gates of Kaifa's palace. And leaving the palace a short time later.

After his visit to the palace, which was already aglow with lamps and torches, and in which the holiday bustle was in full swing, the young man began to walk even more briskly, more cheerfully, and hastened back to the Lower City. On that very corner where the street opened onto the market square, in the midst of the bustle and the crowd, he was overtaken by a slender woman in a black shawl pulled over her eyes, who walked with a dancing gait. As she was passing the handsome young man, the woman pushed her shawl up for an instant and gave the young man a sidelong glance, but rather than slow her stride, she actually quickened it, as if trying to conceal herself from the man she had overtaken.

The young man did not merely notice the woman, no, he recognized her, and having done so, he shuddered and stopped, gazing after her in bewilderment, and then immediately set off to catch up with her. After nearly knocking over a passerby carrying a jug, the young man caught up with the woman and, breathing heavily from excitement, called out to her, "Niza!"

The woman turned, narrowed her eyes as her face expressed cold annoyance, and replied dryly in Greek, "Oh, is that you, Judas? I didn't recognize you at first. But that's all to the good. We have a saying that he who is not recognized will become a rich man..."

So excited that his heart began to flutter like a bird under a black shawl, Judas asked in a halting whisper, afraid that the passersby would overhear, "Where are you going, Niza?"

"And why do you want to know?" replied Niza, slowing her step and looking arrogantly at Judas.

Then a childlike tone crept into Judas's voice as he whispered to her in dismay, "What is this? We had arranged to meet. I wanted to come see you. You said you'd be home all evening..."

"Oh, no, no," replied Niza, willfully making her lower lip protrude, which made her face, the most beautiful Judas had ever seen, even more beautiful. "I got bored," she continued. "You have a holiday, but what am I supposed to do? Sit and listen to you sighing on the terrace? And be afraid that the servant will tell my husband? No, no, and so I decided to take a walk outside the city to listen to the nightingales."

"What do you mean, outside the city?" asked Judas, at a loss. "Alone?"

"Of course, alone," replied Niza.

"Let me go with you," asked Judas breathlessly. His thoughts became muddled, he forgot about everything around him and gazed with pleading eyes into Niza's light-blue eyes, which now seemed black.

Niza said nothing in reply and quickened her step.

"Why don't you speak, Niza?" asked Judas plaintively, trying to keep pace with her.

"But won't I be bored with you?" asked Niza suddenly and stopped. Here Judas's thoughts became utterly confused.

"Well, all right," said Niza, finally softening, "Let's go."

"But where, where to?"

"Wait... let's step into this yard here and decide, otherwise I'm afraid that someone I know will see me and say later that I was out on the street with my lover."

And here Niza and Judas disappeared from the marketplace. They talked in whispers in the gateway of some courtyard.

"Go to the olive estate," whispered Niza, pulling her shawl down over her eyes and turning away from some man with a pail who was entering the gateway, "to Gethsemane, beyond Kedron, do you know where I mean?"

"Yes, yes, yes."

"I'll go on ahead," Niza continued, "but don't follow right behind me, keep a distance between us. I'll leave first... When you cross the stream... you know where the grotto is?"

"Yes, I know, I know..."

"Go up past the olive press and turn towards the grotto. I'll be there. Only don't follow at my heels. Be patient, wait here awhile." And with these words, Niza left the entranceway as if she had never spoken to Judas.

Judas stood there alone for awhile, trying to collect his scattered thoughts, one of which was how he would explain his absence from the holiday table to his family. Judas stood and tried to think up some lie, but in his excitement he couldn't think of anything suitable, and his legs moved of their own accord and carried him out of the gateway.

Now he changed his route, and instead of heading for the Lower City, he turned back toward Kaifa's palace. The holiday was already in full swing in the city. Not only were lights glittering in all the windows around Judas, but prayers and blessings could already be heard. Latecomers were urging on their mules, whipping them, and shouting at them. Judas's legs carried him along by themselves, and he failed to notice the fearsome moss-covered Antonia towers as they flew past him, he did not hear the blast of trumpets in the fortress, and he paid no attention to the Roman cavalry patrol whose torch flooded his path with quivering light.

When Judas turned after passing the tower, he saw that two gigantic five-branched candelabra had been lit above the temple at a dizzying, fearsome height. But Judas saw them through a haze as well, and it seemed to him that ten immense lamps had been hung up over the city and were competing with the light of the single lamp rising higher and higher over Yershalaim—the moon.

Now the only thing that mattered to Judas was to get to the Gethsemane Gate, and he wanted to leave the city as soon as possible.

At times he thought he could see a dancing figure up ahead as it darted among the faces and backs of the passersby, showing him the way. But it was an illusion—Judas knew that Niza must be far ahead of him. Judas ran past the money-changing shops and finally arrived at the Gethsemane Gate. Once there, burning with impatience, he was nevertheless forced to halt. Camels were entering the city, followed by a Syrian military patrol, which Judas cursed mentally...

But everything comes to an end. The impatient Judas was already outside the city wall. To his left he saw a small graveyard and near it the striped tents of a few pilgrims. After crossing the dusty road, which was flooded with moonlight, Judas hurried toward the Kedron stream, intending to cross it. The water gurgled softly at Judas's feet. Jumping from stone to stone, he finally made it over to the Gethsemane bank, and to his great joy saw that the road alongside the gardens was deserted. Not far away could be seen the tumbledown gates of the olive estate.

After the stuffiness of the city, Judas was struck by the intoxicating smell of the spring night. From the garden beyond the fence a fragrant wave of myrtle and acacia came drifting in from the Gethsemane fields.

There was no one guarding the gates, no one there at all, and in a few minutes Judas was running beneath the mysterious shadows of the huge, spreading olive trees. The road led uphill, Judas went up it, breathing heavily, occasionally emerging from the darkness onto the patterned carpets of moonlight, which reminded him of the carpets he had seen in the shop of Niza's jealous husband. In a while the olive press with its heavy stone wheel and pile of barrels appeared in a clearing to Judas's left. There was no one in the garden. Work had stopped at sunset and now a chorus of nightingales pealed and broke into song over Judas's head.

Judas was near his goal. He knew that in the darkness to his right he would soon hear the quiet whisper of falling water in the grotto. And so it was, he heard it. The air was getting cooler and cooler.

Then he slowed his step and called out softly, "Niza!"

But instead of Niza, a thickset male figure detached himself from the fat trunk of an olive tree, and jumped onto the road. Something gleamed in his hand for a second and then was extinguished. Judas gave a weak cry and tried to run back, but a second man blocked his way.

The first man, the one in front, asked Judas, "How much did you get just now? Talk, if you want to save your life!"

Hope flared up in Judas's heart, and he cried out in desperation, "Thirty tetradrachmas! Thirty tetradrachmas! That's all I got, I have it with me. Here's the money! Take it, but spare my life!"

The man in front immediately snatched the purse out of Judas's hands. And at the same instant a knife flew up behind him and struck the would-be lover under the shoulder blade. Judas was pitched forward, his arms raised and his fingers clutching the air. The man in front caught Judas on his knife and plunged it to the hilt into Judas's heart.

"Ni... za..." said Judas in a low, reproachful rasp that was quite unlike his own high, clear, youthful voice, and never uttered another sound. His body hit the ground so hard it began to hum.

Then a third figure appeared on the road. He was wearing a hooded cloak.

"Don't delay," he ordered. The assassins quickly wrapped up the purse with a note given them by the third man in a piece of leather skin and tied it crosswise with twine. The second man thrust the bundle in his bosom, and then both assassins ran off the road in different directions and were swallowed up by the darkness of the olive estate. The third man crouched down beside the body and gazed at the dead man's face. In the shadows it looked as white as chalk and had a kind of spiritual beauty.

Seconds later there was not a living soul on the road. The lifeless body lay with its arms flung out. A patch of moonlight fell on his left foot, making every strap of his sandal clearly visible. The whole Gethsemane garden rang with the singing of nightingales. No one knows where Judas's two assassins went, but the route taken by the third man in the hood is known. After leaving the road, he plunged into a grove of olive trees and headed south. He climbed over the garden wall far from the main gates, in its south corner, where the top layer of stones had fallen out. He soon reached the bank of the Kedron. Then he entered the stream and walked along in the water until he saw two horses silhouetted in the distance and a man standing next to them. The horses were also standing in the stream. The water washed over their hooves. The man tending the horses mounted one of them, and the man in the hood mounted the other. As the two of them headed slowly into the stream, one could hear the horses' hooves scraping on the stones. After the riders came out of the stream, they went up the Yershalaim bank, and followed the city wall at a walking pace. Then the groom broke away and galloped ahead while the man in the hood stopped his horse, dismounted on the deserted road, took off his cloak, turned it inside out, removed a flat, uncrested helmet from its folds, and put it on. The man who now mounted the horse wore a military chlamys and a short sword on his hip. He touched the reins, and his spirited cavalry mount set off at a trot. The rider did not have far to go—he was approaching the southern gates of Yershalaim.

The restless flame of torches danced and played under the archway of the gates. The sentries from the second century of the Lightning Legion were sitting on stone benches, playing dice. They jumped up when they saw the mounted officer, he waved to them and rode into the city.

The city was flooded with holiday lights. Candle flames flickered in all the windows, and the blessings coming from within blended into a discordant chorus. The rider would occasionally glance into the windows that looked out on the street and see people at their holiday tables, set with kid's meat and cups of wine placed between dishes of bitter herbs. Whistling a soft tune, the rider made his unhurried way through the deserted streets of the Lower City, heading toward the Antonia Tower, occasionally glancing up at the unique five-branched candelabra burning above the temple, which were not to be seen anywhere else in the world, or gazing at the moon, which hung even higher up than the candelabra.

The palace of Herod the Great was taking no part in the Passover night celebration. In the auxiliary rooms that faced south, where the officers of the Roman cohort and the Legate of the Legion were quartered, lights were burning and there was a feeling of activity and life. The front section, occupied by the sole and involuntary resident of the palace—the procurator—with its colonnades and gold statues, seemed blinded by the extremely bright moon. Here, inside the palace, darkness and quiet reigned. And the procurator, as he had told Afranius, preferred not to go inside. He had ordered that a bed be made up for him on the balcony where he had dined that evening and conducted the interrogation that morning. The procurator lay down on the couch that had been prepared, but sleep would not come to him. The naked moon hung high overhead in the clear sky, and the procurator was unable to take his eyes off it for several hours.

Around midnight sleep finally took pity on the Hegemon. With a convulsive yawn, the procurator unfastened his cloak and threw it off, removed the strap with its sheathed broad steel knife that belted his tunic and placed it on the chair beside the couch, took off his sandals, and stretched out. Banga immediately got up on the bed and lay down beside him with his head next to his, and the procurator, putting his arm around the dog's neck, finally closed his eyes. Only then did the dog fall asleep too.

The couch stood in semidarkness, shielded from the moon by a column, but a ribbon of moonlight stretched from the stairway to the bed. And as soon as the procurator lost touch with the world of reality around him, he quickly set out on a shining road and ascended it straight to the moon. He even laughed in his sleep with happiness, so splendid and unique was everything on that light-blue, transparent road. He was accompanied by Banga, and walking alongside him was the vagrant philosopher. They were arguing about something complex and important, and neither one of them could convince the other. They did not agree about anything, and that made their dispute all the more engaging and endless. Today's execution, needless to say, turned out to have been a complete misunderstanding—after all, the philosopher who had conceived the absurd notion that all people were good was walking beside him, so he had to be alive. And besides, the very idea that such a man could be executed was utterly horrible. The execution had not taken place! No! Therein lay the charm of this journey up the stairway of the moon.

They had as much time as they needed, and the thunderstorm would only come towards evening, and cowardice was, undoubtedly, one of the most terrible of vices. Thus spoke Yeshua Ha-Notsri. No, philosopher, I disagree with you: it is the most terrible vice!

For example, the present procurator of Judea, and former tribune of the legion, had not been a coward back then, in the Valley of the Maidens, when the furious Germans had almost hacked Ratkiller the Giant to pieces. But, excuse me, philosopher! Could you with your intelligence really imagine that the procurator of Judea would ruin his career over a man who had committed a crime against Caesar?

"Yes, yes," said Pilate, moaning and sobbing in his sleep.

Of course he would. He would not have done it in the morning, but now, at night, having weighed everything, he would be glad to do it. He would do anything to save the totally innocent mad dreamer and physician from death!

"Now we shall always be together," he heard in his sleep from the vagrant philosopher, who had appeared inexplicably on the Knight of the Golden Spear's path. "Where you find one, you'll find the other too! When people remember me, they will immediately remember you too! Me—a foundling, the son of unknown parents, and you—the son of an astrologer-king and a miller's daughter, the beautiful Pila."

"Yes, please don't forget, remember me, the son of an astrologer-king," implored Pilate in his sleep. And when the pauper from En-Sarid, who was walking beside him, gave him a nod of assent, the cruel procurator of Judea wept and laughed with joy in his sleep.

All this was good, but it made the Hegemon's awakening all the more horrible. Banga began howling at the moon, and the light-blue road, slippery and oily-smooth, vanished in front of the procurator. He opened his eyes and the first thing he remembered was that the execution had taken place. The first thing the procurator did was, as usual, to grab for Banga's collar, then, with aching eyes, he began searching for the moon and saw that it had moved slightly to the side and turned silver. Its light was being disrupted by an unpleasant, restless light playing on the balcony right in front of him. It came from a flaming, smoking torch held by Centurion Ratkiller. He glowered with fear and loathing at the dangerous beast ready to lunge at him.

"Stay, Banga," said the procurator with a sickly voice, and he coughed. Shading his eyes from the flame, he continued, "Even at night and in the moonlight, I have no peace. O gods! You too have a bad job, Mark. You maim soldiers..."

Mark looked at the procurator with profound astonishment, and the latter came to his senses. In an effort to smooth over the gratuitous words he had spoken when not fully awake, the procurator said, "Don't take offense, Centurion. My position, I repeat, is even worse. What do you want?"

"The chief of the secret service is here to see you," Mark reported calmly.

"Send him in, send him in," ordered the procurator, coughing to clear his throat, and feeling for his sandals with his bare feet. The flame played over the columns, the centurion's caligas clattered on the mosaic. The centurion went out to the garden.

"Even at night and in the moonlight, I have no peace," said the procurator to himself, his teeth clenched.

The man in the hood took the place of the centurion on the balcony.

"Banga, stay," said the procurator quietly, pressing the back of the dog's head.

Before he began to speak, Afranius, as was his custom, took a look around and stepped into the shadow, and when he had assured himself that apart from Banga, he and the procurator were the only ones on the balcony, he said softly, "I ask that you bring me to justice, Procurator. You were right. I was unable to save Judas of Kerioth. He was murdered. I ask to be tried and discharged."

Afranius felt as if he were being watched by two pairs of eyes—a dog's and a wolf's.

He pulled a bloodstained purse with two seals out from under his chlamys.

"Here is the bag of money the murderers threw at the high priest's house. The blood on it is the blood of Judas of Kerioth."

"I'm curious, how much money is there?" asked Pilate, nodding at the purse.

"Thirty tetradrachmas."

The procurator gave a laugh and said, "Not very much."

Afranius said nothing.

"Where is the slain man?"

"That I don't know," replied the man who never parted with his hood, with calm dignity. "We'll begin our investigation this morning."

The procurator shuddered, and let go of the sandal strap that refused to be fastened.

"But you know for certain that he was killed?"

To this the procurator received a dry reply, "I have worked in Judea for fifteen years, Procurator. I began my service under Valerius Gratus. I don't have to see the corpse to know that a man has been killed, and I am here to report that the man called Judas from the city of Kerioth was murdered a few hours ago."

"Forgive me, Afranius," replied Pilate. "I'm still not properly awake, that's why I said what I did. I sleep badly," the procurator gave a laugh, "and I keep seeing a moonbeam in my dream. It's so absurd, imagine... I seem to be walking along that moonbeam. And so, I would like to know what your thoughts are on this matter. Where do you intend to look for him? Sit down, Chief of the Secret Service."

Afranius bowed, moved a chair closer to the bed and sat down, his sword clanking.

"I intend to look for him near the olive press in the garden of Gethsemane."

"I see. And why there, precisely?"

"Hegemon, by my reasoning, Judas was killed neither in Yershalaim itself, nor very far away from it. He was killed on the outskirts of Yershalaim."

"I consider you one of the leading experts in your field. I cannot speak of Rome, of course, but in the colonies you are without equal. Explain to me, why?"

"It is inconceivable to me," said Afranius, speaking softly, "that Judas would have fallen into suspicious hands within the city limits. You don't stab someone clandestinely on the street. That means he must have been lured into some cellar somewhere. But the secret service has already looked for him in the Lower City, and if he were there, they would surely have found him. I can assure you that he is nowhere in the city. And if he had been killed far away from the city, they wouldn't have been able to throw back the packet of money so soon. He was murdered not far from the city. They managed to lure him out of the city."

"I don't see how they could have accomplished that."

"Yes, Procurator, that is the most difficult question of all, and I don't even know if I'll be able to solve it."

"A mystery indeed! On the evening of a holiday a believer forsakes the Passover meal and goes out of the city for some unknown reason, and there he perishes. Who could have lured him and how? Could it have been a woman?" asked the procurator with sudden inspiration.

Afranius answered calmly and gravely, "Absolutely not, Procurator. That possibility is ruled out entirely. One must reason logically. Who would have an interest in Judas's death? Vagrant dreamers, a group of them, a group, first of all, that doesn't include any women. One needs money to get married, Procurator, money is also necessary to bring someone into the world, but to murder someone with a woman's help, one needs a great deal of money, and vagrants don't have money. No woman was involved in this affair, Procurator. What's more, I would argue such a hypothesis can only serve to throw us off track, impede the investigation, and complicate things for me."

"I see your point completely, Afranius," said Pilate, "and I was only taking the liberty of offering my supposition."

"It is, alas, a mistaken one, Procurator."

"But, then, what other possibilities are there?" exclaimed the procurator staring at Afranius with avid curiosity.

"I think it was still the money."

"A remarkable idea! But who could offer him money at night outside the city? And for what?"

"Oh, no, Procurator, it didn't happen like that. I can offer only one supposition, and if it's wrong, then I probably won't come up with any others." Afranius leaned closer to the procurator and added in a whisper, "Judas wanted to hide his money in a safe spot only he knew about."

"A highly subtle explanation. That must have been how it happened. Now I follow you; it wasn't people who lured him out of the city, but his own idea. Yes, yes, that must have been it."

"Precisely. Judas didn't trust anyone. He wanted to hide his money."

"Yes, in Gethsemane, you said. But why is it precisely there that you intend to look for him—that, I confess, I can't understand."

"Oh, Procurator, that is the simplest thing of all. No one is going to hide money on a road or in an empty, open place. Judas wasn't on the road to Kedron or to Bethany. He needed to be in some safe, secluded spot with trees. It's so simple. And there's no place like that near Yershalaim except Gethsemane. He couldn't have gone far."

"You've convinced me completely. So, what is to be done now?"

"I'll start an immediate search for the murderers who followed Judas out of the city, and in the meantime, I will, as I have already reported, turn myself over for prosecution."

"What for?"

"My men lost him this evening in the marketplace after he had left Kaifa's palace. How that happened, I do not know. It has never happened to me before. He was put under observation right after our talk. But in the vicinity of the marketplace he got away and covered his tracks so thoroughly that he vanished without a trace."

"I see. But I am informing you that I do not deem it necessary for you to be prosecuted. You did everything that you could, and no one in the world,"—here the procurator smiled—"could have done more than you did! Reprimand the men who lost Judas in the marketplace. But here, too, I warn you: I do not wish you to reprimand them too severely. After all, we did everything we could to look after that good-for-nothing! Oh, yes, I forgot to ask," said the procurator, wiping his forehead, "how did they manage to throw the money back at Kaifa?"

"You see, Procurator... That wasn't particularly difficult. The avengers went to the back of Kaifa's palace, where the street looks down over the rear courtyard. They threw the packet of money over the fence."

"With a note attached?"

"Yes, exactly as you had imagined, Procurator. And, by the way,"—here Afranius broke the seals on the packet and showed its contents to Pilate.

"Take care what you're doing, Afranius. After all, they're temple seals!"

"The Procurator need not trouble himself about this question," replied Afranius, closing the packet.

"You mean you have all their seals?" asked Pilate, laughing.

"How could it be otherwise," replied Afranius dryly, with no trace of laughter.

"I can just imagine Kaifa's reaction!"

"Yes, Procurator, it caused quite a stir. I was summoned immediately."

Even in the semidarkness, Pilate's eyes could be seen glittering.

"That's interesting, interesting..."

"I beg to differ, Procurator. It was not interesting at all. It was a supremely tedious and wearisome business. When I questioned them as to whether money had been paid out to anyone in Kaifa's palace, they told me categorically that it had not."

"Is that so? Well, then, if the money wasn't paid, it wasn't paid. It will be that much harder to find the murderers."

"Quite true, Procurator."

"You know, Afranius, something just occurred to me: couldn't he have killed himself?"

"Oh, no, Procurator," replied Afranius, leaning back in his chair in surprise. "That is, if you will pardon me, highly unlikely!"

"Ah, in this city anything is possible! I would argue, in fact, that in no time at all rumors to that effect will be spreading throughout the city."

At this point Afranius gave Pilate that particular look of his, thought for a moment, and replied, "That may be, Procurator."

The procurator obviously could not relinquish the subject of the man from Kerioth's murder, even though it was already clear what had happened, and he commented wistfully, "I wish I could have seen how he was killed."

"He was killed with great artistry, Procurator," replied Afranius, giving him a somewhat ironic look.

"How do you know that?"

"Just take a look at the bag, Procurator," replied Afranius. "I can promise you that Judas's blood flowed freely. I've seen my share of murdered bodies, Procurator!"

"So, then, of course he will not arise?"

"No, Procurator, he will arise," replied Afranius with a philosophic smile, "when the trumpet of the Messiah, whom they await here, sounds above him. But until that he will not arise."

"Enough, Afranius! This subject is clear. Let's go to the burial."

"The executed men have been buried, Procurator."

"Oh, Afranius, it would be a crime to prosecute you. You deserve the highest reward. How did it go?"

Afranius began an account of how, while he was busy with the Judas affair, a secret service team under the command of his assistant got to the hill before nightfall. One body was missing from the hilltop. Pilate shuddered and said hoarsely, "Ah, why didn't I foresee that!"

"It is not worth getting upset about, Procurator," said Afranius and continued his account.

The bodies of Dismas and Gestas, their eyes pecked out by birds of prey, were picked up, and then a search was undertaken for the third body. It was soon located. Some man had...

"Levi Matvei," said Pilate, stating rather than questioning.

"Yes, Procurator..."

Levi Matvei had been hiding in a cave on the northern slope of Bald Skull, waiting for it to get dark. He had Yeshua Ha-Notsri's naked body with him. When the men entered the cave with a torch, Levi flew into a fit of rage and despair. He shouted that he had committed no crime and that anyone had the right, according to the law, to bury the body of an executed criminal if he wished to. Levi Matvei kept saying that he did not want to part with the body. He was agitated, and kept shouting something incoherent, begged, then threatened or cursed..."

"Did they have to seize him?" asked Pilate gloomily.

"No, Procurator, they did not, answered Afranius very soothingly, "The daring madman was calmed when it was explained that the body would be buried."

Levi, after absorbing what had been said, quieted down, but declared that he wasn't going away, and wanted to take part in the burial. He said he would not go away even if they were going to kill him, and even offered them the bread knife he had with him for this purpose.

"Did they chase him off?"

"No, Procurator, they did not. My assistant allowed him to take part in the burial."

"Which of your assistants was in charge?" asked Pilate.

"Tolmai," replied Afranius, adding with alarm, "Did he perhaps make a mistake?"

"Go on," replied Pilate, "there was no mistake. In general, I am beginning to feel somewhat at a loss, Afranius, since apparently I am dealing with a man who never makes mistakes. And that man is you."

They put Levi Matvei into the cart along with the bodies of the executed men, and two hours later they arrived at a deserted canyon north of Yershalaim. There the men worked in shifts and in about two hours they had dug a deep ditch and buried all three of the bodies.

"Were they naked?"

"No, Procurator. The men had brought chitons for that very purpose. Rings were put on the fingers of the corpses. Yeshua's ring had one marking, Dismas's two, and Gestas's three. The ditch was filled in and covered over with rocks. Tolmai knows what the identifying marker is."

"Ah, if only I had foreseen it!," said Pilate, frowning. "I would have liked to have seen that Levi Matvei."

"He is here, Procurator."

Pilate's eyes widened and he stared at Afranius for some time before he said, "Thank you for all that was done in this matter. Please have

Tolmai sent to me tomorrow, and in the meantime tell him that I am well pleased with him. And I ask that you, Afranius," —here the procurator took a ring from the pocket of his belt, which was lying on the table, and handed it to the chief of the secret service—"accept this as a token of my esteem."

Afranius bowed and said, "It is a great honor, Procurator."

"I ask that you reward the men who took care of the burial. And reprimand those responsible for losing Judas. Now send me Levi Matvei. I wish to hear more details about Yeshua."

"Certainly, Procurator," replied Afranius, and he began bowing as he withdrew. The procurator clapped his hands and shouted, "Come here! Bring me a lamp in the colonnade!"

By the time Afranius had reached the garden, lights were seen flickering behind Pilate in the servants' hands. Three lamps were placed on the table in front of the procurator, and the moonlit night retreated into the garden, as if Afranius had taken it away with him. Taking Afranius's place on the balcony was a short, scrawny stranger and beside him was the giant centurion. The latter, at a glance from the procurator, withdrew to the garden and disappeared.

The procurator studied the new arrival with avid, and slightly fearful eyes. It was the kind of look one gives someone one has heard of and thought a lot about, and whom one is meeting for the first time.

The newcomer was about forty, ragged, black, caked with dried mud, and glaring wolfishly from under his brows. In short, he was very unprepossessing and resembled hundreds of other beggars in the city who flocked around the temple terraces or marketplaces of the dirty, noisy Lower City.

The silence between them lasted for some time and was broken only by the strange behavior of the man who had been brought before Pilate. A change came over his face, he tottered, and would, in fact, have fallen if his dirty hand had not grabbed onto the edge of the table.

"What's wrong with you?" Pilate asked him.

"Nothing," Levi Matvei replied, and made a movement that looked as if he had swallowed something. His dirty, bare neck bulged out and then sank in.

"What's wrong, answer me," Pilate repeated.

"I'm tired," Levi replied and stared gloomily at the floor.

"Sit down," said Pilate, pointing to the chair.

Levi looked distrustfully at the procurator, moved over to the chair, cast a frightened eye over its gilded arms, and then chose to sit not on it, but on the floor beside it.

"Why didn't you sit on the chair?" asked Pilate.

"I'm filthy, I'll soil it," said Levi, staring at the ground.

"Then I'll get you something to eat right away."

"I don't want to eat," replied Levi.

"Why lie?" asked Pilate softly. "You haven't eaten for a whole day, perhaps longer. All right, then, don't eat. I sent for you because I wanted you to show me the knife you had."

"The soldiers took it away from me when they brought me here," replied Levi sullenly, adding, "Get it back for me. I have to return it to its owner. I stole it."

"Why?"

"To cut the ropes," replied Levi.

"Mark!" shouted the procurator, and the centurion stepped into the colonnade. "Give me his knife."

The centurion removed a dirty bread knife from one of the two sheaths on his belt and handed it to the procurator. He then withdrew.

"Who did you steal the knife from?"

"From a bread store at the Hebron Gate, right on the left as you enter the city."

Pilate looked at the wide blade, tested its sharpness with his finger for some reason, and said, "Don't worry about the knife, it will be returned to the shop. And now I want something else: show me the parchment you carry around with you, where Yeshua's words are written down."

Levi looked at Pilate with hatred and smiled such a malicious smile that his face became all distorted.

"You want to take that away? My last possession?" he asked.

"I didn't say: hand it over," replied Pilate, "I said: show it to me."

Levi rummaged inside his shirt and pulled out a roll of parchment. Pilate took it from him, unrolled it, spread it out between the lamps, and with a frown on his face began studying the barely decipherable ink markings. The scrawly lines were hard to follow, and Pilate frowned as he bent over the parchment, running his finger over the lines. He did manage to make out that the writing was a disconnected set of sayings, dates, household jottings, and poetic fragments. He was able to read: "There is no death... Yesterday we ate sweet spring figs..."

Grimacing from the effort, Pilate squinted, and read, "We shall see the pure stream of the water of life... Mankind will gaze at the sun through transparent crystal..."

Here Pilate shuddered. In the parchment's concluding lines he could make out the words, "...greater vice... cowardice.'

Pilate rolled up the parchment and handed it brusquely back to Levi.

"Take it," he said, and after a brief silence, added, "You are, as I can see, a learned man, and there is no reason why you, who are alone, should be wandering about in rags without any place to go. I have a large library in Caesarea, I am very wealthy, and I want to take you into my service. You will arrange and care for the papyri, and you will be well fed and clothed."

Levi stood up and replied, "No, I don't want to."

"Why?" asked the procurator, his face darkening. "Do you find me unpleasant, are you afraid of me?"

The same malicious smile contorted Levi's face, and he said, "No, it's because you'll be afraid of me. It won't be easy for you to look me in the face after you killed him."

"Be quiet," said Pilate, "take some money."

Levi shook his head in refusal, and the procurator continued, "You, I know, consider yourself a disciple of Yeshua, but I can assure you that you have learned nothing from what he tried to teach you. Because if you had, you would certainly have accepted something from me. Remember that before he died, he said that he didn't blame anyone,"— Pilate raised his finger meaningfully, and his face twitched. "And he himself would undoubtedly have taken something from me. You are cruel, and he was not a cruel man. Where will you go?"

Levi suddenly walked over to the table, rested both hands on it, and, staring with burning eyes at the procurator, whispered to him, "Know, Hegemon, that I am going to murder a certain man in Yershalaim. I am telling you this so you will know there will be more blood."

"I, too, know there will be more blood," replied Pilate. "Your words do not surprise me. You, of course, wish to murder me, isn't that so?"

"I would not be able to murder you," replied Levi, baring his teeth in a smile, "and I am not stupid enough to expect that I could. But I shall murder Judas of Kerioth, even if it takes me the rest of my life."

A gleam of pleasure shone in the procurator's eyes. Beckoning Levi Matvei closer, he said, "Don't worry yourself, you won't succeed. Judas was already murdered this very night."

Levi jumped back from the table, his eyes staring wildly, and cried out, "Who did it?"

"Don't be jealous," replied Pilate, baring his teeth, and rubbing his hands, "I'm afraid you weren't his only admirer."

"Who did it?" repeated Levi in a whisper.

"I did it."

Levi's mouth fell open, and he gaped at the procurator, who said quietly, "It wasn't very much, of course, but nevertheless it was I who did it." And he added, "Well, will you take something now?"

Levi thought for awhile, relented, and finally said, "Tell them to give me a piece of clean parchment."

An hour passed. Levi was gone from the palace. Now the only thing that disturbed the early morning silence was the quiet sound of the sentries' footsteps in the garden. The moon was rapidly fading, and at the other edge of the sky the whitish speck of the morning star appeared. The lamps had long been extinguished. The procurator lay on his couch. He slept with his hand under his cheek, breathing soundlessly. Banga slept beside him.

Thus the dawn of the fifteenth day of Nisan was greeted by the fifth procurator of Judea, Pontius Pilate.

XXVII

The End of Apartment No. 50

WHEN Margarita got to the final words of the chapter— "...Thus the dawn of the fifteenth day of Nisan was greeted by the fifth procurator of Judea, Pontius Pilate,"—morning had arrived. From the yard came the cheerful, excited, morning sounds of sparrows conversing in the branches of the white willow and the linden tree.

Margarita got up from her chair, stretched, and only then realized how worn out her body was and how much she craved sleep. It is interesting to note that Margarita's soul was in perfect shape. Her thoughts were not in disarray, and she was not at all unnerved by having spent the previous night supernaturally. Memories of her time at Satan's ball did not disturb her, nor did the fact that the Master had been returned to her by a kind of miracle, that his novel had risen from the ashes, and that everything was back in place in the basement apartment, from which the informer Aloisy Mogarych had been expelled. In short, her encounter with Woland had caused her no psychic distress. Everything was seemingly as it should have been.

She went into the adjoining room, assured herself that the Master was sleeping deeply and peacefully, turned off the desk lamp, which was no longer necessary, stretched out on the small couch along the opposite wall, and covered herself with an old, torn sheet. A minute later she was asleep, and that morning she had no dreams. All the rooms in the basement were silent, the private home builder's entire small house was silent, and silence also reigned in the deserted lane outside.

Meanwhile, at the same time, that is, at dawn on Saturday, an entire floor of one of Moscow's official buildings was wide awake, and its windows, which looked out on a large, asphalt-covered square being cleaned by the whirring brushes of special, slow-moving machines, were all lit up with a stark light that outshone the rising sun.

The entire floor was busy with the investigation of the Woland case, and lamps in ten offices had been burning all night long.

Strictly speaking, the rudiments of the case had been clear since the previous day, Friday, when the Variety Theater had to be closed due to the disappearance of its entire administrative staff and the disruptive events surrounding the notorious performance of black magic. But the fact of the matter was that new material kept pouring in to the sleepless floor.

Now it was the task of those investigating this strange case, which blended elements of utterly obvious deviltry with hypnotic trickery and blatant criminality, to take all the various and muddled incidents that had occurred all over Moscow and mold them into some kind of coherent whole.

The first to be summoned to the electric glare of the sleepless floor was Arkady Apollonovich Sempleyarov, the chairman of the Acoustics Commission.

After dinner on Friday, the telephone rang in his apartment on Kamenny Bridge, and a man's voice asked for Arkady Apollonovich. His wife, who answered the phone, replied sullenly that Arkady Apollonovich was unwell and resting, and could not come to the phone. But Arkady Apollonovich had had to come to the phone. When asked who it was that was calling Arkady Apollonovich, the voice at the other end of the line had said who in no uncertain terms.

"This second... right away... just a minute..." babbled the customarily arrogant wife of the chairman of the Acoustics Commission, and she flew into the bedroom like an arrow to rouse Arkady Apollonovich from his bed, where he lay suffering the torments of hell whenever he recalled last night's performance and the ensuing scandal, when his niece from Saratov had been expelled from the apartment.

To tell the truth, it took Arkady Apollonovich not a second, not a minute, but a quarter of a minute to get to the phone. Wearing only underwear and a slipper on his left foot, he babbled into the receiver, "Yes, it's me... I will, I will..."

His wife, forgetting for the moment the many disgusting crimes of infidelity in which the unfortunate Arkady Apollonovich had been implicated, stuck her frightened face through the hall door and, waving a slipper in the air, whispered, "Your slipper, put on your slipper... Your feet will catch cold." Waving his wife away with his bare foot and giving her a ferocious look, Arkady Apollonovich mumbled into the phone, "Yes, yes, yes, of course I understand... I'm leaving now..."

Arkady Apollonovich spent the entire evening on that floor where the investigation was being conducted. His conversation with the investigators was painful and extremely unpleasant because it necessitated his talking frankly not only about the vile performance and the fight in the loge, but also, among other things, about Militsa Andreyevna Pokobatko from Yelokhovskaya Street, his niece from Saratov, and much else besides, which caused Arkady Apollonovich inexpressible misery.

It goes without saying that the testimony provided by Arkady Apollonovich—an intelligent and cultured man, an eyewitness to the disgraceful performance, an experienced and articulate witness, who gave an excellent description of the mysterious masked magician himself and his two knavish assistants, whose splendid memory had retained the magician's name, Woland—contributed significantly to the advance of the investigation. When Arkady Apollonovich's testimony was collated with that of others, including those women who had been casualties of the performance (the one in the violet underwear who had astounded Rimsky and, alas, many others), and Karpov, the messenger who had been sent to apartment No. 50 on Sadovaya Street—it became immediately apparent where the perpetrator of all these misadventures should be sought.

Apartment No. 50 was visited, and more than once, and not only did it receive a thorough search, but its walls were tapped and its chimney flues inspected, in an attempt to locate secret hiding-places. However, none of these measures yielded any results, and no one was ever found in the apartment during any of the visits, although it was patently clear that someone was living there, despite the fact that everyone whose job it was to be informed of the whereabouts of foreign stage performers while in Moscow stated flatly and categorically that no black magician named Woland was in Moscow, nor could he be.

He had certainly never registered anywhere upon his arrival, or showed anyone his passport, or any other documents, contracts or agreements, and no one had heard anything about him! Kitaitsev, the head of the program department of the Entertainment Commission, swore by everything holy that the missing Styopa Likhodeyev had never sent him the program of any Woland for approval, nor had he ever called to inform Kitaitsev of the arrival of any such person. Thus he, Kitaitsev, did not know and could not understand how Styopa could have allowed such a performance to take place at the Variety. When he was told that Arkady Apollonovich had seen the magician in performance with his own eyes, Kitaitsev merely spread his hands and raised his eyes to heaven. And one could see and safely say from Kitaitsev's eyes alone that he was as pure as crystal.

Prokhor Petrovich, the chairman of the Entertainment Commission...

Incidentally, he had returned to his suit right after the police entered his office, to the ecstatic joy of Anna Richardovna and to the great consternation of the police who had been called for no reason. Again incidentally, when Prokhor Petrovich was back inside his gray striped suit, he gave his full approval to all the memos drafted by his suit during his brief absence.

...and so, Prokhor Petrovich, had absolutely no knowledge of any Woland.

The outcome, say what you will, was preposterous: thousands of spectators, the entire staff of the Variety Theater, and, finally, Arkady Apollonovich Sempleyarov, a highly cultured man, had all seen the magician, along with his thrice-cursed assistants, and yet it was impossible to find him anywhere. What, then, if one may ask: had he fallen through the earth after his disgusting performance, or, as some people claimed, had he never come to Moscow at all? To accept the first explanation meant that he had taken the entire top management of the Variety with him when he vanished, whereas the implication of the second explanation was that the managers of the ill-starred theater had themselves disappeared from Moscow without a trace, after first performing some dirty trick (recall, if nothing else, the smashed window in the office and the behavior of Ace of Diamonds).

Credit should be given to the person in charge of the investigation. The missing Rimsky was found with astonishing speed. All that had to be done was to juxtapose Ace of Diamond's behavior at the taxi-stand near the movie theater with certain time data, such as when the performance ended and when Rimsky could have disappeared, in order to dispatch a telegram to Leningrad. The answer came an hour later (on Friday evening) that Rimsky had been located on the fourth floor of the Astoria Hotel in Room 412, which was next door to the room occupied by the repertory director of one of the Moscow theaters then on tour in Leningrad, a room which was known for its gilded, gray-blue furniture and its magnificent bath.

Found hiding in the wardrobe of Room 412 at the Astoria, Rimsky was arrested immediately and interrogated there in Leningrad. Following which, a telegram reached Moscow stating that the Variety's financial director was not responsible for his actions, that he either could not or would not answer questions coherently, and that he kept asking to be put away in an armored room under armed guard. Moscow telegrammed a reply, ordering that Rimsky be transported back to Moscow under guard, as a result of which, Rimsky did leave Leningrad under guard on the Friday evening train.

By Friday evening they were on Likhodeyev's trail as well. Telegrams had been sent to all cities, inquiring about Likhodeyev's whereabouts, and Yalta had sent a reply saying that he had been there, but had left by plane for Moscow.

The only trail that was cold was Varenukha's. The illustrious theater manager, known to all of Moscow, seemed to have dropped into the sea.

In the meantime, they had to deal with what had happened in other parts of Moscow, beyond the confines of the Variety Theater. Explanations had to be found for the strange case of the singing office clerks (incidentally, Professor Stravinsky cured them in two hours with the help of subcutaneous injections), for the individuals who had passed off the-devil-knows-what as money to other individuals or institutions, and finally, for the people who had been victimized as a result.

Needless to say, the most distasteful, the most scandalous, the most baffling incident of all was the theft in broad daylight, of the late writer

Berlioz's head, right out of the coffin on display in the Griboyedov hall.

A twelve-man team conducted the investigation, trying to pick up, with a knitting needle, as it were, all the infernal stitches spread all over Moscow, of this complicated case.

One of the investigators went to Professor Stravinsky's clinic and asked, first of all, for a list of all those who had been admitted to the clinic in the last three days. This led them to Nikanor Ivanovich Bosoi and the unfortunate emcee whose head had been wrenched off. The two of them, however, took up little of their time, since it had been easy to establish that they had both been victims of the mysterious magician and his gang. Ivan Nikolayevich Bezdomny, on the other hand, was of great interest to the investigators.

Early on Friday evening the door of Ivanushka's room, No. 117, opened and in walked a young man with a round face, who was calm, gentle-mannered, and who looked nothing like an investigator even though he was one of the best in Moscow. He saw a pale, drawn-looking young man lying on the bed, whose eyes were indifferent to what was going on around him, whose eyes turned outward, to some spot far above and beyond the room, or inward, into the young man himself.

The investigator introduced himself amiably and said he had come to see Ivan Nikolayevich to discuss the events of two days before at Patriarch's Ponds.

Oh, how triumphant Ivan would have felt, if only the investigator had come to see him a little earlier, say, late Wednesday night, when Ivan had been trying so frantically and passionately to get someone to listen to his story about Patriarch's Ponds. Now his dream of helping catch the foreign consultant had come true, and he did not have to run after anyone any more since they had come to see him themselves, to hear his tale about what happened Wednesday evening.

But, alas, in the time that had elapsed since Berlioz's death Ivan had undergone a complete change. He was ready and willing to answer all the investigator's questions politely, but his indifference was evident in his eyes and in the way he spoke. The poet was no longer moved by Berlioz's fate.

Ivanushka had been lying in a doze before the investigator's arrival, and a number of visions had passed before him. He had seen a strange, incomprehensible, non-existent city with blocks of marble, worn-down colonnades, and roofs sparkling in the sun, with the somber and pitiless black Antonia Tower, the palace on the western hill, sunk almost to the roof in the tropical greenery of a garden, with bronze statues towering above that greenery and burning in the setting sun, and he had seen armor-clad, Roman centurions marching beneath the walls of the ancient city.

A man had appeared before Ivan in his sleep, a man sitting motionless in a chair, clean-shaven, with a yellow, troubled-looking face, wearing a white mantle with a red lining, and gazing hatefully at the lush and alien garden. Ivan had also seen a yellow, treeless hill with empty cross-beamed posts standing on top of it.

And what had happened at Patriarch's Ponds no longer interested the poet Ivan Bezdomny.

"Tell me, Ivan Nikolayevich, how far were you from the turnstile when Berlioz fell under the streetcar?"

An apathetic, almost imperceptible smile flickered over Ivan's lips, and he replied, "I was far away."

"Was the man in checked trousers close to the turnstile?"

"No, he was sitting on a bench nearby."

"Are you sure he didn't go over to the turnstile just as Berlioz fell?"

"Yes, I'm sure. He didn't go anywhere. He was sprawled on the bench."

These were the investigator's final questions. When he was finished, he stood up, gave Ivanushka his hand, wished him a speedy recovery, and expressed hope that he would soon be reading more of his poems.

"No," replied Ivan quietly. "I won't be writing any more poems."

The investigator smiled politely and took the liberty of assuring the poet that although he was in a slight depression at the moment, it would soon pass.

"No," countered Ivan, looking not at the investigator, but at a point in the distance on the darkening horizon, "it will never pass. The poems I wrote were bad poems, and I realize that now."

The investigator left Ivanushka after having received very important information. By tracing the thread of events backwards, from finish to start, he finally succeeded in reaching the source of all the events that followed. The investigator was certain that everything started with the murder at Patriarch's Ponds. Of course, neither Ivanushka nor the fellow in checks had pushed the unfortunate chairman of MASSOLIT under the streetcar. Physically speaking, no one had facilitated his fall under the wheels. But the investigator was convinced that Berlioz had thrown himself under the streetcar (or fallen under it) while in a hypnotic trance.

Yes, there was a great deal of information, and they already knew who should be apprehended and where. But the hitch was that it had proved impossible to apprehend him by any means whatsoever. Admittedly, there was no question that someone was, indeed, living in the thrice-cursed apartment No. 50. Phone calls to the apartment would at times be answered by a nasal, or by a cracked voice, windows would be opened, and a phonograph would be heard playing, But every time they went over to investigate, they found no one there. And they had been there many times, at all hours of the day and night. Not only that, they had combed the apartment and looked in every corner. The apartment had been under suspicion for a long time. Guards had been posted along the route that led through the gateway into the courtyard, and at the back entrance as well; not only that, guards had been posted up on the roof, next to the chimney pipes. Yes, apartment No. 50 was up to no good, but there was nothing anyone could do about it.

Thus the case dragged on until after midnight Friday when Baron Maigel, wearing evening dress and patent leather shoes, made his grand entrance into apartment No. 50 as a guest. The baron was heard being admitted to the apartment. Precisely ten minutes after that they entered the apartment without any advance warning, but not only did they find no residents, there was not even a trace, which was already utterly bizarre, of Baron Maigel.

And so, as has been said, the case dragged on this way until dawn on Saturday. Some new and very interesting facts then emerged. A six-seater passenger plane landed at Moscow airfield from the Crimea. One of the passengers who got off was rather strange. He was a young man, his face overgrown with stubble, who had not washed for three days, had inflamed and frightened eyes, no luggage, and was rather queerly dressed. He was wearing a Caucasian-style fur cap, a felt cloak over a nightshirt, and brand-new, just purchased, blue leather bedroom slippers. They approached him as he stepped off the gangway. They had been expecting him, and shortly after that, the unforgettable director of the Variety Theater, Stepan Bogdanovich Likhodeyev, appeared before the investigators. He added some new information. It now became clear that Woland had gotten into the Variety disguised as a performer, by hypnotizing Styopa Likhodeyev, and had then contrived to spirit the aforementioned Styopa out of Moscow, God knows how many kilometers away. This added to the mounting evidence, but things did not become any easier as a result, and, may in fact have become even more difficult, since it was becoming obvious that it was not going to be easy to capture someone capable of pulling that kind of stunt on Stepan Bogdanovich. In the meantime, Likhodeyev was locked up in a strong room at his own request, and appearing before the investigators was Varenukha, who had just been arrested at his apartment, where he had returned after an unaccountable absence of almost two days.

Despite the theater manager's promise to Azazello never to lie again, he began with a lie. Although one should not judge him too harshly for that. After all, Azazello had forbidden him to tell lies and be rude over the telephone, but in the given instance the manager was speaking without the aid of such an instrument. His eyes wandering, Ivan Savelyevich declared that on Thursday afternoon he had gotten drunk alone in his office at the Variety, after which he had gone somewhere—but where he couldn't recall, had drunk some more Starka vodka, flopped down under a fence somewhere, but where—he again couldn't recall. It was only after the manager had been advised that his stupid and ill-considered conduct was impeding the investigation of an important case and that, naturally, he would have to take the consequences, that Varenukha broke into sobs and, with a trembling voice, his eyes darting all around, he whispered that he was lying out of fear alone, that he was petrified of the vengeance of Woland's gang, into whose clutches he had already fallen, and that he begged, pleaded, and prayed to be locked up in an armored room.

"What the devil! They've all got armored rooms on the brain!" growled one of the chief investigators.

"Those villains scared them out of their wits," said the investigator who had visited Ivanushka.

They calmed Varenukha as best they could, said they could insure his safety without recourse to an armored room, and at this point it came out that he had not been drinking Starka under any fence, but had been beaten up by two men, one with red hair and a fang, the other—fat...

"Who looked like a cat?"

"Yes, yes, yes," whispered the manager, faint with fear and looking around at every second, and he gave more details of how he had spent two days in apartment No. 50, serving as a vampire-bait, and how he had almost caused the death of financial director Rimsky...

At this time they brought in Rimsky, who had been transported from Leningrad by train. However, this terror-stricken, psychologically unbalanced, gray-haired old man, who bore little resemblance to the former financial director, had no desire to tell the truth and was very stubborn in this regard. Rimsky maintained that he had not seen any Hella in his office window that night, just as he had not seen Varenukha, but that he had simply felt unwell and gone to Leningrad in a daze. It need hardly be said that the ailing financial director concluded his testimony by pleading to be locked up in an armored room.

Annushka was arrested just as she was attempting to hand a ten-dollar bill to a cashier at a department store on the Arbat. They listened attentively to Annushka's story about people flying out the window of the building on Sadovaya Street, and about the horseshoe which, according to her, she picked up in order to take it to the police.

"Was the horseshoe really gold with diamonds?" Annushka was asked.

"As if I don't know diamonds when I see them," she replied.

"But did he give you, as you claim, ten-ruble bills?"

"As if I don't know what they are," replied Annushka.

"So when did they turn into dollars?"

"I don't know anything about any dollars, and I never saw any," Annushka replied shrilly. "I was in my rights! I got the money as a reward and was using it to buy some chintz cloth..." She then went off on a tangent about how it wasn't her fault that the house management had let an evil power take over the fifth floor and make life there impossible.

Here the investigator waved Annushka away with his pen, since by then they were all heartily sick of her, and wrote her an exit pass on a green chit of paper, following which, to everyone's relief, she disappeared from the building.

After this came a whole string of people, including Nikolai Ivanovich, arrested solely because of the stupidity of his jealous wife, who at daybreak had reported him missing to the police. The investigators were not particularly surprised when Nikolai Ivanovich produced the prank certificate stating that he had spent the night at Satan's ball. Nikolai Ivanovich strayed from the truth somewhat in his account of how he had flown through the air with Margarita Nikolayevna's naked maid on his back, transporting her to some devils' den on the river for a swim, and how, prior to that, Margarita Nikolayevna had appeared naked in the window. For example, he did not deem it necessary to mention his appearance in the bedroom, holding Margarita's discarded chemise in his hands, nor did he say he had called Natasha Venus. His version of the story was that Natasha had flown out the window, climbed on his back, and lured him out of Moscow...

"I was forced to do it, I had to obey," said Nikolai Ivanovich, and he concluded his tale with a plea that not one word of it be told to his wife. He was promised that it would not.

Nikolai Ivanovich's testimony made it possible to establish that Margarita Nikolayevna and her maid Natasha had disappeared without a trace. Measures were taken to try to locate them.

Thus the round-the-clock investigation extended into Saturday morning. Meanwhile, utterly preposterous rumors sprang up which had a tiny grain of truth buried beneath layers of plush fabrication and they spread around the city. The rumors said that following a performance at the Variety, an audience of two thousand had rushed out on the street as naked as babes, that a printer's shop which made magic counterfeit bills had been uncovered on Sadovaya Street, that a gang had kidnapped the five directors of the entertainment sector, but that they had been found immediately by the police, and much else besides which I don't wish to repeat.

It was getting on toward dinner time when the phone rang in the investigation room. The call came from Sadovaya Street to report that there were again signs of life in the accursed apartment. The windows had been opened and sounds of a piano playing and voices singing were heard coming from the apartment, and a black cat could be seen sunning himself on the windowsill.

Around four in the afternoon of that same hot day a large party of men, dressed in civilian clothes, emerged from three cars that had stopped a short distance from 302B Sadovaya Street. They then broke up into two smaller groups, one of which went through the motor entrance and across the courtyard directly to main entrance No. 6, the other of which opened a small door that was normally boarded up and led to the back entrance. Using separate stairways, the two groups began their ascent to apartment No. 50.

In the meantime, Azazello and Korovyov, the latter no longer in evening dress but wearing his usual attire, were sitting in the dining room of the apartment, finishing breakfast. As was his habit, Woland was in the bedroom, and the cat's whereabouts were unknown. Judging, however, from the crash of pots and pans coming from the kitchen, it could be deduced that Behemoth was there, playing the fool, as was his habit.

"What are those footsteps I hear on the stairs?" asked Korovyov, jiggling the spoon in his cup of black coffee.

"Oh, that's them coming to arrest us," replied Azazello as he downed a shot of brandy.

"Ah yes, well, well," was Korovyov's reply.

By then, those ascending the front staircase had already reached the third-floor landing. There, what looked like two plumbers were fiddling with the radiator. The men on the staircase exchanged meaningful glances with the plumbers.

"They're all at home," whispered one of the plumbers, tapping the pipe with his hammer.

Then, the man in front proceeded to pull a black Mauser from under his coat, and the one beside him produced a skeleton key. All those entering apartment No. 50 were suitably armed. Two of them had easily-deployable, fine silk nets in their pockets. Another had a lasso, and yet another had gauze masks and ampules of chloroform.

In a second the front door to apartment No. 50 was opened, and those who entered found themselves in the hall. The door that banged in the kitchen at that moment signaled the timely arrival of those who had come up the back stairs.

This time, at least, they met with some limited success. The men immediately spread out over all the rooms, finding no one anywhere, but they did find the remains of an apparently interrupted breakfast in the dining room, and in the living room a huge black cat was sitting on the mantelpiece next to a glass pitcher. He was holding a primus stove in his paws.

The men contemplated the cat for some length of time in total silence.

"Mmm, yes... he really is impressive," whispered one of them.

"I'm not doing any mischief, I'm not bothering anyone, I'm just fixing the primus," said the cat with a hostile scowl, "and I consider it my duty to warn you that a cat is an ancient and inviolable creature."

"Exceptionally fine work," whispered one of the men, and another said loudly and distinctly, "Well, then, inviolable ventriloquist cat, come over here!"

A silk net was unfurled and tossed in the air, but to everyone's utter surprise, the man who threw it missed his target and ensnared only the pitcher, which crashed into jangling pieces.

"Forfeit!" howled the cat. "Hurrah!" Here he put the primus aside, and pulled a Browning from behind his back. In a flash he had it trained on the man nearest to him, but before the cat could shoot, there was a flash in the man's hand, and when the Mauser went off, the cat fell head-first off the mantel onto the floor, dropping his Browning and tossing away his primus.

"It's all over," said the cat in a weak voice, as he stretched out languidly in a pool of blood. "Leave me be for a second, let me bid the earth farewell. O Azazello, my friend!" groaned the cat, his blood streaming out. "Where are you?" The cat turned his dimming eyes toward the dining room door. "I was outmatched and you did not come to help me. You abandoned poor Behemoth, forsaking him for a glass of admittedly very fine brandy! Ah, well, may my death be on your conscience, but I bequeath you my Browning..."

"The net, the net, the net," whispered the men anxiously who were standing around the cat. But the net, the devil knows why, got caught in someone's pocket and would not come out.

"The only thing that can save a mortally wounded cat," said the cat, "is a swig of kerosene..." And, taking advantage of the general confusion, he pressed his lips to the round opening in the primus and drank his fill of kerosene. The blood streaming out from under his left front paw stopped immediately. The cat jumped up, alive and well, tucked the primus under his foreleg, and leapt back onto the mantel. Then, he began crawling up the wall, ripping the wallpaper with his claws, and in two seconds he was high overhead, sitting on the metal curtain rod.

In a flash hands grabbed at the curtain and tore it down together with the rod, letting the sunlight burst into the darkened room. But neither the fraudulently revived cat nor the primus fell down. The cat, still holding on to his primus, managed to swing through the air and land on the chandelier that was hanging in the center of the room.

"Get a ladder!" voices shouted from below.

"I challenge you to a duel!" bellowed the cat, soaring over their heads on the swaying chandelier, the Browning appearing in his paws again, and he set the primus down between the arms of the chandelier. The cat took aim, and, swinging like a pendulum over the heads of the men, opened fire on them. Thunder shook the apartment. Shards of crystal rained down from the chandelier on the floor, the mirror over the fireplace cracked into stars, clouds of plaster dust billowed, empty cartridges bounced over the floor, windowpanes broke, the bullet-ridden primus began to spurt kerosene. Taking the cat alive was now out of the question, and the men shot back at him furiously and accurately, aiming their Mausers at his head, stomach, chest, and back. The shooting caused a panic in the courtyard down below.

But it lasted for only a short time and began to subside of its own accord. The fact was that the shots harmed neither the cat, nor the men who had come to catch him. Not only was no one killed, no one was even wounded; everyone, including the cat, remained completely unhurt. To verify this once and for all, one of the men fired five rounds into the accursed head of the beast, whereupon the cat shot back a vigorous reply. And the same thing happened—no one felt the slightest effect. The cat swung back and forth on the chandelier in ever-diminishing arcs, blowing into the muzzle of his Browning for some reason, and spitting on his paw. An expression of complete befuddlement spread over the faces of the men standing in silence below. It was the only instance, or one of the only instances, when shooting had no effect whatsoever. It was possible, of course, to conclude that the cat's Browning was a toy of some sort, but that would certainly not have applied to the Mausers. The cat's first wound, and of that there could not be the slightest doubt, had been nothing other than a trick and a swinish bit of playacting, as was his drinking of the kerosene.

One last attempt was made to catch the cat. A lasso was thrown, it caught on one of the candles, and the chandelier fell down. The crash it made seemed to shake the whole building, but again with no effect. Shards of glass hailed down on those present, and the cat sailed through the air and settled high under the ceiling, atop the gilded frame of the mirror over the mantel. He showed no signs of wanting to make a getaway. On the contrary, he went so far as to address them once again from the relative safety of his perch.

"I simply cannot understand," he said from on high, "why you are treating me so harshly..."

Just as he began his speech, it was interrupted by a low, heavy voice coming from no one knew where, "What's going on in this apartment? It's disturbing my work."

An unpleasant, nasal voice replied, "Naturally, it's Behemoth, the devil take him!"

A third, quavering voice said, "Messire! It's Saturday. The sun is setting. It's time for us to go."

"Excuse me, but I can't talk any longer," said the cat from atop the mirror. "We have to go." He threw his Browning and shattered both windowpanes. Then he splashed down the kerosene, which ignited of itself and sent a wave of flame shooting up to the ceiling.

The blaze broke out with a speed and intensity unusual even for kerosene fires. The wallpaper began smoking immediately, the curtain heaped up on the floor ignited, and the frames of the broken windows began smoldering. The cat curled himself up to spring, meowed, jumped from the mirror to the windowsill, and then disappeared out the window with his primus. Shots came from outside. The man sitting on the iron fire escape that ran alongside the apartment windows sprayed the cat with bullets as the latter flew from windowsill to windowsill, heading for the drainpipe at the corner of the building, which, as already noted, was built in the shape of the cyrillic letter "П." The cat then climbed up the pipe to the roof. There the men guarding the chimney pipes sprayed him with additional bullets, again with no effect, and the cat disappeared in the setting sun that was flooding the city.

Meanwhile, back in the apartment the parquet floor caught fire under the men's feet, and in the flames, on the spot where the cat had sprawled with his phony wound, there gradually materialized the body of the former Baron Maigel with protruding chin and glassy eyes. It was no longer possible to pull him out.

Those in the living room jumped over the burning squares of parquet, slapping their smoking chests and shoulders with their palms, and retreated into the study and the front hall. Those in the dining room and the bedroom ran out through the hallway. Those in the kitchen also rushed out into the front hall. The living room was already smoking and in flames. On his way out someone managed to dial the number of the fire department and shout tersely into the receiver, "Sadovaya Street! 302B!"

They could not delay any longer. The flames swept out into the hall. It became hard to breathe.

As soon as the first streams of smoke sifted through the broken windows of the bewitched apartment, cries were heard out in the courtyard, "Fire! Fire! We're on fire!"

People in various apartments of the building began screaming into their phones, "Sadovaya Street! Sadovaya, 302B!"

As the sound of bloodcurdling sirens filled Sadovaya Street, and long red engines descended upon it from all parts of the city, the people milling about in the courtyard saw smoke coming out of a fifth floor window and flying out with it, three dark, apparently male silhouettes and one of a naked woman.

XXVIII

The Final Adventures of Korovyov and Behemoth

WHETHER the silhouettes were actually there or were merely fantasies of the terror-stricken residents of the ill-starred building on Sadovaya Street is, of course, impossible to say with exactitude. If they were there, then where they were headed is also unknown. Nor can we say at what point they separated, but we do know that approximately fifteen minutes before the fire started on Sadovaya Street, a tall man in a checked suit and a huge black cat showed up at the plate-glass doors of the Torgsin Store at the Smolensk Market.

After winding his way deftly through the crowd of passersby, the man opened the outer door of the store. But here a short, bony, and extremely inhospitable doorman barred his way and said angrily, "No cats allowed."

"I beg your pardon," crackled the tall man, and put his gnarled hand to his ear as if he were hard of hearing, "Cats, did you say? Where do you see any cat?"

The doorman's eyes bulged, and with good reason: there was no longer any cat at the man's feet, but instead, from behind his shoulder a fat man in a torn cap, whose face did look a bit catlike, was pushing and shoving his way into the store. In the fat man's hands was a primus stove.

For some reason the doorman-misanthrope took an instant dislike to these two.

"Foreign currency only," he rasped, looking out angrily from beneath his shaggy, gray eyebrows, which looked moth-eaten.

"My dear man," crackled the tall man, his eye sparkling through his cracked pince-nez, "and how do you know I don't have foreign currency? Are you judging by my suit? Don't ever do that, my precious watchman! You might make a mistake and a very serious one at that. If you don't believe me, have another look at the story of the famous caliph, Harun al-Rashid. But leaving that aside for the moment, let me say that in the present instance I shall lodge a complaint against you with your superior and shall tell him some things about you that might force you to give up your post here between these shiny plate-glass doors."

"Maybe I have a whole primus full of foreign currency," joined in the catlike fat man in a whiny voice as he pushed his way into the store.

The people in back of him were angry and already pushing to get in. Looking at the odd pair with hatred and uncertainty, the doorman moved aside, and our friends, Korovyov and Behemoth, found themselves inside the store. Here they first got their bearings, and then Korovyov announced in a booming voice that could be heard throughout the store, "A splendid store! A very, very, fine store!"

Customers turned away from the counters and for some reason stared at the speaker in astonishment even though his praise of the store was completely justified.

Hundreds of bolts of the most richly colored chintz were on display in floor cases. Behind them towered piles of calico, chiffon, and cloth for uniforms. Stacks of shoe boxes stretched into the distance, and several women were sitting on low stools trying on shoes—their right feet in their old, worn-down shoes, and their left ones in shiny new little boats which they tapped anxiously on the carpet. Somewhere around the corner, in the bowels of the store, gramophones played and sang.

But shunning all these delights, Korovyov and Behemoth headed straight for the specialty food and confectionery departments. Here there was plenty of room, and women in kerchiefs and berets were not crowding against the counters, as they were in the dry-goods department.

A shortish, completely square little man in horn-rimmed glasses was standing in front of the counter, bellowing something in a commanding voice. His face was shaven to a blue sheen and he was wearing a crisp, new hat with an immaculate headband, a lilac-colored overcoat, and red kid gloves. A clerk in a fresh white coat and dark-blue cap was waiting on the lilac customer. With an extremely sharp knife, very similar to the one stolen by Levi Matvei, he was removing the snakelike, silver-flecked skin from a fat, juicy, rose-colored salmon.

"This department is magnificent too," acknowledged Korovyov in solemn tones, "and the foreigner is nice," he said, pointing a well-meaning finger at the lilac back.

"No, Fagot, no," replied Behemoth pensively, "You're wrong, my friend. In my opinion there's something lacking in the lilac gentleman's face."

The lilac back shuddered, but it was probably just a coincidence since a foreigner could not possibly have understood what Korovyov and his companion were saying in Russian.

"Iz goot?" asked the lilac customer sternly.

"The best," replied the clerk, teasing the skin up playfully with his knife.

"Goot I like, bat, no," said the foreigner sharply.

"But of course!" was the salesman's enthusiastic reply.

At this point our friends moved away from the foreigner and his salmon and walked over to the confectionery counter.

"It's hot today," said Korovyov to a young, red-cheeked salesgirl and received no response from her. "How much are the tangerines?" he then asked her.

"Thirty kopecks a kilo," replied the salesgirl.

"Outrageous," remarked Korovyov with a sigh, "Oh well, too bad..." After some further deliberation, he said to his companion, "Try one, Behemoth."

The fat man tucked his primus under his arm, grabbed the tangerine at the top of the pyramid, gobbled it down, skin and all, and then reached for another.

The salesgirl was seized with mortal terror.

"You've gone out of your mind!" she screamed, the color draining from her cheeks. "Give me your receipt! Your receipt!" she said dropping the pair of tongs she was holding.

"My dear, my sweet girl, my beauty," rasped Korovyov, leaning himself over the counter and winking at the salesgirl, "We're all out of foreign currency today... what can you do! But I give you my word, we'll settle everything in cash next time, by Monday at the latest! We live close by, on Sadovaya, where the fire was..."

After gulping down a third tangerine, Behemoth thrust his paw into an ingenious arrangement of chocolate bars, pulled one out from the bottom, causing the whole pyramid to collapse, and swallowed it whole along with its gold wrapper.

The clerks at the fish counter stood petrified, their knives in their hands, the lilac foreigner turned to face the thieves, thereby revealing that Behemoth had been mistaken: rather than lacking something, his face, on the contrary, had rather more than was needed—of hanging jowls and darting eyes.

Turning completely yellow, the salesgirl shouted out miserably to the whole store, "Palosich! Palosich!"

Customers from the dry-goods department came running in response to her screams while Behemoth, abandoning the seductions of the confectionery counter, thrust his paw into a barrel of "Choice Kerch Herring," pulled out a pair and gulped them down, spitting out the tails.

"Palosich!" came another desperate cry from the confectionery counter, and at the fish counter a clerk with a goatee barked out, "What the hell do you think you're doing, scum?!"

Pavel Iosifovich was already hurrying to the scene. He was an imposing man in a clean white coat, like a surgeon, and with a pencil sticking out of his pocket. Pavel Iosifovich was clearly an experienced man. When he saw the tail of a third herring sticking out of Behemoth's mouth, he sized up the situation immediately, knew exactly what was going on, and forswearing any altercation with the brazen creatures, waved into the distance and gave the order, "Blow your whistle!"

The doorman flew out of the plate-glass doors to the corner of Smolensk Boulevard and burst out with an ominous whistle. The customers surrounded the scoundrels, and then Korovyov entered the fray.

"Citizens!" he shouted in a thin, tremulous voice, "What's this all about? Huh? Let me ask you that! This poor man," Korovyov added a quaver to his voice and pointed to Behemoth, who then put on a pathetic expression, "this poor man's been fixing primus stoves all day long; he's starved... and where can he get foreign currency?"

In response, Pavel Iosifovich, usually calm and restrained, shouted sternly, "Oh come off it!" and waved furiously to the doorman. The whistles at the entrance trilled more gaily.

But Korovyov, unperturbed by Pavel Iosifovich's rebuke, continued. "Where can he get it? I'm asking you that! He's tortured by hunger and thirst! He's hot. So the poor guy goes and samples a tangerine. A tangerine that costs all of three kopecks. And already they're whistling like nightingales in spring, disturbing the police, taking them away from their jobs. But that guy over there can have what he wants, right?" and here Korovyov pointed to the lilac fat man, causing the latter's face to register extreme alarm. "Who is he anyway? Huh? Where did he come from? And what for? Were we too bored without him? Did we invite him to come? Of course," the former choirmaster bellowed at the top of his lungs, twisting his mouth sarcastically, "he, you see, is wearing a fancy lilac suit and is all bloated with salmon, stuffed to the gills with foreign currency, but what about our fellow citizen here, our compatriot?! This makes me bitter! Bitter! Bitter!" wailed Korovyov like the best man at an old-fashioned wedding.

This whole extremely foolish, tactless, and no doubt politically dangerous speech made Pavel Iosifovich shake with rage, but, strange as it may seem, one could tell from the eyes of many of the other customers that Korovyov's words had aroused their sympathy! And when Behemoth put his torn and dirty sleeve up to his eye and cried out tragically, "Thank you, true friend, for standing up for a victim!" a miracle took place. A quiet, very proper little old man, poorly but neatly dressed, who was buying three almond pastries at the confectionery counter, was suddenly transfigured. His eyes flashed with martial fire, he turned crimson, threw his package of pastries on the floor, and shouted, "It's the truth!" in a thin, childlike voice. Then he grabbed a tray, threw down what was left of the chocolate Eiffel Tower destroyed by Behemoth, brandished it, tore the foreigner's hat off with his left hand, and used his right to hit him flat on top of his bald head with the tray. A sound rang out like that of sheet metal being thrown off a truck. The fat man paled, fell backwards, and plopped down in the barrel of Kerch herring, sending up a fountain of brine. Then came a second miracle. The lilac fellow who had fallen into the barrel was screaming in perfect Russian with no trace of an accent, "They're trying to kill me! Police! Bandits are trying to kill me!" The shock of what had happened had obviously given him instantaneous mastery of a language previously unknown to him.

Then the doorman's whistle stopped blowing, and two police helmets were seen advancing through the crowds of excited customers. But the perfidious Behemoth poured kerosene from the primus over the confectionery counter, just as water is poured from a tub over the bench in a steam bath, and it ignited spontaneously. The flame flared up and began running down the counter, devouring the pretty paper ribbons on the baskets of fruit. The salesgirls rushed out from behind the counter with shrieks and just as they did, the linen blinds on the windows caught fire, and the kerosene on the floor started burning. The customers let out a desperate shriek, dashed out of the confectionery department, crushing the now unnecessary Pavel Iosifovich, and the clerks from the fish department trotted single-file out the service exit with their sharpened knives. The lilac fellow extricated himself from the barrel, and, covered with herring brine, rolled over the salmon on the counter and followed the clerks out. The plate-glass entrance doors tinkled and shattered, as they were crushed by the people trying to get out of the store, while both scoundrels—Korovyov, and the arsonist Behemoth—disappeared somewhere, but where—it was impossible to figure out. Later, eyewitnesses who were present when the fire started in the Torgsin at the Smolensk Market said that both hooligans seemed to fly up to the ceiling and then burst there like children's balloons. It is, of course, doubtful that that was what happened, but we can't tell what we don't know.

We do know, however, that a minute after the incident at the Smolensk Market, Behemoth and Korovyov turned up on the sidewalk of the boulevard outside the house of Griboyedov's aunt. Korovyov stopped at the wrought-iron fence and said, "Well! So this is the writers' house! You know, Behemoth, I've heard many good and flattering things about this house. Take a look at it, my friend! How nice to think that a veritable multitude of talent is sheltered and ripening under this roof."

"Like pineapples in a hothouse," said Behemoth, and in order to get a better view of the cream-colored house and its columns, he crawled up onto the cement base of the iron railing.

"Quite true," chimed in Korovyov, agreeing with his inseparable companion, "And a sweet terror clutches your heart when you think that at this very minute the author of a future *Don Quixote*, or *Faust*, or, the devil take me, *Dead Souls* may be ripening inside that house! Huh?"

"A terrifying thought," confirmed Behemoth.

"Yes," continued Korovyov, "one can expect astonishing things from the seedbeds of this house, under whose roof have gathered thousands of devotees selflessly resolved to dedicate their lives to serving Melpomene, Polyhymnia, and Thalia. Just imagine what a sensation it will be when, for starters, one of them presents the reading public with an *Inspector General*, or, at the very least, a *Eugene Onegin!*"

"I can easily imagine that," again confirmed Behemoth.

"Yes," continued Korovyov, and raised a cautionary finger, "but! But— I say and I repeat it—but! Only if some microorganism doesn't attack these tender hothouse plants and eat away at their roots, only if they don't rot! And that can happen with pineapples! Oh, yes, indeed it can!"

"By the way," said Behemoth in an inquiring tone, sticking his round head through a hole in the railing, "what are they doing there on the veranda?"

"They're dining," explained Korovyov, "I forgot to mention, dear fellow, that there's a rather decent and inexpensive restaurant here. And it just so happens that I, like any tourist about to begin a long journey, would like a bite to eat and a large, frosty mug of beer."

"Me too," replied Behemoth, and the two scoundrels set off along the asphalt path under the lindens, heading straight for the veranda of the restaurant, which was as yet oblivious of the disaster to come.

A pale and bored citizeness in white socks and a white beret with a tassel was sitting on a bentwood chair at the corner entrance to the veranda, where an opening had been created in the greenery of the trellis. In front of her on a plain kitchen table lay a thick, office-style register in which, for reasons unknown, she was writing down the names of those entering the restaurant. It was this citizeness who stopped Korovyov and Behemoth.

"Your ID cards?" she asked, looking with astonishment at Korovyov's pince-nez and at Behemoth's primus stove and his torn elbow.

"I beg a thousand pardons, but what ID cards?" asked a surprised Korovyov.

"Are you writers?" asked the woman in turn.

"Of course we are," replied Korovyov with dignity.

"May I see your ID's?" repeated the woman.

"My charming creature..." began Korovyov, tenderly.

"I am not a charming creature," interrupted the woman.

"Oh, what a pity," said Korovyov with disappointment, and he continued, "Well, then, if you do not care to be a charming creature, which would have been quite nice, you don't have to be. But, here's my point, in order to ascertain that Dostoevsky is a writer, do you really need to ask him for an ID? Just look at any five pages of any of his novels, and you will surely know, even without any ID, that you're dealing with a writer. And I don't suppose that he ever had any ID! What do you think?" Korovyov turned to Behemoth.

"I'll bet he didn't," replied the latter, standing the primus stove on the table next to the register and wiping the sweat from his sooty brow.

"You are not Dostoevsky," said the citizeness, who was becoming addled by Korovyov.

"Well, but how do you know, how do you know?" replied the latter.

"Dostoevsky is dead," said the citizeness, but not very confidently.

"I protest!" exclaimed Behemoth hotly. "Dostoevsky is immortal!"

"Your ID's, citizens," said the citizeness.

"Excuse me, but this is, after all, absurd," said Korovyov, refusing to give in. "It isn't an ID that defines a writer, but what he has written! How can you know what ideas are fermenting in my brain? Or in his?" and he pointed at Behemoth's head, whereupon the latter immediately removed his cap so that the citizeness could get a better look at it.

"Let people in, citizens," she said, already nervous.

Korovyov and Behemoth stepped aside and let some writer pass who was wearing a gray suit and a tieless white summer shirt, the collar of which was open and splayed over the collar of his jacket, and who had a newspaper tucked under his arm. The writer gave the woman a friendly nod, scribbled something in the register she held out for him as he passed, and proceeded to the veranda.

"Alas, not to us," began Korovyov sadly, "but to him will go that frosty mug of beer that we, poor wanderers, so dreamed of. Our situation is a sad and difficult one, and I do not know what to do."

Behemoth merely shrugged bitterly and put his cap back on his round head, which was covered all over with thick hair very like cat fur. At that moment a soft but commanding voice sounded above the woman's head, "Let them in, Sophia Pavlovna."

The citizeness with the register gave a startled look: in the greenery of the trellis the white dress-shirt and wedge-shaped beard of the pirate had appeared. He gave the two dubious ragamuffins a welcoming look and even gestured for them to come inside. Archibald Archibaldovich made his authority felt in the restaurant he managed, and Sophia Pavlovna asked Korovyov submissively, "What is your name?"

"Panayev," replied the latter politely. The citizeness wrote it down and looked questioningly at Behemoth.

"Skabichevsky," squeaked the latter, pointing at his primus stove for some reason. Sophia Pavlovna wrote that down too and pushed the register over to the guests to get their signatures. Korovyov wrote "Skabichevsky" opposite "Panayev," and Behemoth wrote "Panayev" opposite "Skabichevsky."

To Sophia Pavlovna's utter amazement, Archibald Archibaldovich smiled seductively and led the guests to the best table at the other end of the veranda, the table where there was the most shade and where the sunlight played merrily through one of the openings in the trellis.

Blinking with astonishment, Sophia Pavlovna spent a long time studying the strange inscriptions left in the register by the unexpected visitors.

Archibald Archibaldovich astonished the waiters as much as he had Sophia Pavlovna. He personally pulled the chair back from the table when inviting Korovyov to be seated, winked at one waiter, whispered to the other, and both of the waiters then began fussing over the new guests, one of whom had put his primus stove down on the floor beside his rusty-brown boot.

The old tablecloth with yellow stains immediately disappeared from the table, and another one, as white as a Bedouin's burnous and crackling with starch, billowed in the breeze, while Archibald Archibaldovich leaned over and whispered softly but expressively into Korovyov's ear, "What can I get for you? I have some choice smoked sturgeon fillet... I salvaged it from the architects' convention..."

"You... um... can just give us some hors d'oeuvres... um..." murmured Korovyov cordially as he made himself comfortable in his chair.

"I understand," replied Archibald Archibaldovich significantly, closing his eyes.

Seeing the treatment these dubious-looking visitors were getting from the boss, the waiters put all their suspicions aside and got down to serious work. One offered a match to Behemoth, who had pulled a butt out of his pocket and stuck it in his mouth; the other flew up to the table with tinkling green glassware and began setting it with liqueur and wineglasses, and those delicate goblets one so enjoyed sipping Narzan from under the awning of the unforgettable Griboyedov veranda.

"May I offer you some fillet of grouse," purred Archibald Archibaldovich musically. The guest in the cracked pince-nez fully concurred with the frigate commander's suggestion and gazed benignly at him through his useless lens.

At a neighboring table the writer Petrakov-Sukhovei, dining with his wife, who was finishing her escallop of pork, noticed with a writer's keen powers of observation that Archibald Archibaldovich was showering attention on the guests at the next table, and was very surprised indeed. But his wife, a most honorable lady, simply became jealous of the pirate's attention to Korovyov and even began tapping her spoon on the table, as if to say, "What's the delay... It's time for our ice cream! What's the problem?"

Archibald Archibaldovich, however, merely gave Madame Petrakov a seductive smile and sent a waiter over to her, choosing himself to stay with his dear guests. Ah, Archibald Archibaldovich was smart, all right! And not one whit less observant than the writers themselves. Archibald Archibaldovich knew about the performance at the Variety Theater and had heard about many of the events that had occurred recently, but unlike everyone else, he had not let the words, "checked" and "cat" pass unnoticed. He had guessed immediately who his visitors were.

And as a result, he naturally had no desire to quarrel with them. But what a prize that Sophia Pavlovna was! Imagine trying to bar those two from the veranda! But what could you expect from her anyway!

Haughtily poking her spoon into the melting ice cream, Madame Petrakov looked on disgruntledly as the table in front of the two apparent buffoons piled up, as if by magic, with delicacies. Shining, wet lettuce leaves, washed to a sheen, protruded from a bowl of fresh caviar... a minute later a sweating silver bucket appeared on a small, separate table that had been moved over especially for this purpose.

Only when he was convinced that everything had been done to perfection, only when the waiters had brought in a bubbling, covered skillet did Archibald Archibaldovich permit himself to leave the two mysterious visitors, but only after whispering to them, "Excuse me! I'll only be a minute! I want to see to the grouse fillets myself."

He flew from the table and disappeared into the inner passageway of the restaurant. If anyone had observed Archibald Archibaldovich's subsequent movements, he would certainly have found them rather mystifying.

Rather than head for the kitchen to see to the grouse, the boss went directly to the storeroom. He opened it with his key, locked himself inside, and carefully, so as not to soil his cuffs, removed two heavy smoked sturgeon from the ice-chest, wrapped them up in newspaper, tied them carefully with a string, and put them aside. After that he checked in the next room to see if his hat and silk-lined summer coat were in their proper place, and only then did he proceed to the kitchen where the cook was zealously preparing the grouse promised the guests by the pirate.

It must be said that there was nothing the least bit strange or mystifying about any of Archibald Archibaldovich's actions, and only a superficial observer could have found them so. Archibald Archibaldovich's actions followed logically from everything that had preceded. His knowledge of recent events, to say nothing of his phenomenal intuition, told the boss of the Griboyedov restaurant that his two visitors' dinner, though lavish and extravagant, would nevertheless be of extremely short duration. And that intuition, which had never deceived the former pirate, did not deceive him now.

Just as Korovyov and Behemoth were clinking their second glass of splendid, ice-cold, double-filtered Moscow vodka, the reporter Boba Kandalupsky, famous in Moscow for his startling omniscience, appeared on the veranda in a state of sweaty excitement, and proceeded to join the Petrakovs at their table. After laying his bulging briefcase on the table, he put his lips to Petrakov's ear and began whispering some extremely juicy tidbits. Dying of curiosity, Madame Petrakov also pressed her ear to Boba's puffy, fleshy lips. And he, looking around furtively from time to time, kept on whispering and whispering, and occasionally one could catch a separate word or two, such as, "I swear! On Sadovaya, Sadovaya," Boba lowered his voice even more, "bullets don't stop them! Bullets... bullets... kerosene... fire... bullets..."

"They ought to take those liars who spread filthy rumors," bellowed Madame Petrakov in a louder contralto than Boba would have wished, "and give them a good talking to! Oh, well, never mind, that will happen in good time, they'll be set straight! What vicious liars!"

"What liars are you talking about, Antonida Porfiryevna!" exclaimed Boba, distressed by her refusal to believe what he was saying, and he began hissing again, "I'm telling you, bullets don't stop them... And now the fire... They flew through the air... the air," hissed Boba, having no suspicion that the people he was talking about were sitting at the next table and thoroughly enjoying his hissings.

However, their enjoyment was short-lived. Three men, coming from inside the restaurant, dashed out on the veranda, their waists tightly buckled, wearing leggings and carrying revolvers. The one in front gave a loud, terrifying shout, "Nobody move!" Then all three opened fire on the veranda, aiming at Korovyov's and Behemoth's heads. Both targets immediately dissolved into the air, and a column of flame shot up from the primus to the awning. A kind of gaping maw with black edges appeared in the awning and began spreading all over it. Leaping through the awning, the fire rose up to the very roof of Griboyedov House. Some folders with papers that were on the second-floor windowsill of the editorial room suddenly burst into flame, followed by the blind, and then the fire, roaring as if someone were fanning it, swept in columns into the aunt's house.

Just seconds later, writers who had not finished their dinners, the waiters, Sophia Pavlovna, Boba, and the Petrakovs were running down the asphalt paths out to the iron railings on the boulevard, from whence Ivanushka, the first harbinger of misfortune, who could not get anyone to understand him, had come on Wednesday evening.

Having exited through a side door, without running or hurrying, and with time to spare, like a captain obliged to be the last to leave his burning ship, Archibald Archibaldovich stood calmly in his silk-lined summer coat, two logs of smoked Balyk sturgeon tucked under his arm.

XXIX

The Fate of the Master and Margarita is Decided

A T SUNSET, high above the city, on the stone terrace of one of the most beautiful buildings in Moscow, a building built about a hundred and fifty years ago, were two figures: Woland and Azazello. They could not be seen from below, from the street, since they were shielded from unwelcome stares by a balustrade decorated with stucco vases and stucco flowers. They, on the other hand, could see almost to the very edge of the city.

Dressed in his black soutane, Woland was seated on a folding taboret. His long broadsword had been rammed vertically into the crack between two flagstones, thus forming a sundial. The sword's shadow lengthened slowly and steadily as it crept up to the black slippers on Satan's feet. With his sharp chin resting on his fist and one leg folded beneath him, Woland sat hunched on the taboret, staring fixedly at the vast assortment of huge buildings, palaces, and shacks condemned to destruction.

Azazello had shed his contemporary attire, that is, his jacket, bowler hat, and patent-leather shoes, and like Woland was dressed in black. He stood motionless, not far from his master, and like him, stared at the city.

Woland spoke, "What an interesting city, don't you think?"

Azazello stirred and replied respectfully, "Messire, I prefer Rome!"

"Yes, it's a matter of taste," answered Woland.

A short while later his voice sounded again, "What's that smoke over there on the boulevard?"

"That's Griboyedov burning," replied Azazello.

"One must assume, then, that the inseparable pair, Korovyov and Behemoth, paid them a visit?"

"No doubt about it, Messire."

Again there was silence, and the two on the terrace watched as the broken, blinding sun caught fire in the westward-facing, upper-storey windows of the massive buildings. Woland's eye burned like one of those windows, even though he had his back to the sunset.

But something made Woland turn away from the city here and focus his attention on the round tower on the roof behind him. Emerging from the tower wall was a somber, mud-stained, black-bearded man wearing a torn chiton and homemade sandals.

"Hah!" exclaimed Woland, looking mockingly at the man who had entered. "You're the last person one would have expected to see here! What brings you here, uninvited, but expected guest?"

"I've come to see you, Spirit of Evil and Sovereign of the Shadows," replied the man, looking sullenly at Woland from under his furrowed brows.

"If you've come to see me, then why haven't you greeted me and wished me well, former tax collector?" said Woland in a stern voice.

"Because I don't want you to be well," was the newcomer's impudent reply.

"Nevertheless, you'll have to reconcile yourself to the fact that I am," retorted Woland with a twisted smile. "No sooner do you appear on the roof than you blab nonsense, and I'll tell you what it is—it's in your intonation. You pronounced your words as if you refuse to acknowledge the existence of either shadows or evil. But would you kindly ponder this question: What would your good do if evil didn't exist, and what would the earth look like if all the shadows disappeared? After all, shadows are cast by things and people. Here is the shadow of my sword. But shadows also come from trees and from living beings. Do you want to strip the earth of all trees and living things just because of your fantasy of enjoying naked light? You're stupid."

"I won't argue with you, old sophist," replied Levi Matvei.

"You can't argue with me because of what I just said—you're stupid," replied Woland, and asked, "Well, tell me briefly, without tiring me, why have you appeared?"

"He sent me."

"What did he order you to tell me, slave?"

"I am not a slave," replied Levi Matvei, becoming more enraged, "I am his disciple."

"We are speaking different languages, as always," rejoined Woland, "but that doesn't change the things we talk about. So?..."

"He has read the Master's work," began Levi Matvei, "and asks that you take the Master with you and grant him peace. Is that so difficult for you to do, Spirit of Evil?"

"Nothing is difficult for me to do," replied Woland, "as you well know." He was silent for a moment and then added, "But why aren't you taking him with you to the light?"

"He has not earned light, he has earned peace," said Levi in a sad voice.

"Tell him that it shall be done," replied Woland, and added, his eye suddenly flashing, "and leave me this instant."

"He asks that you also take the one who loved him and who suffered because of him," said Levi to Woland, imploring for the first time.

"We would never have thought of that without you. Leave."

Levi Matvei disappeared after this, and Woland called Azazello and commanded him, "Fly to them and arrange everything."

Azazello left the terrace and Woland remained alone.

But his solitude was not of long duration. Footsteps and animated voices were heard on the terrace, and Korovyov and Behemoth appeared before Woland. But now the fat man was without his primus stove, but was loaded down with other things. Under his arm was a small landscape in a gold frame, over his arm a badly singed cook's smock, and in his other hand a whole salmon, skin on and tail attached. Korovyov and Behemoth both reeked of smoke, Behemoth's mug was covered with soot and his cap was half-singed.

"Salutations, Messire!" cried the indefatigable pair, and Behemoth waved his salmon.

"You're a fine sight," said Woland.

"Imagine, Messire," began Behemoth, shouting joyfully and excitedly, "They thought I was a looter!"

"Judging by what you've got with you," replied Woland, looking at the landscape, "you are a looter."

"Can you believe, Messire..." began Behemoth in a heartfelt voice.

"No, I can't believe," was Woland's curt reply.

"Messire, I swear I made heroic efforts to save everything I could, but this was all I could salvage."

"You would do better to tell me, how did Griboyedov catch fire?" asked Woland.

Korovyov and Behemoth both spread their arms and raised their eyes skyward, and Behemoth cried, "I have no idea! We were sitting peacefully, perfectly quietly, having a bite to eat..."

"And suddenly—bang! bang!" chimed in Korovyov. "They were shooting at us! Frightened out of our minds, Behemoth and I ran out into the street, the pursuers ran after us, and we made a dash for Timiryazev!"

"But a sense of duty," inserted Behemoth, "overcame our shameful fear, and we went back!"

"Ah, you went back, did you?" said Woland. "So, of course then, the building burned to the ground."

"To the ground!" affirmed Korovyov sorrowfully. "That is, literally to the ground, Messire, as you so accurately phrased it. Nothing left but smouldering chips!"

"I headed straight," Behemoth recounted, "for the assembly hall— that's the one with the columns, Messire—expecting to save something valuable. Oh, Messire, my wife, if only I had one, risked being widowed twenty times over! Fortunately, Messire, I am not married, and I'll tell you frankly—I'm happy not to be. Oh, Messire, who would exchange the freedom of bachelorhood for a yoke around the neck!"

"The nonsense has begun again," observed Woland.

"I'm listening and continuing with my story," replied the cat, "yessir, here's a small landscape. It was impossible to remove anything else from the hall, the flames were in my face. I ran to the storeroom and salvaged the salmon. Ran to the kitchen and salvaged the smock. I consider, Messire, that I did everything I could, and I fail to understand the skeptical look on your face."

"And what was Korovyov doing while you were looting?" inquired Woland.

"I was helping the firemen, Messire," replied Korovyov, pointing to his torn trousers.

"Ah, if that's true, then naturally, they'll have to build a new building."

"It will be built, Messire," answered Korovyov, "I can assure you of that."

"Well, then, all that is left is to hope that the new one will be better than the old," remarked Woland.

"And so it shall, Messire," said Korovyov.

"Believe me, it will," added the cat, "I'm a regular prophet."

"In any case, we're back, Messire," reported Korovyov, "and we await your instructions."

Woland got up from his taboret, went over to the balustrade, and, turning his back on his retinue, gazed silently into the distance for a long time. Then he went back, sat down on his taboret again, and said, "There will be no instructions—you have done everything you could, and for the time being, I have no further need of your services. You may rest. A thunderstorm is coming, the last thunderstorm, and it will accomplish everything that needs to be accomplished, and then we will be on our way."

"Very well, Messire," replied the two buffoons and disappeared somewhere behind the central round tower in the middle of the terrace.

The thunderstorm that Woland had mentioned was already gathering on the horizon. A black cloud had risen in the west and cut off half the sun. Then it covered it completely. It got cooler on the terrace. Soon thereafter, it got dark.

This darkness, which came from the west, enveloped the huge city. Bridges and palaces disappeared. Everything vanished as if it had never existed. A single streak of fire ran across the whole sky. Then a clap of thunder shook the city. It was repeated, and the storm began. Woland ceased to be visible in its darkness.

XXX

Time to go! Time to go!

"You know," Margarita was saying, "just as you fell asleep last night, I was reading about the darkness that had come in from the Mediterranean... and those idols, oh, those golden idols! For some reason, they give me no peace. I think it's going to rain now too. Can't you feel it getting cooler?"

"All this is fine and good," replied the Master as he smoked and chased the smoke away with his hand, "—and as for the idols, forget about them... but what will happen next, is quite incomprehensible!"

This conversation took place at sunset just as Levi Matvei came to Woland on the terrace. The window of the basement apartment was open, and if anyone had glanced in, he would have been taken aback by the strange appearance of the two speakers. Margarita was wearing a black cape over her naked body, and the Master was in hospital underclothes. This was because all Margarita's things were back at her house and she had absolutely nothing else to wear, and although the house was not far away, there was, naturally, no question of her going back there to get her things. And the Master, all of whose suits were still in the closet as if he had never been away, simply did not feel like getting dressed, preoccupied as he was with telling Margarita that he was convinced something quite weird was about to happen. True, he was clean-shaven for the first time since that autumn night (his beard had been trimmed with clippers at the clinic).

The room looked strange too, and it was hard to make anything out in all the chaos. There were manuscripts all over the rug and the sofa. A book was splayed spine upwards in the armchair. The round table was set for dinner, and a few bottles stood among the hors d'oeuvres. Neither Margarita nor the Master knew where the food and drink had come from. They had awakened to find it all on the table.

Having slept until sunset on Saturday, the Master and his beloved both felt completely restored, and the only reminder they both had of the previous night's adventures was a slight ache in the left temple.

Psychologically, they had both undergone dramatic changes, as anyone who overheard their conversation in the basement apartment would have realized. But there was absolutely no one to overhear them. The good thing about the yard was that it was always empty. The willow and the lindens outside the window were getting greener every day and their spring fragrance was blown into the basement by a rising breeze.

"Well, what the devil!" exclaimed the Master unexpectedly. "When you think of it, this is really...," he put out his cigarette in the ashtray, and pressed his hands to his head. "No, listen, you're an intelligent person and you were never crazy. Do you seriously believe that last night we were the guests of Satan?"

"Quite seriously," replied Margarita.

"Of course, of course," said the Master ironically, "that means that now we have two lunatics here, instead of just one! The husband and the wife." He raised his hands to heaven and cried, "No, only the devil knows what this is all about! The devil, the devil, the devil!"

Instead of answering, Margarita collapsed on the sofa, burst out laughing, waved her bare legs, and cried out, "Oh, I can't stand it! I can't stand it! If you could only see what you look like!"

Having laughed her fill while the Master sheepishly hitched up his hospital long johns, Margarita then grew serious.

"You just spoke the truth without knowing it," she began, "The devil does know what this is all about, and believe me, the devil will fix everything!" Her eyes suddenly caught fire, she jumped up, began dancing up and down and shouting, "How happy I am, how happy I am that I made that deal with him! O devil, devil!... And you, my dearest, you'll just have to live with a witch!" She then rushed over to the Master, threw her arms around his neck and began kissing him on the lips, nose, and cheeks. Streams of uncombed black hair cascaded onto the Master, and his cheeks and forehead were hot from kisses.

"You really have become like a witch."

"That I don't deny," replied Margarita, "I am a witch and I'm very pleased to be one!"

"Well, good," said the Master, "so you're a witch. Fine and splendid! So, that means I was abducted from the hospital... Also very nice! They've brought us back here, let's grant that too... Let's even assume we won't be missed... But in the name of all that's holy, tell me how we'll live and on what? In saying that, I'm concerned mainly about you, believe me!"

Just then a pair of square-toed boots and trouser legs appeared in the basement window. The trousers then bent at the knee, and an ample rear end blocked out the light of day.

"Aloisy, are you home?" asked a voice outside the window from somewhere above the trousers.

"See, it's beginning," said the Master.

"Aloisy?" asked Margarita, going up closer to the window. "He was arrested yesterday. But who's asking for him? What's your name?"

The knees and rear end vanished in a second, the gate made a knocking sound, after which everything returned to normal. Margarita collapsed on the sofa and laughed so hard that tears rolled down her cheeks. But when she had calmed down, her face changed completely, she began speaking seriously, and as she did, she slid down off the couch and crawled over to the Master's knees, and, looking into his eyes, she began stroking his head.

"How you've suffered, how you've suffered, my poor man! I'm the only one who knows how much. Look, you have streaks of gray in your hair and a permanent line by your mouth. My only one, my darling, don't think about anything. You've had to think too much, and now I'll do the thinking for you! And I promise you, I promise, everything will be spectacularly fine!"

"I'm not afraid of anything, Margot," replied the Master suddenly, and he raised his head and looked just as he had when he was writing about what he had never seen but knew for certain had happened. "I'm not afraid because I've already been through everything. They frightened me too much and they can't frighten me with anything else. But I feel sorry for you, Margot, that's the problem, and that's why I keep coming back to the same thing. Come to your senses! Why ruin your life over a sick man and a beggar? Go back home! I feel pity for you, that's why I'm saying this."

"Oh, you, you," whispered Margarita, shaking her disheveled head, "you unhappy man of little faith. I spent last night naked and shivering because of you, I lost my entire nature and became something different; for months I sat in a dark hole of a room, thinking about only one thing—the thunderstorm over Yershalaim, I cried my eyes out, and now when happiness has come, you want to chase me away? Well, fine, I'll go, I'll go, but know that you are a cruel man! They ravaged your soul!"

Bitter tenderness welled up in the Master's heart, and for some unknown reason he began to cry as he buried his head in Margarita's hair. She whispered to him, crying, and her fingers skipped lightly over the Master's temples.

"Yes, streaks, streaks... your head is turning snow-white before my very eyes... oh, my, my long-suffering head! Just look at your eyes! There's a wasteland in there... And your shoulders, they're weighted down... They've crippled you... crippled you." Margarita's speech was disjointed, she was shaking with tears.

Then the Master wiped his eyes, lifted Margarita off her knees, got up himself, and said in a firm voice, "Enough! You've put me to shame. I won't let myself be fainthearted anymore, and I won't bring up the subject again, don't worry. I know we're both victims of a mental illness that I may have given you... Well, no matter, we'll go through it together."

Margarita pressed her lips to the Master's ear and whispered, "I swear by your life, I swear by the astrologer's son, divined by you, that everything will be all right."

"Well, fine, fine," answered the Master, adding with a laugh, "Of course, when people have been stripped of everything, as you and I have been, they look to otherworldly powers for salvation! Well, all right, I'm willing to do that."

"That's it, now you're your old self again, you're laughing," replied Margarita. "To the devil with your learned words. Otherworldly or not otherworldly—isn't it all the same? I'm hungry."

And she took the Master's hand and pulled him over to the table.

"I'm not convinced that the food won't fall through the floor or fly out the window," said the Master, who was now completely calm.

"It won't fly away!"

And at that moment a nasal voice was heard at the window, "Peace be unto you."

The Master shuddered, but Margarita, already accustomed to the unusual, cried out, "That must be Azazello! Oh, how nice this is, how good!" and she whispered to the Master, "You see, you see, they haven't forsaken us!" She hurried to open the door.

"Pull your cape around you," the Master called after her.

"I don't give a damn about that," replied Margarita, already out in the little hallway.

And then Azazello was bowing and greeting the Master, his walleye beaming at him, and Margarita exclaimed, "Oh, how happy I am! I've never been so happy in my life! But please excuse my nakedness, Azazello!"

Azazello told her not to worry, assuring her that he had seen not only naked women, but women who had been completely skinned, and he took a seat at the table after first placing a bundle wrapped in dark brocade in the corner by the stove.

Margarita poured Azazello some cognac, and he drank it gladly. Not taking his eyes off him, the Master would now and then quietly pinch his left wrist under the table. But the pinching did not help. Azazello did not evaporate into thin air, and, to tell the truth, there was no reason for him to do so. There was nothing terrifying about this short, red-haired man, except perhaps for his walleye, but such things can occur even without sorcery—or except perhaps for his not quite normal clothes—some kind of cassock or cloak—but then again, if one thinks about it seriously, there are people who dress like that. And he drank his cognac as all good men do, that is, downing each glass in one swallow, without eating anything. That same cognac made the Master's head buzz, and he began thinking, "No, Margarita's right! Of course this fellow in front of me is an emissary of the devil. After all, wasn't I just trying to prove to Ivan, two nights ago, that it was Satan whom he had met at Patriarch's Ponds. But now, for some reason, the thought frightens me and I start babbling about hypnotists and hallucinations. What the devil kind of hypnotists are these!"

He began examining Azazello closely and became convinced that some constraint showed in his eyes, some idea which he had not as yet proposed to them. "He's not here just to pay a visit, he's here on some mission," thought the Master.

His powers of observation had not betrayed him.

After downing a third glass of cognac, which seemed to have no effect on Azazello whatsoever, the visitor began as follows, "A devilishly comfy little basement! I have only one question. What are you going to do in this little basement?"

"That's precisely what I was saying," replied the Master, laughing.

"Why are you upsetting me, Azazello?" asked Margarita. "We'll manage somehow!"

"Please, please," cried Azazello, "I never meant to upset you. I even agree with you—you'll manage somehow. Oh yes! I almost forgot... Messire sends his greetings. He also asked that I invite you to go on a little outing with him, if, of course, you wish to. So, what do you say to that?"

Margarita nudged the Master with her foot under the table.

"I accept with pleasure," replied the Master, studying Azazello, while the latter continued, "We hope Margarita Nikolayevna won't refuse our invitation?"

"Of course I won't," said Margarita, again nudging the Master's foot with her own.

"That's wonderful!" exclaimed Azazello. "That's what I like! One, two, and we're off! Not like that time in Alexandrovsky Park."

"Oh, don't remind me, Azazello! I was stupid then. But I shouldn't be blamed too severely—after all, it's not everyday you meet up with an evil power!"

"That's for sure!" confirmed Azazello. "How nice it would be if it were everyday!"

"It's the speed I like," said Margarita excitedly, "the speed and the nakedness. Like a shot from a Mauser—bang! Ah, what a shot he is!" cried Margarita, turning to the Master. "He can hit a seven card underneath a pillow and on any of its markings!" Margarita was starting to get drunk, which made her eyes flash.

"And again I forgot something," said Azazello loudly, slapping himself on the forehead, "I must be overtired! Messire sent you a gift," here he turned to the Master, "a bottle of wine. Please note that it's the same wine the procurator of Judea was drinking. Falernum."

Naturally, such a rarity provoked the Master's and Margarita's interest. Azazello took a moldy jug out of a piece of dark, funeral brocade. They sniffed the wine, poured it into glasses, and looked through it at the light in the window, which was fading in the approaching storm.

They saw how everything was stained the color of blood.

"To Woland's health!" exclaimed Margarita, raising her glass.

All three touched their lips to their glasses and took a long drink. The pre-storm light began to fade in the Master's eyes, his heart skipped a beat, and he felt the end approaching. He saw Margarita, now mortally pale, helplessly stretch out her hands to him, drop her head on the table, and then slide to the floor.

"Poisoner..." the Master managed to shout. He wanted to grab a knife from the table to stab Azazello, but his hand slid helplessly off the tablecloth. Everything around him in the basement turned black, and then vanished completely. He fell backwards, and as he did, cut his temple on the corner of the desk.

When the two who had been poisoned were still, Azazello went into action. The first thing he did was dash to the window and seconds later he was in the house where Margarita Nikolayevna had lived. Always careful and precise, Azazello wanted to make sure that everything that was necessary had been done. Everything was completely in order. He saw a morose woman, who was waiting for her husband to come home, walk out of her bedroom, suddenly turn pale, clutch her heart and cry out helplessly, "Natasha! Someone... help me!" She fell on the living-room floor, without reaching the study.

"Everything's in order," said Azazello. A minute later he was back with the prostrate lovers. Margarita lay with her face buried in the carpet. With his iron grip, Azazello turned her over like a doll, so that she was facing him, and scrutinized her. The face of the poisoned woman changed before his eyes. Even in the dusk of the gathering storm he could see the temporary witch's squint and the cruelty and wildness of her features disappear. The dead woman's face brightened and, finally, softened, and her smile was no longer predatory, but more that of a woman who had gone through a lot of suffering. Then Azazello pried open her white teeth and poured a few drops into her mouth of the same wine he had used to poison her. Margarita sighed, started to raise herself without Azazello's help, sat up, and asked in a weak voice, "Why, Azazello, why? What have you done to me?"

She saw the Master lying there, shuddered, and whispered, "I didn't expect this... murderer!"

"No, no, you've got it all wrong," replied Azazello, "He'll get up in a minute. Ah, why are you so nervous!"

The red-haired demon sounded so convincing that Margarita believed him right away. She jumped up, strong and alive, and helped give the prostrate Master a drink of the wine. Opening his eyes, the latter gave a glowering look and with hatred in his voice repeated his last word, "Poisoner..."

"Ah, well! Insults are the usual reward for good work," replied Azazello. "Are you blind? If so, recover your sight quickly."

The Master lifted himself up, looked around with bright, keen eyes and asked, "What does this new scenario mean?"

"It means," replied Azazello, "that it's time for us to go. Can't you hear the thunder? It's getting dark. The horses are pawing the ground, your little garden is trembling. Say good-bye to your basement, and do it quickly."

"Ah, I see," said the Master, looking around, "You killed us, we're dead. How clever of you! How timely! Now I understand everything."

"Oh, please," replied Azazello, "is that you I'm hearing? After all, your beloved calls you the Master, you are thinking at this moment, how can you be dead? Do you have to be sitting in a basement in a shirt and hospital long johns to think you're alive? That's absurd!"

"I understand what you've said," cried the Master, "Don't say any more! You're a thousand times right!"

"Great Woland!" seconded Margarita, "Great Woland! His idea was a lot better than mine. But the novel, the novel," she shouted to the Master," take the novel with you wherever you're flying."

"I don't have to," replied the Master, "I remember it by heart."

"But you won't forget a word of it, not a single word?" asked Margarita, pressing herself to her lover and wiping the blood away from the cut on his temple.

"Don't worry! Now I shall never forget anything," he replied.

"Then it's time for the fire!" cried Azazello, "Fire with which everything began and with which we are ending everything."

"Fire!" shouted Margarita in a terrifying voice. The basement window banged, the wind blew the blind aside. A short burst of thunder clapped merrily in the sky. Azazello thrust his clawed hand into the stove, pulled out a smoking log and set fire to the tablecloth. Then he set fire to a bundle of old newspapers on the couch, and then to the manuscript and the curtain on the window.

The Master, already intoxicated by the thought of the coming ride, threw a book from the shelf onto the table and ruffled its pages in the burning tablecloth. It went up in merry flames.

"Burn, burn, former life!"

"Burn, suffering!" cried Margarita.

The room was already shimmering in crimson columns, and the three of them ran out through the door along with the smoke, up the stone stairs, and out into the yard. The first thing they saw was the landlord's cook sitting on the ground; scattered around her were potatoes and several bunches of onions. The cook's condition was understandable. Three black horses were snorting by the shed, quivering, and kicking up fountains of dirt. Margarita was the first to mount, then Azazello, and the Master last. The cook let out a groan and was about to lift her hand to make the sign of the cross, but Azazello shouted threateningly from the saddle, "I'll cut your hand off!" He whistled, and the horses soared upwards, smashing the linden branches, and dove into a black, low-hanging cloud. Just then smoke began pouring out of the tiny basement window. From below came the faint, pathetic cry of the cook, "We're on fire!"

The horses were already flying over the roofs of Moscow.

"I want to say good-bye to the city," shouted the Master to Azazello, who was riding in front. Thunder swallowed up the end of the Master's sentence. Azazello nodded and urged his horse into a gallop. A cloud was coming straight toward the riders, but still without a sprinkle of rain.

They flew over the boulevard, looked down and saw tiny figures running all over the place, seeking shelter from the rain. The first drops began to fall. They flew over the smoke, which was all that was left of Griboyedov. They flew over the city being flooded by darkness. Lightning flashed above them. Then the rooftops gave way to greenery. Only then did the rain gush down and transform them into three huge bubbles in the deluge.

Margarita was already used to the sensation of flight, but the Master was not, and he was amazed at how quickly they reached their destination, where the man was whom he wanted to say good-bye to because he had no one else. Through the veil of rain he immediately recognized Stravinsky's clinic, the river, and the wood on the opposite shore that he had come to know so thoroughly. They landed in a grove in the meadow not far from the clinic.

"I'll wait for you here," shouted Azazello through cupped hands, now lit up by flashes of lightning, now submerged in a shroud of gray. "Say good-bye, but do it quickly!"

The Master and Margarita jumped down from their saddles and flew across the clinic garden, flickering like watery shadows. A moment later, the Master's practiced hand was moving aside the balcony grille of Room 117. Margarita was right behind him. They entered Ivanushka's room, invisible and unnoticed, while the storm was crashing and howling. The Master stopped by the bed.

Ivanushka lay motionless, just as he had the first time he watched a thunderstorm from this haven of rest. But he was not crying now as he had been then. After looking carefully at the dark silhouette that had entered his room from the balcony, he raised himself up, stretched his arms out and said joyfully, "Ah, it's you! I've been waiting and waiting for you. And now here you are, my neighbor."

To this the Master replied, "I am here! But unfortunately, I cannot be your neighbor anymore. I am flying away forever and I have only come to say good-bye."

"I knew that, I guessed it," replied Ivan softly and asked, "Did you meet him?"

"Yes," said the Master, "I came to say good-bye to you because you are the only person I've talked to recently."

Ivanushka brightened and said, "It's good that you stopped by. I'll keep my word, you know, I won't write any more silly poems. Something else interests me now," Ivanushka smiled and stared with crazed eyes into the distance, past the Master. "I want to write something else. While I've been lying here, you know, I've come to understand a great deal."

These words excited the Master, and he sat down on the edge of Ivanushka's bed and began speaking, "That's good, that's good. You'll write the sequel about him!"

Ivanushka's eyes flashed.

"But won't you be writing that yourself?" Here he lowered his head and added thoughtfully, "Ah, yes, of course, why am I asking such things." Ivanushka gazed down at the floor, looking frightened.

"No," said the Master, and his voice sounded unfamiliar and hollow, "I won't be writing about him anymore. I'll be busy with something else."

A distant whistle pierced through the sound of the storm.

"Do you hear that?" asked the Master.

"The noise of the storm..."

"No, they're calling me, it's time for me to go," explained the Master and got up from the bed.

"Wait! One more word," begged Ivan, "Did you find her? Had she been faithful?"

"She's right here," replied the Master and pointed to the wall. A dark Margarita detached herself from the white wall and came over to the bed. She looked at the young man lying there, and sorrow showed in her eyes.

"My poor, poor dear," whispered Margarita almost soundlessly, and she bent over the bed.

"What a beautiful woman," said Ivan without envy, but with sadness and a kind of quiet tenderness, "You see, everything worked out well for you. But it didn't for me." Here he thought for a minute and added pensively, "But maybe it has..."

"Yes, yes," whispered Margarita, bending down to him, "I'm going to kiss you on the forehead, and everything will work out as it should... take my word for it, I've seen everything already, I know everything."

The young man put his arms around her neck and she kissed him.

"Farewell, disciple," said the Master barely audibly and began melting into the air. He vanished, and Margarita vanished with him. The balcony grille closed.

Ivanushka became restless. He sat up in bed, looked around anxiously, even groaned, began talking to himself, and then got up. The thunderstorm was raging with increasing fury, and, apparently, had agitated his soul. It also upset him that his ears, accustomed now to perpetual silence, caught the sounds of anxious footsteps and muffled voices coming from outside his door. In a nervous state, he called out, trembling, "Praskovya Fyodorovna!"

As she came into his room, Praskovya Fyodorovna gave Ivanushka an anxious and inquiring glance.

"What is it? What's the matter?" she asked. "Is the storm upsetting you? Well, never you mind, never you mind... We'll make you feel better right away. I'll call for the doctor."

"No, Praskovya Fyodorovna, you don't have to call for the doctor," said Ivanushka, looking restlessly not at Praskovya Fyodorovna, but at the wall. "There's nothing particularly the matter. I understand everything now, don't be afraid. But won't you tell me," asked Ivan with feeling, "what just happened next door, in Room 118?"

"In 118?" repeated Praskovya Fyodorovna, and her eyes began darting all around. "Why, nothing happened there." But her voice sounded fake. Ivanushka noticed that immediately and said, "Oh, Praskovya Fyodorovna! You're such a truthful person... Do you think I'm going to fly into a rage? No, Praskovya Fyodorovna, that won't happen. Why don't you just tell me. I can sense what's going on through the wall anyway."

"Your neighbor just died," whispered Praskovya Fyodorovna, unable to overcome her innate truthfulness and goodness, and clothed in the brilliance of the lightning, she looked in fear at Ivanushka. But nothing terrible happened to Ivanushka. He simply raised his finger meaningfully and said, "I knew it! I can assure you, Praskovya Fyodorovna, someone else just died in the city. I even know who." Here Ivanushka smiled mysteriously. "It was a woman."

XXXI

On Sparrow Hills

THE thunderstorm had passed without leaving a trace, and a multicolored rainbow had formed an arch over the entire city and was drinking water from the Moscow River. High on a hill between two groves of trees three dark silhouettes could be seen. Woland, Korovyov, and Behemoth sat mounted on black horses, gazing at the city that stretched out on the other side of the river, at the fragmented sun gleaming in the thousands of windows facing westward, toward the gingerbread towers of Novodevichy Convent.

There was a rustle in the air, and Azazello, along with the Master and Margarita who were flying behind him in the black tail of his cloak, landed next to the waiting group.

"We were forced to upset you a little, Margarita Nikolayevna and Master," began Woland after a brief pause, "but please don't hold a grudge. I don't think you'll have any cause for regret. Well, then," he said addressing the Master alone, "say good-bye to the city. It's time for us to go." Woland pointed a black-gloved hand toward the other side of the river where countless suns were smelting the glass, and where the sky over these suns was thick with mist, smoke, and the steam from the city left incandescent by the day's heat.

The Master dismounted quickly, detached himself from the group, and ran over to the precipice of the hill. His black cloak trailed behind him on the ground. The Master began to look at the city. In the first few seconds an aching sadness wrenched his heart, but it soon gave way to a feeling of sweet disquiet, the excitement of gypsy wanderlust.

"Forever! That must be fully comprehended," whispered the Master, and he licked his dry, cracked lips. He began to listen carefully and pay close attention to everything that was happening in his soul. His excitement, it seemed to him, had turned into a feeling of deep and deadly resentment. But it was short-lived, it passed, and gave way for some reason to a feeling of proud indifference, which, in turn, became a presentiment of permanent peace.

The group of riders waited for the Master in silence. The group of riders watched the gesticulations of the long, black figure at the edge of the precipice, who at times raised his head as if trying to encompass the whole city with his gaze and peer beyond its boundaries, and at others dropped his head as if studying the stunted, trampled grass beneath his feet.

The silence was broken by Behemoth who had become bored.

"May I have permission, *maître,*" he said. "to give a whistle of farewell before we ride off?"

"You might frighten the lady," replied Woland, "and, besides, don't forget that today's disgraceful antics are over now."

"Oh, no, no, Messire," said Margarita, sitting in the saddle like an Amazon, her hand on her hip, her pointed train reaching down to the ground, "Give him permission to whistle. Thinking about the long road ahead makes me sad. That's natural, isn't it, Messire, even when you know that happiness awaits you at the end of the road? Let him make us laugh, or else I'm afraid this will all end in tears, and everything will be spoiled before we set out on the road!"

Woland nodded to Behemoth, who got very animated, jumped off his horse, put his fingers in his mouth, puffed out his cheeks, and whistled. Margarita's ears began ringing. Her horse reared up, dry branches broke off in the grove, flocks of ravens and sparrows flew up into the sky, a column of dust spiraled towards the river, and several of the passengers on a riverboat that was going past the landing below had their caps blown off into the water.

The whistle made the Master shudder; however, he did not turn around, but began gesticulating even more wildly, raising his fist skyward as if he were threatening the city. Behemoth looked around proudly.

"That was a real whistle, I won't argue," remarked Korovyov condescendingly, "a real whistle, but, objectively speaking, it was pretty mediocre!"

"Well, but I'm not a choirmaster," replied Behemoth with dignity, puffing himself up, and unexpectedly giving Margarita a wink.

"Let me give it a try, if I can remember how," said Korovyov, rubbing his hands and blowing on his fingers.

"But just be careful," said Woland sternly from astride his horse. "No broken limbs!"

"Believe me, Messire," rejoined Korovyov, his hand pressed to his heart, "it's just for fun, I assure you..." Whereupon he stretched as if he were made of rubber, twirled the fingers of his right hand in an ingenious way, twisted himself up like a corkscrew, and then, after suddenly unwinding, let out a whistle.

Margarita did not hear the whistle, but she saw its effects when she and her fiery steed were thrown more than twenty yards to the side. An oak tree next to her was torn up by the roots, and fissures spread over the ground to the river. A huge chunk of riverbank, together with the landing and the restaurant, was uprooted into the river. The water bubbled and heaved, and an entire riverboat was thrown up on the green, low-lying opposite shore, the passengers completely unharmed. A jackdaw killed by Fagot's whistle landed at the feet of Margarita's neighing horse.

This whistle scared the Master away. He grabbed his head and ran back to join his waiting companions.

"Well, then," said Woland, addressing him from atop his horse, "are all your accounts settled? Have you completed your farewell?"

"Yes, I have," replied the Master, and having regained his composure, he looked boldly and squarely into Woland's face.

And then the terrifying voice of Woland boomed over the hills like a trumpet call, "Time to go!" followed by the sharp whistle and laughter of Behemoth.

The horses set off, and the riders soared upwards, breaking into a gallop. Margarita could feel her frenzied horse chomping and straining at the bit. Woland's cloak billowed out over the heads of the entire cavalcade and began filling the vault of the evening sky. When the black covering moved aside for just an instant, Margarita, still galloping, looked back over her shoulder and saw that everything behind them was gone, not only the multicolored towers with the airplane whirring overhead, but the city itself, which had vanished into the ground and left only mist in its wake.

XXXII

Absolution and Eternal Refuge

Gods, my gods! How sad the earth is at eventide! How mysterious are the mists over the swamps. Anyone who has wandered in these mists, who has suffered a great deal before death, or flown above the earth, bearing a burden beyond his strength knows this. Someone who is exhausted knows this. And without regret he forsakes the mists of the earth, its swamps and rivers, and sinks into the arms of death with a light heart, knowing that death alone...

Even the magical black horses had tired and were carrying their riders slowly, and the inevitable night was beginning to catch up with them. Sensing the night at his back, even the irrepressible Behemoth had fallen silent and was flying along, serious and silent, his claws dug into his saddle, his tail fluffed out behind him.

Night began covering the forests and meadows with its black kerchief. The night ignited sad little lights somewhere far below, alien lights that were no longer of any interest or use either to Margarita or the Master. Night overtook the cavalcade, spreading over them from above and scattering white specks of stars here and there in the saddened sky.

Night was thickening, flying alongside the riders, grabbing at their cloaks and pulling them off, unmasking all illusions. And whenever Margarita, buffeted by the cool breeze, opened her eyes, she saw the changes that were taking place in the appearances of all who were flying to their destination. And when the crimson full moon rose up to meet them from behind the edge of the forest, all illusions vanished and the magical, mutable clothing fell into the swamp and drowned in the mist.

Korovyov-Fagot, the self-titled interpreter for the mysterious consultant who never required any interpretation, was hardly recognizable now in the figure who was flying beside Woland, to the right of the Master's beloved. In place of the fellow who had left Sparrow Hills in a torn circus outfit under the name of Korovyov-Fagot, there now galloped, his gold reins clinking softly, a dark-violet knight with an extremely somber face that never smiled. He flew along beside Woland with his chin on his chest, not looking at the moon and taking no interest in the earth below, but, rather, completely immersed in his own thoughts.

"Why is he so changed?" Margarita softly asked Woland to the whistling of the wind.

"That knight once made a joke that fell flat," replied Woland, turning his quietly smoldering eye toward Margarita. "While conversing about darkness and light he made up a pun that was not entirely satisfactory. And after that, he was forced to work a bit longer and harder at making his jokes than he imagined. But tonight is the kind of night when accounts are settled. The knight has paid his bill and closed his account!"

Night had also torn off Behemoth's fluffy tail, stripped him of his fur and scattered clumps of it over the swamps. The one who had been the cat who amused the Prince of Darkness turned out to be a lean youth, a demon-page, the best jester the world has ever known. Now he, too, had fallen silent and was flying noiselessly, his young face raised to the light flowing from the moon.

Over to the side of the rest, the steel of his armor gleaming, flew Azazello. The moon had transformed his face as well. The absurd ugly fang was gone, and the blind eye turned out to have been fake. Both Azazello's eyes were alike, empty and black, and his face was cold and white. Azazello was now flying in his true aspect, as the demon of the waterless desert, the demon-killer.

Margarita could not see herself, but she could certainly see how the Master had changed. His hair looked white in the moonlight and was gathered behind him in a queue that flew in the wind. Whenever the wind blew the Master's cloak away from his legs, Margarita could see the stars flickering on the spurs of his jackboots. Like the demon-youth, the Master flew with his eyes fixed on the moon, but he was smiling at it as if it were someone he knew and loved, and he was mumbling to himself, a habit acquired in Room 118.

And finally, Woland, too, was flying in his true aspect. Margarita could not have said what his horse's reins were made of and thought they might have been moonbeam chains, and his horse—just a clump of darkness, and the horse's mane—a cloud, and the rider's spurs—the white specks of stars.

They flew in silence like that for a long time until the landscape below began to change. The mournful forests drowned in the darkness of the earth, taking with them the dull blades of the rivers. Down below boulders appeared, and began giving off reflections, and in between the boulders were gaps of blackness where the moonlight could not penetrate.

Woland set his horse down on a stony, joyless, flat summit, and then the riders went forward at a walk, listening to the clop of their horses' hooves on the stones and pieces of flint. The moon flooded the area with a bright green light, and in the deserted expanse Margarita could make out an armchair and in it the white figure of a seated man. The seated figure appeared to be either deaf or too sunk in thought. He did not hear the ground trembling under the weight of the horses, nor was he disturbed by the approaching riders.

The moon was a great help to Margarita, it gave better light than the most powerful electric street lamp, and Margarita saw that the seated figure, whose eyes seemed blind, was spasmodically rubbing his hands and gazing with unseeing eyes at the disk of the moon. Now Margarita could see that next to the heavy stone chair, which seemed to sparkle in the moonlight, there lay a huge dark dog with pointed ears who, like his master, was gazing anxiously at the moon. At the feet of the seated figure were shards of a broken jug and a blackish-red puddle that would never dry up.

The riders stopped their horses.

"They have read your novel," began Woland, turning to the Master, "and they said only one thing, that, unfortunately, it is not finished. So I wanted to show you your hero. He has been sitting here for about two thousand years, sleeping, but, when the moon is full, he is tormented, as you see, by insomnia. And it torments not only him, but his faithful guardian, the dog. If it is true that cowardice is the most grave vice, then the dog, at least, is not guilty of it. The only thing that brave creature ever feared was thunderstorms. But what can be done, the one who loves must share the fate of the one he loves."

"What is he saying?" asked Margarita, and her utterly tranquil face was covered by a veil of compassion.

"He says," Woland's voice rang out, "the same thing over and over. That the moon gives him no peace and that he has a bad job. That is what he always says when he cannot sleep, and when he does sleep, he always sees the same thing—a path of moonlight, and he wants to walk on that path, and talk with the prisoner Ha-Notsri, because, as he keeps maintaining, he did not finish what he wanted to say long ago, on the fourteenth day of the spring month of Nisan. But, alas, for some reason, he never does manage to walk on the path, and no one comes to see him. So there is nothing for him to do except talk to himself. Some variety is necessary, however, so when he talks about the moon, he frequently adds that he hates his immortality and unprecedented fame more than anything in the world. He maintains that he would gladly change places with the ragged wanderer, Levi Matvei."

"Twelve thousand moons for that one moon long ago, isn't that too much?" asked Margarita.

"Is this that story with Frieda all over again?" said Woland. "But in this case, Margarita, you need not upset yourself. Everything will be made right, that is what the world is built on."

"Let him go," suddenly shouted Margarita piercingly, just as she had shouted when she was a witch, and her cry dislodged a boulder on the mountainside and sent it hurtling down the slopes into the abyss with a thunderous crash. But Margarita could not tell whether it was the crash of the boulder she heard or the thunder of satanic laughter. In any event, Woland was laughing as he looked at Margarita and said, "One must not shout when in the mountains. Anyway, he's used to avalanches, and it won't disturb him. You need not plead for him, Margarita, because the one he wants to talk with already has." Woland again turned to the Master and said, "Well, then, now you can finish your novel with a single sentence!"

The Master seemed to have been waiting for this as he stood motionless, looking at the seated procurator. He cupped his hands over his mouth like a megaphone and shouted so that the echo rebounded over the desolate and treeless mountains. "Free! Free! He is waiting for you!"

The mountains transformed the Master's voice into thunder, and the thunder destroyed them. The accursed rocky walls caved in. The only thing that remained was the summit with the stone chair. Above the black abyss, where the walls had vanished, blazed a vast city dominated by glittering idols that towered over a garden gone luxuriantly to seed during these thousands of moons. The path of moonlight long awaited by the procurator led right up to the garden, and the dog with the pointed ears was the first to rush out on it. The man in the white cloak with the blood-red lining got up from his chair and shouted something in a hoarse, broken voice. It was impossible to make out whether he was laughing or crying, or what he was shouting, but he could be seen running down the path of moonlight, after his faithful guardian.

"Is that where I'm to go?" asked the Master anxiously, touching his reins.

"No," replied Woland. "Why pursue that which is already finished?"

"Does that mean back there then?" asked the Master, who turned and pointed back to where the city they had just left displayed itself with its gingerbread monastery towers and its sun broken to smithereens in the glass.

"Not there either," replied Woland, and his voice thickened and began to flow over the cliffs. "Romantic Master! The one whom the hero you created and just released so yearned to see has read your novel." Here Woland turned to Margarita and said, "Margarita Nikolayevna! It is impossible not to believe that you tried to devise the best possible future for the Master, but I assure you that what I am offering you, and what Yeshua has requested for you, is better still. Let the two of them be alone," said Woland, leaning across his saddle over to the Master's saddle and pointing toward the departed procurator. "Let's not disturb them. Maybe they will come to some agreement." Woland then waved his hand toward Yershalaim, and it was extinguished.

"And there too," said Woland, pointing backward. "What would you do in your little basement?" The fragmented sun dimmed in the glass. "Why go back?" continued Woland in a firm and gentle voice. "O

Master, thrice a romantic, wouldn't you like to stroll with your beloved under the blossoming cherry trees by day and then listen to Schubert by night? Wouldn't it be nice for you to write by candlelight with a quill pen? Wouldn't you like to sit over a retort, like Faust, in the hope of creating a new homunculus? Go there! Go there! There where a house and an old servant already await you, where the candles are already burning, but will soon go out because you are about to meet the dawn. Take that road, Master, that one! Farewell! It is time for me to go."

"Farewell!" shouted Margarita and the Master in reply to Woland. Then the black Woland, forswearing all roads, plunged into the gap, and his retinue noisily rushed down after him. Nothing remained around them, not the cliffs, nor the summit, nor the path of moonlight, nor Yershalaim. The black horses vanished as well. The Master and Margarita saw the promised dawn. It began immediately, right after the midnight moon. In the radiance of the first rays of morning, the Master and his beloved were walking over a small, moss-covered stone bridge. They crossed the bridge. The stream was left behind by the true lovers, and they walked along a sandy path.

"Listen to the silence," Margarita was saying to the Master, the sand crunching under her bare feet. "Listen and take pleasure in what you were not given in life—quiet. Look, there up ahead is your eternal home, which you've been given as a reward. I can see the Venetian window and the grape-vine curling up to the roof. There is your home, your eternal home. I know that in the evenings people you like will come to see you, people who interest you and who will not upset you. They will play for you, sing for you, and you will see how the room looks in candlelight. You will fall asleep with your grimy eternal cap on your head, you will fall asleep with a smile on your lips. Sleep will strengthen you, you will begin to reason wisely. And you will never be able to chase me away. I will guard your sleep."

Thus spoke Margarita as she walked with the Master toward their eternal home, and it seemed to the Master that Margarita's words flowed like the stream they had left behind, flowed and whispered, and the Master's anxious, needle-pricked memory began to fade. Someone was releasing the Master into freedom, as he himself had released the hero he created. That hero, who was absolved on Sunday morning, had departed into the abyss, never to return, the son of an astrologer-king, the cruel fifth procurator of Judea, the knight Pontius Pilate.

Epilogue

B UT still, what happened next in Moscow after that Saturday evening at sunset when Woland and his retinue left the capital and disappeared from Sparrow Hills?

It's pointless to speak of the preposterous rumors that buzzed loudly and long throughout the city and spread quickly to the most distant and remote parts of the provinces. It's even sickening to repeat them.

The writer of these truthful lines has himself heard, while on a train to Feodosiya, a story about how in Moscow two thousand people walked out of a theater naked in the literal sense of the word and then went home in taxis in the same state.

Whispers of an "evil power" were heard in lines at dairy shops, in streetcars, stores, apartments, kitchens, suburban and long-distance trains, at stations large and small, in dachas, and on beaches.

Needless to say, truly mature and cultured people did not tell these stories about an evil power's visit to the capital. In fact, they even made fun of them and tried to talk sense into those who told them. Nevertheless, facts are facts, as they say, and cannot simply be dismissed without explanation: somebody had visited the capital. The charred cinders of Griboyedov alone, and many other things besides, confirmed that.

Cultured people shared the point of view of the investigating team: it was the work of a gang of hypnotists and ventriloquists magnificently skilled in their art.

Both inside Moscow and beyond, prompt and energetic steps were, of course, taken to insure their capture, but, most regrettably, produced no results. The man who called himself Woland vanished along with his henchmen and never again returned to Moscow nor did he ever show himself or make an appearance anywhere else. Quite naturally there was speculation that he had escaped abroad, but he never showed up there either.

The investigation of his case went on for a long time. Say what you will, it was certainly a hellish one! Apart from the four buildings burned to ashes and the hundreds of people driven insane, there were also fatalities. Two were known for sure: Berlioz and that unfortunate civil servant in the Moscow Bureau of Sightseeing for Foreigners, the former Baron Maigel. Those two had certainly been killed. The charred bones of the latter had been discovered in apartment No. 50 on Sadovaya Street after the fire had been put out. Yes, there had been victims, and that called for an investigation.

But there were other victims as well, even after Woland had left the capital, and, sad to say, they were black cats.

A hundred or so of these peaceful animals, useful and devoted to man, were shot or otherwise destroyed in various parts of the country. More than a dozen of them, some in extremely mangled condition, were delivered to police stations in various cities. For example, a citizen in Armavir brought in one such innocent creature with its front paws tied up.

The man had caught the cat just as the animal was looking furtive (So what can be done if that's the way cats look? It's not because they're guilty, but because they fear that creatures stronger than they—dogs or people—will harm them in some way. And that's not hard to do, but it's nothing to be proud of, I assure you. No, not at all!) and, yes, wearing such a furtive look, the cat was about to bound into a burdock patch for some reason.

As the citizen pounced on the cat and tore off his tie in order to tie him up, he venomously and menacingly muttered, "Gottcha! So, mister hypnotist, you've decided to pay us a little visit in Armavir, have you? Well, we're not afraid of you here. And don't pretend to be mute. We already know what a fine fellow you are!"

The citizen took the cat to the police station, dragging the poor creature by its front paws, which had been tied together with a green necktie, and giving it little kicks so it would walk on its hind legs.

"Cut it out," shouted the citizen, as boys followed him hooting, "stop playing the fool! It won't work! Walk like everyone else!"

The black cat merely rolled its martyred eyes. Deprived by nature of the gift of speech, it had no way to defend itself. For its salvation the poor beast was indebted, first of all, to the police, and secondly to its mistress, a respected elderly widow. Once the cat was at the station, the policeman could see that the citizen who had brought it in reeked of alcohol, which immediately cast doubt on his testimony. Meanwhile, the widow, after learning from her neighbors that her cat had been hauled off, ran to the police station and managed to get there in time. She gave the cat the most flattering recommendation, explained that she had known it for five years, ever since it was a kitten, vouched for it as much as for herself, and proved that it had never been implicated in any misconduct and had never been to Moscow. It had been born and raised in Armavir, and had learned to catch mice there.

The cat was untied and returned to its owner, after, it's true, having gotten a taste of trouble first hand—a practical lesson in the meaning of mistaken identity and slander.

Besides the cats, there were a few people who suffered some minor unpleasantness. Several arrests were made. Among those held briefly in custody were: citizens Volman and Volper in Leningrad; three Volodins in Saratov, Kiev, and Kharkov; a Volokh in Kazan; and in Penza, no one knows why, a doctoral candidate in chemistry named Vetchinkevich. True, he was enormously tall, dark-haired, and swarthy.

In addition to the above, nine Korovins, four Korovkins, and a pair of Karavayevs were caught in various locales.

At the station in Belgorod a certain citizen was taken off the Sevastopol train in handcuffs. This citizen had taken it into his head to entertain his fellow passengers with card tricks.

In Yaroslavl a man appeared in a restaurant just at dinner time carrying a primus stove which he had just retrieved from a repair shop. When the two doormen on duty spotted him in the cloakroom, they took off and ran out of the restaurant, with all the patrons and staff following at their heels. During this, all the cashier's receipts mysteriously disappeared.

A lot of other things happened, but one can't remember everything. There was great intellectual ferment.

Again and again one must give the investigators their due. Everything was done not only to catch the criminals, but to explain all their actions as well. And they were all explained, and one can't but concede that the explanations were both reasonable and irrefutable.

Investigation spokesmen and experienced psychiatrists established that the criminal gang members, or perhaps one in particular (suspicion fell chiefly on Korovyov) were hypnotists with unprecedented powers, capable of appearing not where they actually were, but in illusory, displaced locations. In addition, they could easily convince whoever came in contact with them that certain objects or people were present in places where really they were not, and conversely, they could remove from sight those objects or people that actually were in sight.

In the light of such explanations, everything became absolutely clear, even that which had disturbed the citizens the most, namely, the seemingly inexplicable invulnerability of the cat who had been riddled with bullets in apartment No. 50 during the attempt to take him into custody.

There had, of course, been no cat on the chandelier, and no one had even thought of returning his fire. They had been shooting into the air, while Korovyov, who had duped them into thinking that a cat was raising hell on the chandelier, could easily have been positioned behind those who were shooting, showing off and revelling in his own tremendous, if criminally misapplied, powers of suggestion. And it was he, of course, who had poured the kerosene around the apartment and set fire to it.

Styopa Likhodeyev had naturally not flown to any Yalta (even Korovyov couldn't have pulled off a stunt like that), nor had he sent any telegrams from there. After being tricked by Korovyov into seeing a cat with a pickled mushroom on his fork and fainting with fright as a result, Styopa had lain unconscious in the jeweller's widow's apartment until Korovyov, making a fool of him once again, had yanked a felt hat over his head and sent him off to the Moscow airport, having previously convinced CID members that Styopa would get off the airplane arriving from Sevastopol.

True, the Yalta CID maintained that they had taken the barefoot Styopa into custody and had sent telegrams about him to Moscow, but not one copy of those telegrams was ever found in the files, which led to the sad, but utterly unshakable conclusion that the band of hypnotists was able to practice long-distance hypnosis and not just on individuals, but on whole groups of people at one time. This being the case, the criminals were able to drive the most mentally stable people out of their minds.

Why bother mentioning, therefore, such things as the deck of cards that turned up in the pocket of some stranger in the audience, the ladies' clothing that vanished, or the meowing beret and other such things! Any professional hypnotist of average ability can perform tricks like that on any stage, and that includes the simple trick of tearing off the emcee's head. The talking cat was also downright nonsense. All you need to get such a cat to perform is an elementary knowledge of ventriloquism, and no one could seriously doubt that Korovyov's skills went far beyond the basics.

No, the decks of cards or the forged letters in Nikanor Ivanovich's briefcase were not the issue. Those were mere trifles! And it was he, Korovyov, who had pushed Berlioz to certain death under the streetcar. It was he who had driven the poor poet, Ivan Bezdomny, out of his mind, he who had made him imagine things and have tormenting dreams about ancient Yershalaim and about sun-scorched arid Bald Mountain with its three men hanged on posts. It was he and his gang who had made Margarita Nikolayevna and her maid, the beautiful Natasha, disappear from Moscow. Incidentally, the investigators had given this matter special attention. They had to determine whether the women had been abducted by the gang of murderers and arsonists or whether they had run off with the criminal band of their own free will. Based on the absurd and muddled testimony of Nikolai Ivanovich and taking into account the bizarre and insane note Margarita Nikolayevna had left her husband, in which she said she had gone off to be a witch, and considering the fact that Natasha had disappeared without taking any of her things, the investigators concluded that mistress and maid had both been hypnotized, along with so many others, and abducted by the gang while in that state. The quite likely possibility also arose that the criminals had been attracted by the women's beauty.

However, the motive behind the gang's abduction of a mental patient calling himself the Master from a psychiatric clinic still remained a mystery for the investigators. They could not find an explanation for that, nor could they learn the name of the abducted patient. Thus he vanished into the files under the lifeless tag, "No. 118 from Block One."

And so, almost everything was explained, and the investigation came to an end, just as, in general, all things do.

Several years passed, and the citizens began to forget about Woland, Korovyov, and the others. Many changes took place in the lives of the victims of Woland and his associates, and however petty and insignificant those changes may have been, they still deserve mention.

George Bengalsky, for example, recovered and went home after a three-month stay in the hospital, but he was forced to give up his job at the Variety Theater, and at the most hectic time when the public rushed the theater for tickets—memories of black magic and its exposés were still too fresh in his mind. Bengalsky gave up the Variety because he realized that to appear every evening before two thousand people, to be inevitably recognized and endlessly subjected to snide questions about whether he preferred having his head on or off—was too painful for him.

Yes, and besides that, the emcee had lost a sizable portion of the cheerfulness necessary for his line of work. He was left with the unpleasant and burdensome habit of falling into a state of anxiety every spring during the full moon, when he would suddenly grab at his neck, look around fearfully, and weep. Although these attacks passed quickly, they made it impossible for him to work at his former job, so he went into retirement and began living on his savings, which, according to his modest calculations, would last him for fifteen years.

He left and never again saw Varenukha, who had won universal popularity and affection for his incredibly polite and considerate attitude toward others, rare even among theater managers. Recipients of complimentary passes, for example, regarded him as a father-benefactor. Whoever called the Variety Theater at whatever time of day or night was always greeted by a soft but sad voice that said, "How can I help you?"—and when Varenukha was called to the phone that same voice would readily reply, "I'm at your service." But Ivan Savelyevich's courteousness has brought him suffering!

Styopa Likhodeyev no longer has to talk on the phone at the Variety. After being discharged from the clinic where he spent eight days, Styopa was transferred to Rostov, where he was appointed manager of a large specialty foods store. Rumor has it that he has sworn off port completely and drinks only vodka steeped in black currants, which has greatly improved his health. They say that he has become taciturn and avoids women.

Stepan Bogdanovich's removal from the Variety did not give Rimsky the joy he so fervently dreamed of for so long. After a spell in a clinic and a rest cure at Kislovodsk, the aged and decrepit financial director with the shaking head put in for retirement from the Variety. Interestingly, it was his wife who turned in his retirement application to the theater. Even in daylight, Grigory Danilovich did not have the strength to be in the same building where he had seen the cracked windowpane flooded with moonlight and the long arm feeling its way along the lower latch.

After retiring from the Variety, the financial director joined the children's puppet theater in Zamoskvorechye. There he was no longer forced to deal with the esteemed Arkady Apollonovich Sempleyarov in regard to acoustical matters. The latter had been speedily transferred to Bryansk and made the head of a mushroom-processing plant. Now Muscovites eat his salted saffron milkcaps and marinated white mushrooms, praise them to the skies, and could not be more delighted about his transfer. What's past is past, and it can now be said that Arkady Apollonovich's performance in acoustics was never really a success, and no matter how hard he tried to make improvements in acoustics, they still remained the same.

Besides Arkady Apollonovich, Nikanor Ivanovich Bosoi should be included among those who severed their ties with the theater, although the only connection between Nikanor Ivanovich and the theater was his fondness for free passes. Not only does Nikanor Ivanovich not attend the theater either with a paid ticket or a free pass, his face actually changes whenever the theater is even mentioned. Besides the theater, his hatred for the poet Pushkin and for the gifted actor Savva Potapovich Kurolesov has increased rather than diminished. He hates the latter so much that last year when he saw a black-bordered announcement in the paper to the effect that Savva Potapovich had died of a stroke at the height of his career, Nikanor Ivanovich got so red in the face that he almost followed in Savva Potapovich's footsteps, and then he let out a roar, "Serves him right!" That same evening, moreover, Nikanor Ivanovich, for whom the popular actor's death brought such a flood of painful memories, went all by himself, with only the full moon over Sadovaya Street for company, and got roaring drunk. With each glass he drank, the accursed list of people he detested grew longer and longer, and on it were Sergei Gerardovich Dunchil, the beautiful Ida Gerkulanovna, the red-haired owner of the fighting geese, and the outspoken Nikolai Kanavkin.

Well, so what happened to all of them? Mercy me! Absolutely nothing happened to them, nor could it have since they never existed in reality, just as the likable emcee never existed, nor the theater itself, nor the old skinflint aunt, Porokhovnikova, who let foreign currency rot in her cellar, nor, of course, did the gold trumpets and the insolent cooks. Nikanor Ivanovich had just dreamed it all under the influence of that rogue Korovyov. The only living person in the dream had been Savva Potapovich, the actor, and he had gotten into the dream just because he had been on the radio so much that he stuck in Nikanor Ivanovich's memory. He did exist, but the others did not.

So, maybe Aloisy Mogarych did not exist either? Oh, no! Not only did he exist, he does still, and in the very job that Rimsky left, that of financial director of the Variety Theater.

About twenty-four hours after his visit to Woland, Aloisy came to his senses in a train somewhere near Vyatka and decided that he had left Moscow in a daze for some reason and thus had forgotten to put on his trousers, but what he couldn't understand was why he had stolen the private-home-builder's tenants book, which was of absolutely no use to him. He paid the conductor a colossal sum of money for a greasy old pair of trousers, and turned back at Vyatka. But, alas, he could not find the private-home-builder's house. The dilapidated old wreck had been burned to the ground. Aloisy, however, was an extremely enterprising man. Two weeks later he was settled in a splendid room on Bryusov Lane and a few months after that, he was sitting in Rimsky's office. And just as Rimsky was once tormented by Styopa, so Varenukha is now harassed by Aloisy. Ivan Savelyevich has only one dream, namely, that Aloisy be removed to someplace far from the Variety and out of sight, because, as Varenukha sometimes whispers to close friends, he has "never in his life met such a bastard as that Aloisy, who is capable of absolutely anything."

But the manager may be prejudiced. Aloisy doesn't seem to be involved in any shady business, or in any business at all for that matter, not counting, of course, his appointing a new bartender to replace Sokov. Andrei Fokich died of cancer of the liver in the First Clinic of Moscow University Hospital about nine months after Woland's appearance in Moscow...

Yes, several years have passed, and the events truthfully described in this book dragged on for awhile and were then forgotten. But not by everyone, not by everyone!

Every year, as the spring holiday moon turns full, a man appears toward evening beneath the lindens at Patriarch's Ponds. He is a man of about thirty or so, reddish-haired, green-eyed, modestly dressed. He is a fellow of the Institute of History and Philosophy, Professor Ivan Nikolayevich Ponyryov.

When he gets to the lindens, he always sits down on the same bench he was sitting on that evening when Berlioz, long forgotten by everyone, saw the moon, shattering into pieces, for the last time in his life.

The now whole moon, white at the beginning of the evening, and then golden, with a dark dragon-horse imprinted on its face, floats above the former poet, Ivan Nikolayevich, while at the same time staying in one place overhead.

Everything is clear to Ivan Nikolayevich, he knows and understands everything. He knows that in his youth he was the victim of hypnotist-criminals and that he had to go in for treatment and was cured. But he also knows that there are things he cannot cope with. For example, he cannot cope with the spring full moon. As soon as it draws near, as soon as the heavenly body begins to expand and to fill with gold just as it did long ago when it towered over the two five-branched candelabra, Ivan Nikolayevich becomes restless, anxious, loses his appetite, has trouble sleeping, and waits for the moon to ripen. And when the full moon comes, nothing can keep Ivan Nikolayevich at home. Towards evening he goes out and walks to Patriarch's Ponds.

Sitting on his bench, Ivan Nikolayevich openly talks to himself, smokes, and squints alternately at the moon and at the turnstile he remembers so well.

Ivan Nikolayevich spends an hour or two like that. Then he gets up, and walking with vacant, unseeing eyes, always taking the same route via Spiridonovka, heads for the side streets around the Arbat.

He walks past the oil shop, turns at the corner with the rickety old gas lamp, and creeps over to the fence beyond which he sees a luxuriant garden not yet in bloom and a gothic-style house, colored by the moonlight on one side, where the bay window with the triple casements juts out, and dark on the other.

The professor does not know what draws him to the fence or who lives in the house, but he does know that he cannot resist his impulses during the full moon. He also knows that in the garden beyond the fence he will invariably see the same thing.

He sees a respectable-looking, middle-aged man with a beard and a pince-nez and slightly piggish features sitting on a bench. He is a resident of the gothic house and Ivan Nikolayevich always finds him in the same dreamy pose, his gaze directed at the moon. Ivan Nikolayevich knows that after admiring the moon, the man on the bench will turn his gaze to the bay window and stare at it as if he expects it to burst open any minute and have something unusual appear on the windowsill.

Ivan Nikolayevich knows what will happen next by heart. Here he has to crouch down lower behind the fence, because the man on the bench will start whirling his head, trying to catch something in the air with his wandering eyes, will smile ecstatically, and then in a kind of sweet anguish, will suddenly clasp his hands and murmur plainly and rather loudly, "Venus! Venus!... Oh, what a fool I was!..."

"Gods, gods!" Ivan Nikolayevich will start whispering from his hiding place behind the fence, his inflamed eyes still fastened on the mysterious stranger, "there's another victim of the moon... Yes, another one like me."

And the man on the bench will continue murmuring, "Oh, what a fool I was! Why, why didn't I fly away with her? What was I afraid of, old ass that I am! I got a certificate! So you can suffer now, you old idiot!"

And so it will continue until a window bangs open in the dark part of the house, something whitish appears, and an unpleasant female voice calls out, "Nikolai Ivanovich, where are you? What kind of craziness is this? Do you want to catch malaria? Come have your tea!"

The man on the bench will, of course, then come to his senses and reply in a false tone, "Air, my darling, I just wanted a breath of air! The air is very pleasant out here!"

Then he gets up from the bench, shakes his fist furtively at the downstairs window as it closes, and drags himself into the house.

"He's lying, he's lying! Oh gods, how he's lying!" mumbles Ivan Nikolayevich as he moves away from the fence. "It's not the air that lures him into the garden at all, it's something he sees on the moon and in the garden, when the spring moon is full, high up above. Oh, what I'd give to learn his secret, to find out who the Venus is that he lost and now tries to catch by waving his arms pointlessly in the air!"

And the professor returns home utterly ill. His wife pretends not to notice his condition and hurries him off to bed. But she herself stays up and sits by the lamp with a book, gazing at him with bitter eyes as he sleeps. She knows that at dawn Ivan Nikolayevich will wake up with a tortured scream, and that he will start crying and toss about. That is why she keeps a hypodermic syringe soaking in alcohol on the cloth beneath the lamp in front of her, and an ampule filled with something the color of strong tea.

Tied to a gravely ill man, the poor woman will then be free and can go to sleep without any misgivings. After his injection, Ivan Nikolayevich will sleep until morning, and he will look happy as he dreams rapturous and happy dreams she knows nothing about.

It is always the same thing that causes the scholar to wake up on the night of the full moon and to let out a pitiful scream. He sees an unnatural, noseless executioner leap up with a hoot and put a spear into the heart of Gestas, who is tied to a post and has lost his reason. But the most terrifying thing in the dream is not so much the executioner as the unnatural light coming from the stormcloud that is seething and pressing down on the earth, such as only happens during world catastrophes.

After the injection everything the sleeper sees changes. A broad path of moonlight stretches from his bed to the window and heading up this path is a man in a white cloak with a blood-red lining who is walking toward the moon. Walking beside him is a young man in a torn chiton with a disfigured face. The two of them are engaged in heated conversation, arguing about something, and trying to reach some kind of agreement.

"Gods, gods!" says the man in the cloak as he turns his haughty face to his companion, "What a vulgar and banal execution! But please," here his face turns from being haughty to imploring, "tell me it didn't really happen! I beg you, tell me, it didn't happen, did it?"

"Of course it didn't happen," answers his companion in a hoarse voice, "you only imagined it."

"And you can swear to that?" asks the man in the cloak in an ingratiating way.

"I can!" replies his companion, his eyes smiling for some reason.

"I don't need anything else!" cries out the man in the cloak in a broken voice, as he ascends higher and higher toward the moon, taking his companion with him. Walking behind them, calm and majestic, is a huge dog with pointed ears.

Then the path of moonlight starts frothing, and a river of moonlight gushes forth and spreads out in all directions. The moon rules and plays, the moon dances and romps. Then a woman of matchless beauty emerges from the stream and walks toward Ivan, leading a man by the hand who has an overgrown beard and is looking about fearfully. Ivan Nikolayevich recognizes him immediately. He is No. 118, his night visitor. In his sleep Ivan stretches his arms out to him and asks avidly, "So that was how it ended?"

"Yes, it was, my disciple," replies No. 118, and the woman comes over to Ivan and says, "Of course. Everything ended and everything ends... And I'm going to kiss you on the forehead, and everything will work out as it should."

She leans over Ivan and kisses him on the forehead, and Ivan stretches toward her and stares into her eyes, but she draws back, draws back and walks off with her companion toward the moon...

Then the moon goes on a rampage, it hurls streams of light directly at Ivan, sprays light in all directions, a moonlight flood begins to inundate the room, the light sways, rises higher, and drowns the bed. Only then does Ivan Nikolayevich sleep with a look of happiness on his face.

The next morning he wakes up silent, but completely calm and well. His ravaged memory quiets down, and no one will trouble the professor until the next full moon: neither the noseless murderer of Gestas, nor the cruel fifth procurator of Judea, the knight Pontius Pilate.

1929-1940

A NOTE ON THE TEXT

There are two main texts of this novel, the one prepared by Anna Saakyants for the 1973 *Romany* Moscow edition, and the one prepared by Lidiya Yanovskaya, first published in 1989 by Dnipro Publishers in Kiev (*Izbrannye proizvedeniia v dvukh tomakh*), then used for the 1990 Moscow edition (*Sobranie sochinenii, t. 5*). I have drawn on both of these versions to differing degrees: the Yanovskaya version has been used as the basic text in terms of paragraphing, punctuation, etc., but at crucial points the Saakyants version has been consulted as well. Since Bulgakov rewrote until he became too ill to do so, many variants exist of a given section (the first paragraph is a good case in point); I have generally chosen what appears to be the final version, i.e., Yanovskaya's. However, where a fragment from an earlier redaction helps the reader understand the novel better (such as the section in Chapter 13 about Aloisy Mogarych), and appears to have been cut due to self-censorship, I have included it, but with a note of explanation.

Bulgakov finished work on the main typescript of the complete novel in 1939, but he had not finished his final proof when he died in March of 1940. He probably would have coordinated some late changes with earlier occurrences in the text had he lived (some of them will be remarked upon), but what his final decision would have been on certain previously crossed-out sections is not predictable. However, his earlier work shows clearly that sometimes he returned to an earlier draft version of a scene, and that he remembered the differences quite well. He appears to have completed the final changes on the first part of the novel, but not the second part. We will never know, of course, what would have been his version of the final redaction, but we do know what areas he concentrated on when he knew he had little time left, namely the first and last chapters of Part II. When examining what Bulgakov chose to leave out, it is important to remember that he was constantly anticipating future censorship.

Where line readings differ in meaningful ways between these two texts, I have chosen the one most consistent with Bulgakov's general usage. All such major differences will be mentioned in the notes below. While responsibility for the translation lies with the translators of this volume, the choice of texts is entirely mine.

E. P.

COMMENTARY

These notes are not intended to be exhaustive; names which are easily looked up in any encyclopedia are not glossed. The emphasis is rather on difficult references, especially Russian ones, and on information which will send the reader in the direction of possible subtexts in this novel. While some of my work here is original, I owe a great debt to all previous commentators to the Russian editions of this novel, and to all Bulgakov scholars as well. I also wish to thank Mary Ann Szporluk and Joseph Placek for their editorial and scholarly help on both the translation and the commentary.

CHAPTER 1

Epigraph—While Bulgakov incorporates many Faustian elements (many from Gounod's opera, *Faust*, rather than from Goethe's poem), his use of this material is far from straightforward.

In addition to the direct reference to Goethe's work about a devil-tempter who comes to a scholar, the epigraph introduces the theme of heresy, one which will be reinforced throughout this novel by means of allusions to historical figures accused of heresy. Goethe believed in the theory of polarities which is essentially a version of Manichean thought. In the Manichean view, there are two cardinal principles in the world, the light and the dark, the good and the evil. In this scheme of things, as stated by Mephistopheles in Goethe's *Faust*, God dwells in eternal light, the devils are consigned to darkness, and human beings have only day and night. This sort of dualistic thinking was unacceptable to the Christian faith, which requires that good be stronger than evil, not equal to it; therefore this kind of worldview was considered heretical.

Never Talk to Strangers—this is not only a piece of maternal wisdom, it is a specific marker for the xenophobia of the Soviet era. During this time talking to strangers, foreign strangers especially, could get you arrested on the grounds that they and you were spies for a foreign power.

First paragraph—Bulgakov rewrote the opening of the novel many times. The variant of the opening paragraph used in previous editions (based on the draft typed by Elena Sergeevna Bulgakov) is found nowhere in the notebook containing Bulgakov's different versions. This translation uses what Yanovskaya deems to be his final version, which differs in minor ways from previously published texts.

Patriarch's Ponds—a real location in the heart of old Moscow. While this was a place where Bulgakov spent a lot of time when he first came to Moscow, the location has double significance for the novel—it is named in honor of the Patriarch of the Russian Orthodox Church. Most of the places Bulgakov describes in this novel can still be found in today's Moscow (although many street names have changed), which has led to an entire Bulgakov tour industry. However, sometimes the author moves streets when it suits him, and relocates buildings, thus befuddling many critics who want the topography to be entirely accurate. Bulgakov consciously mixes realia of Moscow life typical of both the 1920s and 1930s.

Mikhail Alexandrovich—Russian names are formally given as first, patronymic, and last. When respect is being accorded, the full first name and patronymic are used. Berlioz's initials match Bulgakov's own.

MASSOLIT—a very funny acronym in Russian, which might be best conveyed in English as LOTSALIT. Bulgakov found the Soviet passion for acronyms very funny, and made up various absurd ones throughout his career, although the real ones were bizarre enough.

Bezdomny—this name literally means "Homeless," and brings to mind an entire series of famous pseudonyms, starting with Maksim Gorky ("the Bitter") and ending with Demyan Bedny ("the Poor"). Bedny is apposite in that he was known for especially egregious antireligious works, such as the 1925 *The New Testament without Defects of the Evangelist Demyan*. Although some have sought historical prototypes for every character in the novel, few of those suggested for the main characters are convincing. Bulgakov's main characters tend to be a blend of many sources, and sometimes are deliberate abstractions (the Master himself is a good example of this). Minor characters, however, do tend to have recognizable sources in a single figure.

What the devil—seemingly unmarked expressions of surprise involving the devil proliferate in the novel. Less obvious to the English-speaking reader are all the sounds that relate to the word for minor devil, *chyort*, especially the root of the Russian word for black, *chyornyi*. On the first page, for example, Berlioz has black frames on his glasses, and Bezdomny has black sneakers.

a long antireligious poem—part of the humor of this particular narrative line is that in the 1920s and 1930s in Russia, in the name of Communism, there was a well-developed propaganda campaign to discredit all religious belief. In most ways this campaign was successful. In the intellectual Marxist world, faith seemed old-fashioned, retrograde, something allowed only the uneducated country folk. It is typical that the editor has ordered a poem on this subject just in time for what would be Easter—this was one way propaganda dealt with the persistence of religious holidays.

Berlioz's remarks on the subject of Jesus are quite close to the real views espoused by many journalists of the time who published in such real journals as *The Atheist* and *The Godless One*. Although a number of real figures have been proposed as the single prototype for Berlioz (named for Hector Berlioz, composer of a number of works which have resonance here, including the *Symphonie fantastique* and *The Damnation of Faust*), he seems to be an amalgam of a number of well-known Soviet hacks, including the famed journalist Mikhail Koltsov. The careful reader will notice that Berlioz can be seen as a Christ parody, having, among other things, twelve disciples who sit around the MASSOLIT table waiting for him, etc. When Berlioz (who shows off his erudition by citing a number of gods of ancient cultures, ranging from the Egyptian Osiris to the Aztec Uitzilopochtli) discusses god myths he is on solid ground, in terms of what the mythological school, as it was called, thought about the story of Jesus. When he turns to historical references, however, he is often in error, which Bulgakov leaves the reader to find out—the reference to Jesus in Tacitus, for example, was not considered fraudulent by all scholars of the times. The conflict between the historical school (Jesus really existed) and the mythological school (just another virgin birth, another creation legend, etc.) which was raging in biblical studies' circles from the eighteenth century onward, is here submerged in a greater theme: what happens when an entire culture is forced to deny belief in God—but meets up with the devil in the flesh.

Kant's proof—the philosopher Immanuel Kant postulated three proofs of the existence of God, rejected them and came up with the one least likely to convince either the devil or a Muscovite of the 1930s: that God is to be postulated for the moral will. Bulgakov is either joking or miscounting here. Woland mentions *five* proofs, which makes Kant's own the sixth—and the proof Woland provides, the seventh. This entire discussion, indeed this entire chapter, is the nucleus of the philosophical and thematic structure of the novel.

Strauss—refers to David Strauss (1808-74), the famed German Bible scholar whose *Life of Jesus* was used by Bulgakov in his work on this novel. Strauss belonged to the historical school, which attempted to separate historical fact from mythic elements in the Gospels.

Solovki—the nickname given to a famous prison in the north of Russia on the Solovetsky Islands in the White Sea. Originally it was famous for its monastery, but in the 1920s a famous and terrifying prison was established there and it became shorthand for the worst possible fate. There is another level to this reference, one which fits in with one of the main subtexts of this novel: as a monastery, it had a bloody history in Old Russia. At the time of the liturgical reforms in the sixteenth century, the monks of this monastery refused to accept the changes which were to bring the Russian Orthodox Church into compliance with Greek Orthodox forms of worship—such people were called Old Believers—and the monks were massacred after a ten-year siege.

Your relatives start lying to you—readers of Russian literature will see in this brief narrative of how one loses control and dies a clear echo of Tolstoy's story "The Death of Ivan Ilyich."

a member of the Komsomol—the Komsomol was the youth organization run by the Communist Party. A female Komsomol member would be pure of heart and motive, something like a political Girl Scout, which is why Berlioz thinks Woland is joking.

"I suppose I'm a German..."—one of many motifs in this chapter which point to the Faust legend. Both Goethe's poem and Gounod's opera are used as sources of Faustian moments and details to provide hints that Woland is a Mephistopheles figure. The poodle-headed cane, the triangle on the cigarette case, the offering of diverse brands, and many other things, are connected to various Faust-related sources. Woland's name is important in this respect as well—Bulgakov makes the point in Russian that the name begins not with a V (as in the German source, Valand, one of the names of the devil, specifically used in Goethe), but with a roman W. And the W upside down is an M.

Gerbert of Aurillac—real name of Pope Sylvester II, who reigned from 999-1003, and was a leading scholar of his time. Early in his career he was accused of being a Manichean dualist on the basis of the contents of his *Epistolae*. Relevant to Bulgakov's interest is the fact that after his death the rumor arose that he was a necromancer, since his learning was so remarkable that it was assumed by the ignorant that the devil must have played a part in it.

CHAPTER 2

Nisan—the first month of the synagogal year (seventh in the civil year) in the Jewish lunar calendar, roughly corresponding to the end of March and part of April.

O gods, gods—this rhetorical refrain, taken from Verdi's opera *Aida*, a favorite source for refrains in a number of Bulgakov's works, occurs at several crucial points of the novel, and is spoken by different characters, a sure sign of hidden connections among them. In the opera Aida calls on the gods to help her in "Numi, pietà," and the gods are implored by other characters in this way as well.

Sinedrion—Bulgakov deliberately uses the unusual Greek form instead of the Russian *sovet* for what is normally known in English as the Sanhedrin, at this time the Jewish equivalent of a Supreme Court. Throughout these chapters the author is defamiliarizing this material for the Russian reader by using unusual, yet understandable forms. If the Greek is customary, he uses the Aramaic or the Latin, etc. Since Jerusalem at the time of Christ was a polyglot city (Hellenized Jews spoke Greek, the locals spoke Aramaic, and the Roman rulers spoke Latin), the mixing of languages is justified, even within one conversation. It is noteworthy that the only main character to be given a Hebrew version of his name is Yeshua Ha-Notsri, called Isus in the Russian Bible. Another unusual name transcription choice is the version Levi Matvei, which is a purely Russian non-biblical form of Matthew the Levite. In many cases periphrasis is used: instead of the Fulminata Regiment—the Lightning Regiment; instead of Gethsemane—the olive grove, etc.

In his research Bulgakov appears to have relied on the Russian translations of several main works of Christology (the lives of Jesus by Strauss and Farrar), various encyclopedias, famous literary works about the subject (such as Anatole France's *Pontius Pilate*), and the main ancient histories (Flavius Josephus, Tacitus). His research was not, however, confined to historical sources—when something in folklore or the apocryphal books of the Bible struck him he used it, as will become clear.

Despite his efforts to be (or, rather, seem) accurate, there are necessarily occasional errors and misunderstandings, such as naming a gate which was not yet built at the time of his story, etc. Given the complexity of the sources, however, Bulgakov did a remarkable job for an amateur who knew virtually none of the languages involved.

Ratkiller—this is Bulgakov's witty Russian translation of the Latin term of abuse for a cowardly soldier *muricidus*—literally, mousekiller.

turma—the Latin term is used in Russian here. Bulgakov is careful to use precise Roman terms for parts of the army throughout the Pilate chapters. A *maniple* was made up of 120 to 200 men. The term *ala*, which will be encountered later, refers to the cavalry in general, numbering either 1,000 or 500 men. These were then divided into 24 or 16 *turmae*. These units usually had names indicating the source country of the recruits, the emperor or general who had raised them, and sometimes were named in honor of their weapons. The infantry was organized into cohorts *(cohors)*, with there being ten cohorts in a legion, which were then divided into centuries. The majority of the troops described carefully in the Pilate chapters are *auxilia*—troops raised outside of Italy and lightly armed. Over time they lost their native character, but at this point they were important in controlling the empire. Their commanders were either prefects or tribunes, and under them were centurions. Bulgakov, who had briefly been in the military (on several sides) during the Civil War, had an especial fondness for the cavalry troops.

Idistaviso—(Idistavisus Campus) literally, this translates as Valley of the Maidens, as Bulgakov periphrastically refers to it, or female spirits (elves) of the lakes and rivers. This is a reference to the location of a famous battle between the Roman leader Germanicus, who triumphed over the German tribes led by Arminius in A.D. 16.

On top of this bald head was a gold crown—the old man at Capreae who appears to Pilate as he hears the second charge is the Emperor Tiberius, who suffered from leprosy according to one of Bulgakov's sources. This little section has a strong connection to a story about death at sea (also mentioned in Bulgakov's first novel), Bunin's "The Gentleman from San Francisco," in which there is also a reference to Capri and Tiberius. Heads are important throughout this novel, which features a prominent beheading. In apocalyptic thought the head was often a symbol for Rome itself.

Judas of Kerioth—Following the French writer Renan *(La Vie de Jésus)*, Bulgakov is at pains to use an explanatory name, instead of the more usual Judas Iscariot.

Lit the candles...—according to Jewish law, a trap for criminals had to be well-lit, to avoid mistaken identity. By this Bulgakov is indicating an entire subtext in Pilate's understanding of who Judas really is, and who has employed him.

Dismas, Gestas—these names are mentioned in the *Apocryphal New Testament of Nicodemus*, which Bulgakov drew on in addition to the historically acceptable sources.

Bar-rabban—Bulgakov uses this instead of the *Varavva* of the Russian Bible; again, Renan is the likely source. This name means simply "son of the father," another messianic reference; both Bar-rabban and Yeshua are thus seen as messianic figures by their followers, and the authorities simply have to decide which is the more dangerous.

Knight—Pilate is a member of the *ordo equester* (equestrian class), the usual category for a man who became a procurator (prefect) in Roman times. This word, *usadnik*, may be translated as horseman, cavalryman, rider or knight. In the sense that it means belonging to an elite group, it is normally translated as knight. The figure of the cavalryman or knight is encountered in many of Bulgakov's works, and clearly had a special autobiographical meaning, as well as a clear connection to the famous four horsemen of the Apocalypse.

Solomon's Pool... insignia...—these are old wounds between the two antagonists. This entire conversation between Pilate and the high priest is saturated with references to previous struggles between the Jews and the Roman government. Philo of Alexandria and Flavius Josephus (two of Bulgakov's main sources) describe these incidents, which involve either insensitivity on the part of Pilate to local religious custom, or deliberate provocation to revolt, which then the procurator might brutally repress. In one case the Jews protested the image of the emperor carried on the insignia of the soldiers entering Jerusalem, since it was against their religious belief. In the end, the insignia were removed. In the other case, concerning Solomon's Pool, Pilate had an aqueduct built extending from the pool to the city, a distance of 37 kilometers. Pilate confiscated temple property to pay for the aqueduct, in direct conflict with the priests who protested, and an uprising was the result. This revolt was put down by Pilate's soldiers with great cruelty.

ten o'clock in the morning—a mysterious phrase, given that we know it is almost noon from other remarks. Bulgakov made relatively few changes in the Pilate chapters from version to version, so it is unlikely that an important final phrase would be an error. In all versions of this chapter the sentence was to be pronounced at noon, with the sun blazing over Pilate's head. What did begin at ten o'clock, of course, is the interrogation of Yeshua. It may be that we are meant to be taken back to the beginning of everything, in which the sense of this phrase could be "it happened" at ten o'clock in the morning.

CHAPTER 3

The Metropole—the beautiful turn-of-the-century hotel in Moscow's center, used at this time for high-ranking foreigners.

And the devil doesn't exist either?—the Manichean theme begun in the epigraph is here restated. If there is no God, there is no Devil; but the atheist Berlioz, as the reader by now knows, has just spent time with the devil.

He just caught a glimpse of the gilded moon high above—solar and lunar themes multiply in this novel. Some characters are tortured by the sun, some by the moon. This is one of several motifs which recur almost musically in different contexts—roses, severed heads, knives, the colors black, red, and yellow, etc.

CHAPTER 4

The threesome—Woland, the choirmaster, and the cat are an unholy trinity, and Ivan is about to have a baptism in the Moscow River (at the very location where the Church of Christ the Redeemer had earlier stood), followed by his version of the Stations of the Cross. There are many details here which are allusions to events of the New Testament—events which are not described in the Pilate chapters, but which are given in parodic form in the Moscow chapters, a pattern which will continue throughout.

building No. 13—an inside joke. Bulgakov and his first wife had lived in a wretched communal apartment in a building No. 13. Various characters, including the Annushka who spilled the sunflower oil come from this part of Bulgakov's life. An attempt to solve the housing crisis, a communal apartment was an infernal living arrangement, not unlike a boarding house. Six or seven families, sometimes more, would share the common areas of kitchen and bathroom, often resulting in personality clashes as people of wildly different backgrounds and habits were forced to live together.

the omnipresent orchestra—at this time all Moscow apartments had radio receivers which received the same station. Music, and especially opera, which Bulgakov loved, will play a role throughout the novel, often as a counterpoint to comically banal action. Opera is connected to the characterization through voice type as well: Woland's bass emerges in odd contexts (sometimes without his name being mentioned), and Yeshua's hoarseness is underscored.

CHAPTER 5

Griboyedov—the name of the building housing the writers' organization is clearly meant to evoke Herzen House, which in the 1920s and 1930s was the location for many literary organizations. It had a nice restaurant, which prompted satire from the poet Mayakovsky in the poem named "Herzen House." Alexander Herzen was a famous literary and political figure of the previous century, as was Alexander Griboyedov, but Bulgakov had other reasons for choosing the latter. Griboyedov's great play *Woe from Wit* (1822-24), was a favorite reference point for Bulgakov, himself a playwright. In this chapter Ivan is again caught in a literary situation parody, this time a pathetic version of the brilliant Chatsky in Griboyedov's play who is considered insane because he speaks the truth.

The other important aspect of this chapter is its wonderfully accurate portrayal of what it meant to be a coddled Soviet writer, and the kind of jealousy provoked by the various privileges the Writers' Union could confer.

Perelygino—read Peredelkino, even now the prestigious location outside of Moscow for the intellectual elite. The Klyazma is the river nearby.

Amvrosy—the Russian version of Ambrose, a very unusual and somewhat humorous name, as are most of the others in this chapter—Hieronymus Poprikhin not only has a peculiar first name for Russian, his last name contains the root meaning "fidget."

twelve writers—another parody situation: twelve writers are arguing over who will get a place at the writers' summer resort, as opposed to the Last Supper, when the discussion is of who will be prominent in the kingdom yet to come.

Hallelujah—Bulgakov uses this song several times in this novel, usually as the theme of the inferno arrives. The specific reference is to Vincent Youmans' song *Hallelujah!* which was published in Russia in 1928. This is another example of traditional religious motifs turning up in parodic form. *Alleluia* means something quite different in its traditional context—praise to the Lord.

Glukharyov began dancing—this little paragraph owes a great deal to Gogol (as do many other touches in the novel). The list of names and descriptions combine to give the reader the impression that hundreds of people are dancing. Most of the names have funny associations: Glukharyov (wood-grouse), Dragunsky (Dragoon), Cherdachki (attics), Pavianov (baboon), Bogokhulsky (blasphemer), Sladky (sweet), Spichkin (matches), Buzdyak (rowdy).

Ioann from Kronstadt—Archpriest Ioann of Kronstadt (1829-1908) was a famed preacher who was also said to be a miracle worker.

zubrovka—Polish bison-grass vodka.

Ryukhin—this name is a negative one, having at its root the meaning to crash, fall down.

cabdriver—the driver of a horse-drawn carriage. In this case the Russian is *likhach*, meaning the highest class of the three classes of cabbies competing against taxis in the late 1920s in the capital.

CHAPTER 6

wrecker—a key political code word for the period, meaning a person who actively worked against the regime, damaging equipment, etc. not unlike the similar "saboteur" (who sabotaged less actively, by not working, for example), the always popular "enemy of the people," "kulak" (rich peasant), etc. Politically correct people were encouraged to seek out such persons and "unmask" them to the authorities. The result was sometimes arrest.

Soar...Unfurl—these poems are clearly paeans to the Soviet banner.

metal man on a pedestal—reference to the statue of Pushkin on Pushkin Square. This jealous, Soviet second-rate poet is to some degree an amalgam of a number of figures, but he is clearly meant to at least partially evoke Mayakovsky, the poet of the Revolution. As he looks at the statue and broods about why Pushkin got famous ("Storm with mist" is a line from a famous poem by Pushkin, much loved by Bulgakov), there is a connection to Mayakovsky's poem "Jubilee" (1924), in which Mayakovsky revises his previously negative view of the great poet. Although Bulgakov and Mayakovsky had opposing views of Russian culture, all evidence indicates that Bulgakov nevertheless thought Mayakovsky, whom he knew personally, was a real poet, unlike Ryukhin. Ryukhin is of such primitive culture that he refers to the man who killed Pushkin in a duel in 1837 as a *white guard*, a contemporary term of abuse, meaning those who fought on the side of the monarchy during the Russian Civil War, a term which actually applies to Bulgakov who was briefly on the White side after the Revolution. Mayakovsky, who committed suicide in 1930 (an event which much struck Bulgakov), had earlier referred to Bulgakov satirically in his play *The Bedbug*, and this appears to be Bulgakov's settling of accounts with him.

Abrau champagne—Soviet champagne, usually known by its full name as Abrau Dyurso.

CHAPTER 7

Likhodeyev—derived from an old noun meaning "evil-doer." Styopa (nickname for Stepan) and his hangover parallel that of the state and the character of Stiva Oblonsky in Tolstoy's *Anna Karenina*.

six-storey building on Sadovaya Street—Bulgakov has located the evil apartment in the building he lived in during his wretched early years in Moscow, when he and his wife lived in a communal apartment with a motley group of people who were to inspire some of his most negative portraits.

people started disappearing—although the casual reader might not really focus on it, disappearance, arrest, interrogation, and punishment occur suprisingly often in this work (although often displaced to the Pilate chapters), reflecting well-known features of everyday life as the 1930s wore on. Bulgakov is consciously mixing details and atmosphere of the two decades, since he began the novel in 1928, and worked on it throughout the 1930s. Arrests became much more widespread among the people he knew, or knew of, after the killing of Kirov in 1934 which triggered massive "reprisals" (some evidence indicates that Stalin had the popular boss of Leningrad killed himself). Bulgakov's friends were not spared, and it was common to have a suitcase packed in advance in case of a knock on the door in the middle of the night. The narrator is amusingly ingenuous here when referring to obviously politically motivated acts as witchcraft. Such events were nonetheless mysterious in reality in that no logical reasons were required for someone to be held or arrested.

Pyramidon—trademark name for aminopyrine, a drug used as aspirin would be later.

And here I am!—The first words spoken by Mephistopheles in the Russian libretto of Gounod's *Faust*.

a seal on the door—so that nothing will be touched before a police investigation. Styopa is assuming that Berlioz has been arrested.

Azazello (also Azazel)—demon of the waterless desert or the ritual scapegoat, according to several mentions in the Old Testament; Satan's standard bearer (in Milton's *Paradise Lost*, for example); and, most relevant here, also identified as the fallen angel who taught men magic and women how to paint their faces.

Messire—a French term of address, used to indicate respect; "sir" would be an equivalent in English. Bulgakov is deliberately using the French in the Russian text.

CHAPTER 8

Dr. Stravinsky—another musical name, that of the composer Igor Stravinsky.

Ivan—in the course of this chapter Ivan begins to seem more and more like the folklore Ivan, called Ivanushka, who seems a fool but always turns out to be right.

There are some smart people even among the intelligentsia—as a young proletarian poet, Bezdomny has been trained to believe that the intelligentsia are useless. This was a serious issue for Bulgakov who spent much of his career defiantly defending his class.

CHAPTER 9

Nikanor Ivanovich Bosoi—*bosoi* means barefoot in Russian, and clearly points to the peasant nature of this character. This character and his milieu are drawn from Bulgakov's experiences with Moscow's communal apartment life in the early 1920s. For Bulgakov, the Moscow housing crisis was a moral category of its own, as people spent years trying to get a room in a good location, or searched obituaries to see who had died—and left an apartment empty. Bosoi is the chairman of the house committee, which means he is in charge of all basic changes within the building. Although the chairmen were supposed to be elected by the inhabitants of the building, they in fact turned into permanent tyrants who entered apartments without permission, controlled how many people could live in an apartment, whether things were fixed, and whether bribes were required to get them fixed.

pelmeni—small meat-filled dumplings.

Today I'm unofficial, but tomorrow...—a remark reflective of the reality of the mid-1930s when high (and low) officials were replaced with stunning rapidity as the political fortunes of their protectors rose and fell; many of them lost not only their positions but their freedom as well.

Korovyov—this character has a number of literary associations. He is dressed like the shabby devil found tormenting Ivan in Dostoyevsky's *The Brothers Karamazov*, and certainly shares that character's impudent, over-familiar manner. Bulgakov is on record as having said that undue familiarity was a characteristic he could not bear. Korovyov's other name in the novel is Fagot (meaning a bassoon), a musical reference in Russian, but in French and Italian the name also means a silly person, or a trickster. This character is later identified as a choir-master, which brings another literary figure to mind, that of E. T. A. Hoffmann's Kapelmeister Kreisler. While Hoffmann's *Kater Murr* is also a possible source for the talking cat, Behemoth (the Russian word for hippopotamus), Bulgakov himself was surrounded by cats during his second marriage to the animal-loving Lyubov Belozerskaya, and was a close observer of animals in general (see his *Heart of a Dog*).

a temporary residence permit—due to the housing shortage (and a need to keep the provincial population from flooding the large cities), Russia had very strict rules concerning residency in cities and movement within the country in general. This was all the more true for foreigners, who were carefully tracked at all times. Bosoi is taking a big chance here, unless he clears it with the secret police.

CHAPTER 10

Varenukha—this name is based on that of an intoxicating vodka-based berry beverage.

"the cliffs, my refuge..."—a line from Schubert's "Refuge," with words by Ludwig Rellstab, from the Romantic composer's last song cycle, *Schwanengesang*. Schubert had special significance for Bulgakov. See note to Chapter 32.

CHAPTER 12

George Bengalsky—another humorous name, suggesting a Bengal tiger, among other things; the first name in Russian is the Frenchified *Zhorzh* instead of the Russian *Georgy*. Bengalsky is also a character in a famous Russian novel from the beginning of the century, Sologub's *The Petty Demon*. This character represents a type who aroused Bulgakov's aversion as he visited popular entertainments (which did indeed include foreign magic acts)—this sort of a master of ceremonies was often more a political worker than an entertainer, and was there to guarantee the educational value of a given event.

Fagot—meaning bassoon in Russian. See note to Chapter 9 under **Korovyov**.

Behemoth—while this is the Hebrew name given to a beast in Job (which is apparently a mishearing of the Egyptian word for the hippopotamus), and he is listed as the Grand Cup-bearer to Satan in sources on magic, there is another more likely source for the name. In Goethe's *Faust* a poodle (Mephistopheles in disguise), turns into a hippo at the very moment when Faust translates from the Gospels.

chairman of the Acoustics Commission—a made-up organization, but one which was quite possible in these years of bureaucratic control of the theater, when many were employed in meaningless jobs.

Luisa—refers to the role of Luisa Miller in Schiller's play *Treachery and Love*.

the...provocative words of the march—the words are from an 1839 vaudeville piece, reprinted in 1937, called "Lev Gurych Sinichkin, or a Provincial Debutante."

CHAPTER 13

Enter the Hero—literally, "The Appearance of the Hero." Here Bulgakov himself underscores that he is aware how odd it is to have a major figure (whose name is used in the title) first appear more than a third of the way through a novel. Up to this point one could easily conclude that Woland or Ivan is the real hero. Certain aspects of the Master are very Bulgakovian—his need for quiet, his dislike of certain critics (all given names which hint at real critics), being attacked in print for something that was only partially published, etc. Bulgakov was quite different in temperament, however, quite far from the Master's passivity, and unlike his hero, he had a sense of humor. Certain things about the Master (his state of mind, his burning of the novel) bring to mind not only Bulgakov himself, but his favorite writer, Nikolai Gogol. In earlier variants of the novel the Gogol allusion was made explicit, but here it is merely a trace, an association.

the opera *Faust*–Gounod's *Faust* was one of Bulgakov's favorite works, and was a crucial thematic element of his first novel, *White Guard*. In the sense that *The Master and Margarita* is operatic in style and structure, Gounod's work is more important for the novel's atmosphere than Goethe's poem.

I am the Master–this phrase can be translated as "I am a master." The sense is both master as opposed to apprentice, and master in the sense of teacher and artist.

a private home builder–a very special class of people. During the New Economic Policy (NEP), instituted in 1921, certain lucky people were allowed to engage in private construction of small buildings and actually to own the building. This situation did not last very long, due to abuses on the part of entrepreneurs and to the Party's need to reassert control. Bulgakov exhibited a consistently negative attitude towards the profiteers of NEP, both in his journalism and in his artistic works. Bulgakov himself rented one of his apartments from a private home builder.

a sink...–the Master is said to be proud of this sink "for some reason." The reason is that in communal apartments sinks were normally only in the shared areas of kitchen and bathroom. Unlike many people, the Master could wash in private.

disturbing yellow flowers–mimosa. The symbolic color scheme in this novel is chiefly based on red, black, and white. Margarita's flowers are a symbol of misery–dark yellow being the color of the madhouse, as well as the color of betrayal. The only other important yellow-black combination is that of the yellow M sewed on to the Master's black cap–which he does wear in the madhouse. In Bulgakov's symbolic system, the best flowers are red roses (also important in *Faust*, and Berlioz's *The Damnation of Faust*) which stand for immortal beauty. However, Pilate's cape-lining and the pool of wine at his feet are blood-red, of course, and point to an opposite meaning.

Tverskaya–the main street leading down to the Kremlin area, called Gorky Street for much of the Soviet period, and now once again known as Tverskaya. Although many landmarks in this novel are related to realia of Moscow (the restaurant mentioned in this section is the Prague, for example), Bulgakov freely changes geographical reality when he needs to, just as he does in the Pilate sections. The aim is verisimilitude rather than accuracy, a point to keep in mind at all times.

my secret wife–twentieth-century Russians refer to any serious partner as a husband or wife, whether or not the marriage has been legalized. The idea is that the serious nature of the relationship is indicated by these words. Margarita is, of course, married to someone else, but she is more than a lover to the Master.

a novel on such a strange subject–there is much that is autobiographical here. Bulgakov's first novel, *White Guard*, was only partially published in a journal in 1925, but he read it to various literary groups, whose general reaction was that one could never get a work on such a subject published. The real attacks, however, came in 1926 when Bulgakov turned the novel into a hit play for the Moscow Art Theater, under the name *The Days of the Turbins*. Indeed, nothing could have been stranger than Bulgakov's subject, namely the fate of a pro-monarchist family in Kiev during the Civil War. The attacks described in this section of *The Master and Margarita* are clearly distillations of the ones various critics made on Bulgakov's plays, up to and including the play *Molière*, which was banned after a few performances in 1936.

Ariman–Bulgakov has given a real critic (Averbakh) the name of the Zoroastrian evil spirit.

something about slanting rain and despair–the adjective slanting as applied to rain here has attracted the notice of Russian critics, who see in this section a reference to Mayakovsky's poem "Homeward" (magazine variant), in which he talks about wanting to be understood by his country, but if he isn't–he will pass by on the side as slanting rain does. The words "something about" here do seem to indicate a hidden meaning.

"I remember it..."–the Yanovskaya text leaves this paragraph out as not belonging to the final draft, but without it the Master is being attacked for an *unpublished* work. Later in this chapter (in the version Yanovskaya does use), Margarita is said to be asking the Master's forgiveness for having advised him to publish an excerpt—obviously this section is needed for that remark to make sense. Saakyants leaves it in. It is impossible to know which version Bulgakov would have chosen if he were not worrying about censorship. While it was theoretically possible to be attacked for an unpublished work, Bulgakov's own experience was of being attacked for the partially published *White Guard*, and the plays which were performed, even if only through the dress-rehearsal stage.

Pilatism—the Russian here has the suffix *china*, which is hard to convey in English, but is extremely insulting.

Old Believer—see note to Solovki in Chapter One. As the son of a professor of theology, Bulgakov was knowledgeable about those who continued, even under Soviet power, to rebel against the change of liturgy initiated in 1653. The reforms in the religious practices aroused cries of Antichrist and apocalypse among the Old Believers, for whom true faith was inalterably tied to correct *forms* of worship.

"Completely joyless autumn days...such a chapter will not do—these three paragraphs are in the Saakyants text, but are not included in the Yanovskaya text. Yanovskaya looked at various drafts and decided that this section did not belong in the final one. However, I feel that this description of the treacherous neighbor is essential, and that very likely self-censorship played a role if Bulgakov really planned to leave it out. It is unlike Bulgakov to give so little information about the author of the Master's misfortune. The time of year is meaningful for Russian readers, since autumn and spring were times of increased arrests, as the government tried to distract the populace from the regime's economic and agricultural failures.

Aloisy Mogarych—Aloisy is funny to the Russian ear—Aloysius in English— and Mogarych is a fake patronymic which has the meaning of a drink or bribe provided by the receiver of a good deal in business.

started to burn them—Bulgakov himself did this with a number of his manuscripts in 1930, when he was effectively banned from the theaters. Many of the details of the Master's anxiety are autobiographical. In the mid-1930s Bulgakov suffered from agoraphobia and was treated by various methods.

in the middle of January—the Master has clearly been arrested, as the detail of the coat with the buttons torn off shows (Soviet prisons of the time habitually cut off all buttons on the clothes of prisoners), as does the meaningful "knock at the door." The Master appears to have been held only three months, and was then sent to the clinic. Drafts indicate Bulgakov originally intended that the Master be gone a total of one year and two months, part of which was spent in the clinic. It would appear that Bulgakov was trying to elude censors with the three month gap, although there were cases of people being held briefly.

CHAPTER 14

"Ai-Danil" wine—fittingly, this table wine comes from Yalta.

fortochka—a small hinged pane found at the top of Russian double windows, opened in winter to let in a small amount of fresh air.

CHAPTER 15

foreign currency—it was a crime for a private Soviet citizen to possess foreign currency at this time without special permission. The state preferred to absorb all hard currency itself, through special stores, the Torgsins, which at this time dealt not only in hard currency, but in gold, silver, and precious stones.

a dream—this dream is apparently based in reality. One of Bulgakov's good friends was caught in a random round-up in the early 1930s meant to root out those who had hidden gold or jewels. Typically a large group would be kept in a room, given something salty to eat and then denied water or a bathroom. Very quickly confessions of hidden valuables would be coaxed out of them. Of course, arrest and imprisonment were the lot of some of the unlucky people caught up in these dragnets.

speculators—the Russian here is *valiutchiki*, from the word *valiuta*, which earlier simply meant currency, but which under the Soviets came to mean not only foreign "hard" currency, but gold tsarist coins, which were supposed to have been exchanged for Soviet currency—at a loss, of course. Campaigns in the press were organized around the concept of unmasking valiuta-profiteers.

Pushkin—Bulgakov often cites Pushkin in his works, and this poem about a miser is very appropriate.The use of the poet here is also time-specific—1937 was the hundredth anniversary of Pushkin's death, and the entire country was involved in literary celebrations.

CHAPTER 16

Hebron Gate—one of several anachronisms. This gate was not yet built.

your true and only disciple—while the Russian word *uchenik* can be translated as disciple in English, the more literal translation would be pupil or student. The Russian word does not carry as much of a biblical association as the word disciple does in English—*uchenik* is fairly neutral.

Levi, the former collector of taxes—Bulgakov has combined two figures from two Gospels: in Matthew and Luke this personage is called Matthew, but in Mark he is called Levi. Despite the fact that these chapters use historical sources, it is wise to keep in mind that Bulgakov freely blends the elements, all in the name of what he might consider a higher truth, but certainly in the name of what the reader will *feel* is true.

a razor-sharp bread knife—knives are important in many of Bulgakov's works, often a Finnish knife, which is used to stab a character in the back metaphorically. Here the knife is a bread knife, possibly because in the Christian tradition the bread represents the body of Christ.

Valley of Gion—also known as Valley of Hinnom, or Gehenna.

Darkness covered Yershalaim—in the Gospels it is reported that Christ's death was accompanied by an earthquake and darkness.

CHAPTER 17

Bureau of Foreigners—this name is a mixture of two real ones, one from the 1920s—the Bureau of Service to Foreigners—and one formed in 1929—Intourist, which translates as foreign tourist. These organizations fulfilled both travel agent and spy functions.

Vagankovsky Lane—many of the geographical locations in the Moscow strand of the novel have associations for those who know the city well. While most of them are beyond the scope of this commentary, this one deserves mention. Vagankovsky is associated both with the area where entertainers and clowns gathered, and with the cemetery which was founded during the plague year of 1771.

A glorious sea—lines from a famous old convict song, "Glorious Sea." It became politically correct after the Revolution.

valerian—a drug made from the heliotrope plant, used widely as a sedative at this time, usually in the form of drops.

Lermontov—famous nineteenth-century romantic poet and prose writer, known as the author of the novel *A Hero of Our Time.*

CHAPTER 18

Department 412—a ridiculously high number. The passport question was a serious one. After a period of no internal passports, they were introduced again in 1932. Movement from one city to another was controlled in this way. The peasants were refused passports, however, so that they could not leave their collective farms.

"Everything...in the Oblonsky household,"—famous line from Tolstoy's *Anna Karenina.*

for Christ's sake—the only mention of Christ in the novel, as opposed to the hundreds of casual mentions of the devil.

bartender—this word in Russian, *bufetchik*, does not have an English equivalent. The buffet in a Russian theater has both liquor and food, and the *bufetchik* would be both bartender and manager. As a practicing playwright, Bulgakov had plenty of opportunity to observe everything about theater life, including the management of a *bufet.*

second-grade fresh—this oxymoronic phrase entered popular usage as soon as this novel was published.

Kuzmin—this entire section was written in the months before Bulgakov's death, which can easily be felt in the discussions of how one should die by poison, etc. Bulgakov himself was treated by a real Prof. Kuzmin, and was obviously not very impressed by him, judging by the satirist's revenge at the end of this chapter.

CHAPTER 19

Margarita—while this character might at first suggest *Faust*'s Gretchen (whose real name is Margarita), she is no innocent. As will become clear, Margarita is also named in honor of Marguerite de Valois (1553-1615), whose marriage to Henri IV triggered the St. Bartholomew's Day Massacre (she was Catholic, he Huguenot). The French queen, also known as Margot, was the heroine of Dumas père's novel *La Reine Margot*, and of Meyerbeer's *Les Huguenots*, an opera much loved by Bulgakov since childhood. In the Dumas novel, and in the edition of letters and memoirs by her which Bulgakov read, the queen is daring and passionate. Historical accounts say she was both brave and compassionate during the massacre. The queen and her best friend were united in misfortune: both their lovers were beheaded for supposedly conspiring against the king. In his novel Dumas uses the legend that the two women subsequently bought the heads and had them embalmed for permanent safe-keeping. Certainly Bulgakov's heroine has the most in common psychologically with Marguerite de Valois. His heroine also has similarities to Bulgakov's last two wives. The first wife, Tatyana Lappa, who endured all of his early miseries with him, is not reflected here (unless she is the one whose name the Master can't remember); the second wife, Lyubov Belozerskaya, had emigrated and then returned after many adventures abroad, and was physically daring and loved action; the third, Elena Sergeevna Bulgakov was a born hostess and as dedicated to Bulgakov's creative work as Margarita was to the Master's.

a log hut—to a Russian reader it would be clear from this section that Bulgakov is describing the Master either in a camp or in exile, although he is careful to make it a dream.

Lovelace—Samuel Richardson's English novel *Clarissa Harlowe* was very influential in Russia, and led to the use of the major negative character's name, Lovelace, as a synonym for a womanizer, the equivalent of Don Juan in English.

Ah, really I'd sell my soul to the devil—the Faustian moment of the bargain, but this time the one who is saying the fateful words is a woman. Faust's motivation is profoundly different from Margarita's.

Have you come to arrest me?—a historical marker for the Russia of the Great Terror. Margarita's question would seem a normal reaction to Russians from this period: although it is clear she has done nothing wrong, she is prepared to be arrested anyway.

CHAPTER 20

Azazello's Cream—since Azazello (also Azazel) is the fallen angel who taught women to paint their faces, it is clear why he, and not Behemoth, must deal with Margarita at this point.

CHAPTER 21

oil shop—a period detail. Oil shops at this time sold kerosene (for home dry cleaning), and alcohol for various kinds of lamps and stove burners, as well as soap, matches, etc. When electricity and gas became available to all apartment houses the shops disappeared.

Claudine, it's really you, the merry widow!—this Claudine is probably also connected to Marguerite de Valois: the Queen's lady-in-waiting was Claudine, Countess of Tournon.

his friend Guessard's bloody wedding in Paris—a scholar's joke: Guessard was the nineteenth-century editor of Marguerite de Valois's memoirs. The bloody wedding is the St. Bartholomew's Day Massacre. (See note to Chapter 19.)

the most gala reception—there is a Gogolian feel to this section which features Margarita's flight, the man transformed into a hog and a mood of gay enchantment. Bulgakov is theoretically describing a witches' sabbath, but the tone is comic rather than threatening. Many elements here are suggestive of Berlioz's *The Damnation of Faust*, in which the "Dance of the Sylphs" occurs after Méphistophélès sings "Voici des roses," as Faust is supposedly asleep on the banks of the Elbe.

CHAPTER 22

a...French Queen would have been astounded—Marguerite de Valois would certainly have been surprised, since she is said to have been childless. While it is possible Bulgakov is here thinking of Marguerite de Navarre (1492-1549), author of the *Heptameron*, the constant use of the diminutive Margot makes it seem likely that it is Marguerite de Valois Bulgakov has in mind.

seven gold claws—a biblical detail brought into the Moscow strand of the novel—this is the menorah, the Jewish candelabrum.

a finely carved scarab—this is an Egyptian amulet, which in ancient Egypt symbolized evil which led to good.

accursed Gans—i.e., Fool—*die Gans* in German—literally, goose.

Sextus Empiricus...Martianus Capella—two very learned classical authors. The first was a doctor of medicine and a Skeptic philosopher around A.D. 200; the second wrote a famous allegorical work about the Seven Arts around A.D. 439.

the pain in my knee—a Faustian reference to a sabbath on the Brocken, the location for Goethe's Walpurgisnacht. Traditionally, however, it is said that the devil is lame because of his fall from heaven.

My grandmother—a play on words, since a common negative Russian expression is "the devil's grandmother."

A war has broken out—very likely the Spanish Civil War which began in 1936.

Abaddon—"the destroyer," the Hebrew name for the Greek Apollyon, angel of the bottomless pit.

CHAPTER 23

picture of a poodle on a heavy chain—another Faustian reference; Mephistopheles takes the form of a poodle at one point. However, this is also displaced Gospel material, since, unlike Yeshua, Margarita does go through her version of the Stations of the Cross with something heavy around her neck.

Margarita found herself in a tropical forest—these extravagant details of the ever-changing ball scene, which appears to be both an updating of a witches' sabbath and a version of the classic ball scenes to be found in nineteenth-century Russian literature, actually has its source in the author's own life. Bulgakov and his wife attended a ball at the American embassy in 1935, which in terms of everyday life in 1930s Moscow was truly amazing, since it featured live bears and birds, and lavish musical entertainment as well as an enormous amount of food and drink—and a few well-known informers as well.

Vieuxtemps—Henri Vieuxtemps (1820-81) was a Belgian musician and composer who performed in Russia.

Monsieur Jacques—like many of the ball guests, who tend to be either well-documented malefactors, such as medieval poisoners, or fall in the more ambiguous category of alchemists, this character has a historical prototype. Jacques Coeur was *argentier* to the French king Charles VII (1403-61), and after a successful career was said to be an alchemist, counterfeiter, and traitor, and was rumored to have poisoned the king's mistress, Agnes Sorel (who actually died of dysentery).

Count Robert—Robert Dudley Leicester, the lover of Queen Elizabeth I of England, a man suspected of having poisoned his wife.

Signora Tofana (also Toffana)—a legendary poisoner. Aqua Tofana was one of the names for a poison popular in seventeenth-century southern Italy. This school of poisoners (there were several Tofanas) was based in Sicily and Naples. The most notorious among them was Signora Tofana, who was responsible for hundreds of deaths. The poison was placed in special vials bearing the picture of a saint, which were sold freely as a cosmetic, since arsenic (although some think it was opium) was said to help the complexion. Those wives who knew the contents could use it as poison, and the result was a wave of poisonings of husbands by wives.

stuffed the handkerchief in his mouth——this character blends features of Goethe's Gretchen with those of her real-life inspiration, Susanna Brandt, who was convicted of murdering her child, another scholar's joke. Since her name here is Frieda, some have also seen a link to a real-life patient, Frieda Keller, described in *Sexual Questions,* by the Swiss psychologist Forel.

Think of me not as a cat, but as a fish...—in Russian the phrase *quiet as a mouse* becomes *quiet as a fish on ice.*

The marquise—the Marquise de Brinvilliers was beheaded in 1676 for poisoning her father. When her father had her lover put in the Bastille, the lover befriended inmates with knowledge of poisons, specifically ones hard to trace. She poisoned her father and then her two brothers, thereby inheriting everything, but doctors ultimately traced the poison and she was caught.

Lady Minkina—a famous figure of Russian history, she was the favorite of Count Arakcheev, and was notorious for her sadistic treatment of her servants. She was killed in 1825 under mysterious circumstances.

Emperor Rudolf—Rudolf II (1552-1612), of the German Habsburg dynasty, was more interested in the arts and sciences than in ruling his empire. He was said to be an alchemist, probably due to the fact that his private secretary was the alchemist Michael Maier.

Moscow dressmaker—an inside reference to the prototype for the heroine of Bulgakov's own play, *Zoya's Apartment*.

Malyuta Skuratov—this was the nickname of Grigorii Skuratov-Belsky, a notorious favorite of Ivan IV of Russia who was involved in the terror instigated by the *oprichnina*.

Brocken—a Faustian-magical reference. The Brocken is the highest point in Germany's Harz Mountains. Due to an optical effect which appears when the sun is low and huge shadows are cast on clouds or fog in the area, local folklore considers the place mystical. Magic rites were performed long after the introduction of Christianity on the traditional Witches' Sabbath, Walpurgis Night (April 30). Since the very ball scene itself is an echo of these celebrations, the allusion has many levels.

spray the walls of the man's office with poison—a contemporary reference. Genrikh Yagoda, head of the Soviet secret police under Stalin, had been trained as a chemist and pharmacist, with a special knowledge of poisons. After launching the first public purge trials, he fell from grace and was accused of trying to kill his successor Yezhov (under whose rule the Great Terror advanced) by spraying the walls of his office with poison gas; his secretary, P. Bulanov, was also implicated. The trial which featured such startling charges began in March of 1938, and Bulgakov read about it in the newspapers.

on the dish...the severed head—another displaced biblical reference, to the story of Salome and John the Baptist, whose head was served on a platter. This is the culmination of many severed head references. That this head turns into a skull fits with other adumbrations of this theme, specifically the skull on Archibald Archibaldovich's flag. This may all be related to the part of the apocryphal *Gospel of Nicodemus*'s "Legend of the Cross," in which the story of Adam's skull is given, the huge skull which became Golgotha itself.

...each man it will be given according to his beliefs...—a version of lines found in the Gospel according to Matthew.

Baron Maigel—while the citing of real-life prototypes is usually of limited interest for non-Russian readers, this one is an exception. When Bulgakov began to frequent the American embassy gatherings (and American diplomats began to visit him at home), he ran into a high-level NKVD agent, one B. S. Shteiger, known as Baron Shteiger. Shteiger was used by the secret police to deal especially with American ambassadors, as well as important foreigners who had contact with the most famous Russian theaters, such as the Art Theater. On at least one occasion, the Bulgakovs were forced to ride home from the American embassy with him, despite the fact that they lived far apart. While Bulgakov wrote one execution scene, history wrote another—Shteiger was arrested in 1937, and was apparently shot.

...where it spilled, clusters of grapes are already growing—a reverse of the Eucharist, in which the wine is transformed into Christ's blood, and possibly another reference to the "Legend of the Cross," which contains the explanation that Adam's tree (in whose roots the skull was located) became Christ's cross. When He bled from being pierced, that blood soaked into the hill of Calvary/Golgotha, and onto Adam's skull. This in turn freed Adam from his sin of having signed a pact with the devil to stay and work the earth after being expelled from Paradise. Bulgakov's care in using periphrastic designations for Golgotha/Bald Mountain as well as his reliance on the *Gospel of Nicodemus* elsewhere makes such an association plausible.

CHAPTER 24

Manuscripts don't burn—a phrase that went into Russian literary history. Woland is talking about the immortality of a created work, possibly in the sense that sooner or later it will turn up, perhaps even to be given to one writer or another as inspiration from another world.

However, despite this phrase, Bulgakov himself knew very well that manuscripts do burn, since he burned a number of his own in 1930—including the first draft of a novel about the devil—when he lost faith in his future.

No documents, no person—although this phrase had special resonance for a contemporary Russian reader in that documents were all-important to stay out of trouble, the concept can be found in many anti-bureaucratic works of the previous century, especially by such writers as Saltykov-Shchedrin and Sukhovo-Kobylin. The phrase was also used in a work probably known to Bulgakov, Tynyanov's "Lieutenant Kizhe."

Then he rushed...back up the stairs—there is a contradiction here: Mogarych was earlier described as having flown right out Woland's window. There are a number of minor textual discrepancies, especially where material added just before Bulgakov's death is concerned. The entire story of Mogarych was a late addition.

CHAPTER 25

Is it a Falernum—Falernian wines are mentioned in classical Latin literature. They were amber-colored, but were not red. Since they are often referred to as dark, Bulgakov clearly thought this wine was red at first. Later, having learned otherwise, he mentions Cecubum (which is red), but did not make the change everywhere in the novel—see notes to Chapter 30.

To us, to you, Caesar...—this toast, while being historically accurate, would sound very contemporary to a Russian reader of the Stalin era. In general, much that was typical of Russia in the 1930s is displaced into the Pilate chapters: interrogation and beating, political double-dealing, spying, and provocation. In turn, as mentioned above, the Moscow strand of the novel contains much that is a parody of New Testament elements.

Bar is now...harmless—an error. The name Bar-rabban cannot be shortened this way, since Bar means "son of."

were they given a drink—Jewish custom was to give the condemned a drink of wine with sedative herbs mixed into it to ease their suffering. According to Pilate this drink was to be given before the men were hung to the posts, a time about which the narrative provides no information. We have seen in Chapter 16 that Yeshua was given a sponge with water on it, but we have no knowledge of anything else, although the point is made that Matvei was present throughout the execution, at a distance, but able to see. Afranius, a deeply mysterious figure, who, like Woland, has a violent band at his command, may or may not be telling the truth in this chapter. While he does what Pilate tells him to, the descriptions of his expressions during this interview indicate that all is not as it seems. For example, before replying to the question about whether Yeshua was given a drink before being hanged, Afranius closes his eyes at a crucial point, and tortures Pilate by leaving out Yeshua's name. Afranius also leaves out the fact that the last word spoken by Yeshua was *Hegemon*. Bulgakov brings a great deal of the dramatist to these conversations, and the stage directions are as eloquent as the words themselves.

cowardice—seen in the context of all of the author's works, this is a truly Bulgakovian theme, which is found in his earliest stories and most of his plays, as well as in his last novel. The Russian here is *malodushie*, which literally means faint-heartedness or pusillanimity. Later, Pilate will use the specific word *trusost'* which means cowardice.

he will be murdered tonight—like many other tyrant figures in Bulgakov's works (see the plays *Last Days* and *Molière*, for examples), Pilate gives orders indirectly. Pilate is here beginning the myth of Yeshua for his own reasons. On the one hand he wishes to somehow make up for the unjust execution of Yeshua, on the other, he is making sure that Kaifa will have problems resulting from this death.

CHAPTER 26

Banga—a very inside joke. Bulgakov's second wife, Lyubov, was nicknamed Lyubanga. She was also the person who brought animals into Bulgakov's life.

Niza—the meeting between Niza and Judas parallels the one between the Master and Margarita, which in turn echoes Faust's meeting on the street with Gretchen. There are many other parallels between the Moscow strand and the Pilate chapters—color schemes; weather (especially sun and moon descriptions at crucial moments); architectural monstrosities; masters and disciples; the same general time frame; and, of course the power of an off-stage despot.

the olive estate—a periphrastic way of saying Gethsemane.

five-branched candelabra—a historically accurate detail which Bulgakov found illustrated in Farrar's *Life of Jesus Christ.*

Now we shall always be together—when Yeshua says this to Pilate in the latter's dream, he is expressing the thought found in the apocryphal *Gospel of Nicodemus* (also known as the *Acta Pilata*), to the effect that Pilate is linked throughout all eternity with Christ.

the son of an astrologer-king—there are several sources for this genealogy. One is the poem "Pilate," written in Latin, and translated into Russian in collections of apocrypha and medieval Latin literature. A Russian work from the fifteenth century, "A Journey to Florence," includes a legend about Pilate then current in Europe, in which this parentage is mentioned. Since Pilate is one of the few documented historical characters in the central drama of the New Testament, it is fairly amusing—and typical—that Bulgakov chose to bring in folklore apocrypha at this point. The historical Pilate, about whom Bulgakov seems to have known at least what his main source—Farrar—did, was considered by the Jews to be "inflexible, merciless, obstinate" (Philo, *Leg. ad Gaium* 38). The historical Pilate was prefect of Judea from A.D. 26-36. History considers that his condemnation of Jesus was a form of concession to the Jews. He aroused the ire of the governor of Syria after the Samaritans complained about him, and he was summoned back to Rome by Tiberius, but he arrived after the Emperor's death. At this point the historical record is unclear. Eusebius reports that he ended a suicide. Apocryphal accounts have him taking poison, a motif which Bulgakov uses. Some Christian authorities felt him to be a "Christian in his conscience" (see Tertullian, *Apol.* 21.24). There is extensive apocryphal literature about him.

Valerius Gratus—Pilate's predecessor.

couldn't he have killed himself—everything in this discussion is ironic, of course, as Pilate and Afranius agree on what lies to tell, but this line is especially so when one knows that in the New Testament account Judas is said to have hanged himself.

There is no death...sweet spring figs...water of life...crystal—these jottings are meant to be a version of the *Logia,* words supposedly spoken by Jesus which were later incorporated into the Gospels. These particular phrases echo well-known sections of both the New Testament (Jesus mentions the fig tree which gives no fruit) and the Book of Revelation. The Apocalypse carries a message of destruction, but its final conclusion is that there will peace in the age to come: "And God shall wipe away all tears from their eyes; and there shall be no more death, neither sorrow, nor crying, neither shall there be any more pain: for the former things are passed away." However, it is important to keep in mind that Yeshua has already declared that he never said most of what is written on Matvei's parchment.

CHAPTER 27

apartment on Kamenny Bridge—a veiled reference to the so-called "House of the Leaders" built in this area in the early 1930s.

a Caucasian-style fur cap—Styopa is wearing a *papakha* due to an error: in an earlier version of Styopa's story he was sent not to Yalta, but to Vladikavkaz, where it would have been cold.

CHAPTER 28

the Torgsin Store—in its quest to extract all hard currency and valuables from both its citizens and foreign visitors, Russia had stores which specialized in offering in exchange generally unobtainable objects, ranging from clothes to food and drink. However, unlike the Beriozka stores of the late Soviet period, which were off-limits to ordinary citizens, theoretically anyone could go into the Torgsin store, although certainly the guards at the entrance would not let people in who looked unlikely to possess valuables. Bulgakov had recourse to this institution himself when he needed to buy fabric for the dinner clothes he had made for the ball at the American Embassy.

Harun al-Rashid—historically, a caliph of the Abbasid dynasty, but Bulgakov is thinking of the legendary Harun al-Rashid, one of the characters in the *Arabian Nights.* In these tales, the caliph dresses up as a beggar and wanders around Baghdad with various companions—a poet, a musician, and an executioner—and then invites unsuspecting ordinary citizens to the court.

Palosich—the running together of a name and patronymic—Pavel Iosifovich—as it would sound when said quickly.

Bitter! Bitter!—this is said at Russian weddings to force the bride and groom to kiss, to take away the supposedly bitter taste of the food.

Panayev...Skabichevsky—two very second-rate writers of the nineteenth century. Panayev (1812-62) wrote sentimental society tales; Skabichevsky (1838-1910) was a critic and publicist.

CHAPTER 29

one of the most beautiful buildings—easily recognized as the Pashkov House, a mansion built in the 1780s, which was said to be one of the most beautiful buildings of old Moscow. Bulgakov had visited it in the early 1920s when it was the Rumyantsev Museum. It is now one of the buildings of the Russian State Library, formerly known as the Lenin Library. The mansion has a striking setting in downtown Moscow, and there are wonderful views from its rooftop. This is a very operatic setting. Wagnerian motifs—black horses and riders, swords, flight, and Woland's bass voice—are scattered through the last chapters of the book.

Dressed in his black soutane—an interesting, and very specific, choice of dress for Woland, this is the cassock normally worn by the secular clergy of the Catholic church.

shacks condemned—as Bulgakov was writing, this area (where the Cathedral of Christ the Redeemer had been demolished), was to be completely redeveloped to make room for a Palace of the Soviets, which, however, was never built.

I prefer Rome—Azazello is certainly thinking of something specific here—he seldom speaks, but when he does, it is important. While Moscow was supposed to become the "third Rome" according to ancient Russian predictions, an idea recycled by various Russian thinkers over the centuries, this doesn't seem quite enough to prompt Azazello's comment. However, it makes more sense if there is another parallel, another event in Rome at which this band might have been present, namely the famous burning of Rome under Nero in 64 A.D. Bulgakov had originally planned to have the entire city of Moscow burn at the end of this novel, but changed his mind, and had only specific locations go up in flames.

He has not earned light, he has earned peace—this is a crucial statement. Even in earlier drafts, the Master was not intended to go to the light. There are various theories about this, but the one that seems most convincing is that the Master gave up faith in himself completely, a great sin in the eyes of the author of *Faust*, for example, who conveys the message that striving is all. In Dante's *Divine Comedy* the moon, a major fascination of the Master's, is the place for those who have left vows unfulfilled, perhaps as a result of outside pressures over which they had no control, but their vows are unfulfilled nonetheless. One might easily conclude that the Master has not fulfilled his vow to be a writer, to continue to work. Dante underscores that the moon is the abode of those who did not return to their mission as soon as the external pressure was taken away.

a dash for Timiryazev—that is, for the famous statue of K. A. Timiryazev (1843-1920) on Tverskoi Boulevard. Timiryazev was a famous botanist.

CHAPTER 30

Time to go!—another Pushkin reference, to his poem of 1834, "Pora, moi drug, pora!"— "It's time to go, my friend, it's time to go!" This short lyric contains a very appropriate line about there being peace and freedom only in death.

Peace be unto you—another displaced biblical element. These words are found in Luke 24:36, as the resurrected Christ speaks to the apostles—appropriate here, since a resurrection of sorts is to take place.

stained the color of blood—actually, as stated earlier, Falernian wine was amber-colored. Bulgakov planned to change this to the red Cecubum, but had not coordinated the change.

you are thinking—as in Descartes' "I think, therefore I am."

the sign of the cross...I'll cut your hand off—here, rather than in the Pilate chapters, is the Russian adjective from the word "cross," a word previously avoided; here also is the only direct clash of the satanic with the Christian. It may be telling that the Christian tries to perform an action which Azazello stops with words.

Farewell, disciple—the parallel with Yeshua and Levi Matvei is here made clear.

CHAPTER 31

Sparrow Hills—a very famous location in Russian literature, used in a number of works, most famously in Alexander Herzen's (1812-70) memoirs. In 1935 the name was changed to Lenin Hills. Under any name, this location has a wonderful view of Moscow.

CHAPTER 32

Gods, my gods! How sad the earth—this subsequently very famous paragraph was written when Bulgakov knew he was going to die of nephrosclerosis, the same disease which had killed his father at almost the same age. This paragraph's ending, "knowing that death alone...," was apparently deliberately left unfinished by Bulgakov who dictated it to his wife. Earlier versions used Elena Sérgeevna's addition: "would calm him." This section is reminiscent of the end of *Aida*, when the lovers sing the duet "O terra, addio" ("Farewell, Earth") as death is approaching.

That knight once made a joke—of course a play on dark and light is found in the epigraph to this novel.

the best jester—Behemoth may be inspired by the character of Tyl Eulenspiegel, hero of Richard Strauss' symphonic poem and of Charles de Coster's novel of the same name, which was very popular in Russia. Tyl, a legendary Flemish joker, wreaks havoc wherever he goes, first in the market, then among clergymen and pedagogues. He ends by being beheaded.

boulders appeared—Pilate's place of exile appears to be Mt. Pilatus in Switzerland, which is where an apocryphal source called "The Death of Pilate" put him. According to legend, the Romans buried Pilate in the middle of the mountains; on every Good Friday, the devil lifts Pilate's body out of its grave and puts it on a throne of stone, where Pilate makes the gesture of washing his hands.

Twelve thousand moons—this would seem to be an error. Two thousand years would add up to 24,000 moons.

Romantic Master—an important point. Although writing in the time of the triumph and tyranny of Socialist Realism, Bulgakov, like the Master, felt himself to be more akin to Romantic writers of the nineteenth century, such as Gogol, E. T. A. Hoffmann, etc. There are many kinds of Romanticism, of course, but judging strictly by Bulgakov's works, it is clear that a belief in the value of the vision of the individual artist is paramount. Bulgakov felt he was reading about himself in an article he found on Hoffmann, which included the following ideas: a real artist is doomed to solitude; art is powerless in the face of a reality which is destructive to art; the artist is not of the ordinary world; clarity and peace are needed for creation. In this same article on Hoffmann Bulgakov underlined a passage to the effect that the man of genius is caught between two possibilities: if he concedes to reality he will become a philistine, but if he doesn't, he will die before his time or go mad. Bulgakov is also at pains in this novel, however, to present the work of art as a revelation granted to the inspired artist—the Master says that he "guessed" it all, not that he made it all up. Here we are dealing with the ancient idea of the artist as the instrument of divine inspiration.

listen to Schubert—although this Romantic composer, who died very young, set several poems by Goethe to music (including a song from *Faust*), he has additional significance for Bulgakov. Like Bulgakov, Schubert suffered from constant defeat in his life as a composer, and was profoundly depressed for personal reasons as well. He produced beautiful melodies marked by spontaneity and joy, but melancholy, suicide and death became his frequent themes. Like Bulgakov, Schubert worked right up until his death, and only long after his death were the true dimensions of his talent revealed to the musical world. There is every reason to believe that Bulgakov identified strongly with Schubert's fate, both personal and professional.

Woland...plunged into the gap—parallels the hell ride which is the high point of Berlioz's *The Damnation of Faust*.

Sunday morning—i.e., Easter Sunday. Like *Faust* and *The Divine Comedy*, *The Master and Margarita* is an Easter novel. Easter is the most ancient and holy day of the Christian calendar, and, like Passover, is based on calculations involving both lunar and solar calendars. Since the calculations have been done differently at different times, it is hard to say whether Bulgakov truly means the Pilate narrative to be occurring at precisely the same time as the Moscow one.

Certainly the days of the week involved are the same, Wednesday through early Sunday. The Yanovskaya text contains a serious error here, possibly one of proofreading. Throughout this work, and especially in the Pilate narrative, Bulgakov has carefully avoided words like "cross," "resurrection," etc., and here the Russian is easily mistaken. The Yanovskaya text says Pilate was absolved on the morning of the *resurrection*. The difference between "Sunday" and "resurrection" is one letter in Russian. The author has been meticulous about time markers throughout the novel's action, which makes a Sunday reference logical. There is no reason to think that Bulgakov would suddenly introduce religious categories he had so assiduously avoided up to this point.

EPILOGUE

But still, what happened next—the narrator who has been in and out of the novel is back with a vengeance, and echoes many famous nineteenth-century narrators—especially those of Dostoyevsky and Gogol. The final version of the epilogue was written not long before Bulgakov's death and was pasted in on the last page of the bound manuscript. Many have objected to the jarring dissonance of tone here, and wonder if Bulgakov would have kept the epilogue if he had lived. Since the epilogue brings the total number of chapters to the meaningful number of 33 (Christ's age at his death), it is very likely that Bulgakov would have kept it. The epilogue suddenly expands the time frame of the novel—some eight years have passed, judging by Ivan's age. And Ivan is very much the point—the novel must come back to its beginning, and to the one person who could learn something of importance from the story of the Master and his Margarita.

cultured people—this use of "cultured" is equivalent to "educated people," and does not necessarily have anything to do with real culture. It is meant to distinguish the middle class from the hopeless vulgarians.

a hundred or so...were shot—although the subject is supposedly cats, it is hard not to see a political subtext here, since Bulgakov is writing during the terror.

Margarita...disappear from Moscow—this may or may not be an error, but it is certainly a mystery—the reader has already read that Margarita died of a heart attack in her apartment.

Absolutely nothing happened to them—Bulgakov is slyly reminding the reader that some parts of the novel didn't happen, a deeply ironic enterprise.

Institute of History and Philosophy—in reality there was no such institution, but if there had been, Ivan would have been perfect for it, since the Pilate chapters and the Master's story belong to both these areas.

Ponyryov—only the second mention of Ivan's real last name, which has the associations of "dive" and "downcast."

Everything is clear to Ivan—a possible indication that he is a failed disciple: Ivan has accepted the rational explanations his world has provided him with, and he will never be an artist because of it.

the knight Pontius Pilate—the Saakyants text has a slight difference in phrasing between the ending of Chapter 32 and the Epilogue. The chief difference is that the name Pontius is spelled differently—*Pontiiskii* instead of *Pontii*. This matters because if the endings are different, and only one matches what the Master said the last words of his novel would be—and it is hard to believe that Bulgakov would not remember such an essential phrase—then only that one, specifically the ending to Chapter 32, is the real ending to the Master's novel. Yanovskaya states that Bulgakov's own last text did end with the different form of Pontius, but that the author's widow, Elena Sergeevna, entered the change which made both the Epilogue and Chapter 32 end with identical words. For many reasons it makes sense that Chapter 32 is the end of the Master's work, and the Epilogue the end of Bulgakov's. This point, like so many other textual differences, will have to be left unresolved. In either case, it would be hard to convey such a difference in English—*Pontian* is the closest equivalent in English.

BIOGRAPHICAL NOTE

MIKHAIL AFANASIEVICH BULGAKOV was born in Kiev in 1891, the son of a Russian lecturer in theology, and the grandson of priests on both sides. Medicine, religion, and education were the dominant careers in his family. Despite an early interest in literature and the theater, Bulgakov chose to become a doctor. In 1914, as a medical student, he volunteered with the Red Cross during World War I. After graduating from the University of Kiev in 1916, he served in the White Army during the Civil War, and briefly forcibly mobilized by the Ukrainian Nationalist Army. These experiences during the chaos of the Civil War in Kiev and the Caucasus had a profound effect on the writer and his work. His two younger brothers disappeared during the fighting around Kiev, and later surfaced in Europe. In 1919, while in the Caucasus, he made the decision to leave medicine for literature; soon after he almost emigrated, but was prevented from doing so by illness, which he took as a sign. By 1921 he was in Moscow where his literary career began in earnest. The *Diaboliad* collection, published in 1925, was his major publication of this time, since his masterpiece, *Heart of a Dog*, could not get past the censorship. This same period saw the partial publication of his novel about Kiev during the Civil War, *White Guard*. Publication ceased when the journal serializing the novel was shut down; however, enough had come out to arouse the interest of the Moscow Art Theater, which commissioned a play based on *White Guard*. This play, *The Days of the Turbins*, was the source of Bulgakov's fame for the rest of his life, and was a major sensation both due to its vivid characterizations and its portrayal of a monarchist family in a sympathetic light rather than as monsters, which was the norm at this time. By the late twenties, when he had a number of other plays in production (*Zoya's Apartment, Flight* and *The Crimson Island*), Bulgakov had drawn down the wrath of the leftist critics who felt that everything he wrote was essentially anti-Soviet. This was a period of extreme polarization, and Bulgakov's career was destroyed by 1929. He would have one more original play, *Molière,* staged in his lifetime (it was quickly withdrawn from production due to the critics), but all publication of his prose ceased after 1927. In 1930, in a time of despair when he burned his works in manuscript, he wrote his famous letter to the Soviet government, defending his right to be a satirist, and asking that his country let him emigrate if it could not use his abilities. To everyone's astonishment, Stalin, who had seen *The Days of the Turbins* many times, answered this letter with a phone call, and soon afterward Bulgakov had employment with a small theater. The Moscow Art Theater then found work for him, but most of the projects he worked on came to nothing, and the last eight years of his life were full of stress and disappointment. He broke with Stanislavsky and the Art Theater after the *Molière* debacle, and returned to *Theatrical Novel* (begun earlier, then resumed) as a way of venting his spleen. He went to work for the Bolshoi Theater as a librettist, which also proved frustrating, as project after project remained unproduced. From 1928 on, Bulgakov had worked only sporadically on his major work, *The Master and Margarita;* in 1937 he dropped *Theatrical Novel,* which would remain unfinished, and concentrated on the novel about the devil in Moscow. In 1938 under pressure from the Art Theater he wrote a play about the young Stalin, *Batum,* which was not only a compromise on his part, but adversely affected his failing health when it was rejected. When he died of nephrosclerosis (which had killed his father at the same age) in 1940, he had finished the writing of *The Master and Margarita,* although not the final editing, which he worked on up to months before his death. This novel, which is now considered one of the best Russian novels of the twentieth century, was not published until 1966-67 (and then in censored form in a Moscow journal), twenty-six years after Bulgakov's death. *Heart of a Dog,* however, was not published until 1987, the height of glasnost—more than sixty years after it was written—a true indication of just how threatening satire could be to a totalitarian regime. Bulgakov is now one of his country's most popular writers.

Bulgakov the magician confidently steps out on the stage of a theater he has constructed himself and begins his performance. Its success depends on the successful implication of the audience itself. What the audience-reader notices in the exuberant, intricate extravaganza that is *The Master and Margarita* is how Bulgakov the magician spares no resources in his effort to make *us* believe—but on first reading we are left unsure of both his intentions and his beliefs. This is a very cinematic work, respecting no unities of geography or epoch, full of dazzling humor and startling shifts. At the end of this work we have been profoundly amused by both the situations and characters, but we have also been disturbed. In this afterword I will concentrate on the sources of that disturbance, not because it is more important than the buoyancy on display, but because its sources are harder to fathom.

Thanks to the work of numerous critics and scholars, we know much more now about Bulgakov's most famous novel than we did when it was first published in English. Bulgakov worked sporadically on different versions of *The Master and Margarita* from 1928 up until 1940. The main text was completed in the summer of 1938, but Bulgakov continued making corrections up until a few months before his death. Although he had moments of thinking he might be able to get the novel published, most of the time Bulgakov wrote with full awareness that this novel would not be published in the foreseeable future. But Bulgakov was counting on the unforeseeable future—which caught up with him in 1966, twenty-six years after his death, when a censored version of the text was serialized in a Moscow journal. The Russian literary world was stunned by the unexpected transformation of a dramatist of the 1920s into a major novelist and an unnerving influence on the culture as a whole. To this day Russians use key phrases from the novel ("second-degree freshness"), and label certain kinds of banal-yet-mysterious events "Bulgakovian."

Throughout his career Bulgakov specialized in genre mutations: plays that were dreams, science fiction that was neither science nor fiction, adaptations that were actually original. So it is no surprise that *The Master and Margarita* is dense with mystery, ambiguity and irony, a subversive work which fits no genre neatly. The question of genre is essential to Bulgakov's magic: because we don't know what category this work belongs to, we don't know what expectations to bring to it. But it is a mark of the quality of this work that both the ignorant and initiated may find entertainment equally—it is not necessary to solve all the mysteries to enjoy *The Master and Margarita*.

Like the writers literary history has come to label modernists, Bulgakov is writing in the post-Einsteinean universe, and in many ways he fits the general profile of Anglo-American modernism. Because he is usually discussed as a Soviet writer, albeit an aberrant one, he is rarely placed in this context. Like the modernists, Bulgakov was inclined to parody the forms of the earlier masters, and in this novel he certainly uses myth to impose order of sort—only then to explode the myth itself. Like T. S. Eliot, Bulgakov had no desire to subvert traditional human-ism—to the contrary, he longed to reestablish it in a country where it was held in contempt. But his art actually reveals the typical concerns of modernism, so it is not surprising that irony and ambiguity of motiva-tion are central to *The Master and Margarita*. To some degree these ap-proaches are present in earlier Russian writers, especially Dostoyevsky and Gogol, but Bulgakov adds truly modern anxiety: the knowledge that there is no stable society against which to rebel, there is only entropy, visible everywhere.

Bulgakov's narrator at first seems to promise an old-fashioned story. However, this narrator is as misleading as his style. Bulgakov's style demonstrates a remarkable ability to combine seemingly disparate ele-ments, especially language levels, in such a way that the reader accepts the whole as harmonious—although this style is not particularly smooth. This is rhythmic, musical prose, full of rich sound play, but it features unexpected words in unexpected order. The tendency to put the key word at the end of the sentence, often the verb, is quite un-Russian, but very Bulgakovian in that it creates suspense on the level of a phrase. This is nervous, modern prose. For all the ways in which it continues the clas-sic themes of Russian literature, Bulgakov's novel lacks many of the ele-ments we associate with that literature. No one has a childhood in *The Master and Margarita*, no one's character evolves profoundly over time, no souls are probed deeply. We are shown an adulterous love which ap-pears to have no physical side to it. Nor is this the Gogolian world of grotesque "types," although Gogol is a major influence on Bulgakov (as well as a possible model for the Master). Very realistic minor characters intermingle with archetypal or deliberately abstract figures. The reader notices few of these things, so caught up is he in this strange narrative. The difficulty of this novel is partly due to something Bulgakov could never have envisioned: the role the postponement of his literary appear-ance would play in the critical reception of the novel, and the persis-tence of the biographical fallacy which would make many assume that the Master was merely a stand-in for the author, and therefore must be heroic. These two elements have clouded readers' visions from the novel's first appearance in 1967-68, and understandably so—Bulgakov was much more modern than anyone was prepared to see.

The first chapter is a good example of the playwright at work. When Berlioz, Ivan and Woland meet on the park bench, the major worlds of this novel meet. The discussion about theology which appears merely to be a pretext for Woland to make fun of the atheism of the two Soviet writers is, in fact, filled with clues to the author's intentions when telling the story of Pontius Pilate, but like Matvei and Ivan, the reader is unable to understand these clues until he has finished the novel. The themes touched on in this opening chapter—fate, the existence of God and the Devil, and Bezdomny's strange ability to write in a believable way about Jesus Christ—are part of the overture. Bulgakov's style in Russian in this chapter is brilliant and unconventional, his dialogue quickly characterizes the speakers, and nothing is irrelevant: a suspenseful opening act.

The second chapter is something few readers are prepared for, especially after the humor of the first. The chapter is entitled "Pontius Pilate," so when we read the words "the accused is from Galilee?" we think we know what is coming, all of it colored by romantic irony. But this Yeshua is not *that* Jesus, just as this Woland is not *that* Satan. The style of the Pilate chapters, with its majestic rhetoric and almost transcendental irony, is the skin covering the muscle of Bulgakov's scholarship. These chapters are a *tour de force*, and represent Bulgakov the mystificator at his most dazzling, as well as the amateur historian. While Bulgakov sprinkles parodistic echoes from the Gospels throughout the Moscow narrative, he scrupulously strips away everything that can be called messianic or mythic from the Pilate chapters, leaving us with a pitiful yet compelling Yeshua, who is historically plausible. Bulgakov then promptly undercuts this historical tendency by incorporating apocryphal material in what appears to be his straight historical narrative. There are many scholarly in-jokes here, a few of which I have mentioned in the Commentary.

Bulgakov's works as a whole, and what we know of his biography reveal him to be a believer in the need for religious feeling, but not necessarily an admirer of organized religion itself. Kaifa is a typical religious figure for this author, who portrayed worldly, politicized priests in many of his works. It is not surprising that many Russian Orthodox readers consider this novel blasphemous. But Bulgakov, like Tolstoy, Mandelstam and many other artists of his time, was more interested in Christ than in the religion created in his name.

The Pilate chapters are clearly included within the Moscow narrative for a reason, and there are certainly many stylistic and thematic parallels between them, but we are at first unable to see the connection. We certainly notice the similar paradigm of teacher/failed disciple/betrayer in both plots, as well as myriad motifs which recur like operatic phrases. Displacement is pervasive: there are no last suppers, baptisms, or twelve disciples in the Pilate chapters, but these motifs are all to be found in parodic form in the Moscow strand.

The narrator's direct addresses to the reader at the most unexpected points of the story are part of the magician's diversion. This is a wildly unreliable narrator, an actor whose aims are as obscure as Woland's. But the author's aims are there for us to see if we look closely. Underneath the humor, fantasy, and deep lyrical sadness, is a philosophical structure. This structure is not meant to be perceived separately from what surrounds it, of course, but in order to reveal Bulgakov's main feat of magic here a bit of analysis is in order—always keeping in mind that he is not a philosopher or a scholar, no matter how well he impersonates one, but an artist.

There are many questions which come to mind when reading this work. For example, why is the novel called *The Master and Margarita* when those two characters arrive very late in the narrative? What is Woland's real purpose in Moscow, and what does it have to do with Pontius Pilate? How many statements which the reader takes seriously are actually meant ironically? Are these simply loose ends, sloppy plotting? Bulgakov had finished the novel in terms of structure, but he would certainly have continued to coordinate the minor changes he began in the first part of the novel with the second part if he had lived. The changes he was in the process of making before he died were not substantive, and I doubt that they would have done anything to change the general impression that the two parts of the novel are quite different, the first seeming more concrete and dense, the second more abstract and fantastic. Before concluding that everything unclear or seemingly contradictory is a mistake, we have to look at the text more carefully.

One way to understand this work is to consider Bulgakov's other artist heroes. Dymogatsky, the dramatist in *The Crimson Island* is appalled at what the censor and the director are doing to his play, but gives in; Molière, in the play of the same name, grovels before his king; the playwright in *Theatrical Novel* is unable to defend his play against the director; Pushkin in the play *Last Days* is humiliated by the Tsar. Consistently, Bulgakov's artist heroes feel themselves crushed by greater force. Their only salvation is the act of creation itself. Bulgakov himself was familiar with all of these humiliations, and his own worst compromise with his conscience was probably the writing of the play *Batum*, about Stalin as a young revolutionary.

The Master is a distillation of this line of somewhat autobiographical heroes: like them, he is naive about the likely reception of his work, and is unable to deal with the attacks of the critics. Unlike these other characters, the Master stops writing: he is completely broken by his encounter with both the critics and the police. The point is made that it is not his experiences, but rather his *reaction* to them that is the problem, the fear itself. The Master is no conventional hero, he is barely characterized, his attitude to himself is sadly ironic (as when he shows his profile to Ivan, something Behemoth will do later in a gesture rhyme), and his novel is the only remarkable thing about him. But it is enough. It is the justification for his existence. Metatistic was characteristic of Bulgakov from the start of his career—fictionalized accounts of his early attempts to be a writer, plays within plays, plays within novels, works about writers, or their analogues, creative scientists. Here in Bulgakov's last novel we have the writer's text itself, as separate from the surrounding narrative. The Pilate "novel" is revealed in many different ways and through different consciousnesses, as if it were an ur-text waiting to be discovered—but it is clearly the Master's work, and meant to be understood as such, judging by all of the internal indicators, no matter how it is presented. That the chapters are scattered throughout the larger narrative means that once again the reader is implicated. The reader's consciousness must provide the coherence between widely spaced sections, remembering details, and, most of all, wanting to know how this story, so familiar yet so new, will develop.

The only real characterization of the Master is to be found in his creation, a point generally overlooked. The Master as author does not appear to be interested in the fantastic, but rather the political and the psychological. The Master approaches the New Testament as *literature* rather than revelation, and proceeds to rewrite it in a way which makes better sense to him. The dialectic implicit in the contradictory world-views of Yeshua ("All men are good") and Pilate ("All men are bad," with "including myself" understood) is never resolved. The tension between these points of view continues into the outer novel, as the two protagonists ascend the moon path, still arguing. Throughout this narrative the emphasis is on the fact that Yeshua is extraordinary only in his sensitivity and his naive belief in the goodness of man. It is a defenseless human being who is beaten and hung on the cross, not the Messiah. We know that the Master, like Woland, was a historian in his former life, and his novel certainly demonstrates this. The Master has taken what is normally perceived as religious material and given it a social context; his novel is not about Jesus Christ and His divinity as revealed by His time on earth, but about the unseen forces of politics and morality which lead to the death of a historically plausible figure—and the creation of the myth which will be the basis of a major world religion. If we try to comprehend the Master through his novel, we must conclude that he is essentially a pessimist. A case can be made, using only his text, that while wishing that Yeshua were right about humanity, he ultimately agrees with Pilate. In addition to the text of his novel, we have the Master's story of his love affair, a strange blend of ironic cliché and real emotion, and later, when things are going badly for him, he and Margarita appear to grow apart. We are given two other facts about the Master which are more important than they might at first seem: he can't remember his first wife's name, and he got his start as a writer by a remarkable turn of luck—he won the lottery. Fate—or Woland—provided him with the possibility of creating his novel, but he himself must rise to the challenge the critical reception poses. Unlike virtually everyone else in the novel, the Master guesses right away that Woland is the devil, but he nevertheless demonstrates little understanding of Woland's function, or of what is taking place. And what is taking place? A drama of identity, a recognition plot.

When the novel opens, we read the epigraph from *Faust* and we make at least two assumptions: first, that there will be something Faust-like in this novel; second, that the epigraph is meant seriously. As we read on, we are barraged by allusions to *Faust*, sometimes to the opera (which Bulgakov saw over forty times), sometimes to Goethe's poem, sometimes to the original sources. Bulgakov has gone to a lot of trouble to lead us to the conclusion that Woland's role is identical to that of Mephistopheles. By this time a fellow magician would know the main trick is being readied. These allusions are so distracting that we forget to ask: is Woland really Mephistopheles, is he really the embodiment of the force opposed to good? As the novel continues, we see that his role is quite dissimilar. We are comfortably superior to Ivan and Berlioz, as they fail to recognize the very literary figure who is telling them the story of Pontius Pilate, but what do we ourselves really know? The Master and Margarita seem to recognize Woland fairly quickly, but at first they both expect something terrible. Only after the ball has Margarita come to understand something of this personage, although, significantly, she is ready to trust him if it will help her lover. Margarita is the most active figure in the novel, the one most willing to take risks. As for the Master, only after death does he say the words "Now I understand everything."

To begin to see what the Master now "understands," we have to trace one of the essential themes of this work.

The manipulation of the reader-audience begins early, at the time of Berlioz's death. Berlioz is obnoxious and arrogant, everything that a writer like Bulgakov could not tolerate, and it seems that the reader would be glad to see him go. But his death, like so many here, is described in a jarringly violent way. Is the reader really happy to see that severed head rolling on the street? Or to see the loathsome master of ceremonies, Bengalsky, have his head torn off during the Variety performance? Perhaps Bulgakov is merely settling scores like Dante, killing off his enemies in print, instead of in life? We are in the position of the Variety audience here, and even they beg for mercy for Bengalsky. Is Margarita enchanting when she destroys Latunsky's apartment? Pilate fits into this context of revenge as well. Unlike Levi Matvei, Pilate is capable of understanding what Yeshua has tried to teach, but he rejects it and insists on retribution, using the mysterious Afranius who is pursuing his own ends. Pilate, like many Bulgakov heroes before him, experiences guilt over the fact that he gave into his fear and let Yeshua go to his death. The procurator is forced to suffer long to expiate his sin, and is not freed until the Master is instructed by Woland to finish his novel with a single line: "Free! Free! He is waiting for you!" which brings us to the question of who is in charge. Yeshua *intercedes* for Pilate, and *requests* a specific outcome for the Master and Margarita. Paradoxically, Yeshua does not appear to be more powerful than Woland, and it is left quite unclear whether there is a power higher than Woland himself.

The reader is so convinced that Woland is the devil he knows, that even Woland's consistent actions are not quite enough to awaken the reader's suspicions. Woland, like his creator, is inexhaustibly ironic. When Margarita is instructed to show no preference for any one at the ball, for example, this is to see if her compassion will shine through even in the face of prohibition. When Woland rewards her despite her favoritism toward Frieda, and complains that compassion leaks through the cracks, he is being disingenuous: he rewards Margarita because she has passed the *real*, not the stated, test.

The violence in this novel is meant to disturb the reader, so that eventually, he, like the Master and Margarita, will understand that even Mark Ratkiller is indeed a good man, as Yeshua claims. The characters and the reader are meant eventually to see beyond apparent identity to the real identity, to understand that Woland and Yeshua bring the same message. Woland gives everyone, especially Margarita, the same test, and to pass it, one must show compassion *even to the worst humanity has to offer*, from the hell of the dance at Griboyedov, to the hell of the criminals at the ball, to Pilate suffering torture in the relentless sun. Yeshua teaches by example, Woland by provocation, but they are both teaching that compassion is preferable to revenge. Read in this light, the barbed conversation between Woland and Levi Matvei about the need for shadows assumes new significance, as does the way in which the Master comes to regard his neighbor, the betrayer Aloisy. The very *process* of reading the novel is meant to educate the reader, to lead him to a state of enlightenment in which the division of humanity into good and evil is no longer useful and the transcendence of the need for retribution is the goal.

This issue of the process of perception was also important in Bulgakov's first novel. A crucial dream (left out of the English translation) in *White Guard*, written when the Civil War was still very much a recent memory, contains the same sentiment, although no one but the narrator is able to voice it. In the dream a character named Zhilin is in heaven and asks God why He is willing to welcome even the Bolsheviks who don't even believe in Him. God's answer is curious. He says that it is all the same to him whether the soldiers believe in Him or not: "Zhilin, here you have to understand that for me you are all identical—killed on the field of battle. This, Zhilin, must be understood, but not everyone does." The characters in *White Guard*, who at first divide the world into the categories of good and evil based on what army they fight for, are just as unaware of the meaning of their sufferings as the Master is, and partial understanding is available only through their dreams.

In an early draft of *The Master and Margarita* Bulgakov planned to have a major scholarly character write a work about the "secularization of ethics." This was an essential concern of Bulgakov's generation, including those who were committed Marxists. Bulgakov's much-loved stepfather was an atheist, who demonstrated that such beliefs were not incompatible with the highest ethics. To Bulgakov's mind, however, the Soviet era seemed to abound in disturbing examples of what happens when ethics are divorced from the religious impulse and attached to the vagaries of political expediency. Pilate, as he struggles with his conscience and his fear, solidly based in what he knows awaits him if he allows a man who talked against the emperor to go free, in this way seemed quite contemporary. Bulgakov's entire novel is in a sense a polemic with the dominant force of his time, the belief in enlightened rationalism which in his country ended in a totalitarian structure.

The key to this aspect of the novel is Berlioz, who, as the novel begins, represents the smugness of the ideologically orthodox literary world. The editor is clearly educated and possesses a certain degree of intelligence. Berlioz's world is rational, he feels safe and in control, and his belief system protects him against the unknown. The rigidly rationalist and materialist nature of the philosophical-political system he lives under makes him quite unprepared to deal with even Bezdomny's degree of imagination (we must remember that this work opens, significantly, with a discussion of literary talent and censorship) as Berlioz explains to the poet that he has somehow made Jesus come alive, as if he had actually existed, which is ideologically incorrect. All of the things the Soviet ideology denied—the irrational and the unconscious—are about to inundate Berlioz in the person of Woland.

How is it that Bulgakov came to the desire for the philosophical reconciliation of opposites which we see in *The Master and Margarita*, an idea so unacceptable to his times? The answer lies more in life than in literature. No matter how flexible his intelligence, I do not think Bulgakov would have ever conceived of a universe in which Yeshua and Woland are working toward the same end if he had not lived through a remarkable era, enduring experiences which powerfully affected his point of view on politics and life. Born into the monarchist family of a lecturer in theology, Bulgakov received a good scientific education and went to medical school. When World War I came he went to the front as a young medic with the Red Cross, where he saw first-hand what the human results of modern war were. After the revolution Bulgakov lived through twelve changes of government in his native Kiev. In the course of a year he joined the White Army to defend Kiev against the Ukrainian Republican troops; in February 1919, he was forcibly mobilized by the Ukrainian army as well, but managed to escape at the risk of his life; finally, in autumn of 1919 he was again mobilized by the Whites, and sent to the Caucasus as an army doctor. These are the events we are sure of— it is quite likely that there are others Bulgakov told no one about. When he left his first wife, he made her swear to tell no one of his past, and I doubt that even she was told everything—Bulgakov was very secretive. At the start of this political-philosophical education Bulgakov was no doubt conventional in his monarchist beliefs, but by the time he had witnessed the behavior of White officers who abandoned their men, and examples of atrocities on all sides, his point of view shifted dramatically. During these dangerous years Bulgakov saw a great deal of torture and death. The theme of the witness who is too cowardly to do anything to help a suffering victim clearly has its roots in events during this period, events which Bulgakov did not discuss openly, but which found almost compulsive description in his early prose and plays. What dominates is a Christian—and Manichean—theme, that of cosmic responsibility. Bulgakov's particular emphasis is always on the issue of personal responsibility, no matter what the social context. The degree to which this concern is autobiographical is strikingly supported by a quote from the recently published extracts from his diary of 1924, which came to light because the secret police had made a copy of it while it was in their hands (Bulgakov burned the original after getting it back with great difficulty some years later). This quote is from an entry about how suddenly in the middle of another conversation in Moscow five years after the event, he remembered the death of his tsarist colonel:

> ...I saw... the day I was shell-shocked under the oak tree and the colonel was wounded in the stomach.... In order not to forget and so that posterity should not forget, I am recording when and how he died. He died in November 1919 during the campaign for Shali-Aul and his last words were addressed to me: "Don't try to comfort me. I'm not a boy." I was shell-shocked an hour after that.

This was only one of many terrible things Bulgakov saw in this period, and I suggest that it was precisely these experiences that made him rise above his identity as a monarchist White officer and understand that the Civil War was a tragedy for all sides. The general movement in Bulgakov's works over time is from the pain of the cowardly moment, which eternally tortures his early characters, to the possibility of atonement, and, finally in this last novel, the experience of grace and absolution.

While the horrors of World War I served as a marker for the break with the past in the West, Bulgakov's generation suffered revolution and bloody civil war, extraordinary upheavals which culminated in a totalitarian culture which was comparable only to fascist Germany's. Bulgakov's generation had lost the certainty of science and religion, but unlike their

European counterparts they did not have the luxury of thinking that a change in the social order would improve things—the Russian intelligentsia was living that change and it was terrifying. Bulgakov would have agreed with the hero of Joyce's *Ulysses* that history was a nightmare from which he was trying to awake. He and his generation often made the point that they had been born in the nineteenth century, and that their worldview was decided by this. This was a remarkable group, which included Tsvetaeva, Akhmatova, Mandelstam, Mayakovsky, and Pasternak, to name but a few of those born in the same five-year period from 1889 to 1893. They met the Revolution and Civil War in very different ways, but they all felt a profound break in their world. Mandelstam gave voice to this sense in his famous poem from 1923, "The Age": "My age, my beast, to whom will it be given/To behold the pupils of your eyes,/To connect two centuries together,/Giving of his blood to glue their spines?"

More than one writer of Bulgakov's time pointed out in private correspondence that the Russian intelligentsia was now living in the ideal future as imagined by the character Shigalyov in Dostoyevsky's *The Possessed*: a state in which society is controlled through spies and denunciations. Many artists in Russia at this time wanted to continue the themes (but not necessarily the forms) of the classical Russian cultural tradition, but in the politically polarized Soviet society of the 1920s choosing the wrong theme could be dangerous to your career; in the 1930s, it was dangerous to your life. The very nature of the concept of *The Master and Margarita* marks Bulgakov as a risk-taker of the first order. Characteristically, his response to this fear-struck era was a multi-faceted joke.

The atmosphere of terror deepened all through the years Bulgakov was working on what he referred to as his "sunset" novel. Friends and acquaintances were arrested and exiled. Many writers gave up during this period, switching to translation or children's literature, not even daring to write for the drawer. But unlike the Master, Bulgakov continued to work on a novel which had no hope of being published in his lifetime—although like others, he sometimes lulled himself with the idea that soon the terror would run out of steam, soon things would change. More to the point, this novel could easily have gotten him arrested, as could the fact that he socialized with American diplomats. The knowledge that Stalin had liked his play *The Days of the Turbins* might have provided a kind of protection at first since the secret police tried not to dispose of people the leader might one day inquire about. But after Mandelstam's first arrest in 1934 Bulgakov could have had no illusions about safety. In the early 1930s even those who should have known better sought logical meaning in these arrests, and speculated about the "cause" of a given arrest. According to Nadezhda Mandelstam, the poet Anna Akhmatova (whom Bulgakov knew and liked), very early on countered these questions by saying *"What for?* What do you mean, *what for?* It's time you understood that people are arrested for nothing!" Bulgakov, like Akhmatova, had his ear to the ground, he knew what form the social architecture was taking before it was completed, and as a man who actually had fought against the Bolsheviks during the Civil War, he knew what danger he was in. So why did he continue? Perhaps in order not to be

like the Master, a character who represented his own worst side, the side
which dominated when Bulgakov had a series of what we would call nervous breakdowns, during which he was afraid to go out on the street,
and during which he could not work. His letters and conversations
quoted in memoirs suggest that he considered himself weak in every
area but his work. Others would not have agreed with him: they saw a
witty man who joked until the end, a brilliant mimic and storyteller, who
summoned the last of his energies to finish work few could have imagined would ever be published. Bulgakov was determined to accomplish
what he felt his fate required of him. This sense of destiny often provoked humor from fellow writers who thought Bulgakov took himself
too seriously. He was tense and prickly, quick to see an affront to his
honor in the way in which a theater would deal with his text, for example. But when one examines just how difficult it was for him to become a
writer in a time actively hostile to people of his political background, this
seriousness becomes understandable. The early years in Moscow were
especially difficult, as this quote from a diary entry of 1923 demonstrates:

> David, who is always singing psalms [in Fenimore Cooper's *The Last of the
> Mohicans*], led me to think of God. Perhaps the strong and the daring don't need
> Him, but for people like me life is easier with the thought of Him. My illness has
> developed complications and is protracted. I am in very low spirits. Illness may
> prevent me from working, which is why I am afraid of it, which is why I hope in
> God.

He was over thirty before his career really began, he was in constant
ill-health, and was a hypochondriac as well. Only now, thanks to the
diary entries, do we know that shell-shock played a role in his nervous
condition—although some would consider the arrests proceeding all
around him as the 1930s wore on reason enough. He appears to have always had fears that he would die early, as his father had. There is a sense
in his letters of time running out, of trying to accomplish his main
work—even when he was not quite sure of what it was. Of course when
he identified in himself the symptoms of the kidney disease his father
had died of, few took him seriously. But it was these symptoms which
made him determined to finish the novel he considered his main work.

Fate, for Bulgakov, is a central mystery which cannot be penetrated
by the human mind, only submitted to, as one gradually begins to sense
its form. Yeshua blames no one for his death, he accepts his fate; Berlioz
does not, but it comes to him anyway. In the play *Molière*, a work that ex-
plores many of the same themes as *The Master and Margarita*, we see a
writer destroyed by both his society and his own character flaws. At the
end of the play, the chronicler of Molière's troupe writes in his register
and asks himself what was the cause of Molière's death, and answers:
"The cause was fate." This line was censored in Soviet texts, fate being
one of those things which scientific systems of organizing humanity prefer to ignore.

In Anglo-American literary studies we refer to "the anxiety of influence"; in totalitarian Russia the appropriate phrase would have been
"the anxiety of destruction." All of Bulgakov's literary energy and creative will were concentrated on proving something that his environment

contradicted: that manuscripts don't burn, that art outlasts the tyrants, that entropy doesn't triumph over the creative spirit. In the view of some of his friends this was touching naivete, not unlike Yeshua's, or perhaps it was a kind of cosmic whistling in the dark.

But not everyone saw this belief as quixotic. In 1935 at a private literary gathering, Boris Pasternak said he wanted to drink to Bulgakov. The hostess protested that the first toast should be to the respected older writer, V. V. Veresaev. "No," said Pasternak, "I want to drink to Bulgakov. Veresaev is a great man, of course, but he is a lawful phenomenon, while Bulgakov is an unlawful one."

Who at that party in 1935 would ever have believed that from the late 1960s through the 1990s Bulgakov's works would be translated around the world that he never got to see, that his plays would be made into movies, that there would be a cult surrounding him and his works in Russia, that his old house in Kiev would become a museum, that he would be more popular than Gorky? Not Pasternak—not anyone.

Bulgakov's novel reached its audience twenty-six years after his death. Only now do we have some insight into how that work began, thanks to the diary fragments published in 1990, fifty years after that death. A diary entry of January 1925 finds the writer visiting the editorial office of the magazine *The Atheist*. He bought most of the 1924 issues, went home to look through them, and wrote down his amazed reactions:

...I was stunned. Not by the blasphemy, although it is boundless, but that is merely a superficial aspect. The essence of the matter lies in an idea which can be proved by citing the actual documents: Jesus Christ is depicted as a swindler and a scoundrel, and the attack is focused on him. It is not difficult to see whose work this is. This is a crime like no other.

The fantastic nature of *The Master and Margarita* itself is Bulgakov's answer to his era's denial of imagination and its wish to strip the world of divine qualities. Fittingly, it was his own final act of magic.

picador.com

blog
videos
interviews
extracts